ANNE RILEY

SPENCER
HILL
PRESS

Spencer Hill Press

Contact: Spencer Hill Press, 27 West 20th Street, Suite 1102, New York, NY 10011

Please visit our website at www.spencerhillpress.com

First Edition: 2016
Anne Riley
Pull / by Anne Riley – 1st ed.
p. cm.

Summary: Rosie Clayton is in London because of her dying grandfather when she meets a mysterious group of crime-fighting teens with the ability to rewind time – now if only she could figure out why it is her life they keep saving.

Cover Design: Jenny Zemanek
Interior layout by Jenny Perinovic

ISBN 978-1-63392-045-3 (paperback)
ISBN 978-1-63392-046-0 (ebook)

Printed in the United States of America

FOR ALL OF THE DARK KNIGHTS WHO HAVE WILLINGLY STEPPED INTO DANGER'S PATH FOR THE SAKE OF ANOTHER.

ONE

FOR MOST TEENAGERS, SPENDING EVERY SUMMER IN London would be a dream come true. For me, it's less a dream and more a relief—from Tennessee's scalding heat, from my grease-filled waitress job at The Chicken Cottage, and from Mom and Dad's increasingly frantic conversations about my brother. If I hear the words *emotionally damaged* whispered across a sink full of dirty dishes one more time, I'll fire his sorry excuse for a counselor myself.

Not that I actually have the power to do that, but still. It's a nice thought.

My friends think I spend my London summers doing ridiculously cliché things, like flirting with chimneysweeps and gulping down pints of Boddington's. But instead of partying with hot Englishmen at one of Leicester Square's nightclubs, my evenings tend to be fairly tame—mint ice cream with my grandparents, Yorkshire Tea paired with an Austen novel, or late-night reruns of *Big Brother*. And the heath, of course. A summer in London wouldn't be complete without long afternoons lounging on its wide, grassy spaces or taking a stroll down one of its pathways.

For all practical purposes, the heath is just a park without benches or shrubs or anything, really. But to me, it's a beat of rest in a city that pulses with commotion. It's a place to breathe after an entire day of being crammed into various vehicles with a hundred other passengers.

It's also the inspiration for the name of Papa and Nana's village, Blackheath. Nestled in the southwest corner of London, Blackheath is a cozy collection of cafés, bookstores, and restaurants serving traditional English fare. I could hang out forever in one of its low-lit pubs, chowing down on some authentic fish and chips while traffic meanders past the windows.

But things won't be so simple this time.

Papa, my dad's father, is sick.

I remember how Dad's face drained when Nana called so early that morning, and the way he stared at the refrigerator with his phone smashed against his ear and mumbled to no one in particular: *pancreatic cancer. Three months to live.* I was the only one with him in the kitchen, and when that first tear rolled down his stubbly cheek, it felt like my whole world was ripping apart.

I'd never thought much about cancer until two weeks ago. But here I am, cruising toward London on an express train from Gatwick Airport, preparing to watch this disease take Papa's life.

It smells like sweaty Englishmen in every direction—probably because there *are* sweaty Englishmen in every direction—and there's a drippy stain next to my leg on the blue velour seat. Vomit, maybe, or some kind of milk-based drink. There's no way I'm going to let it touch my jeans, so I shift closer to my brother, Paul. He's sitting up, but his eyes are closed and his breathing is deep and even. A disgruntled rapper with gold teeth glares at me from the front of his black T-shirt; I guess Mom has given up trying to convince him to wear a button-down.

He looks so peaceful with his mouth slightly open and his head lolling to the rhythm of the train. A square of sunlight passes over his sharp features as we round a corner. I wish I could fall asleep like that, right in the middle of everyone's chatter, with full sunlight beaming through the window and a seat that cuts off the circulation in my legs.

"Stop trying to snuggle, Rosie," he mutters, and I startle at the sound of his voice. "You smell like a fast-food place that failed its health inspection."

This is probably true. I had McDonald's right before we boarded the plane in Philadelphia, and the scent of Big Mac has clung to my skin ever since.

I nudge his gangly arm. "Are you pretending to be asleep so you don't have to talk to me?"

He cracks open one eye. The pupil contracts in protest at the sudden light, allowing the soft brown iris to take over almost completely. "Maybe."

"Why?"

"I just am." Then, in typical Paul fashion, he shifts toward the aisle and tugs his Thug Life beanie over his eyes. "I'm really going to sleep now, so stay on your side."

"Fine." I inch away from him. Better to brave the drippy stain than to risk upsetting the precariously balanced apple cart of my brother's emotional state. Although I'm not sure how we'll keep him stable when Papa—

If, not when.

If Papa dies.

It's possible the doctors will work a miracle and Papa will be okay. That ten-percent survival rate has to come from somewhere, right?

But if he doesn't live, we only have three months with him.

Three months. Twelve weeks. One quarter of a year.

That's hardly enough time to hear all the stories he's never told. When are we supposed to discuss the latest mystery novel he read? When will we have a chance to debate Agatha Christie versus Sir Arthur Conan Doyle?

The train rocks and I clutch my stomach. All this travel is messing with my inner ear, but I'm not sure how much better I'll feel once we arrive. The prospect of seeing Papa sick—*really* sick—has kept me in a mild state of nausea ever since we found out.

I wish I'd spent more time with him before now. Yes, we've seen him every summer, but he's involved in so many things—the Blackheath Community Improvement Committee, Friends of the North Greenwich Library, and the Thames River Beautification Board, just to name a few. It seems like he's always shuffling out the door with his navy cardigan slung over his shoulder, giving us his wide, toothy grin and calling, "Off to the library. Back before you know it, my loves!" only to return hours later. Three months is hardly enough time, but I'm going to make the best of it.

I close my eyes and lean my head against the window. It's an exhausting task, trying to be positive when everything is crap.

The plexiglass feels cool on my forehead, and for a moment it tempers the headache brewing behind my eyes—but then the tremor of the engine starts to rattle my teeth, so I sit up and watch the ancient brick row houses zip past my window. They're dotted with flags for all kinds of soccer—I mean, *football*—clubs, but I only recognize the bright blue of Chelsea and a couple of red Arsenal ones. Some people have their laundry hung out to dry— thick black socks and gauzy floral skirts, a pair of jeans, a white cotton blouse. The images register as incomplete snapshots of the whole picture, and I wonder who wears those gauzy skirts, what her life is like, and if she's happy.

Three months. Two and a half, now.

People you love shouldn't come with an expiration date.

We roll into London Bridge station two minutes past our nine o'clock arrival time. The platform is crowded with dozens of men in crisp dark suits, women in sleek jackets, and two glowering men in baseball caps who appear to be delivering someone's new bed. *Wentworth Bed Shop*, the enormous box reads in blocky letters. *Prompt delivery with a cheery smile!*

"Right," Dad says as the train comes to a full stop. "Everyone got everything? Suitcases, wallets, mobiles?"

Dad's English accent is always present, but the moment we set foot on British soil, it seems to gain back the strength it lost during his time in America. It's like his inner Briton spends all year in Nashville wadded up in a cocoon, only unfurling its tea-stained wings when it senses dreary weather and breakfasts of toast with baked beans.

"It's called a phone," Paul mutters, peeling the knitted cap off his eyes. His forehead is embossed with the fabric's striped pattern. "And yes, for the fifteenth time, we have everything."

After eight hours on a plane and another two on trains, even my patience for Paul's snarky comments is wearing thin.

"He's just making sure," Mom says, holding her hand up like she does to our cat, Wally, when he tries to jump on the kitchen counter. "There's no need to get snippy."

Paul rolls his eyes and turns toward the window. Good—if he keeps his mouth shut, I probably won't rip into him the way I'd like to.

This is London Bridge, says a posh English recording over the intercom, but the buzz of the passengers makes it difficult to hear. *The next stop is Waterloo East.*

The doors hiss open and we're caught up with the mass of bodies exiting the train. Everyone jostles around with their bags and briefcases, stepping carefully over the gap between the train car and the platform as the next batch of aggressive commuters swarms the doors.

As we push through to the other side of the crowd, I register the symptoms of all-day travel that have crept into our appearances. Mom's normally flawless blonde hair has a cowlick in the back from napping on the plane, Dad's carefully pressed button-down is rumpled and halfway untucked, and Paul—well, give him a few scars and some blood around his mouth and he's a dead ringer for a zombie.

We wind through the station until we reach the main atrium, which is a wide-open space lined with news kiosks, bathrooms, and a couple of fast-food stands. Dad leads us to our usual regrouping spot by the escalators, where we drop our bags and breathe a collective sigh of relief. At least, it's a sigh of relief for me. I'm not sure about the rest of my family; their eyes are shifty.

"Do I look as fabulous as all of you?" I pull a lock of blonde hair away from my head. It falls limply back to my shoulder. "Because y'all look like the cast of *The Dead Life*."

Dad gives me a tired smile. "Is that one of your zombie shows?"

"It's *the* zombie show. I only have one." Thank goodness he's smiling. A week ago, he wasn't even getting out of bed. Not that I blame him. The weight of Papa's diagnosis crushes my chest at least a dozen times a day.

"Coffee would be good, I think," Mom says, eyeing Dad's sagging shoulders. "We could all use a little pick-me-up."

Paul huffs. "More coffee. What a shock."

I turn to him with a frown. Maybe he'll see the disapproval on my face and keep the rest of his comments to himself.

Of course, if it were this time last year, he never would have given Mom a hard time. He wouldn't have a reason to be *emotionally damaged*, or whatever godforsaken label they've condemned him with. If it were this time last year, his friend Carter would still be…well, normal. And Papa wouldn't be sick. And Stephen would be preparing to tell me he loved me for the first time.

I close my eyes against a wave of longing. God, what I wouldn't give for Stephen to be here right now.

When I open my eyes, Mom has a hand on her hip. She's arching her overly plucked eyebrows at my brother. "Is there a problem with us getting coffee?"

"You just had coffee at the airport!" he shouts. "How much of that stuff do you need? You're like a car with an oil leak. Always needing a refill and it's never enough."

I get that he's been traumatized by what happened to his friend—really, I do. But surely he has enough self-control to keep his mouth shut once in a while. I grab his arm and give it a little shake.

"Stop it," I say. The words come out with more venom than I mean them to, but I'm too tired to check myself. "If Mom wants coffee, that's none of your business. Why are you shouting at her about it?"

He rakes his fingers through his messy brown hair. It falls into his eyes, and he shakes it back like a dog ridding its fur of water. "I want to go to sleep. I don't understand why we're going to the hospital right now instead of tomorrow."

I lift my eyes to Dad's face. He's staring at the screen above our heads as if the departures and arrivals information is absolutely captivating. His lips are tight in a way that means he's about to explode, and he doesn't trust himself to speak. Over the years, Dad's learned to control his rage a little better, but now that his father is sick…Will he be able to control himself? I don't know, and I'm not looking forward to finding out.

I follow Dad's eyes to the screen and scan the list of departures. Brighton, Birmingham, Newcastle, plus a dozen more. Part of me wants to get back on a train, any train, and ride it all the way to the end of the line. I could get away from this stupid argument. I could stop worrying about Dad's next temper tantrum. I could forget about my brother.

Except, of course, that I couldn't. Not really.

"There's a Starbucks just outside the station," Dad says tersely, and I exhale. Thank God he didn't lose it. He wipes his tortoiseshell glasses on his shirt, puts them back on, and squints at his watch. "We're a little late to meet Nana at the hospital, but I'll text her."

We lug our bags to the Starbucks, which sits right across the street from Guy's Hospital. It feels weird to detour for coffee when Papa is *right there*, but since our family is on the brink of self-destruction, I guess it's worth it. After all, nothing keeps family members from turning on each other like a hearty dose of caffeine.

We heap our bags together on the sidewalk and Paul collapses on top of his like it's a beanbag chair. He crosses his arms over his knees and stares blankly at the brick hospital across the street. A black cab slows hopefully as it passes us—we're clearly from out of town and sick of lugging our stuff around—but I shake my head and wave it on.

"Paul and I can stay with the bags," I say, using my hand as a visor against the sun. "As long as someone gets me a vanilla latte, of course."

Mom gives me a grateful smile while fiddling with one of her earrings. "Sure. Paul, what do you want?"

"To be left alone," he snarls.

For a second, Mom's eyes narrow and her lips part as if she's finally angry enough to stand up for herself. After ten months of his increasingly malicious behavior, I'm ready to see her tell him to shove it—even if it's in her trademark passive-aggressive style.

But instead, she takes a deep breath, clears her throat, and says, "Okay then. We'll be just a minute."

Of course. I should have known better than to hope for discipline from Mom. Her reins on Paul have loosened considerably since Carter's accident, and even though Dad still tries to keep him in check, he gets away with a lot more than he used to.

Paul stares at the hospital with his back to me while Mom and Dad go inside. A group of cyclists whizzes by, all skin-tight outfits and bright helmets. Their sunglasses show a distorted reflection of the street, almost an alternate-universe kind of thing. If I could magically walk into an alternate version of London, would Papa still be dying? Or would he be okay, and my brother would be whole again, and everything would be perfect?

Entering an alternate reality is probably not an option, so I'm better off dealing with the situation in front of me—even if that situation seems steadfastly determined to ignore me.

"Want to talk?" I say to the back of my brother's head. He doesn't even flinch.

According to the counselor, we're supposed to give him every possible opportunity to talk about his feelings. Even if his words aren't positive, I'd rather have him acting out than sitting in silence. I don't know what he's thinking about when he's quiet. Is he planning to run away? Planning to hurt someone? Hurt himself?

"Hey." I kick the bag beneath him. He shifts his foot to catch his balance, but doesn't turn around. "Come on.

Talk to me. How was Carter last week? Has he made any progress with walking?"

This is another thing we're supposed to do—ask him about his best friend. The counselor says it's dangerous for Paul to internalize his anger over what happened to Carter. But he visits him every Saturday, so he's constantly thinking about him, both the way he is now and the way he was before the car accident that took most of his mind last August.

Paul fidgets and tightens his crossed arms. "Nope. Still falls into random pieces of furniture like he doesn't even see them."

I wince at the harshness in his voice. "He'll get better. He's got a great therapist, right? They'll keep working with him, and—"

He whips around with a vicious glare. "Carter doesn't even know who I am, Rosie. I go over there every week, and he just stares at me like I'm a total stranger. I won't be able to see him all summer because I have to be here instead, so by the time we get back, it'll be a lost cause." He shakes his head. "I might as well stop trying."

The Paul Clayton I know is tenderhearted, with warm brown eyes that invite you to sit down and tell him all about your day. But this guy? He's got eyes of stone that threaten to freeze the blood in my veins. I don't recognize him. And I'm not sure he recognizes me anymore.

"I know," I say in a small voice. "I'm sorry."

"Yeah, well." He stands up and puts his hands on his hips, then wraps his arms around his torso like he's trying to keep from shattering. "Lotta good that does me."

I close my eyes with a sigh. I've got to figure out how to break through his walls before it's too late.

"It's not fair," he says, and I meet his cold stare. "I'm his best friend, and he can't even say my name. He has no idea we used to sit by each other in history class, or that we used to spend every afternoon trying to catch fish in the creek behind his house. How does someone forget everything they ever knew, just like that?"

He stares at me like he's waiting for an answer.

I open my mouth, but nothing comes out. I'm desperate to say something—anything—to make this better, to give him hope. But what could I possibly say? I don't know how it happens any more than he does.

So I close my mouth and shrug.

"Exactly." He shakes his head at the ground. "Nobody knows the answer because there isn't one."

My heart feels like it's ripping in two. I want so badly to bundle him up in my arms like I did ten months ago, when he found out that Carter and his mom had been hit by a drunk driver. His face looks a little older now, but as he wipes his suddenly damp eyes with the sleeve of his T-shirt, I still see the trembling boy that clung to me that afternoon while we waited to find out if Carter would survive like his mom.

"I wish he would've just died in that stupid wreck," he mutters.

My insides turn to ice. "You don't mean that."

"I do!" His expression is feral. "It's not fair. Nobody should have to deal with this. It's not fair. It's *not fair.*"

I don't know if he means Carter or himself, but either way, I can't stop from throwing my arms around his heaving shoulders. He tries to push me back, but I hold him tighter. There's no way I'm letting go of him. Not now, not ever.

"It's okay," I whisper in his ear. "Take a deep breath, all right? Just focus on one breath at a time. In and out. Nice and steady."

He breathes, but it's ragged and forced.

"That's good," I lie. "Do that again. In and out. Don't think about anything else."

I feel him squeeze his eyes shut on my shoulder, and whatever was left of my strength crumbles to dust.

In and out.

In and out.

"I don't want to see Papa," he whimpers.

A giant sob rips from his throat, and I stroke the back of his head and say, "Shh, shh," like Mom did when we were little. Tears roll down my face in spite of my efforts to stop them. Not only has my brother watched his best friend turn back into a toddler, but now he's got to watch his grandfather die.

The door to Starbucks swings open behind us, and Paul catapults out of my arms. He turns back toward the street and faces the wind. I bet he's hoping it will dry his cheeks before someone notices. That's what I do when I cry in public, anyway.

"Vanilla latte," Dad says, offering me a paper cup with a plastic lid. Mom follows him back to our pile of bags and takes a long swig of coffee while Dad nods at the hospital. "I'll just text Nana that we're coming up."

I tip back my cup, relishing the heat of the coffee as it slides down my throat. Dad fishes his phone out of his pocket with a frown. He pokes at the screen with too much force, as if jabbing it makes him feel better.

"Hang on," he mutters. "She's already sent me a message that Papa is worse. And I've got two missed calls from her—must not have heard the ring in the coffee shop. Better phone her back." He gnaws his bottom lip and lifts the phone gingerly to his ear.

Nana answers instantly. I can hear her from where I'm standing, and it sounds like she's shouting.

"Hold on," Dad yells into the phone. "Slow down. What are you saying?"

He stares at the air in front of him with his mouth slightly open. Nana's voice goes shrill on the other end of the line, and I take a step forward. "What is it?"

A knot has formed in my chest. Dad's strained expression, Nana's piercing shouts—something is very wrong. Paul turns around, but the animosity in his face has been replaced with fearful curiosity. He chews on his thumbnail while staring at Dad. Mom puts a hand on Dad's arm, her eyebrows pinching together in the middle.

"Oh God," Dad whispers and his hand starts to tremble. "Oh God, oh God. We're coming! Just don't—don't let him go yet, okay?"

The knot in my chest jerks tight. "What's wrong?"

"Philip!" Mom says. "What's going on?"

This can't be happening. We have three months. We have *three months.*

Dad draws in a jagged breath and thrusts the phone at Mom. She fumbles, but manages to keep it from hitting the sidewalk. I look from her furrowed brow to Dad's paling cheeks.

"He started crashing ten minutes ago," Dad says, spinning to face the hospital. "He's somewhat stable now, but they don't know for how long. We've got to get up there immediately." He steps toward the building, but stops when we don't follow. He claws at his shirt collar and swallows a stuttered breath. "Now! Let's go!"

Mom scowls at the phone in her hand. "What do you mean, crashing? He can't be— I don't understand—"

Dad bends over and puts his hands on his knees. I want to go to him, but my feet are rooted to the pavement. All I can do is stare at the phone, like Mom. Paul steps toward us, wide-eyed. His chest is rising and falling too quickly. I've seen him like this before, when we thought Carter was going to die. He's panicking. Someone needs to calm him down, but I don't know how. None of us do.

Dad presses a hand to his stomach like he's about to throw up. "Everybody leave your bags—no, that's not right, we should take our bags with us—"

I swallow, blinking back tears. "But he has three months!"

Dad grabs the handle of his rolling suitcase. He jerks it too hard and it flips upside down. His face flushes to a deep red and he throws the suitcase down with a roar of fury.

"Come on!" he screams, hurling himself across the street.

I stumble off the sidewalk and into the road. Mom's in front of me, and I think Paul is to my right—at least, that's where he was a second ago. A car horn blares nearby. I don't know exactly where it came from or how close I came to getting hit. I don't care.

Papa is dying.

We were supposed to have three months.

Papa is dying.

This can't be real.

TWO

THE FEEBLE OLD MAN IN THE HOSPITAL BED CAN'T BE MY grandfather. Edward Clayton would never let himself get so skinny; his love of red meat would ensure that. And his gray hair would be carefully combed and tucked beneath a black-and-white houndstooth golf cap, not splayed across a vinyl-covered hospital pillow scrawled with DO NOT REMOVE in black marker.

But when I force myself to look at his face—the bump on his nose where a cricket ball once broke the bone, the shallow dimple in the center of his chin—it is Papa. Of course it is.

And everything inside me is splintering to dust.

The throbbing that began behind my eyes on the train has strengthened. I press my fingertips to my temples and make small circular motions, letting out a breath when the pain begins to dull. A chasm of hopelessness cracks open somewhere in my heart, but I force it shut quickly. Better to keep it in check as long as I can. Maybe, if I'm strong enough, I can keep it closed forever.

I don't remember much about the hospital lobby or the elevator that brought us to the third floor—just blurred images of metal doors, sleek wooden chairs, and a faceless receptionist. But now that we're in the room, every detail takes root in my brain with brutal clarity. Canvas shades cover the single window, sheer enough to allow some light, but no glare. The white linoleum beneath our feet is dotted with green and gray, a subtle attempt at design that makes the floor look dirty. And the smell—part bleach, part stale blankets, all cold and sterile. It's too similar to the day we put our black lab down and I passed out in the waiting room. Same smell and a similar environment, but on an infinitely worse scale.

Nana is perched on the edge of a chair with her knobby fingers wrapped around Papa's hand. She's wearing the periwinkle cardigan Mom sent her for Christmas last year and her coral lipstick is smeared past the corners of her mouth. Tears leave wet trails through her makeup before they *drip drip drip* onto the white bedsheets. One splatters onto Papa's wrist and rolls all the way to his elbow. He moans softly as his glassy eyes roam the ceiling.

They said he was stable for the moment, but to me, he looks about as stable as a gasping fish on the bottom of a boat.

Two nurses in light green scrubs stand by the bed with matching grimaces. One of them, a tall girl with red hair that frizzes at the ends, checks the monitors and scribbles on a clipboard. The other, a stout man with black hair and olive skin, hangs a plastic bag full of fluid on a metal pole. He connects it to a tube that runs to a needle in Papa's arm.

"Morphine," he explains to Nana in a soft voice. "So he'll be comfortable."

Papa opens his mouth wide and shouts, "No! Not the bus!" Then he rolls halfway onto his side and lets out a little yelp. His expression twists and he settles onto his back again, but his legs fidget.

"Nana?" I say, nearly choking on her name. Paul brushes against my arm; he's staring at Papa with wide eyes. His chest rises and falls like he's just run a mile. A thick fringe of dark hair hangs halfway over his eyes, but he doesn't brush it away.

Nana looks up. "Rosie. Oh, thank the stars you're all here."

I lurch across the room and loop my arms around her narrow shoulders. Nana's always seemed young as far as grandmothers go, but she's aged a lot since last summer. Her gray hair seems faded, her curls less springy, the wrinkles around her eyes and mouth more pronounced. How much of that transformation has occurred in the weeks since Papa's diagnosis?

"I don't know what happened," she whispers, clutching Papa's hand tighter. "I keep saying it's not possible for something to move that quickly, and they keep arguing—" she puts a hand to her mouth, speaking through her fingers "—that this is just what pancreatic cancer does sometimes." She sniffles into her palm as fresh tears follow well-worn paths down her face.

"It's okay," I say, even though I'm not sure if she's apologizing, or defending herself, or what. "We're here now."

Her hand falls from her mouth and she plants a wet kiss on my cheek. "Thank goodness," she manages. "I'd be lost without you."

Her eyes shift over my shoulder to Dad. I know it's him because I hear his too-loud breathing right behind me. I move to the side, and he slumps into her arms. They say nothing, but the tight line of Nana's lips and the stiffness in my dad's back fill in the blanks.

"Edward," Mom whispers, approaching Papa's bed. She lays a couple of fingers on his arm, but his eyes stay fixed on the ceiling as he groans. Mom cups a hand over her mouth and squeezes her eyes closed. "How could this happen?"

"I just need to do it again," Papa murmurs. A thread of saliva stretches between his lips with each word. "Just let me try again. I can do it. It was the bus, it was. Too fast."

Paul sinks back to the wall with his arms crossed. His eyes are shifty and round, like a child who's lost his mom in a crowded department store.

"The bus!" Papa cries out, and everyone jumps.

"Yes, Papa," I say as my heart pounds in my throat. "The bus. It was going too fast, wasn't it?"

Mom gives me a questioning look as I approach Papa's bed. I shrug at her; of course I have no idea what he's talking about, but it's obvious he wants us to know about this bus. Or at least, he wants us to know about whatever bus he's picturing in his disease-addled mind. If it will make him happy to think I've understood him, then I'll pretend.

I'll do anything to ease his final moments.

I settle on the edge of the bed opposite Nana. His hand is smooth and cool when I take it in mine; I don't think I've ever held Papa's hand before. He turns to me, but I'm not sure he even knows who I am. At least he's quiet now. I scoot a little closer and bend toward his wrinkled face.

"Can you see me?" I search his watery gray eyes—almost perfect reflections of my own—for any sign of lucidity.

He blinks once, twice. Then he gives me an almost imperceptible nod.

"God," Dad hisses behind me. I turn to find him watching Papa over my shoulder. "He's still rational."

I start to stand up, gesturing at my spot on the bed. "Do you want to…?"

"No, no." Dad waves me off. "You're doing well. Keep talking to him."

I sit down and lean close to Papa's face again. He can see me, but does he recognize me? What if he doesn't know who we are?

"Papa," I say. "It's me. Rosie."

His lips twitch with a hint of a smile. He opens his mouth like he's going to talk, but then he sucks in a sudden breath and expels a violent, racking cough. It's followed by another, and then another, and soon he's clinging to his pillow while his face reddens, unable to catch his breath.

"Edward!" Nana cries, leaping to her feet. She waves at the nurses, who are already flanking Papa's bed. "Help him! Do something!"

I stumble off the mattress as one nurse—Roderick, according to the red plastic nametag pinned to his shirt—guides me to the chair next to Nana. The other nurse, the girl with red hair, hurries to Papa's side and puts her hands on his chest and shoulder.

"Just sit here," Roderick says, lowering me into the chair. "We'll handle it."

I can't sit down. My grandfather wants to say something to me, and if they can't stop this coughing fit, I might never find out what it is. I stand back up. "Papa?"

"Please stay back, miss," the redheaded nurse barks. She makes a shooing motion with her hand, and a burst of anger flares inside me. I open my mouth to retort, but Dad puts his arm around me before I can argue with her.

"It's all right," he says, tugging me out of the way. "They'll get him sorted out. Just give them a minute, yeah?"

His voice is too high. It's the same voice he uses on Mom almost every time he says he'll cut the grass. He's lying, but not just to me. He's lying to himself. And I can tell by the tension around his eyes how badly he wants to believe it.

"Okay," I say, nodding. My voice sounds a little shrill, too. Maybe we share the same tell.

The redhead straps an oxygen mask over Papa's nose and mouth. He rolls from side to side, but the movement grows calmer, and the nurses' expressions are less frenzied. Finally, he lies still and closes his eyes.

"Is he okay?" Dad croaks. He releases my shoulders. "Or is he—"

"He's all right." Roderick turns to Dad with a tight-lipped frown. "For the moment."

Papa looks like he's falling asleep. I let out a long, slow breath, and relax my shoulders for the first time since we walked in. The muscles in my neck are tight from being clenched for so long. I roll my head left to right and close my eyes.

When I open them a second later, Papa is staring at me.

Rosie.

The word is a whisper inside my head—sharp, hurried. Papa's oxygen mask is strapped securely onto his face, yet I'm sure he spoke somehow.

Rosie. Can you hear me?

What in the world is happening?

If you can hear my voice, nod.

No one is watching me. Dad's opening the cabinets against the wall and glowering at their contents. Mom's looking at Papa and wiping mascara from beneath her eyes. Paul's still leaning against the wall like he's hoping it will absorb him completely.

I look back to Papa, and I nod.

He opens his mouth a little. No actual words come out, and even if they did, the oxygen mask would muffle them. Still, I hear—feel? see?—more words, louder now: *Keep your eyes on mine, and listen to what I tell you.*

Two compulsions war against each other in my mind. The first urges me to turn away and accept the fact that I'm having some kind of stress reaction to Papa's condition. But the other one…

The other one urges me to consider another, more startling, possibility—that Papa is actually speaking into my mind.

Are you listening? Do you hear me?

The words come through a little muddled this time, as if they're traveling through water. I nod again.

For several seconds, nothing happens.

Then—

A rush of energy like a wave knocking me down at the beach. I clamp my eyes shut. There's a giant pressure on my chest, a squeezing, like the whole thing is about to implode. My knees weaken and I stagger to the left—

—but then the pressure lets up, and I gasp.

My talent is yours, dear girl. Take it and conquer.

I step back until my heels hit the wall. "What?"

Mom's eyes snap to me. "What's wrong?"

Her voice is static in my ears. White noise. And Papa's voice seems to be slipping away, no matter how much I try to focus on it. Mom's mouth opens again, and I hold up my hand, palm out. She makes an indignant huffing noise, but doesn't speak.

A strange word comes: *Mortiferi.*

I shake my head. I don't understand.

Mortiferi.

Papa's eyes widen like watchful sentries on either side of his mask. The nurses adjust the monitor on his chest. The word, whatever it means, seems thin and full of holes.

Mortiferi.

I don't even know if I'm hearing it right.

Fight them. Fight them with all you have. And whatever you do, always protect our secret.

The redheaded nurse walks around Papa's bed to the heart monitor, and as she passes between the two of us, our eye contact is momentarily interrupted. Something almost tangible, like an invisible cord, snaps in two—

The connection is gone.

Papa roars into his mask.

"Sir!" Roderick cries. Then, to the redhead, "What happened?"

The tubes and monitors jerk as Papa struggles to escape his bed. An alarm wails somewhere in the room, and I'm shoved into the corner as a gaggle of nurses swarms around him. Two of them pin his arms down while another tries to talk him into submission; the rest set about adjusting switches and checking monitors.

"Hold steady, Mr. Clayton!" Roderick shouts over his screams. "Please, you've got to stop! Sir! Please!"

But Papa doesn't seem to hear him. He claws at his bedsheets as if he's trying to break free and run from us, from this place. Instead of words, he produces muffled grunts from within the oxygen mask—but his horror-struck eyes communicate everything his mouth can't.

Nana materializes next to me and stands, hands over her mouth, between the nurses and me. "Oh God," she whimpers. "This is it, isn't it?"

I shake my head, but I can't convince myself she's wrong. I'm pretty sure this is it, too. Papa was just saying a mysterious word inside my head and I might never talk to him again. I have to stop this. I have to calm him down so he can begin treatment and get cured. But I can't.

I'm helpless.

The heart monitor starts to give off a series of short, earsplitting beeps. One of the nurses says, "He's crashing again!" Feet pound down the hallway and the clatter of a cart echoes close behind. People burst into the room, so many people, all barking orders at each other.

"He's going into cardiac arrest!" someone shouts.

"Edward!" Nana screams. Mom makes a choking noise in the back of her throat, and then Dad's phone—which she has been holding all this time—drops to the floor. One of the nurses kicks it under a chair and Mom doesn't move to pick it up. Paul is the one who sidles over to the chair and reaches for the phone with his long, trembling fingers. Dad's eyes are wide. He's shaking his head the way you do when a character in a horror movie is about to walk into the wrong room and you know there's nothing you can do to stop it.

Except this isn't a movie, and Papa isn't an actor playing a part, and there won't be any credits to signal the end of this nightmare.

I'm frozen, barely breathing. All the times Papa read to me when I was little swim to the front of my mind—the lilting rhythm of his voice, his fingers running over my hair. I always thought we had a special connection, but it was never anything like the current of desperation I felt coming from him as he spoke into my mind. I wish he would say something else, tell me what "Mortiferi" means—but a horde of people stands between us, and any chance we had of re-establishing that mental cord is gone.

"Not breathing," someone announces, and Nana crumples into my arms, gripping my elbows with her bony fingers. Several pairs of gentle hands guide us into the hallway as her quiet tears become guttural sobs.

"Wait here," one of the nurses says before hurrying back into Papa's room. She closes the door, and watching the scene from the outside, in a silent hallway, is worse than being in the middle of things. I want to go back in, look into Papa's eyes, and hear him speak thoughts to me again.

I keep one arm around Nana while I stare through the window. Mom has her purse pinned between her elbow and her ribs; her mouth hangs slightly open. Dad's jaw works as he stares at Papa's door. Paul shuffles to the other side of the hallway and examines a map of brightly colored fire escape routes.

If only we had an escape route from Papa's cancer.

The nurses in his room fly around the bed, injecting something here and checking a monitor there. But no matter how many buttons they push or how many chest compressions they do or how many times his body jerks from the defibrillator, their expressions remain strained.

Finally, the doctor straightens and shakes her head. She motions for the others to stop. A short blonde nurse with wet eyes silences the heart monitor.

The team stands quietly aside as the doctor walks out to us and says, "We did all we could, but he simply couldn't hold on any longer." Her eyes droop, and she puts a hand on Nana's shoulder. "I'm so sorry."

THREE

DEATHLY SILENCE DRAPES US AS WE ARRIVE AT PAPA and Nana's—or, just Nana's, I guess—townhouse. I still expect Papa to be here when we open the door, even though I just watched him die. Surely he'll greet us with a hearty "At last!" from his favorite armchair in the sitting room, and then he'll stand up and gather us into his strong arms while Nana puts the kettle on. I can't imagine walking into this house any other way. I don't *want* to imagine it any other way. But I'm seconds from stepping into this new reality, whether I like it or not, so I take a deep breath and rub my arms even though it's not cold.

Mom and Dad stare at the ground while Nana jabs her key at the brass deadbolt. She misses one-two-three times before finding her mark. Paul bites his bottom lip and looks away; maybe he's crying again, and if he is, I certainly won't blame him. He's endured too much heartache for a fifteen-year-old. I start to put an arm around him, but then pull back. He'll just shake me off like he did on the train. The possibility that this was the last straw for him, that Papa's death will be the thing that finally shuts him down for good, is too much to consider.

I have to keep him from falling apart.

Nana finally coaxes the door open with a loud *squeak*—the same squeak that made me cry the first time I came here as a baby. According to Mom, the only thing that distracted me from my fear was the door's bright blue color, although now I can't look at it as we lug our bags inside. Its cheerfulness sickens me.

Mom and Dad drop their suitcases by the door and walk straight to the kitchen with Nana; I'm guessing they'll make some tea and sit around the small wooden table, rehashing Papa's death and trying to figure out the next step.

Mortiferi.

What could it possibly mean? Did Papa really speak into my mind?

My talent is yours, dear girl. Take it and conquer.

What talent? And what am I supposed to conquer? That pressure on my chest, the wave of energy that crashed into me—what was all that?

I close my eyes and force myself back to that hospital room with the green spots on the floor. Papa's face floats to the front of my mind.

Mortiferi.

I shut the front door and turn to ask Paul if he's okay, but he's already at the top of the stairs with his ratty JanSport backpack slung over his shoulder. The floor squeaks as he walks to his bedroom—Dad's old room, the one that overlooks the cramped townhouses of Nana's street, Camden Row. The bedroom door clicks softly shut and something thuds to the floor—his backpack, probably. Knowing Paul, that's the last we'll see of him until dinner, or maybe until tomorrow morning. I'd like to sleep for the next sixteen hours too, but my mind is racing and I'll end up just staring at the ceiling. I need to go to the heath. But first, I need to call Stephen.

I duck into the sitting room and call him, closing my eyes in relief when he picks up and says, "Hello?"

"You have no idea how happy I am to hear your voice," I say with a sigh.

The second I open my eyes, I'll lose my mental image of him lying on his bed, arms crossed behind his head and phone on speaker next to him. I know that's what he's doing because it's the only way he talks on the phone. I shut my eyes tighter, imagining his ruffled hair and the way his smile always looks adorably sleepy.

A girl giggles in the background. It's fleeting and quiet, but definitely there.

My eyes fly open and the mental image shatters. "Who's that?"

"Uh, no one," he says, and there's a pause. Then his voice again, closer, as if he took me off speakerphone: "Just Hope."

Hope is Stephen's youngest sister. She's nine, and that definitely wasn't the giggle of a nine-year-old. I've heard that giggle before, six weeks ago, at the prom afterparty. I know exactly who it belongs to. But maybe, just maybe, I'm wrong. Maybe the distance between our phones is playing tricks on my ear.

"Great," I say lightly. "Put her on, I'd love to say hello."

Another pause, longer this time. "Well, she's actually using the bathroom right now."

Surely this is not happening. Not now, when I need him the most. "If she's using the bathroom, why did I just hear her laugh?"

There's a loud snort, then more giggling.

Stephen whispers *shut up*.

Six weeks ago, when I walked into Rebecca Evans's bedroom by accident (I was trying to find the bathroom), I found Rebecca and Stephen sitting on her bed together. Nothing was *obviously* wrong; they were both fully clothed and her desk lamp was on. But the door had been shut, and her hair was kind of messy, and Stephen had told me he was going outside to check the score of the Braves game. There was better reception outside, he said.

When I asked how he'd ended up in Rebecca's bedroom, he said they were talking. And then Rebecca giggled.

"Stephen," I say. My voice is scratchy. "Who are you with? And don't say Hope."

Silence.

"Is it Rebecca?" Please, please say no.

He sighs. "Look, I know you don't like her, but Rebecca and I are—"

"Stop."

Rebecca and I. He said it like it's a thing. Like they're some kind of unit.

After I found them together that night, things were different between Stephen and me. We still went out on the weekends, still kissed in the driveway when he dropped me off, still talked and laughed as if everything was okay.

But it wasn't.

I asked about the Rebecca incident one other time, a couple weeks after prom. Stephen told me to stop accusing him of cheating.

I'm starting to think my suspicions were valid.

"Actually, Rosie," he says evenly, "we need to talk."

My stomach plummets to my toes. Sure, our relationship has been a little rocky lately, but we've been together almost two years. He knew Papa was sick. He knew how torn up I was about it. Surely he's not going to break up with me now.

"So talk." I clutch the delicate gold necklace he gave me last summer. I never take it off, not even to shower.

Most of what he says doesn't fully register in my mind. He compliments me a lot, and Rebecca's name weaves through his words, just like she probably wove her fingers through his hair the moment I left town. I manage a few *uh huh*s and one or two *okay*s, but the only thing I really hear is his last sentence: "I don't think we should be together anymore."

I stare at the carpet and run my thumb along the necklace. I say, "My grandfather died today."

Then I hang up.

"MOM? ARE YOU IN HERE?"

I'm creeping down the hallway toward the kitchen. My voice is like a cannon. I never knew a house full of people could feel so empty. I never knew *I* could feel so empty.

She's sitting at the table with Nana, who's clutching a bunch of tissues in one hand and a cup of hot tea in the other. Both of their eyes are red-rimmed and glassy, and Mom's knee is bouncing under the table.

My mother is many things, but never a fidgeter.

"I need to go out," I say. Thankfully, my voice is even and I'm pretty sure my eyes are dry. I can't bear to tell them about Stephen—not now.

"Out where?" Mom says.

The frown lines around her mouth seem deeper than before, or maybe she's just frowning more than usual. I should stay; I know I should. But I can't.

"The heath?" I say, not meaning for it to come out like a question. I swallow and try again. "The heath. Just for a little while."

Dad's leaning against the counter next to a cup of tea that must be his, but it's still full and he hasn't put milk in it yet. The carton sits next to his elbow with the cap still on while Dad glares at the floor. He huffs and shakes his head as if my request is the most asinine thing he's ever heard. Mom looks at him like she's expecting an outburst, but it doesn't come. Instead, he picks up the still-unused milk, rips open the refrigerator door, slings the carton onto the shelf, and slams the fridge closed.

We wait in silence as he stomps out of the room.

"I guess it's okay if you go out," Mom says, refusing—as always—to acknowledge Dad's anger. "But I want you back before dark."

I squint through the kitchen window. The sky is already streaked with pink and orange. How did it get to be so late?

"That doesn't give me much time," I say.

Mom tilts her head with a sigh. "You're really going to argue with me right now?"

Her eyes start to tear up again. I can't take it—I've got to go, even if it's just for half an hour.

"No, I'm not arguing." I back out of the kitchen toward the entryway. "See you in a bit."

I grab my green hoodie out of my bag and slip out the front door. The grief in the house is a quiet monster with claws and teeth, shredding our souls to dust. And the grief inside me—mostly over Papa, but also over Stephen—is wrapped around my organs, squeezing the life out of me one millimeter at a time.

At some point, I'll have to deal with Papa's death, and I can't distract myself forever from the strange things that happened in that hospital room. But as I pull on my hoodie and tug the zipper all the way up, striding past carefully manicured gardens and surly cats weaving around trashcans, I don't care. Tonight, I want a distraction. I want to breathe the cool evening air that's such a contrast to Nashville's soupy summer nights. I want to walk around the heath and think about anything but Papa. Anything but Stephen.

I stride past the line of tiny Renaults and Smart Cars that crowd Camden Row, then start up the hill that leads to the heath, taking comfort in the small things—the brick wall half-covered with ivy; the shaggy black dog at the house with the huge garden, barking at everything that moves; the neatly trimmed shrubs that sit inexplicably paired with wild, overgrown rosebushes.

As I crest the hill and look to my right, I actually manage a smile.

The heath—green, crisscrossed with pathways, and gloriously plain. This place carries a hint of magic I can't sense anywhere else. As the breeze curls around my shoulders and the twilit sky stretches overhead, the ache in my heart eases.

Tonight, the heath is empty except for the trees that dot its perimeter and the old stone church, All Saints, which sits off to the right. There are usually more people out, but I'm kind of glad to be alone with the first batch of twinkling stars; I don't have much time before nightfall, so I need to walk quickly.

I cross the street and set off down the nearest path. It runs through the interior and will take me to Duke Humphrey Road, where I'll loop around the apartments on Talbot Place and head back home. This has been my route since I was twelve or so—whenever Mom and Dad started letting me indulge my introverted side by walking alone. It's familiar, but not boring. The open air is already loosening the tension in my chest.

I reach up to the necklace that still hangs around my neck—the necklace I should have taken off the moment

I hung up on Stephen. It's two small interlocking gold rings on a delicate gold chain.

Stephen.

The pain of losing him rips through my chest. Our breakup is easier to deal with than Papa's death, so I allow myself to start there as I walk. I let myself hate Rebecca Evans, and I let myself cry—for Stephen, yes, but then for Papa. My tears come with such force that I can't keep walking. I can hardly see. Papa's face, the way he screamed into his oxygen mask—

Something moves on the other side of the heath.

My heart rams the inside of my chest and alarms wail in my mind—the result of Dad's constant lectures on nighttime safety in Nashville whenever I go to dinner with my friends. But the thing moving is just a girl walking toward me, looking at her phone. She's using one hand to keep her pleated skirt from blowing up in the wind while texting someone with the other, and she hasn't noticed me.

She also hasn't noticed the two guys coming from the other side of the heath.

They're laughing and pushing each other the way Paul used to do with his soccer teammates after a goal. The weak light doesn't reveal details, but I can tell that one is tall and lanky with longish hair and the other is short, stocky, and bald.

The bald guy looks in the girl's direction and lets out a long wolf whistle. I roll my eyes—why do men think that kind of thing is charming? The girl crosses her arms with her phone still in her hand and picks up her pace, eyes locked on the ground.

"Oi, gorgeous!" calls the lanky one. He mutters something to his friend, and they both laugh. "Where you off to?"

A vague sense of dread forms in the pit of my stomach. I stop walking. I don't like the way these two are moving at an angle that will allow them to intercept the girl, nor the leering tone in their voices. They haven't seen me yet, but they will—and then what?

The girl starts running as best she can in her wedge heels. The bald guy takes off after her and catches her by the arm. I swear under my breath as my stomach clenches with panic. This is Blackheath, for crying out loud. Crime is way down on their list of concerns, right below alien invasion, yet this girl is getting attacked. She screams and tries to wrench her arm free, but he twists her elbow to the point that all she can do is shake her head, mouth open in a silent cry. Her knees buckle and she falls to the grass as his accomplice moves in on her.

"Hey!" I shout. "Get away from her!"

Either they don't hear me or they don't care. I run toward them, reaching for my phone to call the police—but it's not in my back pocket where I normally keep it. It's not in any of my pockets. I must have left it in the sitting room after I talked to Stephen.

The girl starts to get up, but the two thugs push her back down, hard. Her head slams to the ground and she rolls to the side, her skirt wafting in the breeze.

"Stop it!" I scream, and this time they look up. They're only distracted for a split second, but the girl makes her move.

Taking full advantage of her chunky shoes, she lands a solid kick to the bald guy's groin. He doubles over, and for a moment, she's free—but he snags her ankle before she can stand up, and the lanky guy rams his knuckles into her nose. She crumples to the ground like a ragdoll.

I swallow my terror and launch myself toward them, churning my legs as fast as they'll go. The bald guy hooks his hands under the girl's thin arms and scuttles across the grass with her. He's headed toward a tiny black car with a dented front fender parked on the side of the road. Both guys glance at me, probably trying to judge whether I can get to them before they can get in the car.

I can't. I'm still too far away. I have to do something, anything, to keep the girl out of that car.

"I called the cops!" I yell. My voice jars with the pounding of my feet. "They're on their way, and I gave them your license plate number!"

The bald guy looks at his friend. Maybe they believe me. Maybe they'll drop the girl and drive away, and everything will be all right.

But that would be too easy.

They shove the girl into the backseat of the car and the bald guy climbs in with her. She screams—but it's cut off with an abruptness that sends chills up my spine. The interior of the car is dark, but I can see her silhouette as she struggles against him. I have a feeling she won't make it out of this alive unless I come up with a plan in the next five seconds.

Make that two seconds, because now the lanky guy's glare has shifted to me. I slow down as his narrowed eyes slice into mine and his thin lips press together. With one long-fingered hand, he pulls a switchblade out of his pocket and flicks it open. His expression seems so empty, as if he couldn't care less about stabbing me in order to get away. He flips the handle over in his palm without looking at it, twirling the knife like it's nothing more than a harmless stick. The blade glints orange in the last rays of the sun.

I squeeze my eyes shut for a second, trying to muster the courage to fight two guys who have at least one knife, maybe two. But in order to muster courage, the courage has to be there in the first place—and I think I left all mine in Papa's hospital room.

I turn around and throw myself into a sprint. The village is just down the road. If I can make it there, I can borrow someone's phone; there's no way this guy will stab me in the middle of town.

Will he?

My legs churn harder and I force my lungs into a steady rhythm. In and out. In and out. Just like I said to Paul outside Starbucks this morning. I keep running, pushing thoughts of the mugger's switchblade out of my mind. Getting into town—that's my goal. Find a phone. Call for help. Try not to die.

But when I cross into the long shadows of All Saints Church, something stops me.

The air thickens. My legs push against some massive invisible pressure. It's like I've run straight into quicksand, except that my gray running shoes are still on solid ground. I turn to see if the lanky guy and his knife are gaining on me, but the motion is slow and strained. I can't get my head around.

My stomach begins to implode.

I sink to the ground and curl into a ball. It feels like my bones and organs are collapsing. The trees and sky blur together and a hurricane-force wind rushes past. Colors swirl across my vision: the green of the heath, the orange and pink of the sky, and a black silhouette—the guy with the knife.

My ears fill with a *whooshing* sound like a thousand vacuums turned on at once. I cover my face with my hands and shut my eyes tight. The pressure on my body keeps building and I'm starting to struggle for air. In one last frantic attempt to escape the vortex, I claw at the ground, gasping the word *help*.

White light flashes, too bright even through my closed eyelids.

And now—What in the world? How did I get back here?

I'm standing on the heath. My body is perfectly intact, and the *whooshing* has stopped.

The girl is walking toward me again. Her pleated skirt swishes in the wind while she struggles to tame it and her purse dangles from her shoulder.

And there are the two muggers, shoving their way across the grass, laughing. The bald guy whistles at her. Then comes the shout: "Oi, gorgeous!"

I press my hand to my head and take a few steps back. This isn't possible. I've seen it all, just like this, a few minutes ago. It's already happened.

So how can it be happening again?

The girl breaks into a run, just as she did a few moments ago, and the bald guy catches her arm, just as I knew he would—

But this time, another figure appears from behind the church. I'm sure it's a guy, judging from his powerful frame and the loping way he slinks along the church wall, but he's too deep in the shadows for me to see his face.

He is very still. Watching. Crouching lower.

Then he erupts from his hiding place and sprints across the field. He tackles the bald guy, driving them both into the lanky guy. They hit the ground hard.

"Run!" the stranger shouts at the girl. "Get out of here!"

She sprints in the direction of the village.

I stumble toward the church, hunkering down in the same shadows that concealed the girl's savior a moment ago. I should leave, but I need to know what happened— what's *happening*. If I'm seeing the same event unfold again, why is it different?

I can't leave until I know.

The three guys are throwing their fists into each other's faces. They look like a tangle of detached limbs, with feet slamming into ribcages and elbows pounding noses. I can hardly tell whose hands are whose and which one is winning, or if everyone is just getting beaten to a pulp. I'm sure the stranger will lose this fight in spite of his size; it's two against one, after all.

Unless I jump in to help.

I push my sleeves up and rake my fingers through my hair. "Okay," I mutter, and take a deep breath while wiping my palms on my jeans. "One, two, th—"

The fight loosens for a moment and I straighten. The stranger isn't losing. Not even close.

The short bald thug is limping, blood streaming from his lip. His friend doesn't seem to be able to catch his breath. But the new guy throws one punch after another, each one delivering just as much force as the one before it. Finally, the bald mugger staggers toward the black car and yanks the door open. He slides into the driver's seat and cranks the engine, easing away from the curb as if he's going to abandon his friend, who scrambles toward the street with a panicked expression.

"Oi!" he shrieks at the moving car. He clambers across the grass and throws himself into the passenger seat. The door slams shut and the tires squeal as the bald guy hits the gas, filling the air with the smell of burning rubber as the black car hurtles toward downtown.

Silence covers me like a blanket.

I ease into the dusky half-light, watching the mysterious stranger. He's standing in the middle of the heath with his arms hanging loosely at his sides. His back is to me, but when he looks down at his bloodied knuckles, I catch the outline of his profile. Straight nose, strong jaw. A sheen of sweat covers his powerful arms, and blood trickles from his short dark hair into his eyebrow.

He looks over his shoulder, and his eyes lock on mine.

Alarms go off in my head: *Danger, danger, get out!*

I'm standing less than ten yards behind him and I'm clearly unarmed. I'd assumed he was a good guy because he beat up the girl's attackers, but what if he's part of some rival gang or something? What if he was waiting for the girl to walk past the church, and he was just mad the other guys got to her first?

I want to run away, but my feet might as well be cemented to the ground. He could kill me with his bare hands. His eyebrows pinch together like he can't believe I'm still here. His fists clench; are they itching for more action? I'm an idiot for staying here just to watch the guys fight, just to try to figure out what happened.

He drags a hand across his mouth and it comes away streaked with blood—his bottom lip is split. "Go home," he says in a voice that rumbles like faraway thunder. "The heath is dangerous tonight."

I manage one step back. "What—what happened? Did you—"

"Go!" He strides toward me, closing the gap between us so that I can see the fury in his eyes. "If they come back, I might not be able to stop them again, yeah? So go!"

His accent is rough around the edges—not the rounded syllables of London's well-to-do areas. This guy is a local, born and bred on the south side.

Just like Papa.

"The pressure," I say, wrapping my arms around myself. "And that noise. What was it?"

His expression shifts from anger to disbelief. "Sorry?"

"It sounded like a giant vacuum, or a hundred hot tubs turned on at once." Wow, that was a genius comparison. "Okay, maybe not hot tubs, but—"

"Go home." He's backing away from me now, and his eyes dart around the heath as if he's waiting for someone else to jump out at us. "Right now. Turn around and run back to your hotel, or wherever you're staying. Don't come back until daylight."

I step backwards, but I can't quite make myself turn around. "I saw two endings," I blurt. "Why?"

He stops.

Then he strides toward me again, fists tight, eyes lit with urgency. "I said *get out!*"

I stumble back and hit the ground on my butt, hard. He's still coming toward me. I can hear my racing pulse in my ears. Asking questions was obviously not a good move; I should have run the moment I knew the girl would be okay. What if this guy hurts me?

I'm not sticking around to find out.

Swallowing the panic that threatens to paralyze me, I plant my hands on the dry earth to push myself up, scramble to recover my balance, and take off for Nana's.

FOUR

M Y HANDS TREMBLE AS I OPEN THE FRONT DOOR AND slip into the hush of the entryway. I'm still shaky over what happened with Papa, but now that I've been to the heath, my insides feel like a giant swarm of bees. Did I really see two outcomes to the same mugging, or was that just a hallucination caused by jet lag and the shock of Papa's death?

I need to go to bed.

"I'm back," I call toward the kitchen as the door clicks shut behind me.

No response.

I stop by the sitting room and retrieve my phone from the couch, exactly where I dropped it after Stephen dumped me. He has called me five times.

I block his number and then erase it from my contacts list. I know myself—if I don't take preventative measures now, I'll end up calling him back.

Everybody else in the house is probably conked out already. Staying awake until a respectable bedtime is nearly impossible on the first day—jet lag usually has us stumbling toward our beds by sundown. But just in case, I peek into the kitchen.

Dad's slouching at the table, wearing a stained undershirt and gray sweatpants. Yet another cup of tea sits in front of him—or maybe it's the same one from earlier, still unconsumed. His face is buried in his hands, and he's wearing one black sock on his right foot. His left foot is bare. I can picture him sitting down to take off his socks—such a mundane thing after a day like today—and getting frustrated at it not coming off quickly enough. He probably threw it across the room and decided not to bother with the other one.

A large part of me doesn't want to talk to Dad, which is terrible but true. I'm torn between pretending I never saw him and locking myself in my room, or doing the right thing and checking on him. Man, I want to choose the easy way out. I could sneak upstairs, unpack my things, and start researching the word "Mortiferi" along with the freaky alternate-ending stuff I think I just experienced. I wouldn't have to deal with Dad's emotions, at least not until morning.

My fingers drum silently against the doorframe. Then I take a deep breath. "Dad?"

He sniffles and looks up. "Rosebud. I didn't hear you come in."

His face is lined and patchy, as if he's been napping since I left. There are red blotches underneath his eyes from where he propped his face on his hands, and his glasses are lying on the table. He puts them on without wiping them on his T-shirt first. I don't think I've ever seen him skip that step before.

I open my mouth to say—what? I'm sorry about Papa? I'm sorry he spoke into my mind—at least, I think he did—and I can't talk about it because *what if I'm crazy?*

I'm sorry I can't tell you what just happened on the heath because I don't know if it was real?

"Stephen and I broke up," I say.

Holy crap. Where did that come from?

Dad's eyebrows lift. "Too bad. You all right?"

"Not really."

He nods. "Sorry about that."

I dig my toe into the floor. If he doesn't ask any follow-up questions, then I don't know what else to say.

"Right," he says, getting up from his chair with a grunt. "Better get to bed."

He moves toward the door, leaving his cup on the table. Tears spring to my eyes. Is it so impossible for him to talk to me about Stephen? Doesn't he care that I've said goodbye to my grandfather and my boyfriend in the same day? I get that he's hurting—he just lost his dad, after all. And I didn't even want to talk to him when I walked into the kitchen. But now that I've confessed what happened with Stephen, I'm desperate for a little fatherly compassion.

"Dad?" I say, hoping I can get him to stay. "Did you want your tea?"

He stops with his back to me. His head turns a fraction—a flicker of movement accompanied by a deep sigh. "If you want me to clean up after myself, then say so."

"No, that's not what I meant. I just—"

He waves me off, and I leave the sentence hanging. How could he have misinterpreted my words that badly? He stalks back to the table and hooks the mug's handle with two fingers, sloshing tea onto the pale oak finish. His lips are turned down at the corners, exactly like a baseball pitcher's before he throws a fastball.

"Wait," I say, holding up a hand. "I didn't mean for you to clean it up, I was just hoping—"

He hurls the mug into the kitchen sink. It slams into the stainless steel and sprays the wall with dark droplets. One chunk of ceramic bounces out of the sink and lands on the counter with a delicate *dink*. The other two chunks slide toward the drain.

"Go up to your room," he seethes.

I know better than to hesitate.

THE ROOM I USE AT NANA'S HOUSE USED TO BE MY AUNT Alison's. It's small, but the walls are almost the same shade of pale green as my bedroom in Nashville, and the carpet is soft and thick. I slip beneath the patchwork quilt Nana made when Aunt Alison was a child. The sheets are cool against my skin, which is still giving off steam from my impromptu sprint to Nana's house. My thighs are going to burn tomorrow.

Dad's temper tantrum ruined any remaining chance of sleep, so I tug my phone out of my pocket and pull up the Web browser. It's time to do some research.

Search term #1: *alternate ending to same event*

My screen fills with links to deleted scenes from the movie *Event Horizon* and the definition of the phrase "alternate ending."

Great. That's really helpful.

Search term #2: *I saw the same event twice*

There's a story about a man who was struck by lightning twice, someone complaining about a country club event being uploaded to a website twice, and a book reviewer's blog post entitled "Why I Read the Same Book Twice (and Enjoyed It!)."

Nope, not what I'm looking for.

Search term #3: *my mind is playing tricks on me*

The first result is a forum on out-of-body experiences, and predictably, it's full of people claiming one crazy thing after another. One guy, "JediWarrior423," swears he can time travel in his bathtub. A woman, "BunnyGirl4U," says she might have been brainwashed by aliens because she can't remember anything from her high school years. Interestingly, she also mentions seeing the aliens more clearly when she takes her "special pills." Somehow, I don't think BunnyGirl4U and I are having the same experience.

Only one girl, "PhoebeMP," says something that lands in the right ballpark. "I hit my head and blacked out," her post reads, "and when I woke up, I felt like I was reliving the past day of my life all over again."

Of course, the comments on her post are full of people telling her to go to the hospital, or see a psychologist, or stop watching *Groundhog Day* on repeat.

I scroll through the rest of the forum, but Phoebe doesn't show up again. Noticing a search box in the top corner of the page, I type in her username, but the only result is the post I've already read. So Phoebe had a weird experience, posted about it on the Internet, got made fun of, and never came back.

Maybe she had legitimate head trauma.

Or maybe she decided it was all a dream.

What happened to me could have been a dream. The swirling colors, the deafening noise, the suctioning in my gut…

Go home. The heath is dangerous tonight.

I've never had a dream that vivid, and anyway, I wasn't asleep.

Search term #4: *Mortiferi.*

I'm assuming that's how it's spelled; it sounds Latin, and thanks to my eighth-grade Latin elective, I know that "mort" is a common root for words related to death, like *mortality*. It would make sense that "Mortiferi" had something to do with dying. And Papa spoke it into my mind right before he died.

Did you mean MODIFIER? asks my search engine.

I bark out a loud "Ha!" and toss my phone on the mattress. If the Internet can't come up with any answers, then I don't know where else to look.

I heave myself out of bed and walk to the full-length mirror on the closet door. My necklace hangs innocently around my neck and I reach up to touch it, torn between throwing it away and keeping it forever. The smooth gold beneath my fingers sends an ache through my heart, and I stop breathing for a second, hoping the pain will pass.

It does, and my fingers fall away from the rings.

"I'll take it off soon," I assure myself in the mirror over my dresser. "Really soon. Like, tonight."

My reflection and I nod at each other, and I look away before I'm forced to acknowledge my own stupidity.

My brain isn't even close to settling down for the night, and my answer to restless thoughts is always the same—tea with scones. Nana keeps scones on hand like most people keep toilet paper or coffee. They're a staple in her kitchen, and to go a day without them would be madness.

Paul's room is next to mine on the top floor. The master bedroom sits down a short flight of creaky wooden stairs. Mom and Dad stay in the guest room on the first floor, and I'm hoping that's where Dad is now; if he's come back out to make more tea he'll never drink, I might just have to take my snack upstairs. He's never hurt any of us—well, not me, anyway. I don't think he's ever hurt Paul or Mom. But his fits of rage are strong enough to make him damage other things, like dishes and electronics, or whatever happens to be in his way at the time.

The steps complain beneath my bare feet as I creep down to the second floor. Nana's door is halfway open, her dainty snore drifting from somewhere in the darkened room. Good—she's getting some sleep.

I glance into the room and notice Papa's reading glasses on the nightstand, illuminated by the dim hallway light coming through the open door. They're delicate gold frames with one broken nose pad he never bothered to replace. It's weird, seeing them and knowing he'll never put them on again. I don't know how Nana can sleep in that bed knowing the other side will always be empty. It must feel so cold.

My eyes start to burn, and I hurry down the rest of the stairs to the first floor.

I don't know if I can handle being in this house all summer.

FIVE

IT's BEEN TWO DAYS SINCE PAPA DIED. TWO DAYS SINCE
a casual walk on the heath turned into a vortex of
impossibility. And now, on my third day in London, I've
entered a different kind of vortex—the kind where my
brother makes a quick trip to the grocery store feel like
never-ending torture.

"Put the beer down, Paul." How many times have I
said that in the past year? "It's not on the list, and you're
not old enough to drink. Not even in Britain."

He shoots me a withering glare while setting a case of
Stella Artois back on the shelf. "I know. I'm just looking.
Why are you being such a mom?"

"Because," I say, adding a pint of milk to the basket
on my arm, "your actual mom isn't here. Somebody's got
to keep you in line. Hey, grab that loaf of French bread
behind you."

Nana wants to cook dinner for us tonight. She has
cried almost nonstop for the past two days, barely holding
back her tears when well-wishers stopped by, and then
starting back up the moment they left. Her friend Irene
came over yesterday evening. They spent nearly three

hours in the back garden, talking over glasses of chilled white wine. What Irene said to her, I have no idea, but Nana's been marginally less weepy ever since.

Since Paul and I have been busy all day with a whole lot of nothing, I volunteered us to walk down to the Costcutter and pick up a few ingredients for dinner. Conveniently, this also gets us out of the house, which has grown gloomier with each passing moment. The depression weighs on my chest when I'm there, like water pressure at the bottom of a pool. I can't take it. I'm going to have to find more excuses to leave.

"What time are Mom and Dad coming home?" I ask, perusing a shelf of pastas. Vermicelli, macaroni, capellini, fusilli…I don't see Nana's requested gemelli, and the boxes are starting to blur together.

Paul shrugs. "Dunno. Before dinner, I guess. Unless Mom decides to follow a rabbit trail."

Our parents have been downtown all day doing research for Mom's latest book on the London working class in the 17th century. She's a history professor at Vanderbilt—or, as her website bio describes her, "one of the leading historians of culture in the early modern British Atlantic world, with a focus on race, slavery, and empire." She's always working on something extraordinarily specific, like 18th century slave clothing or the working conditions of tobacco shops during the Georgian era. This means our London summers often turn into historical scavenger hunts, and after a few unsuccessful attempts to involve Paul and me in the process, she now either goes alone or with Dad.

Today's excursion was probably more of a distraction for Dad than anything else, but Paul's right—if Mom picks up on an interesting rabbit trail, there's no telling when they'll get home.

"Dude!" Paul barks behind me. "Pick out some friggin' pasta."

I snap out of my daze. How long have I been standing in front of this shelf? The girl behind the checkout counter is watching me with a slightly open mouth. I arch my eyebrows at her, and she snaps back to her *OK!* magazine.

"Nana's pasta isn't here," I say, grabbing a bag of fusilli. "This is close enough. You still have the bread? Or have you swapped it out for a six-pack of Corona?"

The words burn as they leave my mouth. I know better.

Paul blinks at the floor and then holds up the bread with a scowl. "I realize I'm a screw-up, but I *am* capable of holding a loaf of bread for two minutes."

Resentment lies thick beneath his words. Yes, my little brother has problems, but nobody deserves to feel like a total failure. I put a hand on his arm and wait for him to look at me. "Hey. Just because you've made some bad choices doesn't mean you're a screw-up."

"Of course not. Which is why I'm starting Camp Loser tomorrow."

London is home to a massive counseling program for teens called SPARK (Southwark Program for Addicted and Rebellious Kids) that also boasts a well-respected grief program. I assume this is because so many addictions and rebellions are rooted in some kind of grief—the death of a loved one, the splitting up of a family, or just a general lack of love. Mom enrolled Paul back in April, a mere two weeks before we found out about Papa's diagnosis. He'll spend six hours a day talking about his feelings with a counselor and playing icebreaker games. Even though he's horrified, I'm confident it will help him.

"Don't call it that," I say with a sigh. "I know it sucks, but you need to be there—it'll be way better than hanging out at Nana's all day. Plus, those people can help you."

"Help me with what?" His voice is high. Redness seeps into his cheeks. "I don't have 'problems,' Rosie. I have a best friend who's pretty much dead. They can't fix Carter, can they? So what's the point?"

I put a finger to my lips as the cashier's eyes dart to us. Then I grab Paul's arm and pull him around a display of pre-packaged dessert cakes.

"What are you doing?" he snaps.

I switch the grocery basket from one arm to the other. "Giving us some privacy. Do you really think you don't need help?"

His eyes flicker to the floor as he licks his lips—a classic Paul Clayton tell that assures me he knows how bad things have gotten, but he's too embarrassed to admit it.

"It doesn't have to be like this," I say.

He shoves his hands into the frayed pockets of his jeans. "Well, it *is* like this. And a stupid camp isn't going to change any of it, especially since Mom and Dad are just using it to keep me out of the way."

"Keep you out of the way? What are you talking about?"

"Come on, Rosie," he says with a bitter laugh. "The professional counselor isn't working. The rehab center didn't work. They know this SPARK thing won't work either, but it'll keep me occupied. That's all they care about."

How can he believe that's true? After everything our parents have done for him, does he really think they just want him out of the way?

"They signed you up before we knew about Papa," I say. "So that has nothing to do with it. Mom and Dad love you. They want you to stop drinking. They want you to pull up your grades and make it to high school graduation." We hold each other's eyes for a moment, and his are full of such hopelessness it almost brings me to my knees. "Don't you know how much they care? How much *I* care?"

For an instant, his expression softens. My heart lifts just a little—maybe I'm finally getting through.

"Paul?" I whisper. "Are you hearing me?"

But then his face tightens back up. He shakes his head and says, "Whatever. Let's pay for this stuff and get out of here."

My shoulders sag as he turns toward the register. I felt so close to connecting with him—like I was an inch away from unearthing the old Paul, buried somewhere inside this stranger I call my brother. I blink at the grocery list in my hand, trying to clear my mind. Then my eyes focus on the last item we're supposed to get.

"Hold on, we need one more thing." *Pistachio ice cream,* it says in Nana's careful cursive. That's funny. None of us likes pistachio ice cream.

Except for Papa.

Does she actually want me to buy it, or was it simply on the list before he died?

It's possible she wants to have it for dessert as a sort of tribute, so I grab the ice cream from the freezer and join Paul at the checkout. The cashier—a slightly built girl with hot pink lipstick and skin so fair it's practically transparent—looks us over as she rings up our groceries. She seems familiar, but I can't figure out why. The only people I know here are friends of Papa and Nana's, or Dad's old buddies from secondary school; she's definitely not one of them. She's probably a couple years older than me, with rings on every finger and fluffy golden hair like a lion's mane.

"What are you two doing in Blackheath?" she asks in a thick Cockney accent. Our groceries zip through her hands and over a scanner. "Are you on holiday or something?"

"Sort of," I say. "Visiting family."

"That'll be twelve pounds nineteen, love. Are you American? Canadian?"

"American." I count out the money and hand it to her, watching her slap it into the register drawer. "We're from Tennessee."

She chews on a metallic-green fingernail. "Wicked. Things are pretty slow around here most of the time, but you still gotta watch your back. Take care, okay?"

"I always do," Paul mumbles as I heft the bag into my arms. He heads for the door, and I'm about to follow him when I place the cashier's face—at least, I think I do. Maybe I'm wrong and she's not who I think she is. But what if I'm right?

"Hey," I say, turning back to the register as Paul exits onto the sidewalk. The door falls closed behind him, and I'm glad because I don't want him to hear this conversation. "This is kind of a weird question, but were you on the heath the other night?"

Her eyes grow wide. "Yeah! You see me on the news yesterday morning?"

Nope. I'd searched for stories about it online, but didn't find anything. She must have done an interview for the local morning news program, *Blackheath Daybreak*, and I slept through it. "Uh, yeah. What did you say to the reporter, again? I can't remember exactly—"

"Oh, it was all about the attack, wasn't it? Bloody scary, that was." She shakes her head slowly, staring at the space between us. "If it hadn't been for that bloke…"

An image of the mysterious stranger's face, bloodied and bruised, flashes through my mind. "What bloke?" I manage. I want to hear her say it out loud. If she confirms what happened that night—even in part—I'll have an easier time believing it myself.

"Surely you heard me talking about him in the interview. The bloke who chased them fellas away. He saved my life."

"Right." I steady myself with one hand planted firmly on the counter. "So the muggers never touched you?"

"Just the one time, when they grabbed my arm. But it could've been quite a bit worse."

Yes, it could have been worse. It *was* worse—more so than she'll ever know. I'll never forget watching her get shoved into the backseat of that car. I'll never forget the way her scream cut off so abruptly, and how helpless I felt, desperate to stop those guys but completely powerless to do so.

The cashier glances out the window and then leans closer to me, eyes wide. "They never found the guy who saved me, you know. I think he was an angel."

I take a deep breath before responding. "Hmm. Maybe. Either way, you're a lucky girl. I'm glad you're okay."

"Me too, mate. Things like that don't normally happen 'round here." She tilts her head and squints at me. "Feeling all right?"

My emotions must be leaking through to my expression. I stand up a little straighter and force a smile.

"I'm fine," I say, too quickly. "Just hungry. I better go."

"Right then. You be careful on your way home, yeah?" Her tone is dark, as if the prospect of walking outside equates to imminent danger. Which, for her, it probably does.

"I'll be fine." I nod toward Paul, who's waiting outside. "I've got my brother."

She gazes at him through the glass. "Hmm, and ain't he fit."

"Um…yes?" The cashier meets my eyes, and we both laugh. Wrapping my head around the idea that Paul could ever be considered *hot* is going to take some time. "He's available, although I'm not sure he's boyfriend material."

"Uh-oh," she says with a grin. "Trouble, is he?"

I amble toward the door. "Like you wouldn't believe."

"Too bad," she mumbles, and goes back to chewing her green nails.

I have to focus on each step as I walk across the floor and push the door open. As soon as I'm outside, I thrust the bag against Paul's chest and take several deep breaths, leaning back against the plate glass window.

He wraps an arm around the groceries. "What's wrong with you?"

"Nothing."

There's no way I can tell him what happened on the heath that night—at least, not yet. The details are still too sketchy in my mind, and even though I know I experienced *something* out there, I don't know what it was.

He frowns at me. "Well, 'nothing' has made you white as a ghost. Are you sure you're okay?"

And there it is. A glimpse of the brother I used to have, the one who cried when I skinned my knee and stayed by my bed when I had the flu, even though Mom did her best to keep him away from my germs. The one who picked violets in the backyard and gave them to me while I sat in time-out, stricken with grief over lying to Dad about how many cookies I'd had before dinner.

Tears sting my eyes, but I blink them back. I would give anything to get the old Paul back—*anything*. If he still talked to me the way he used to, I would have told him everything about the heath, whether I had all the details straight or not.

"I'm okay," I say, looking away from him. "Let's go home."

"Hold on." He puts a hand on my arm. "Did the cashier say something to upset you?"

"No, no," I say, even though this is not exactly true. "We were talking about you, actually. Good news—you've got a date with her any time you want. She thinks you're *fit.*"

He scrunches up his nose. "Hmm. I might be interested, if her hair didn't look like a wild animal's. Did she say whether our date would involve bringing down a wildebeest?"

"Like you have so much room to be choosy," I say, biting back a smile. Paul's giving me a snippet of our old relationship, but the moment he realizes it, he'll stop. "Come on, let's get back to the house. Nana will want to start dinner soon."

"Can we get a movie first?" He nods at the Prime Time video store.

I raise my eyebrows. "From a video rental store? What is this, 2003?"

"It's not like Nana streams movies on her TV," he says, throwing his hands out to his sides. "Dad convinced her to buy a DVD player just for us. It'd be rude of us not to use it."

I want to ask why he suddenly cares about being rude, but I'd better keep my mouth closed. If he wants to get a movie, we'll get a movie—rental store and all.

"Can't argue with that," I say. "Let's go."

We set off down the sidewalk into the village, passing the travel agency and Nana's favorite wine shop on our way to Prime Time Video. Logically, the place should have shut down years ago, but the locals make sure it stays in business. Paul hands me the bag of groceries as we reach the door.

I give him a wry look. "Need both hands for movie browsing?"

"It's a big job, love," he says in a terrible impression of an English accent. "Can't be hampered by groceries and whatnot."

He smiles at me as we push through the door, and I can't help grinning back, which alerts him to his cheerfulness. His expression sours instantly, and the metaphorical cloud settles over his head again. New Paul has returned. But I got to spend a moment with Old Paul, and now I'm even more determined to get him back for good.

The inside of the store is pleasantly cool, with funky red carpet and a circular checkout desk set into the center. I roam the aisles, only vaguely registering the movies lining the shelves. Paul already has his nose in the video games—funny, since he's the one who insisted we get a movie—so it's just me and the groceries, loitering in the drama section. A jingling bell announces someone else's arrival. I turn toward the door.

It's him. The mysterious stranger from the heath. His split lip has halfway healed, and the gash on his eyebrow has been stitched up. Imaginary people don't go to the doctor for stitches. His injuries are real. *He* is real.

Spots cross into my vision and I turn around before he sees me. First I talk to the cashier, who just happens to be the girl who got mugged and then *didn't* get mugged, and now I see the guy who saved her. It feels like fate—or whatever controls the universe—is trying to convince me that everything I experienced that night was real. But as far as I know, it's impossible to see the same event unfold twice with two separate endings. So how can this guy be standing twenty feet away from me? If he's real, and the cashier is real, does that mean all of it was real?

I might throw up.

No. There's no time for vomit. I've got to take advantage of this opportunity to watch him and gather as much information as I can. He was the catalyst that changed the outcome of the mugging last night; he must be connected to the vortex I felt. Maybe he'll say or do something that will give me some clue as to what happened.

I move to the center of the store and drop to the floor in front of a shelf of romantic comedies, clutching the groceries to my chest. There's a gap in the movies that allows me to spy on him through the wire-mesh shelves. He's got short black hair that would be curly if he grew it out, pale green eyes, and evidence of a recent fistfight all over his face. He's so tall that he has to look down when the clerk behind the desk asks if he needs any help, and the clerk isn't all that short. Now that I'm getting a better look at him, I'm not surprised he was able to handle both muggers on his own. Anybody who tried to fight this guy would be asking for a hospital visit.

"Help you find anything?" another clerk bellows as he bursts from the back room, arms loaded with movies and video games.

His question seems to be directed at the store in general, so we all mumble that we're just looking and turn back to the shelves. I peek at the mystery guy while pretending to look at a copy of *You've Got Mail*. A thick black watch wraps around his left wrist—nothing fancy, just a single digital display. A scar, purple and jagged, begins just in front of his left ear and traces a path to the bottom of his jaw. Unlike the fresh bruises on his face, this mark is something he's carried for years.

The bell flies into a frenzy as the door opens again. A tall, stern-looking girl sticks her head in the store, surveys the room for two seconds, and scowls at the mystery guy.

"Albert!" She sweeps her long black hair away from her face. "I thought you knew what you wanted! How long are you planning to faff about in here?"

Aha! His name is Albert. It's not much, but it's more information than I had five seconds ago.

"I can't decide," he says in a slow, casual tone that makes her nostrils flare. "*Pretty In Pink* or *Labyrinth?*"

He flinches as she chucks her white leather purse in his direction. It falls to the floor about three feet in front of him.

"Wicked throw, Case. Signing up for that cricket team soon, are you?" He brings her purse back to her with a grin. She snatches it out of his hand with a reluctant smile, and I notice her eyes are the same pale green as his. Same hair, same eyes…same parents?

"You might be planning to sit at home all night like an old man, but Dan and I have plans," she says, gesturing through the front window. "So come on, then. Don't take all day. And get something good, will you? I can't have a brother who watches shoddy films."

Rising to a half-crouch, I peer over the top shelf toward the front of the store. Two guys are outside, leaning against the window. One of them, a gangly redhead, smashes his nose against the glass and makes a mock-angry face at Albert. Then he presses his mouth to the window and exhales a circle of steam. The other guy—tall and built, with dreadlocks that hang past his shoulders—gazes out at the street with his arms crossed.

"Plans," Albert echoes with arched eyebrows. "So you've finally agreed to go out with Dan."

The girl rolls her eyes and pokes him in the ribs. "We don't have plans with each other, you muppet. Plans with *other people.*"

"All right, all right. Let me pay for this, and I'll be done."

She flounces back out to the sidewalk, shooting a dark look at Albert through the window while talking to the tall redheaded guy. He laughs and says something that makes her slap him on the arm.

Albert makes his selection, and before I can maneuver to a better spot to see what it is, he's paid for it and left—swept down the street by his friends.

"Yo," says a voice behind me.

I jump and drop the groceries. "Jeez, Paul!"

"Relax." He bends down to put everything back in the bag. "I was just going to ask you if *Snatch* is okay. Didn't mean to make you think your life was in danger."

"Sorry. I was just thinking about—I was just thinking. *Snatch* is fine, but I'm not watching it with Nana or our parents. You'll have to get something rated PG if you want this to be a family affair."

He shrugs and stands up with the bag. "I'll just watch it once everybody goes to bed."

"Sure," I say, staring through the window. I wish the mystery guy—Albert—hadn't left so quickly. Not that I was planning to talk to him, but it would have been nice to hear a little more of his conversation. Maybe I could have picked up a few more tidbits about who he is.

Paul's hand waves in front of my face. "What is wrong with you? Aren't you going to tell me I have to go to bed early tonight? Remind me that I have a big day tomorrow at SNARK?"

"SPARK," I correct blandly, forcing my attention back to him. "And yeah, you do have a big day tomorrow. Let's get you home."

SIX

"YOU DON'T HAVE TO DO THIS, NANA," I say as Paul sets the groceries on the kitchen counter. "Cook for us, I mean. We can fend for ourselves."

There's a large pot of water boiling on the stovetop. Nana is bent over with her head inside the refrigerator, rifling through the produce drawer.

"Where is that parsley?" she mutters, sweeping aside a collection of fat-free yogurt cups. "I know it's here somewhere. Refrigerators are like bags, aren't they? Even when you know something is inside, you can't put your hands on it for anything."

I run my fingers along the strangely spotless countertop. Paul ambles over to the table, but instead of pulling out a chair like he usually does, he eyes the whole space as if he doesn't trust it. Everything is so clean—sparkling windows, smudge-free appliances, and no trace of the clutter I've come to expect on every surface in this house. Dad's broken mug has been cleaned up. Did he think better of his actions and do it himself? Or did Mom or Nana have to deal with it?

There isn't one piece of dirt on the floor, not even in the corners, and I know this is unusual because I have distinct memories of dust bunnies under the kitchen table. Paul and I have always joked about how you better wear shoes at dinner, because if you don't, the dust bunnies might nibble your toes off.

Paul places a hand on the back of a chair, then removes it and leans against the wall instead. He's probably afraid he'll mess something up.

"Did you hear me, Nana?" I say as she fishes the pasta out of the grocery bag. "We can just have peanut butter and jelly tonight. There's no reason for you to go to all this trouble. Mom and Dad aren't even back yet."

If she hears me, she doesn't show it. Instead, she rips open the box of pasta and dumps it into the boiling water. Her glasses slip down her nose as she stands over the steam, but she doesn't push them up. She just stirs the pasta with a long wooden spoon, watching it as if it's going to jump out of the pot and run away.

"I know I don't have to cook," she finally says in a wavering voice, and it suddenly hits me that she didn't reply right away because she didn't trust herself to speak. She rubs at a grease spot on the stove with her blue-striped apron and then goes back to stirring. "But cooking helps me think about something other than…well, you know."

"Of course," I say quickly, digging the carton of ice cream out of the bottom of the grocery bag. Nana's not watching, and I'm still not sure if she intended for me to buy it or not, so I sneak over to the freezer and ease the door open. There's another carton of pistachio there already. It's covered in frost. I pick it up, and my hand sags with its weight. It slips from my fingers and lands by my feet with a thud.

"Oh," Nana says, and I look up to see an expression of vague surprise on her face. She raises her eyebrows at the frostbitten ice cream on the floor. "I'm so used to him going through a pint of that stuff a week, I didn't even think about not buying—"

My stomach fills with lead. I cram both cartons into the freezer and shut the door too hard. "No problem," I say. "Someone will eat it, I'm sure."

None of us will eat it. Not a chance.

"Right," Nana says.

A heavy silence falls over the kitchen. Paul pulls a chair away from the table and the scraping sound it makes over the wooden floor seems to fill the room. He slides into his seat and examines his fingernails.

Nana fixes a smile on her face. "Rosie, my dear. I'd love for you to wash and slice that tomato."

"Sure thing."

I grab the tomato off the counter and hold it under the faucet, letting the cold water run between my fingers and over the backs of my hands. I thought dealing with the grief in this house was bad, but Nana's determination to avoid talking about Papa is worse. If there's one thing that makes my skin crawl, it's a fake smile. Seeing one on Nana's face is enough to set all my nerves on edge. But now isn't the time to demand authenticity from her. In our family sessions, Paul's counselor always says to let him grieve in his own time, in his own way. It makes sense to do the same for Nana.

I guess I've learned more from Paul's counselor than I thought. Maybe even more than Paul has.

I place the tomato on the cutting board and pull a sharp knife out of the drawer below me. The outer surface is so smooth beneath my fingers—plump and firm, just the right size. I place the tip of the blade on the tomato's skin and—

"Oh!" Nana cries.

I jump, and the knife slips suddenly toward my hand. "Nana! I almost sliced my thumb open!"

"So sorry, my dear, but I forgot to tell you something Irene said last night."

I catch my expression a nanosecond before it falls into complete horror. "Oh? What?"

"She's got a good match for you, I think," Nana says. "You know, since you've called it off with your boyfriend."

I stab the tomato with my knife and slice off a thick, uneven chunk. Nana's friend Irene is constantly trying to set me up with a "nice English boy," even though I haven't been single in almost two years. Now that I'm not dating Stephen anymore, she'll be particularly aggressive, cornering me in the kitchen with her bright red bifocals and her coffee breath. This so-called "good match" is probably the grandson of one of her knitting club friends who's just "marvelous, such a lovely lad," and I'll be forced to look at a picture of him from three years ago when he had a bowl cut and braces, and then it will take all the avoidance techniques I can summon to keep from committing to a date.

I stare at the tomato. "How do you know about Stephen? I've only told Dad about that."

"He told me yesterday morning. He thought you wouldn't mind."

Paul leaps out of his chair. I'd almost forgotten he was in the room, he's been so quiet.

"You broke up with Stephen? When did this happen? Every detail of my life is public knowledge, but you break up with your boyfriend and no one says anything?" He throws his hands in the air. "I'm going upstairs. Call me when dinner's ready."

Nana and I stare at each other until his bedroom door slams. Her lips pull into a tight line, and I have to stifle a momentary spark of hatred toward my brother for just straight-up abandoning me to this conversation.

"I do hope he makes some progress this summer," Nana says.

I nod. "I think we're all hoping for that."

Everything is quiet for a moment.

She must have forgotten.

Thank you, crazy little brother, for creating enough of a diversion to give me an escape.

"Anyway," Nana says, and I suppress a groan. "Irene is desperate for you to meet this boy James. Apparently he's perfect in every way. Had a bit of academic trouble in his past, but he's sorted it out now and has become a lovely young man. An angel, in her words."

I freeze with my knife hovering over the tomato. The cashier's words float to the front of my mind: *I think he was an angel.*

Nana looks less miserable right now than she has at any other point since Papa died. Maybe setting up this date would be a good distraction for her, and if it had been more than three days since Stephen broke up with me, I might have the strength to indulge her. But I can't. The wound is too fresh.

I slice through the tomato again, more gently this time. "I don't think so. Tell Irene I appreciate the thought, but I *just* broke up with Stephen."

"Ah," Nana says. "Well. It was only an idea."

I set down my knife to scratch my neck, and my fingers decide to make a pit stop at the necklace on their way back down. They touch the golden rings for little more than a second, but Nana sees it. And unlike Mom, Nana isn't afraid to ask questions.

"Are you in love with Stephen?" she asks.

My lip trembles dangerously. I take a deep, shuddering breath. "We were together since the summer before our sophomore year. He was practically part of my soul. And he dumped me the same day Papa died, which I realize isn't nearly as big of a deal, but it hurts." I cut off another slice of tomato and blink back tears.

"Hmm." She eyes me, and I stare through the back window into the garden, thinking about how nice it would be to sit in one of those wrought-iron chairs with a cup of tea—alone. "Do you know how long your grandfather and I had been married?"

I shake my head.

"Forty-two years."

My mind boggles a little. I could live my entire life over again and still not match the time she's spent with Papa. Stephen and I couldn't even hold it together until senior year.

"Forty-two years," she says again, as if the number surprises her almost as much as me. "If I can keep my head up, my darling, then so can you."

My breakup snaps into perspective—although I'm not sure it's fair to compare my dating relationship to her marriage.

"Now, what do you say about meeting this James? Nothing serious, just a bit of fun." She arches an eyebrow at me and opens the refrigerator.

I consider the proposal again as she pulls an enormous carrot out of the produce drawer. Stephen and I weren't together for forty-two years, but my heart is still shattered. I can't fathom sitting across a table from a guy who isn't him. I can't imagine looping my arm through anyone else's, or sitting in anyone else's car, or feeling anyone else's hand on my waist when we dance.

"Maybe," I say, keeping my eyes fixed on the tomato as the blade carves through it. "I'll think about it."

What she doesn't know is that I've already thought about it, and the answer is no.

She leans closer to me. Her perfume, something floral with a hint of fruit, drifts past my nose. "Keep in mind that if you refuse, Irene will interrogate you about it the next time you see her. And I'm hosting knitting club this month, so you'll see her in about two weeks."

She's right about the interrogation. Last time I refused one of Irene's setups, right before Stephen and I became official, she came over for tea and grilled me about my love life for an entire hour. There are few things worse than an old lady with lipstick on her teeth asking about the last time you kissed a boy.

I've got one more possible escape up my sleeve. "Have Mom and Dad met him? You know Dad won't let me go out with a guy he doesn't know."

"Your dad has met him several times," Nana says, smiling at the carrot as she peels it. She's totally onto me. "He grew up with James's mum."

I squeeze my eyes shut; there goes my last hope. "Okay. But," I say, pointing at her with my tomato juice-covered knife, "I'm only committing to one date. I'm not saying yes if he proposes, unless he happens to be a prince and I'd get a royal wedding out of the deal."

"Perfect! You're meeting him at the Hare & Billet at seven o'clock tomorrow night."

I turn to her with my mouth open. My grandmother has set me up on a date without even checking to see if I wanted to go? I believe I've ventured into a whole new level of pathetic. "Nana, what if I had plans?"

"Do you?"

"Well, no."

She pops a piece of carrot into her mouth. "Then there's no reason you can't go, is there?"

The problem with being away from all my friends back home is that I can't come up with plans on the spur of the moment. There's no one in Blackheath I know well enough to send a quick-get-me-out-of-this text.

"No," I mutter. "There's no reason."

"Excellent. I'll let Irene know you're available." Her eyes practically sparkle as she takes my cutting board and rakes the tomato chunks into the pasta. "Dinner will be just a moment, dear, if you'd like to watch a little telly."

I shuffle out of the kitchen and start for the sitting room, but I want something quieter, more secluded. My bedroom has a door that shuts, which is everything I could ask for right now, so I start up the stairs to the top floor—and hear Paul's door click suddenly closed.

Fully aware that meddling in the secret affairs of a fifteen-year-old boy is hugely risky, I climb the rest of the stairs and walk to his door. Maybe our time would be better spent together than apart. Maybe, if I approach him in the right way, I'll get another minute with Old Paul.

"Hey," I say, knocking softly. "Can I come in?"

Nothing.

I knock louder. "Just for a minute, I swear."

"Go away, Rosie," he says, and the moment I hear the slur in his words, I know what he's doing. The bedroom doors at Nana's house don't lock, so I turn the knob and push into the room.

Miniature liquor bottles are scattered across the floor. Well, except for the ones Paul managed to stuff into his backpack before I came in. Mini Smirnoff bottles cascade elegantly from the front pocket onto the beige carpet below.

I wave a hand at the scene. "Why? How? When?"

He glowers at me and shoves the rest of the minis into the backpack. "It's not a big deal, okay? I got them at the airport while Mom and Dad were filling out customs forms."

"While we were supposed to be in the bathroom?"

"Yeah." He shrugs. "There was a duty-free store right by the men's room."

I hold my hands up, eyes closed, trying to unravel what he's telling me. "Wait a second. You're saying the airport duty-free store sold minis to a fifteen-year-old?"

He cuts his eyes to the side. "Not exactly."

I squint at him. "Then how—oh. You stole them."

"They were only, like, a dollar apiece," he fires back. "Big friggin' deal. Nobody's going to send me to jail over that."

This is what drives me crazy—he scrambles to cover his tracks, but when he gets caught, he acts like he hasn't done anything wrong.

"If it's not a big deal," I say, keeping my voice low so Nana won't hear me, "then why were you trying to shove them all into your backpack before I saw them?"

"Because you'll tell Mom."

As if on cue, the front door opens downstairs. Mom's quiet footsteps shuffle around the entryway as she drops her keys on the table and rustles out of her jacket, answering Dad's mumbled questions with one-word answers. I can't hear what they're saying, but Mom's flat tone conveys everything I need to know. Whatever she needed for her research, she didn't find it.

"Maybe I should tell her. Maybe it would do you some good." I pull the door shut and head for the stairs.

If I don't find a way to reach my brother soon, I'm afraid I'll lose him forever.

SEVEN

Paul never came back down to dinner last night. When Mom went up to check on him shortly after they got home, he told her he was resting up for SPARK tomorrow.

Yeah, right.

I almost told my parents about the minis before they went to bed, but they seemed irritated with each other throughout the meal (not surprising, given how scattered most of Mom's research trips are), and I couldn't do it. So now I've decided to tell Mom before they leave for SPARK orientation this morning. Yeah, it sucks to tattle on my brother, especially when he's so fragile—but sometimes you have to sacrifice cool points in the name of helping people.

I'm waiting in the entryway for Mom to come downstairs, running through the speech in my head. *Hey Mom, I know you've got a lot going on right now, but you need to know what Paul has done.* That's how it starts. Her face will wilt with disappointment, but I can't let that stop me. She has to know. *He's still drinking, and it's worse than we thought. Oh, and you can add "kleptomaniac" to his list of compulsions. So there's that.*

Hmm. Better work on that last part.

Finally, the door to Mom and Dad's room opens, and Mom appears wearing full makeup and a maroon pantsuit—the one she's always saying gets hopelessly wrinkled. If you ask me, the whole concept of a pantsuit is a little hopeless, but it actually looks nice on her, rogue wrinkles and all.

I step toward her and open my mouth to rat out my brother, but then the stairway squeaks at the very top as if someone's weight has landed on it. I can't see him from this angle, but Paul is listening.

"Uh, Mom?" I begin, but she's focused on the pearl necklace in her hands and doesn't seem to hear me.

"Rosie," she says, waving the necklace at me. "We're late for orientation. Can you help me with this thing?"

"Sure."

She turns around and shoves her short hair out of the way. The clasp is stubborn, and as I'm trying to coax it open, I hear Paul coming down the stairs. My eyes lift to meet his.

"Did you tell?" he mouths.

I shake my head. Until now, he probably assumed I told them last night.

"Don't," he mouths. "Please."

The fear in his eyes is so heavy. The right thing to do is to ignore the sour feeling in my stomach and tell Mom. But I can't force the words to come. They stick in my mouth.

When the clasp finally cooperates, I pat my mom on the back and smile. "There. You look really nice."

Paul exhales.

"It will do, I guess," Mom says. "Is that what you're wearing, Paul?"

"Um." He looks down at his jeans and Bob Marley T-shirt. "Yes?"

"It's fine," I tell her quietly. "He looks fine." Giving Paul a hard time about his clothes definitely isn't the right way to begin this whole SPARK thing. Hopefully, she'll realize that and drop it.

"All right," she says with a weary sigh. "Let's go."

She grabs a house key off the table and a rush of urgency floods my chest. Mom and Dad made me promise not to keep secrets about Paul back when he first started acting out, and I swore I'd always keep them in the know.

"Mom, can I talk to you later?" I say. My eyes cut to my brother, whose jaw drops in disbelief. "About—something?"

Mom eyes me. "Is something wrong?"

"Well…"

I glance at him again. Suddenly he looks so young, like he did before all this started. More than that, he looks betrayed. And if he feels like I've betrayed him, how will he ever trust me?

I can't do it. I can't rat him out. "I just wanted to find out more about that guy James. The one I'm going out with tonight."

Mom brushes a lock of hair back in place. "I don't know much about him, Rosie. It's your father who knows James's parents, so you should talk to him." She turns to Paul, who's loitering by the stairs. "Come on, honey, we've got to hurry."

As Paul moves to follow her out the door, I catch him in a hug that almost surprises me as much as it seems to surprise him. His muscles tense under my touch.

"Let them help you," I say in his ear. "Remember—it doesn't have to be this way."

He gives me the tiniest of nods and then closes the door behind him.

Even though I need to spend the evening contemplating—yet again—how to stop my brother from getting drunk at every opportunity, and even though Papa's death is a fresh wound on my heart, I can't bring myself to cancel my blind date with James the Angel. Nana's too excited about it and I'm too desperate to get out of the house before everybody gets home. My parents and Nana left a while ago to pick up Paul from SPARK orientation. Once he gets settled in, he'll come home on his own, but today they wanted to ride the train with him.

I'm glad I had the house to myself while I got ready. It made things a little easier, not having to act excited about meeting James. My enthusiasm for this date is still hovering just below zero, and it's raining—so not only do I have to go on a date with a stranger, I have to slog through a downpour to do it.

The prospect of going out with someone who's not Stephen still feels wrong and uncomfortable, like trying to ride a unicycle when you're used to a bike. I would much rather spend the evening in my pajamas, finishing off the Cadbury bars I spotted in the back of the pantry. But I suppose it won't hurt me to get out there and meet someone new. At the very least, I might make a local friend who's younger than fifty.

As I turn away from the door to search for an umbrella, my hand drifts to the interlocking golden rings that still hang from my neck. I take a deep breath and rub them between my thumb and index finger. I didn't take my necklace off the other night, even though I promised myself I would, and I know it will only get harder the longer I wait.

He doesn't love you, I remind myself. *He loves Rebecca.*

The thought rips me open like barbed wire.

Armed with Mom's polka-dot umbrella and Nana's lavender rain boots, I slog down Camden Row and across the grassy area by a cluster of houses called Grotes Buildings. Fat raindrops pound the pavement around me as I splash through puddles and squint into the wind. I cut through a small access road and hang a right by the heath, picking up my pace when I see the flower-filled window boxes hanging over the gold HARE & BILLET sign.

Rounding the corner, I dart through the pub's black doors, which are framed by lanterns and more flowers. I shake the rain from my umbrella onto the sidewalk before letting the door fall shut, then examine the water damage to my outfit. I'm not wearing anything fancy—just a gray T-shirt and jeans—but I sure looked a lot cuter when I was dry. Oh well. Maybe James likes his women on the disheveled side.

Not that I'm looking to impress him, but whatever.

The Hare & Billet is one of those places that brims with vintage charm. Its ceiling is fairly high for a pub and painted a shade of cream that makes the whole space feel open and airy. Clusters of tables sit amongst black columns, and the walls are a soft shade of olive. Wide wooden planks make up the floor, and there's a fireplace set into one of the walls.

Thanks to Nana's explanation of his "dreamy good looks," it's easy to spot James once I look around properly. He's at a table in the middle of the room, slugging down a dark beer and checking his phone. The pub lighting is low, but somehow this only serves to highlight his blond hair, strong jawline, and expensive—maybe even high-end designer?—clothes.

"James?" I say as I approach the table.

He glances up and then looks back down at his phone. His lips remain in a tight line. "You must be Rosie," he says to the screen. He punches a few more icons, then shoves the phone into his pocket and gestures at the chair across from him. I sit down and run a hand through my scraggly hair. The wet weather has made it curl in all the wrong places.

"What'll you have?" he asks with a nod toward the bar. "Gin and tonic? Rum and Coke?"

"I think I'll go with a Coke for now. Minus the rum."

"Just Coke?" he repeats.

"Yeah." When he doesn't get up, I say, "Is something wrong?"

"No, no." He stands, and he's shorter than I expected. "You're sure? Just Coke?"

I try to keep the sting out of my words. "I'm only seventeen. Gotta save the rum for next summer."

If James notices the slight edge in my voice, he doesn't show it. He strides to the bar, where the bartender—a petite girl in a white tank top—waits with a pouty grin. James leans close to her as he orders our drinks; she looks from him to me and then laughs. I feel my eyebrows pinch together. What is she laughing at? Surely I'm not the only one who's come in streaked with rain tonight.

Then I see her lips form the words "Just Coke?" and her nose scrunches up. James shrugs, then props his elbows on the bar and whispers something to her. She rolls her eyes and laughs.

Oh, please. We're two minutes in, and I already hate this guy. Okay, that's not fair—he deserves more of a chance before I label him a total jerk. But that doesn't mean I can't mentally print the label up and have it ready to go.

When he returns to our table holding another beer and my Just Coke, I squash the reluctance bubbling up inside me and give him a smile.

"My grandmother talks about you all the time," I say.

It's a lie; I'd never even heard of James until yesterday. But I'm hoping it will start a conversation that turns this night around.

He lifts his perfectly tweezed eyebrows while taking a long sip of beer. "Really. What has she said?"

"That you're handsome, mostly."

"Interesting." He crosses his arms and leans back in his chair. "Anything else?"

"Not really. You'll have to fill me in." I giggle in an attempt to flirt like the girl at the bar, but it comes out all ditzy and unnatural. James gives me a funny look. I clear my throat. "Have you heard anything about me?"

His eyes travel from my face to my chest, then back. "That you are newly single and gorgeous." He looks away and runs his tongue over his teeth. "Beauty is in the eye of the beholder, I suppose."

I squint at him. Surely he didn't just blatantly insult me. Did I misunderstand him?

He takes a swig of his drink and licks his lips, surveying me with his chin lifted just a bit higher than normal. "Anyway, I'm nineteen years old. Studying law at King's. When I'm not studying, I'm out with my mates. No time for anything else, 'cept the Addicks, of course."

"Ah," I say with a slow nod. Leave it to an English guy to steer the conversation to soccer. "Charlton fan, eh? Wow. That's…"

"Wicked?" he offers with a gleaming smile.

"Not really, considering I go for Crystal Palace."

"Ugh!" His face twists in disgust. "I'd prefer you were a Millwall fan over Crystal Palace, and that's saying quite a lot. I hate Millwall, but Crystal Palace are a load of—"

"Hey," I snap. "I grew up watching Crystal Palace matches with my dad. It's a family thing, and it's special to me. So why don't we talk about something else?"

He looks at me like I'm a leper. "Right. Um…want another drink?"

I shoot a pointed glance at our full glasses. "I'm good."

He sighs and looks away. The silence between us feels like a chasm of awkwardness, even though the pub is swollen with chatter. I stare at the front door. It'd be great if that vortex thingy would come after me again, maybe swirl me out the door and into an alternate version of my current reality. One where James doesn't suck.

I wait for the vortex.

It doesn't come.

The lull in conversation is killing me, so I chug the rest of my Coke and plunk the empty glass on the table. "Okay, now I'll take another drink. Just Coke again."

But James isn't listening. I follow his gaze as a couple of girls walk in. Instead of making them look sloppy the way it did to me, the rain has upped their sexy factor by at least five points. They brush their tousled hair out of their faces and head for a table in the corner.

"Hey, James," I begin, "I'm not feeling so great. Maybe—"

I stop short. He still isn't paying attention to me, but at least he's not staring at the girls anymore. This time, he's completely hidden behind a menu.

"Ordering something else?" I ask, not bothering to sound polite.

He slides the menu to the side and peeks around it. "I used to go out with one of those girls," he whispers. "The blonde. Didn't end well."

"Because?"

He clears his throat. "Because I cheated on her with the brunette."

The words knife my insides as I glance at the blonde girl. He cheated on her just like Stephen did with Rebecca. If, for whatever reason, I wasn't already one hundred percent turned off by James, then that would have been the nail in the coffin.

"Well, everyone makes mistakes," I say, keeping my tone light so my roiling emotions won't betray me. "You should probably try to get her back. I mean, she looks like a supermodel."

"She *is* a supermodel."

Of course she is.

James leans toward me, moving the menu so that both of us are hidden from the girls' view. "You know, Ruthie," he says with a throaty purr.

"Rosie."

"Yes, of course. Rosie." He reaches for my hand across the table. I plant the very tips of my fingers into his palm. As he strokes the back of my hand with his thumb, I notice the diamond-encrusted watch on his wrist. "If you want to look like her, I could tell you what diet she follows," he says. "I still remember. It's sort of a mixture of Paleo, vegan, and Atkins. Works wonders on love handles. I'll write it down, if you're interested."

Oh *hell* no.

I push my chair back with a *screech* and stand up. "Sorry, James, but I don't think this is going to work out."

"What?" he says from behind the menu. A few people at nearby tables are staring at us. "What did I do?"

I glare at him, grab my umbrella, and head for the door. About halfway there, I change course for the table where James's former victims sit.

"Hey," I say, sidling up to them. "Don't y'all know that guy over there?"

I point to the table where James, still cowering behind the menu, is doing his best to disappear. Unfortunately, his watch is exposed. I haven't seen many people in the village wearing that kind of bling.

"Is that James Murphy?" the blonde asks with a scowl.

"Yep, that's him," I say. Their expressions darken. "He was just telling me the two of you might know a good place to pick up some guys. I think his exact words were, 'They've hooked up with every guy in this pub.' So I was just wondering if maybe you could point me in the direction of a good club or something, because I'm looking for…"

I trail off because they're getting out of their chairs, eyes narrowed with catlike disdain. They stride to his table and the brunette snatches the menu out of his hands.

"Rosie!" he calls out to me, but I'm already halfway out the door. Maybe it's cruel to leave him like that, but I don't really care. I just want to get out of here.

Outside, I press myself to the wall of the building to avoid the downpour. How long did my date last? According to my phone, twenty minutes. Great. If Irene thinks James is a nice guy, I shudder to think what her definition of rude might be.

I can't go home yet because my family will be there, and Nana will be upset if she finds out the date turned sour. The handful of acquaintances I have in London are my parents' age or older, and they'd ask too many questions if I showed up on one of their doorsteps. That leaves one option—find somewhere to lurk for about forty-five minutes, then go home and tell Nana I had a good time but I don't think James and I are right for each other.

The nearest place to take shelter is Taste of Raj, the Indian restaurant behind the church. I brace myself against the pounding rain and jog, using my umbrella as a shield, across the muddy grass. Nobody else is crazy enough to be walking around in this weather; once again, I'm mostly alone.

With the heath stretching out to my left, I hurry through the rain to the cluster of willow trees on the corner of Tranquil Vale and Royal Parade, stopping beneath their branches to catch my breath—

Until an arm curls tightly around my neck.

I try to scream but can't conjure more than a squeak. I swing wildly with my umbrella, hoping to connect it with my attacker's head, but then it's wrenched out of my hands. My eyes dart left, right, looking for someone—anyone—who can help. But the few people who have braved the storm are running toward shelter with their eyes down, raincoat collars popped. I'm standing in the middle of the willow trees. No one will see me through the leaves and rain unless they're looking for me.

And no one is looking for me.

I twist with every ounce of strength in my body while clawing at the man's hairy, muscled arm. My voice isn't working, so I mouth the word "no" over and over. This can't be happening. There's no way I'm getting attacked in the one place people won't notice.

Brakes squeal. A car door slams. Another man, speaking some foreign language, shouts to my attacker. He loosens his hold just enough that I can turn to see his face. As I strain to look over my shoulder, a voice echoes in my head: *Notice as much as you can. You never know what tiny detail could save your life.*

I'm sure my father has said this to me at some point; we've certainly had our share of "what to do if you're kidnapped" conversations. But if I'm recalling something he told me, then I'm recalling it in the wrong voice.

It sounds just like Papa.

I catch a glimpse of my attacker's face, and all other thoughts are erased from my mind. He's huge, with shaggy brown hair and bulging muscles. Veins pop out on his forehead and neck. An orange light reflects in his pupils—it must be a streetlamp, but somehow it isn't illuminating us at all.

"Turn around," he growls, and then he hits me in the face so hard his knuckles crack across my cheekbone and lights explode in front of my eyes. The man shouts something to his accomplice, his voice deep and rough. I'm too stunned to understand his words.

He starts dragging me toward the car.

Remember what I gave to you, Papa's voice says again. *Focus. You have the talent, dear girl.*

What talent? What am I supposed to do?

My head lolls to the side. I can barely keep my eyes open. Rain splashes in my face as my feet make feeble attempts to protest the dragging. I hear the *pop* of an opening trunk.

Then a familiar feeling blossoms inside my stomach.

Something is pulling me into myself. There is an unbearably loud *whooshing* sound, even more deafening than when I first heard it. And suddenly my kidnapper isn't holding me anymore. I'm not being held by anything, or standing on anything, or sitting anywhere. I just *am*. My eyes crack open; everything around me is lost in a blur of motion. I try to curl into a ball to keep myself from imploding, but I can't move. I'm too weak.

It's happening again.

Does that mean he will be here?

White light flashes in front of my eyes, painfully bright, as if someone has taken a picture of me from two inches away.

And now I'm running across the heath with my umbrella over my head, approaching the willow trees, just like a couple minutes before—and Albert is sprinting toward me, drenched with rain.

EIGHT

HYSTERICAL SOBS WORK THEIR WAY UP MY THROAT AND I sink to the ground. Fat raindrops pound into my back and onto my head, but I hardly notice them. I don't know if my legs are working anymore. I've never felt such a lack of control over my body, not even as I watched Papa die. But knowing what almost happened to me—knowing that man almost put me in the trunk of his car to take me God knows where—the terror of that almost-reality is crippling. Wetness seeps through the knees of my jeans as I gasp for breath, and my fingers squelch in the mud, leaving two perfect imprints of my hands.

Two attacks in Blackheath in the same week. There hasn't been this much crime here since—well, ever.

Sucking in a deep breath, I remind myself I'm okay. I'm not being hit in the face or loaded up in somebody's car. Nobody has an arm around my neck. And the guy that I'm pretty sure just saved my life is running toward me.

The other two guys I saw through the window at Prime Time—one with red hair, the other with dreadlocks—are jogging across the heath about twenty paces behind him, pointing at the willow trees and nodding at each other.

"Stay where you are!" Albert calls to me, even though I'm barely moving. My knees feel like they're made of overcooked noodles.

He hurries toward me while the other two guys run straight for the trees, their shoes churning up pieces of the muddy ground. I wipe a lock of wet hair out of my face and blink as the sky pelts me with cold, stinging drops of rain. A wheezing sound comes through my chattering teeth. I'm shaking, but not from the cold, even though there is a chill seeping through my clothes. I can't erase the image of that man's face—his horrible eyes as he hit me, the stringy hair that hung like curtains around his square jaw.

Albert barely manages to stop before he skids into me, but I'm too numb with shock to care that he almost ran me over. His soaked green T-shirt clings to him like plastic wrap and his black hair drips water down the sides of his face. The scar by his left ear seems more pronounced than it was in the video store, maybe because he's been running. His waterlogged jeans hang low on his hips and he grabs my elbow, cold fingers digging into my skin. I still don't know whether to trust or fear him, but one thing's for sure—accepting his help is a much better option than getting wrestled into the trunk of a car. He tugs on my arm and I shakily get to my feet.

"Are you okay?" he says in a rush. Thunder booms behind him. He flinches. "Do you feel all right?"

I nod, then point unsteadily at the trees. "Your friends—you have to stop them. There's a—"

"Don't worry about my friends; they can handle themselves. Just come with me."

The redhead has already ducked beneath the droopy branches where my attacker is waiting. The guy with dreadlocks is right behind him. Do they know he's there?

I shake my head at Albert. "No, you don't understand—"

"I do understand," he says, pinning me with a sharp gaze. "And so do they. Let's get out of here."

I tear my arm from his grasp. "Would you please shut up for one second? There's a huge man under those willow trees who attacked me and tried to stuff me into the trunk of a car, and your friends are headed right for him."

My heartbeat throbs in my palms. I can feel it because my fists are clenched, and the adrenaline that must have been pumping through my veins for the past few minutes is surging with fresh strength.

He stiffens. Rain leaks from his hair into his eyes. He rubs a hand over his face, but I don't know if it's because of the water or because of what I've said. He's wearing his watch again, the simple black digital one.

"What are you talking about?" he says in a low voice.

I drop the umbrella, which has hung uselessly from my hand since this conversation started. It thuds onto the soggy earth by my feet. "You tell me."

Thunder rumbles overhead.

"There's nothing to tell," he says.

"So you ran after me and sent your buddies into those trees because you felt like it? You asked if I was okay on a whim?"

There is nothing like a wave of frustrated anger to get my head right again. I've nearly forgotten the terror I felt just a few moments ago.

He shrugs. "Doesn't matter, does it? Important thing is, you're safe. But we need to get you out of this rain."

"It does matter, and a little rain never hurt anyone."

He laughs, although I can tell he's not amused. "That's up for debate."

I step closer and tilt my head so I can look him in the eyes. Even though we're standing in the middle of the heath, there's enough soft light from the nearby streetlamps to show me the outlines of his features.

"Forget about the rain," I say. "Something strange is happening."

He is as still as stone. "Strange how?"

"I'm positive that man under the trees attacked me just a few minutes ago. But before he could finish the job, everything rewound and I was back on the heath, before the attack. And you were running toward me."

"Impossible," he says as a gust of wind sprays drizzle across our faces. "You haven't been attacked at all."

The calm in his voice is maddening. I feel like a child who's just been told the bullies at school are a figment of her imagination. "Then why are you saving me, Albert?"

He steps so close to me, I can hear the rhythm of his breathing and smell the rain on his skin. Part of me wants to back up, but another part—the more powerful one—insists on standing my ground.

The muscles in his arms tense as he clenches and releases his fists. "A better question—how do you know my name?"

Oops.

"I saw you at the video store," I admit. "I heard someone call you Albert. And I paid attention to you because I'd seen you save a girl's life the night before. Funnily enough, she got attacked the first time around, too. I guess when you watch the same event end two different ways, you remember the guy who changed the outcome."

Recognition floods his eyes.

"You told me to go home," I go on. "You said the heath was dangerous. I asked you what had happened, and you wouldn't tell me. Is any of this ringing a bell?"

He lets out a long breath and puts his hands on his hips. Then he looks at the ground. I glance toward the trees, where the redhead and the guy with dreadlocks are quietly dragging my attacker toward a green and white Volkswagen bus. The attacker's stringy brown hair hangs in his face and his legs aren't really working. He's alive, I think, but incapacitated.

"What are they going to do with him?" I ask.

When I turn back to Albert, he's giving me a piercing look, as if he's trying to see past my flesh and into my mind. I'm tempted to break the silence by asking another question, but something stills the words before they leave my mouth. He's about to speak; I can tell by the way the tip of his tongue runs over his lips. Then, so quietly it seems he's talking to himself, he says, "Are you one of us?"

A thrill goes up my spine. "One of who?"

"You're not, then." He wipes the rain from his eyes. "But if that's the case, then how are you aware of it?"

"Aware of what?"

The text message alert goes off on my phone. I ignore it.

Albert raises his eyebrows. "Aren't you going to check that?"

With a sigh, I pull my phone out of my back pocket, trying to shield it from the rain with my hand. The text is from Paul.

Come home ASAP!

Something's happened, something bad. Paul never asks for help unless he has no other options, and considering that today was his first day at SPARK, the possibilities for disaster are absolutely endless.

"I have to go," I say. "Tell me quickly. What am I experiencing? What is it you think I'm aware of?"

He runs a hand through his wet hair. "It's not the kind of thing I can explain in a matter of seconds."

"Why not?"

"I just can't."

We stare at each other in a wordless stalemate. Unbelievably, he breaks first.

"Look," he says with a sideways glance, "let me at least walk you home."

"No, I'll be fine." I step away from him, slipping a little in the squelchy earth.

He points at the willow trees. "You were just attacked out there. And you want to walk home by yourself?"

"I'll be okay. Our house is thirty seconds away."

"Your house? You don't sound like you're from around here."

"I'm not," I say as Paul texts again: *Rosie! Come home!* "I'm fine. I have to go."

"Right," he says with a clipped tone. He glances into the sky, still thick with angry clouds. "Be careful. Don't stay outside any longer than you have to."

"I won't."

I'm not sure what he's more worried about—me getting attacked again, or the storm. He's staring into the sky like it's personally offended him by deciding to produce rain, and when the lightning pulses through the clouds, he flinches.

"What are you going to do with him?" I ask.

He frowns. "Sorry?"

"The man under the trees. I saw your friends put him into their car. What will happen to him?"

Albert gazes across the heath at the Volkswagen bus, which is idling with its headlights on. The lights flicker once, then again, and Albert waves at it.

"You don't want to know," he says. "Trust me."

Of course. No details, nothing that could be considered helpful information. For all I know, they're going to dissect him and put his organs into glass jars.

Wait a minute…

"Are you a serial killer?" I blurt.

He tilts his head back and lets out a single laugh. "That's certainly a good theory, but no, I'm not. Though you don't want to know what I've got in my cellar."

"You certainly have a lot of opinions about what I do and don't want to know," I say. "It'd be nice if I could make those decisions for myself."

Another text from Paul. *Yo! Are you getting these?* I put a hand to my forehead. His timing could not be any worse, but if he's having a crisis, I've got to help him.

"I have to go," I say, and break into a run toward Camden Row. I look over my shoulder once. Albert is still standing there while the rain pours down around him, watching me.

NINE

I SKID TO A STOP AT NANA'S FRONT DOOR WITH A SOLID block of dread in my stomach. Did Paul have a bad day at SPARK and do something stupid in an effort to escape? Or did they all have some kind of accident on their way home from dinner? Nana could have had another breakdown about Papa, or Dad's temper could have gotten out of hand. Maybe he lashed out at Mom. Or, even worse, maybe he lashed out at Paul, and that's why I'm being paged so urgently. My little brother could be cowering in his room, alone, desperately trying to recuperate from whatever soul-stabbing words my father yelled at him.

It certainly wouldn't be the first time that's happened. To either of us.

I burst into the house, soaking wet and gasping from my full-speed run down Camden Row. "I'm here," I call, throwing my key onto the table. "What's going on? What happened?"

Silence.

The entryway is empty. I don't hear any footsteps creaking on the second floor. He did say to come *home*, didn't he? I rip my phone out of my pocket and open Paul's first message—was I supposed to go somewhere else?

No. I'm in the right place. So where is he?

Someone shouts in the backyard—muffled, but clearly a yell. I sprint through the kitchen and erupt onto the covered patio—

—where my little brother is lounging on one of the wrought-iron chairs with his hand on his belly, laughing in great loud guffaws.

The rain is still pouring just like it did the whole way home, but the awning over the patio keeps the area perfectly dry. It wasn't yelling I heard—it was Paul's laughter, but it's been so long since I heard it, I'd forgotten what it sounds like.

Two other guys stand with their backs to me, one in a gray hoodie and the other in a long-sleeved black T-shirt. The one in the hoodie has a shaved head and a stockier build than his friend, whose shaggy black hair skims his narrow shoulders.

The one in the black shirt turns around with a smile that's more of a grimace. He has a hooked nose and droopy eyes, and he's missing a canine tooth. Judging from the wounded state of his gums, he lost it recently. The shorter one looks over his shoulder at me. His eyes are circled with bruises. Both guys have either been in a fight or an accident, but Paul doesn't seem injured, so what—

Hold on.

I know these guys. They're the muggers from the heath, the ones who attacked the girl and then promptly got their tails kicked by Albert. And now they're standing in Nana's backyard.

Oh, crap.

My fingers dig into the doorframe as I try to breathe normally, but the acid in my stomach is boiling. My brother obviously met these guys somewhere, maybe at SPARK, and they hit it off. Now he's brought them home to introduce them as his friends. And, apparently, to parade me in front of them like a first-prize pig at the state fair.

Fabulous.

"Told you she'd come," Paul proclaims with a wide smile. "Rosie, this is Max"—he points at the bald guy— "and Luther." The tall guy—Luther—gives me another gap-toothed smile. "I told them about you, and they wanted to meet you before we went out."

This was the reason for his urgent texts?

"All right, love," Max says. "We've heard quite a lot about you. Didn't expect you to be quite so wet, but I can't say I'm disappointed." His eyes focus on all the wrong sections of my body. I cross my arms to block his view.

"Paul," I say, hoping my voice doesn't betray my brewing panic, "can I talk to you in the kitchen, please?"

He scowls. "Why?"

"I just need to talk to you." *Come on,* I say to him with my eyes. *Please don't be too dense to pick up on the fact that something is terribly wrong.*

He looks from me to his new friends, then back. "Okay."

We walk into the kitchen and I shut the door. It seems weirdly quiet inside after the patter of the rain; maybe the noise will protect our privacy. With a deep breath, I face my brother, doing my best to keep my hands off my hips. The last thing I want is to come off like Mom right now. "First of all, I'm not some kind of eye candy you can show off to your buddies. Got it?"

He rolls his eyes.

"And secondly, where did you meet them?"

"At orientation," he says with a shrug, backing up to lean against the counter. "They were at my table."

I shake my head. "They have to leave. Right now."

"What? Why?"

"Shh! Keep your voice down!"

He crosses his arms and his expression hardens. "Seriously? I make a couple friends at this godforsaken reform camp and you won't even give them a chance?"

I know that tightness in his voice—he's already starting to shut me out. "I saw those guys on our first night here, after we got home from the hospital. They attacked a girl on the heath."

He stares at me like I've sprouted horns. "What girl?"

"Actually, it was the cashier from the Costcutter." I grab a dishtowel from the hook over the sink and start blotting my hair with it. "The one who thought you were 'fit.'"

He blinks. "What are you talking about? Are you making this up?"

"No!" I throw my hands out to my sides, nearly whipping him with the towel. "I saw it happen! I went for a walk, and the cashier was walking across the heath, except I didn't know she was the cashier at that point. And those two guys—your new *friends*—" I put air quotes around the word, which makes Paul roll his eyes again, "—mugged her! They robbed her and beat her up!"

"Okay." He holds up his hands. "I'm going to stop you right there. First of all? You're insane."

"I'm not—"

"And second of all, there's no way you would have seen all that go down and then not say anything about it. You didn't mention it that night when you got home. You didn't mention it the next day. You didn't even bring it up at the Costcutter, while we were talking to the girl who supposedly got mugged. So basically, you're lying to get rid of Max and Luther."

"No!" I'd forgotten Paul was already outside when I asked the cashier about her close call on the heath. "I'm not lying! And why would I want to get rid of them if I didn't have a good reason?"

He leans against the wall with his arms crossed. "Oh, I don't know. The same reason you told me to stop hanging out with Chase Williams in ninth grade because you thought he gave off a 'weird vibe?'"

Paul's eyes shift to something out the back door. Luther is watching us carefully. Max lights a cigarette, and the small flame illuminates his face with a momentary orange glow. He turns toward the garden and puffs into the wet air. I tug on Paul's arm until he follows me to the kitchen table, where we can talk without being observed—although neither of us sits down.

"Chase Williams *did* give off a weird vibe," I hiss as he glowers at me. "And have you forgotten about the meth lab he had in his basement? I was right about him!"

"Fine." He grips the back of a chair. "But you've completely misjudged every guy I've made friends with after that. You accused Robert McNearney of cutting class to make out with his girlfriend, but he was actually tutoring his sister. She was failing math."

"That's only one guy. I haven't—"

"And then there was David Conrad, who you thought was spiking his coffee with Bailey's."

I shove my hands in my pockets. "Well, it smelled Irish."

"It was flavored creamer!" Paul shouts.

"Not so loud," I say, smacking him on the arm. "And okay, I might have jumped to conclusions with some of your friends—"

"We haven't even talked about how you thought Gary Noah was in a gang."

I freeze. "Wasn't he?"

"Working with his church to help former convicts re-enter the workforce," Paul says with a sigh.

Okay, so maybe he has good reason for doubting me.

"You've got to trust me on this one." I step closer to him. "I saw what these guys did. They're bad news."

"Sure, sure." He pushes past me toward the door.

My anxiety spikes into full-fledged panic. Whatever happens, I can't let him leave with these guys. "No, Paul, please don't go anywhere with them."

"Don't worry," he says, opening the door with a *creak*. Max and Luther both look up at the noise. "I'll be home by midnight."

"Ready?" Max asks, stamping his cigarette out on the patio floor. The ash smolders for a few seconds, but then succumbs to the moisture in the air and fades to gray.

Paul holds the door open for them. "Yeah. Let's go."

They clomp inside, and I mentally flail around for a legitimate reason to keep them here. "Wait! Where are Mom and Dad? Where's Nana? You have to get permission before—"

"Relax, dude," Paul says. "I got permission. Everybody's thrilled I've made friends so quickly. But to answer your question, they went to Irene's house for dessert. Mom says they're going to get Nana out of the house every chance they get."

I rub the center of my forehead and puff out my cheeks. Of course they're not here. Not when I'm desperate for backup. I could call Mom and tell her who Max and Luther really are, but she would have the same issues Paul had—like why I didn't mention it sooner, and my questionable track record with judging his friends' character. And if they've already given him permission to go out, they're not likely to take it back now. Rocking Paul's emotional boat isn't something they like to do these days.

"Paul, please stay home." I swallow as Max and Luther look at me. "I need to talk to you about some stuff."

He huffs. "We've done enough talking for one day. Come on, guys."

They stride through the kitchen and down the hallway. Paul opens the front door for his friends, but only Luther moves toward it. Max, on the other hand, is staring at me. My stomach clenches as his beady eyes roam my face.

"Have we met before?" he asks. There's a hint of suspicion in his voice.

"Nope," I say firmly.

I'm still not sure what happened the other night, so I don't know whether they would remember me. In scenario one, they definitely saw me because I shouted about calling the cops and Luther chased me with a knife. But in scenario two, Albert interfered before it got to that point. Did they see me that time? Or are they remembering something from scenario one? Regardless, I've got to divert Max's attention.

"When will Mom and Dad be home with Nana?" I say to Paul.

He throws his hands up. "I don't know. Call them."

"Why didn't they make you go to Irene's with them?" It's possible Mom and Dad really are happy about Paul's new friends, but something about his story doesn't add up. It's not like them to give him full permission to go out on the town with people he just met.

Paul lets out an exasperated sigh. "Look, Captain Twenty Questions. I didn't go with them because I wanted to do something fun. Mom was thrilled when I told her we had a mixer tonight at SPARK."

I give him a dubious look. "You're going to a mixer?"

"Not a chance." A one-sided grin creeps over his lips. "That's just where she *thinks* I'm going."

"She actually believes that?"

"She did when Luther called, pretending to be a counselor." Paul grins at Luther, who puts an invisible phone up to his ear.

"Hello, Mrs. Clayton, this is Devon Summerby with SPARK," he says in an overly polite tone. "Yes, we're just calling to inform you that we'll be having a lovely mixer tonight at the center, and we're hoping Paul can join us. It will be such a good opportunity for him to exercise his social skills."

They all laugh. Mom's a sucker for phrases like "exercise social skills."

"So," he says, sidling up to me with a victorious sneer. "Are we allowed to leave yet, Mom?"

"Stop talking to me like that!" My voice is shrill and does, in fact, sound just like my mother when she's worked up. My pulse is pounding in my head. It's probably a lost cause, but I have to try one more time. "If you leave, I'll tell Mom and Dad you lied to them. I'll blow your mixer story wide open."

Paul barks out a laugh. "Nice. Everybody loves a tattle-tale."

"This isn't kindergarten! You're lying to them while they're trying to cope with Papa's death and planning his funeral! Don't you get why they signed you up for SPARK in the first place?" I blink back angry tears. Getting emotional with Paul definitely won't earn his trust or respect, but I can't help it anymore. "It's because they love you, and they want you to get better. They want you to learn how to deal with what happened to Carter in a healthy way. They love you, Paul. And so do I."

His face is unreadable. He stares at me while Max and Luther shoot amused expressions at each other.

"What's so funny?" I snarl at them. "You think it's funny that I love my brother? Huh? Is that hilarious to you?"

"Shut up, Rosie," Paul says. "You're making a fool of yourself."

The air leaves my lungs in a rush. I feel like he's just slapped me. Paul can be rude, and he can say insensitive things, but he has never told me to shut up.

"Like I told you at the Costcutter, Mom and Dad signed me up for SPARK to get me out of the way," he says, pointing out the door as if that's where we all want him to go—*out*. Away. Somewhere else. He rakes a hand through his hair and tosses his shaggy bangs to the side. "I might as well have as much fun as I can. And if you tell them I lied, you'll regret it."

He yanks open the door and strides into the rainy night with Max and Luther on his heels. The door slams against the wall and stays open long enough for me to watch my brother, small but full of rage, march down the street with two criminals.

TEN

IT IS THE MORNING AFTER MY BROTHER LEFT NANA'S house with Max and Luther. He got home late, but he got home. That's all that matters. He's all right and it's a new day.

Although I'd still like to punch him for the way he walked out on me.

The fortress in front of me is bathed in pink light from the just-risen sun. Mom barely let us finish breakfast at Café Rouge before herding us onto a train and depositing us in front of the Tower of London. Paul, who hates family activities of any kind, has been weirdly compliant during this entire escapade; he's probably hoping it'll make him late for SPARK.

"Seriously, Mom. We've all seen Traitor's Gate before." I stuff my hands in my pockets and lean against the rail. This is probably my fourth or fifth visit to the tower, and I could go a long time without hearing, yet again, the names of every person imprisoned here.

"But not recently," Mom points out, which is true. The last time we stood in this line, I was about to start my freshman year. "And if I'm going to finish writing this essay on the conditions of the Tower of London during Anne Boleyn's imprisonment, I've got to see it again."

"It won't hurt you to be here, Rosie," Dad adds wearily. He looks out over the Thames with a distant expression.

Paul leans against the rail next to me with his arms crossed. His expression seems easy and unburdened, but when he glances at me, the tightness returns to his eyes.

"When is the essay supposed to be published?" I ask, swatting away a group of overly enthusiastic gnats.

"Six months." The wind flutters her hair and she slaps the rogue strands before they get too out of control. "And if it's not good—well, it has to be good. Better than good. It has to be perfect."

Mom's perfectionism has been the bane of my existence since I was in kindergarten. I remember bringing home a picture of a unicorn I'd colored, feeling so proud that each section of its mane was a different shade of pink. Mom had smiled and said, "It's lovely, dear, but why don't we work on keeping your crayon inside the line?" I took it back and folded it four times so that it fit in my pocket. When I got to my room, I threw it in my Strawberry Shortcake trashcan.

I never showed her my pictures again.

"Why does it have to be perfect?" I ask, fully expecting her to shrug and tell me it just does—her usual response.

Instead, she exchanges a hesitant look with Dad. Something in my chest has been wound tight since the day we arrived, and as my parents hold an uncertain conversation with their eyes, it stretches just a little thinner.

"Why?" I say again, looking from Dad to Mom.

"Because," she replies with a sigh, "they're cutting people, Rosie."

Paul looks up.

"Who's cutting people?" I ask.

Dad puts an arm around Mom's shoulders. "We haven't told you because we didn't want this to worry you on top of everything else."

I think I know what they're about to tell me, but maybe, just maybe, I'm wrong. "Haven't told me what?"

"Vanderbilt is laying off professors," Mom says, looking at the river. The corners of her mouth sag so that her frown lines deepen. "Budget cuts."

"But they won't cut you," I say. "You're the best history professor they've got."

"I'm not saying they'll let me go for sure." Her voice is sharp. "I'm just saying there's no room for error here. And I'm sorry you don't want to be here, but—" She chokes the sentence off and stares at the air in front of her. Her lips tremble once before she regains control. "I'm sorry you don't want to be here," she says again, "but I have to. And I'd like to actually spend some time with the two of you this summer."

My heart sinks. Paul looks at the ground and scuffs his sneaker on the pavement. All this time, I've felt like Mom just tolerated Paul and me on her research trips, and here I find out she actually wants to be with us. I want to tell her I'm sorry for complaining, that I should have realized why she brings us along on all her quests—but she's checking her watch and shaking her head, and before I can produce the right words, she opens her mouth.

"Why aren't they open yet? They should have started letting people in ten minutes ago." She glances down the line of tourists that has formed behind us. Judging from the scowls on their faces, they're wondering the same thing. I start to say that maybe they finally realized how morbid it is to turn an execution chamber into a tourist attraction, but a massive yawn comes out instead.

"Why are you so tired, Rosebud?" Dad asks. "Not sleeping well?"

Based on the shadows beneath his eyes, I'm thinking someone needs to ask him the same question.

"Had a busy night," I reply with a glare in Paul's direction. "*Somebody* went out with his new friends, and I couldn't sleep until he came home."

Mom's eyebrows pinch together. "You mean the mixer? It was a SPARK thing, and you know he needs—"

She abandons the sentence with a worried glance at Paul. I know what she was going to say—that he needs friends, he shouldn't have to go through all this stuff with Papa on top of everything else, and we need to encourage him to be social.

But she's not going to say any of that in front of him.

"Seriously, Rosie," Paul says with a scrunched-up nose. "What could possibly happen to me at a SPARK mixer?"

I bark out an incredulous laugh. "You have no shame, do you?"

"What are you talking about?" Dad shoots a sideways look at Paul. "Did you go somewhere else last night? Even though we gave you explicit instructions to come home immediately after the mixer?"

"There was no mixer!" I cry out. "He's hanging out with a couple of punks who attack people on the heath! He made up the whole stupid mixer thing so he could get out of the house!"

"She's lying!" Paul yells. His cheeks flush red.

"But one of the counselors called," Mom says. Then her eyes close with understanding. "It wasn't a counselor, was it?"

"Nope," I say, even though Paul's lips are pressed together so tightly they're turning white at the edges. "I tried to get him to stay home, but he wouldn't listen to me."

Dad grabs my elbow. His fingers tighten so hard it hurts, and his face goes all splotchy. "If you knew what he was doing, why didn't you call us?"

My whole body goes still. "I—I don't know."

"You don't *know*?"

I should tell him Paul threatened me. That he told me I'd regret it if I told them. But the deadly look on my brother's face stops the words in their tracks.

"I thought maybe he would come to his senses," I say. If I play my cards right, I can get Dad to calm down before he loses it. "I didn't want to stress you guys out more than you already are."

Mom and Dad stare at me with matching scowls. Dad's grip loosens on my arm, but he doesn't let go completely.

"I'm sorry," I say. "I made a mistake. It won't happen again."

"No, it won't," Mom says in a chilly voice. "And Paul, you'll have an escort to and from SPARK from now on. Whoever these guys are you're spending time with, you're not allowed to be alone with them."

"They're not gangsters!" Paul snarls. "Rosie's decided they're trouble, so she's made up some crock story about them trying to mug somebody."

"Why would she make up something like that?" Mom says.

Paul gives her a grim look. "Remember what happened with David Conrad and the Irish coffee? Gary Noah and the gang she thought he had joined? Or what about Robert McNearney tutoring his sister while Rosie spread rumors that he was sneaking off with his girlfriend during school? All those guys were my friends until Rosie got in the way. I made a few mistakes, I had one friend who actually got in trouble for something, and she's tried to sabotage all my friendships ever since. All in the name of protection."

He glares at me while my face heats up like a furnace. Mom and Dad let out a collective "Hmm," and that's it— they've sided with Paul. To be fair, it's usually wise to at least pretend you're siding with Paul. Otherwise, you're looking at an explosion in the form of his incendiary emotions. But this time, I need them to see my side of the story, and I need them to back me up, regardless of how poor my timing might be.

I hold up my hands in defense. "Look, I know I've come to some incorrect conclusions in the past. But I *saw* these guys attack a girl on the heath. I saw them hit her and shove her in the back seat of a car. It actually happened."

Dad purses his lips. "There was a girl on the news who was approached by two guys on the heath. It was a local crime segment, I think."

I clap my hands. "Yes! That's her!"

"She said they grabbed her arm," Dad continues. "But there was no hitting, no getting shoved in a car. So what are you talking about?"

I've based this entire thing off of the first version of the mugging, which apparently didn't happen for anyone but me.

Everyone stares at me while I fish around for an answer that makes sense.

"See?" Paul says with a smug grin. "Lying."

I ball my fists. "I'm not lying. It's just…a complicated truth."

Silence.

My parents hold another conversation with their eyes. I hate it when they do this because I have absolutely no warning about what's coming. I can't prepare at all.

"Rosie," Mom says. "I think you and Paul have some things to work out. Why don't you act as his escort to SPARK today? Your dad and I can do Traitor's Gate on our own." She looks at her watch again. "They should be letting us in. I don't understand what the problem is."

A man in a navy and red uniform comes out of the tower and unhooks the rope from across the doorway. "Sorry for the delay, folks," he calls out. "Small rat problem, all sorted out now. Tickets at the ready, please."

Paul is practically burning holes in the concrete with his eyes.

"Okay, little brother," I say. "We've officially been dismissed. Let's go get some coffee and hug it out until SPARK starts."

I've been angry at Paul before, but I've never felt quite as spiteful toward him as I do right now. And apparently the feeling is mutual, because the glower he's fixed on me smolders with hatred.

"Sure you don't want to stay here with the rats and Anne Boleyn's ghost?" he says.

"Oh, I'd pick rats and ghosts over you any day, but Mom and Dad asked me to take you to SPARK. Unlike some people, I actually care about doing the right thing."

Usually.

"Stop it," Dad shout-whispers. "You've got two hours until SPARK opens. Go to a café or something. And for the love of all that is good and right in the world, figure out how to be civil to one another."

I give Paul my most sarcastic jazz hands. "Coffee date with my favorite brother! Should we split a pastry, or would you rather I just stab you in the arm with a fork?"

"Maybe just push me off this bridge," he mutters. "Come on, escort from hell. Let's get this over with."

A few minutes later, Paul and I are on the platform at the Tower Gateway DLR station. Tourists are everywhere, and even though I'm technically one of them, annoyance simmers in my gut as they jabber about how much the London Eye costs and where's that one restaurant that what's-his-name said we have to try.

My fury toward Paul has tempered a bit now that we've ignored each other for several minutes, and instead of wanting to punch his lights out, I'm starting to feel desperate again—just like last night when he left with Max and Luther. It doesn't matter if he thinks I'm a liar or not; I know what those guys did, and I know my brother needs to stay as far away from them as possible. If Paul ever attacked someone, if he ever altered someone's life forever in that way, it would destroy me. It would destroy our parents. And let's face it—Mom and Dad are already on the brink of falling to pieces.

"Listen," I mutter as we pull away from the station. "You and I need to work out a deal."

Paul arches an eyebrow. "I don't make deals with liars."

"Oh, of course. Because you're such an honest person. How many of those little bottles do you still have in your backpack?"

He tries to walk away from me, but there's hardly any room to move, and I catch the sleeve of his T-shirt.

"Just listen to me, okay? If you quit hanging out with Max and Luther, I'll rescue you from SPARK once a week. Nobody will know."

I'm really hoping this will work. If anything will convince him to stay away from Max and Luther, it's time away from SPARK. I'm not even sure I can pull this off, but I'm willing to try.

He shakes his head. "No deal."

"What? Why?" I tighten my grip on the pole as we screech to a halt at Shadwell station.

"Because," he says as people push their way on and off of the train, "you don't get to pick my friends for me."

"They're not friends. They're thugs." The train moves beneath us, knocking me slightly off-balance.

"You know," Paul says, "you should really let that one go. The thing about them mugging some girl on the heath, I mean. We all know it's not true."

"Paul, you've got to believe me; they're bad news."

"I don't have to believe anything, and it's funny you mention news. That's where Dad saw the story about the girl, and she definitely wasn't mugged."

"But she was almost mugged," I point out. Man, I really wish everyone else knew about that first scenario. Sure would make my life easier right now.

We grimace at each other as the train pulls into the Westferry station. People jostle around us on their way in and out of the train car. I only have to deal with public transport eight weeks out of the year, but I'm already over it. Driving my quiet little Hyundai is a million times better than trying to keep my balance on a packed train.

"I don't get why you keep doing this," Paul says. His cheeks are flushing again. "You say you care about me, and then you screw up my friendships, claiming you're trying to protect me. Here's a newsflash—I don't need your protection."

"If you would just listen to me—"

"Are you mad because people actually want to hang out with me? Do you want me to be a loser so you'll feel better about yourself? Are you jealous I've made friends here and you haven't?"

"Jealous?" My eyebrows skyrocket toward my hairline. I'm so stunned at his accusation that I almost fall over when the train starts moving again. "What would I be jealous of? That you're hanging out with a couple of jerks who have serious hair issues?"

Well, that's the final straw. I can tell by the way his neck turns pink and his shoulders stiffen. I hate this whole conversation. I hate that Paul and I fight all the time.

I start to tell him this, but he cuts me off again.

"You know what? I just met Luther and Max, but this is the first time I've actually felt accepted by anyone since Carter. Everybody else back home, including you, thinks I'm an idiot who can't do anything right. Everybody thinks I'm weak. But these guys are different. I have fun with them. And if you don't like it, that's too bad. There's nothing you can do about it."

I hadn't noticed we were stopping again, but suddenly the doors slide open and my brother starts moving toward them.

"Paul!" I shout. "Hey! Where are you going?"

"SPARK," he calls over his shoulder. "Where else?"

"It doesn't start for another hour and a half!"

He ignores me.

I let go of the pole and launch myself into the crowd of people boarding the train. Making progress is impossible; nobody will let me through. I feel like a salmon trying to swim upstream. Somehow, Paul works his way through the crowd, slips through the doors, and strides down the platform toward the station exit.

"Paul!" I get stuck between a couple of large men wearing Yankees hats. "Move, people!"

But it's too late. The doors close, and my brother is gone.

ELEVEN

I've called him a million times. He's not picking up.

I could go after him, but by the time I get to SPARK, his first session will have started and I won't have a chance to see him until lunch. Instead, I stare out the train window and pretend my brother hasn't just walked out on me. It's times like this I'm thankful for Londoners' determination to ignore other people on public transportation. No one will ask if I'm all right, so I won't have to lie.

My plan is to change trains at Greenwich and head for Blackheath, eventually making my way back to Nana's. But when the train stops and I step onto the platform at Greenwich station, I'm furious at my brother all over again. The train ride gave me too much time to think.

I need to walk. To clear my head.

It's a busy day on the High Road, even for the summer tourist season. My shoulders graze dozens of others as I push past St. Christopher's Inn, a backpacker-type hotel with a boisterous downstairs pub. A few summer school students mill around outside Greenwich London College, laughing. I keep my eyes down as I shove through the crowd. Paul's face keeps popping into my mind, bringing with it a surge of anger and worry. Of course he couldn't stay on the train with me. That would be too expected. It would make too much sense. And if I've learned anything about Paul Clayton over the past year, it's that he is chock-full of surprises.

I arrive at Greenwich Park a little sweaty and out of breath, but less inclined to send texts with a lot of four-letter words to my brother. Maybe if I can get a few quiet minutes to myself, I'll be able to deal with him graciously instead of tearing him to shreds.

The sun is out, and as expected, everyone in London is wearing half the clothes they normally would in an effort to soak up the vitamin D. People are sprawled across the park on picnic blankets. Men doze with their shirts off and their sunglasses on. A handful of dogs are scattered around the green while their owners chat and wrap unused leashes around their hands.

This kind of weather is a treasure, and not one I plan to miss out on.

Daffodils have bloomed on the hill just below Greenwich Observatory. Their cheerful yellow color makes me breathe a little easier, somehow. A small piece of beauty in the midst of a strange, unsettling week. I walk up the hill and settle down at the edge of the flowerbed. Here, finally, I can rest. The sunbathers are farther down the hill near the road, and the tourists at the observatory are too far behind me to be a bother.

As I look out over the London skyline, the extent of my exhaustion sinks deep into my bones and I let out a groan. My eyelids seem determined to fall shut, no matter how much I fight them. My weary body doesn't care that I don't have a blanket to lie on; nothing has ever felt as comfortable as the soft grass beneath me, so I kick off my sandals and stretch out with my eyes closed.

It can't be more than one minute later when I hear a familiar voice—rumbly and soft, like distant thunder—coming from somewhere above me.

"You've got nerve, lounging about on your own after what happened on the heath. At least it isn't raining this time."

My stomach lurches and I bolt to a sitting position. Albert is standing in front of me. The guy with the dreadlocks is with him, his dark eyes slightly narrowed. He stands with rigid shoulders and crossed arms, the tightness of his black T-shirt emphasizing the strength of his chest. He's probably not that much more muscular than Albert, but he has a way of carrying himself that makes him seem huge, and it takes everything I've got to keep from edging away.

"Hi," I say. "What are you doing here?"

Albert nods toward the road. "Isaac and I were just out walking."

His friend—Isaac—gives him a look. "That's not exactly true." If Albert's voice reminds me of thunder, Isaac's is like an earthquake, low and threatening. "Albert saw you on the High Road and made me follow you up here. I tried to convince him otherwise, but he wouldn't listen."

He glares at me, and I swallow.

"Easy, mate," Albert says to him.

Isaac shakes his head. "I told you how I felt about all this."

"Yeah, and I told you what she told me." Albert's voice is smooth as glass, the kind of tone I use with Paul when he's about to flip out. "The least you can do is give her a chance."

Isaac's jaw works as he and Albert stare each other down. All I wanted was to enjoy the sun and the daffodils, but now I'm smack in the middle of a testosterone-laden standoff.

"Fine," Isaac says. "Do what you want. I'm going to work." He walks away without looking at me, leaving the air thick with tension.

Albert gives me an apologetic smile. He shifts the watch on his wrist from one side to the other. "Sorry. Isaac is a bit uncertain about all of this."

"You told him about me?"

"After what you said you'd experienced, how could I not?"

It's hard to believe this is the same guy from last night. On the heath, he was a fighter—rugged, powerful, and dangerous. Now he looks almost kind, although he still carries a few bruises and cuts.

"Thank you," I say.

He tilts his head. "For?"

"What you did last night. I never thanked you."

"Oh, that. You're welcome."

He drops to the ground beside me and lies back with his hands folded across his stomach. His sudden nearness unsettles me. Even on the heath in the middle of the rain, when we practically stood nose to nose, I didn't feel his presence quite as acutely as I feel it now. His scar stands out in the sunlight, a deep purplish-pink against his fair skin.

"So," he says. "Who are you?"

I scoff at him. "Are you kidding? If either of us should be answering that question, it's you."

He smiles. "All in good time. You first."

I cross my legs under me and stare out over the park. "I'm a waitress from Nashville who's freaked out about some off-the-charts déjà vu."

"Nashville." He turns to me, squinting against the sunlight. "Country music?"

I hug my knees to my chest. "Yeah, but I hate country music."

"Banjos and hoedowns don't do it for you?"

"Nah, I'm more of a gangster rap kind of girl. Can't you tell?" I wriggle my toes in the grass and cut my eyes over to him. It's always fun to see whether or not people pick up on my humor.

He gives me a one-sided smile. "Yes, gangster rap fans often wear pink T-shirts with stars across the front."

"Are you saying my shirt doesn't give me street cred?"

"Of course not, I would never imply anything of the sort. Anyway, listen, I know you're dying to talk more about last night, but I've got errands to run this afternoon."

Aha! More secrets. "What kind of errands?"

"Nothing worth talking about." He won't make eye contact with me. "I need to go uptown now, in fact, but I'm up for meeting later if you are."

He says it as if we meet up all the time. As if we didn't just have an argument in the middle of a storm about whether or not I'd seen two endings to the same event.

"I don't know," I say. "Even if you tell me what happened, how do I know you're being honest?"

"Good question." He sits up. "I suppose, realistically, you can't know for sure. But I do have an explanation for what you're experiencing—it's not déjà vu, by the way—and I'm very interested to know what you feel when you see two outcomes to the same scenario. It's up to you whether or not to trust me."

So he's going to acknowledge what I told him, then. I expected him to deny it, or at least be vague and irritating about the whole thing.

"It's not that I just see it," I say. "I *live* it again."

He looks at me for a moment. "I feel like I should already know this, but what's your name?"

"Rosie."

"No last name?"

"You'll find out when you prove you're not a serial killer."

He gets to his feet with a grunt. "Fair enough, Rosie. If you want to talk to me tonight, I'll be at the Hare & Billet at six o'clock. If you don't want to talk, I'll have some quality time with myself."

"I can't guarantee I'll be there."

He shrugs. "Not asking you to. If you come, have someone walk with you. It's not a good idea for you to be alone in Blackheath."

"Why?" A sense of foreboding traces its finger down my spine. "Is the man who attacked me still out there? I thought your friends took care of him."

He looks away from me. "We do the best we can. Sometimes it's enough. Sometimes it's not."

What? What does that mean?

He turns his back to me and takes a few steps down the hill before stopping. "Just do me a favor," he says, spinning around to face me, "and don't go running around in the rain again."

"Please," I say. "You might as well tell me to become a hermit. This is London, remember?"

"I'm just telling you to be careful."

"Duly noted."

"Anyway," he says, "mine's Shaw."

I blink at him. "What?"

"My last name. So now you know I don't think *you're* a serial killer, whatever you might think about me."

He strides down the hill and disappears into the shade of the chestnut trees, and once he's out of sight, I get to my feet and hurry toward Nana's.

I have a decision to make.

TWELVE

I'M CURLED UP ON NANA'S COUCH WATCHING MY FIFTH *Big Brother* rerun on Channel 5, alternating between hoping Paul has run away forever and worrying I'll never see him again. The conversation with Albert has played on a loop in my head ever since I got home; should I meet him tonight, or am I better off getting out of this—whatever it is—while I can?

Even though he seems trustworthy, the image of him beating up Max and Luther on the heath is etched in my mind. I can still see the veins in his forearms popping out as he clenched his fists, the coldness in his eyes when he told me to get out of there. He's capable of violence; that much is clear. But if he only becomes violent when he's protecting someone, I'm not sure it's a bad thing.

I glance at the chipped penguin clock on the bookcase—a gift I gave Nana when I was in preschool. The penguin's flippers act as the hands of the clock, and right now, they read 5:22 PM. Paul should be home by now.

As if on cue, the front door opens and he appears in the entryway.

"There you are!" I cry.

He throws his SPARK manual ("Lighting Up the Darkness: How to Ignite the SPARK of Success in Your Life") on the buffet table by the door, drops his keys in the bowl with a loud *clank*, and says, "SPARK gets out at 5:00. Train takes a few minutes. I'm right on freaking time." His nostrils flare a little as he tugs off his toboggan cap. The hair beneath it is a tousled nest of brown waves, and if all this were happening a couple years ago, I'd make fun of him for looking like a shaggy dog that just woke up from a nap.

But it isn't two years ago and New Paul wouldn't take kindly to such a comment.

"Want to talk?" I say carefully.

He hesitates for half a second. My heart lifts with the possibility he'll say yes—but then he barks out "Nope," and clomps upstairs to his room. His door slams so hard it rattles the light fixture over my head.

"Alrighty." I turn back to *Big Brother*. "Good chat. Glad we got everything worked out."

I could stay in all night instead of venturing out to the pub with a guy who may or may not be slightly dangerous; after all, there is bad reality television to be watched and flannel pajamas to be worn. But Paul probably won't come back downstairs, and Dad will probably spend the evening staring at a cup of cold tea. Mom and Nana will warm up one of the ten thousand casseroles brought over by friends and neighbors, and then they'll eat it without speaking to each other because there's nothing left to say.

I'll try to talk to Paul one more time. If he lets me into his room, I'll stay home. But if he doesn't, I'll go to the pub to get whatever answers I can get.

I take the stairs two at a time and knock on his door. "Can I come in?"

Silence.

I try the knob. It turns, but something has been propped against the door from the inside. It won't budge.

"Take a hint," Paul growls from inside the room. His voice is muffled; I bet he's in bed. And once my brother goes to bed, there's no getting him up until he decides he's ready.

Rolling my eyes, I slog back down the stairs and into the kitchen. Mom and Nana are cleaning out leftovers from the refrigerator, stacking disposable containers and foil-covered casserole dishes on the counter. I've only seen a few sympathizers come and go, but judging by the amount of food in Nana's freezer, half of Blackheath has stopped by to offer condolences.

"Mom," I say, leaning against the doorframe, "is it okay if I go down to the Hare & Billet for a while?"

She looks up from a Tupperware full of withered salad. "The Hare & Billet? Why?"

"Let me guess," Nana says. "James has asked you out again?"

This is, in fact, the story I had planned to go with. "Yep. We're meeting in just a few minutes." I look back to Mom. "Is that okay?"

She smiles. "Sure, I think it's great you're going out with him again. I'll drive you over."

The weather is unseasonably cool by the time Mom and I crank up Nana's bright yellow Citroën. She hardly ever drives it, opting instead for the extensive public transit system, but we use it occasionally when we're in town. It's fun, sitting on the wrong side of the car and watching Mom try to adapt to a stick shift.

"So," she says as the car stutters down Camden Row. It almost stalls, but Mom punches the gas pedal with her Nine West peep toe just in time. "You like this James guy, huh?"

Guilt bubbles in my stomach at the relief in her voice. "Uh, yeah. He's pretty great."

"Good. I'll have to meet him sometime."

I wish I didn't have to lie, but here's the thing—my parents ask *a lot* of questions. Especially about boys. So if I told them I was going to meet a guy named Albert—someone they don't know at all—they would ask me where I met him, and I would have to lie. Then they would ask me about his family, and since I don't know anything about them, I'd have to make up something to satisfy their inquisitive minds. Then they would ask Nana if she knew him, and of course Nana would say no, and then they would probably be so overcome with curiosity that they would tail me to the pub and introduce themselves.

And I really can't have that.

Mom drops me off at the sidewalk with instructions to call when I'm ready to come home. She idles at the curb until I open the door of the pub, then eases away with a wave and a hint of a smile.

I can't decide if I'm glad to be alone, or if I'm on the brink of bailing on this whole operation. But Albert has answers—he's made that much clear. And if I don't like the way the evening progresses, I can always call Mom to pick me up.

It's a Tuesday night, so fewer than half of the tables are occupied. A circle of older men roars with laughter as I walk in, eyes sparkling and pints of beer sloshing in their hands. In the center of the pub is a group of younger guys reenacting highlights from some soccer match. Not many girls out tonight, just three of them tucked into a corner, examining something on one of their phones.

I zigzag through the room. Albert isn't at the bar, and I don't see him at any of the tables; maybe he decided not to come. A strange blend of relief and disappointment stirs in my chest at this possibility. But then I spot him at a small table in the dimly lit back corner, reading a tattered copy of *Catch-22* with a pint glass in front of him.

"Hi," I say when I reach him.

He looks up and snaps the book shut. "Hi. Someone walked with you, right?"

"My mom drove me." I sit down across from him. "Maybe you should have asked me to meet you during the day, when it's safer."

He arches an eyebrow and nods. "I would have, but I was busy."

"Oh, right. With your errands." I mirror his arched eyebrow. "What were they, again? Grocery shopping? Dry cleaning?"

A wry smile creeps across his lips. "Something like that. They were so dull, I hardly remember. Would you like a drink?"

I hesitate, remembering the unfortunate Just Coke episode. "I don't know. What are you having?"

"Coke." He holds up the glass of dark liquid.

My mouth twists. "Just Coke?"

"Just Coke." He gives me a suspicious look. "What? Why is that so funny? Would you prefer I do tequila shots or something?"

"No, it's just that you look old enough to drink. I'm surprised that's not a beer."

He looks at his glass and runs a thumb along its side, leaving a transparent trail in the condensation. "I'm eighteen, so it could be. But I don't drink much."

"You're only eighteen?" My eyes run over his powerful shoulders, then up to his face. Maybe it has something to do with the scar, but I would have pegged him at more like twenty-two. The idea that he's the same age as some of my gawky, potty-humor-loving classmates is laughable. "You look older."

He looks up from his glass. "So I've heard."

"So, then," I say, gesturing at the Coke, "why the abstinence policy?"

He leans back and crosses his arms. "Sometimes I find myself in situations that require sharp thinking. Alcohol's not exactly the best choice when you need to be clear-headed."

"Situations that require sharp thinking," I echo.

"Yeah." He grins—the kind of grin that hints at a secret. I know he's got secrets; I've witnessed his peculiarity firsthand. But when his eyes lock on mine and one corner of his mouth twitches, a thrill goes through me anyway. He puts his hands on the table and pushes halfway out of his chair. "Why don't I get you that Coke before you launch into a full-scale interrogation?"

"Fair enough," I say, and he saunters up to the bar.

The bartender—same girl as last time—leans on the counter as Albert orders. She nods with half-lidded eyes, as if to say *Oh, I'll pour you a couple of Cokes, baby*. But as she starts to fill the glasses, Albert turns his back to her and smiles at me. I smile back. The bartender looks at me like I've just crawled out of the Thames with dead fish stuck on my clothes.

"She seems to like you," I say as Albert returns to the table.

He sets my Coke in front of me and plops into his chair. "Matilda? Yeah. I kind of helped her out one time."

"And by 'helped her out,' you mean…" I glance at Matilda, who's watching me with obvious hatred. If only she knew her jealousy was completely unfounded.

Albert shrugs. "Similar situation to the girl you saw on the heath. Some tosser tried to rob the place when she was here alone. She normally wouldn't have been closing by herself, but the other bartender had gotten sick and left. The robber waited till she was closing up, then pulled a knife on her and demanded all the cash in the place. She refused, and he held the knife to her throat." He looks toward the bar. Matilda's face lights up instantly. "That's when I happened to come back for my wallet. I handled the situation and she hasn't forgotten about it."

Clearly.

Albert looks back to me and takes a sip of his drink. I lean forward, putting my elbows on the table. "So now that your errands are done and it's not raining, are you ready to talk?"

He snort-laughs into his Coke. "God, you made me sound like a diva just then."

"Call 'em like I see 'em."

"Yes, I'm sure." He eyes me while running a finger over his chin. "Tell me again what you saw Saturday night on the heath."

"You mean the first time?"

He laughs. "I knew this conversation was going to get a bit sticky. Tell me what you saw both times."

"Okay." I clear my throat and shift in my seat. Then I tell him what I experienced that night—the mugging, the vortex, and the attempted mugging repeat. "And then you came out of nowhere and beat up those two guys," I finish.

"I didn't come out of nowhere," he says indignantly. "I was standing by the church, in the shadows."

"Well, that's very cool and mysterious, but where you were standing isn't really the point, is it?"

A smile twists the corner of his lips. "No, it isn't."

"So?"

He opens his mouth, but it's a few seconds before he says anything. "When you say that you felt like you were getting sucked into a black hole, did you feel…like you were turning inside-out?"

"Yes! Like I was imploding."

"And was there anything else?" His eyes narrow a fraction. "You mentioned a noise."

"Yeah. Like a bunch of vacuums turned on at the same time."

"Huh." He licks his lips. "And just before the scene started over, did anything else happen?"

I squeeze my eyes shut, thinking. "A flash of light. Blinding, as if a giant flashbulb went off in my face."

When I look at him again, he's staring at me with a mixture of fear and intrigue in his eyes. "It's true, then. You really can feel it."

"Oh, I felt it. Whatever *it* is."

He stares at the space in front of him, twisting his watch around his wrist. Then he nods. "All right, look. I'm going to talk low and fast, so you gotta keep up, yeah?"

"Yeah. Go."

He props his elbows on the table. I keep my eyes pinned on his so I won't miss a word.

"What you experienced on the heath that first night, and again last night when you were attacked, is called the Pull. There are only a few people in the world who are capable of Pulling, and I'm one of them."

I blink at him. I've heard the phrase before, but not like that. English guys talk a lot about being "on the pull" and "pulling a bird"—both of which mean hooking up with someone.

"Pulling, huh?" I lift my eyebrows suggestively. "Funny, I didn't notice anyone trying to make out with anyone else during either of those fights."

He laughs. "No, it has nothing to do with kissing, although the name does lend itself to jokes here and there."

"No kissing." I heave an exaggerated sigh. "Too bad. What is it, then?"

He leans back, still grinning. "Basically, I can rewind time and replay a scene that's just happened. If I want to change something, I change it. That's what you felt when you thought you were getting sucked into a black hole—me rewinding the scenario."

I stare at him, feeling numb. All the jokes I was making up in my head about the term "Pulling" have evaporated.

"Please say something," he says.

I sort through the jumble of words in my head, hoping to find at least a few that make sense. "What do you mean, you can rewind time?"

He shrugs. "There's really no other way to say it."

"How far back can you go? Days? Weeks?"

"Only a few minutes at a time, and I can only do it every few hours. It requires a huge amount of energy and focus." He glances at the table next to us. A couple more girls have walked in and are draping their jackets over the chair backs.

"So it's like you're time traveling?" I ask.

He wrinkles his nose. "Sort of, only I'm not going anywhere. I'm pulling time back into itself, if that makes sense. *Everybody* time travels. Everything goes back. Not just me."

I blink at him. "Everyone? As in, everyone in the whole world?"

"Everyone. But most of them have no idea anything happened. A handful of people, if they're near the spot where the Pull originated, might have a sense of déjà vu. But you're the first non-Servator I've ever met who feels what we feel." He pauses. "The first any of us has met, actually. We didn't think people like you existed."

My mind latches onto the one word in his speech that didn't compute. "Servator? What's that?"

"It's a name for people like us," he says in a low voice. "People started using it sometime in the Middle Ages."

"So it's a relatively new thing."

He grins. "Do you always make jokes when you're uncomfortable?"

"Yes." I cover my face with my hands. "I'm sorry."

"It's fine. It's a lot to take in. Frankly, I'm shocked you're still sitting here."

"Me too." I sip my Coke. "Who's 'us?'"

He frowns. "Sorry?"

"You said I'm the first non-Servator any of 'us' has met that can feel the Pull." The word "Servator" strikes me in the same way the word "Mortiferi" did at the hospital—meaningless, yet somehow intriguing.

"Ah, right. 'Us' would be me, my twin sister Casey, and my two mates, Dan and Isaac. Dan thinks he's the world's greatest comedian; Isaac tries to kill people by staring holes through their heads. You remember Isaac from the park, I'm sure," he goes on. "Charming bloke, really warm and friendly."

I smirk at him. "Be honest. He cares for stray kittens in his spare time, doesn't he?"

Albert's head tips back as he barks out a laugh, and I like the way his eyes come alive in the moment, like he's been holding back until now. It feels good to make somebody laugh. Nobody in Nana's house so much as cracks a smile these days.

"Kittens," he echoes. "Not sure I'd trust him to keep anything alive, honestly. Casey, maybe, unless it did something to annoy her. But not Isaac."

"Is it just the four of you?" I ask.

He shakes his head. "There are others out there. We're the only ones in London, but there are more in Paris, Madrid, Dublin…nearly every major city in the world. But—" he grabs the napkin next to his arm and folds it in half, then in half again "—there are only a couple thousand of us worldwide."

He matches the edges of the napkin with precise movements, folding until there's no more room to fold. Then he flicks the square toward the wall and laces his fingers together. This little ritual would probably tell me something about him if I knew him better, like how Stephen always fiddles with the hem of his shirt when he's worried.

But I'm not supposed to be thinking about Stephen.

"And do you always use the Pull to save someone who's in trouble?" I ask. "Or can you use it for anything you want?"

"We can use it for anything we want, but most of us only use it to save a life. I'd be gutted if I Pulled for something stupid, but then needed to save someone a few minutes later and didn't have the energy." He sips his drink; it's more than halfway gone. "And anyway, it's not wise to Pull unless you absolutely have to. What if I changed too many little things and ended up altering the entire course of a person's life? Or the entire course of humanity?" He shakes his head. "It's a bit risky, tampering with time."

"So I would think."

His story makes sense with what I've experienced twice now. I've felt the Pull; I've seen it in action. There's no other explanation. Except that I've lost my mind, of course.

Since Albert obviously operates in a different reality than I do, it's possible he would have some insight into Papa's mysterious words to me in the hospital. He may not know how I heard Papa speaking to me inside my mind—if that's really what happened—but at the very least, I could ask him if he's ever heard the word "Mortiferi."

"Hey," I say. "Do you know the word—"

I stop. Albert's gaze has flown to something over my shoulder. Alarm flashes in his eyes.

"What?" I start to turn around, but then—

Gunshots.

Dozens of them. Hundreds. Shattering the air like missiles. Screams explode from the girls next to us, from the group of guys recapping the soccer match, from my own throat.

Albert shouts, "Get down!"

I scramble to escape my chair. I can't make my arms or legs function properly. One of the girls at the next table hits the floor. I see the hole in her chest, watch the blood puddle around her and seep into the cracks between wooden planks—but I don't understand it.

I'm frozen in place. Paralyzed. And I'm only halfway out of my chair.

Hands on my shoulders. Albert's voice in my ear, shouting at me to get down. He shoves me under the table. I huddle against the wall, curled up on my knees with my forehead pressed into the floor. My hands grip my skull as if they can stop a bullet. I have no protection other than this table.

I peer up at Albert. He's staring at his watch.

Boots come into view through the chair legs. Black, leather, covered in dust. The old men are tangled in a heap, arms and legs flung into unnatural angles. The faces of several of the younger guys stare blankly at the floor or ceiling or wall. Some of them are still alive, hunkered under tables like we are. How long do we have left? A minute? Twenty seconds?

I'm going to die.

But if I'm going to die, I'm going to fight my way to the end.

My fingers find the wood of the floor. I push up until my head hits the underside of the table. Albert is crouched beside me with his eyes closed and his hands held out in front of him, palms up. He blows a stream of air through his lips as gunfire explodes around us, each shot closer than the one before. How can he be so calm when we are seconds away from being blown into shrapnel?

"What are you—" I begin, but his fingers are curling around something unseen, as if he's holding on to a handle. Then he pulls the invisible handle toward his body, slowly, steadily. His arm muscles strain and his jaw clenches.

The inside of my gut transforms into a black hole.

My entire body starts to cave in on itself.

Whoosh.

THIRTEEN

I AM SITTING AT THE TABLE WITH ALBERT, STARING AT the glass of Coke in front of me. He's looking at his watch and muttering numbers under his breath. A single droplet of condensation slithers down my glass and puddles on the table. Laughter bubbles from the groups of people around us, and when I glance to my right, I see one of the girls in the corner toss her head back with a delighted cackle. She swats her friend's arm and then leans over her phone, pointing at something on the screen and laughing again. I'm struck by their cheerfulness, the simple smiles they exchange with no shadow of foreboding in their eyes. Just like the mugging on the heath, no one else realizes something has changed—not even the victims. Albert and I are the only ones who know. I understand why he knows...but why me?

Papa's last words swim through my mind like a school of minnows, picking and nibbling at the memory of that hospital room, grazing the edges of our present reality.

My talent is yours, dear girl. Take it and conquer.

I would give anything to know what he meant.

Albert's eyes are roving the room behind me, but when I look at him, he meets my gaze. "You Pulled?" I whisper.

He nods—a tiny movement full of tension. It's like he didn't have time to be anxious when we were crammed under the table together, so now all the terror of the previous scene has worked its way into his neck muscles, his jaw, his hands. Everything about him seems dangerously taut, like an over-inflated balloon. I have this weird feeling I could poke him with a fork and he'd pop.

"How long do we have?" My arms and legs feel wound up tight.

"Five minutes," he murmurs.

We're leaning toward each other, propped on our elbows, exactly as we were before. His eyes flicker from my face to the door, and I glance over my shoulder. The doorway is empty. My relief is fleeting; the man will come soon, and unless we stop him, death will reach every table.

"How do we keep it from happening again?" I say, crushing my hands together to stop their trembling.

The shock I saw in Albert's face is gone, replaced with a fierce stare and a solid set to his jaw. The intensity in his gaze makes me fidget. I've seen that look twice before, and I know what it means. He's preparing to "handle the situation," as he so delicately put it.

"Get up," he mutters.

Ordinarily, I'd bristle at being ordered around, but I know what happens in the next few minutes. The girl in the ruffled tank who's currently sipping a vodka and tonic will be lying on the floor in a pool of her own blood. Countless others will follow suit. Albert and I will be crouched under the table, waiting to face our own executions.

So I get up.

"This way," he says, nodding toward the back of the pub. I step around the table—every movement feels forced, robotic, like I'm thinking about it way too hard—and take the hand he offers me. His fingers are oddly calloused, and the roughness of the skin anchors me somehow. Walking through the pub feels too risky. Too exposed. I'm fighting to keep breathing, but gripping his hand helps me focus.

"Come on," he says, pulling me toward the wood-paneled alcove that houses the bathrooms. "Quickly. And no matter what happens, stay out of sight."

We hurry to the door of the men's bathroom, where Albert throws one glance over my head to the pub door. No alarm sparks in his eyes; the shooter still isn't here.

"How much longer?" I ask. My whole body is buzzing.

He checks his watch. "Four minutes. Let's hope it'll be enough."

There's a layer of uncertainty in his voice that sends a blast of fear through my chest. "What are you going to do?"

If he Pulled, I assume he's planning to change the scene like he changed the mugging on the heath, but Max and Luther didn't have guns. This is a whole different ballgame.

He pushes open the bathroom door. "I'll take care of it. Stay in here and don't come out unless I come get you."

"What about the others? We can't let them sit out there." Images of the dead pub-goers flip through my mind like a horrific slideshow, bloodied faces and matted hair and splayed limbs. I remember the crunch of the killer's shoes on glass and wood, the thud of bodies hitting the floor.

Instead of answering, he lifts the collar of his T-shirt up to his mouth as if he's about to wipe crumbs off his lips—but then he speaks into it. "Hare & Billet. Now. One of them just came in. I've already Pulled once; were you close enough to feel it?" He stares at the air in front of him. It looks like he's listening to someone whisper a secret into his ear. Then he says, "Nah, mate, this one's got a gun. Definitely a new convert." More listening. "In the men's loo. That's where I'm going to put them all; there's no time to evacuate, and I don't know if there are more outside. Just get here, yeah?"

He's calling for help. Can he not handle this on his own? We have less than four minutes, and we're waiting for backup?

"Albert," I blurt. "What about the police?"

He shakes his head at me. "Can't."

"Why not? That guy is coming back right now, and whatever we can do—" I spread my hands in front of me. My throat is tightening and my voice sounds pinched. "We've got to stop this."

He holds up his index finger, telling me to wait. Sure, I can wait. We have all the time in the world.

"Right," he says into his shirt collar. "I'm going for the others. Let's just hope they listen." He drops his shirt, lets out a quick breath, and looks at me. "Stay in the loo."

I don't even have time to respond before he walks out into the pub, approaches Matilda at the bar, and leans over to whisper in her ear.

Her expression goes from elated to horrified in a matter of seconds. She nods once, then again, and Albert walks out to the middle of the room. He pulls out a chair and uses it to step up to the top of an empty table.

"Ladies and gentlemen," he says, his voice booming across the room almost as if he had a microphone. The noise in the pub shrinks, but it takes him a second time— "Ladies and gentlemen, please—" to reduce it to whispers. Everyone looks at him. "What I'm about to tell you may seem unlikely, but it's the absolute truth. A man is headed this way with a gun. He is extremely dangerous and looking to kill."

No way. Nobody's going to believe him.

Then a voice pipes up from the bar: "Listen to him. I've already called the police."

Matilda. She watches Albert with a strained expression while twisting a dirty dishrag between her hands. But she didn't call the police—I was watching her the whole time Albert spoke into her ear.

The whispers have come to a complete stop. People look from Albert to Matilda. The Guinness clock above the liquor shelves ticks softly, a reminder that the minutes Albert bought are running out.

"We have very little time left—not enough to evacuate, and even if we did, I can't be sure the streets are clear," Albert goes on. "Take your things and move into the men's loo. My friend Rosie is already there and will keep you safe while I handle the situation."

There's that phrase again—*handle the situation*. Like it's a simple matter of taking out the trash. I trust him and his fighting skills far more than I trust myself to keep anyone safe in the bathroom. I have no weapons, no skills whatsoever. If the shooter gets past Albert, and his friends don't arrive soon, there's nothing I can do.

Murmurs fill the room as people turn to each other with frowns, uncertainty plain on their faces. Should they believe this guy? Is this some kind of trick? I swallow and shift my weight, leaning against the doorframe.

"How do you know this man is coming?" a woman shouts. "Why should we believe you?"

Muttered *yeah*s and *exactly*s ripple through the crowd.

"You have no reason, really," Albert says. "You'll just have to trust me. If I'm wrong, you'll simply be inconvenienced. But if I'm right, and you ignore me, you'll be dead."

There is a beat of silence so profound, I could wrap up in it like a blanket.

"If you don't trust me," he pleads, "then trust Matilda. Most of you have known her for years."

Everyone looks at Matilda.

"He's saved my life once before," she says. "If he says something's going to happen, you should listen."

They stare at her. Then they stare at Albert.

And then finally, thank God, they start to move. How long do we have? One minute, maybe less?

One by one, they shoulder their purses, stuff phones into their back pockets, and follow each other to the bathroom. I stand where they can see me, holding the door open with my foot, waving people in. Their eyes brim with insecurity; I'm sure half of them are worried this is a trap, and the other half are too drunk to really understand what's happening, and then there's probably some remainder that are convinced they're about to die.

Here's hoping they're wrong.

Albert follows the last person to the bathroom, and as I take a quick glance around the pub, I'm relieved to see that everyone has followed his orders. Thankfully, there were only about a dozen people here.

"Stay quiet," he says to us.

A hush falls over the crowded bathroom. I let out a shaky breath and stare at the floor.

"Rosie," he says, and I look up. "Make sure everyone stays in here unless you're sure there aren't any more outside. Sometimes these blokes travel in packs, and they keep one or two near the exits to take down escapees."

My stomach bottoms out. I can't talk, so I just nod.

Albert speaks into his collar again. "Hope you're close, lads, because he's nearly here."

He steps back into the pub. I catch the door before it falls shut, leaving it open about an inch. Albert stops in the center of the room. He stretches his fingers out at his sides and then clenches them into fists. His shoulders rise and fall as he takes a long, deep breath. He must have done this countless times before—stepped into a life-threatening situation without knowing whether or not he'll see tomorrow. He could back down. He could let whatever's going to happen, happen. But he doesn't. I'm only brave enough to hide in a bathroom with a dozen would-be victims, which really isn't brave at all.

With a quick "right" and a subtle lift of the chin, he strides toward the door.

It opens.

The man—the killer—stands there, gun held at his side. He is huge, with stringy brown hair and muscles lined with popping veins.

This is the same man that attacked me under the willow trees.

I sag against the doorframe as the memory comes rushing back. It's like I can still feel his bicep digging into my throat, feel the pounding of his fist against my cheekbone. I thought they dragged him toward that Volkswagen bus. I thought Albert said they took care of it.

What happened? Why is he here?

Albert puts his head down and launches himself toward the doorway. Toward the giant man holding a weapon. Toward possible—almost probable—death.

My heart nearly stops. The people behind me who can see through the crack suck in a collective gasp.

"Oh God," Matilda whispers. She's right next to me.

Albert slams into the man's enormous frame with enough force to drive him out of the building. Their voices roar as the front door falls closed and they stumble onto the street. Something thuds against the exterior wall once, then again. Which of them is throwing the other around?

I don't hear gunshots—did Albert get the gun away from the killer?

I let the bathroom door swing shut. Nothing to do now but wait.

FOURTEEN

IT FEELS LIKE A YEAR HAS PASSED BEFORE I HEAR VOICES in the pub again. Five years. A decade.

It's an unfamiliar voice first—male, but not Albert's. At first I'm sure it's my attacker. He's killed Albert and come back to finish off the rest of us; this is it, we're dead. But I barely have time to come to grips with my fate before another voice joins in—rumbly and deep, and thrillingly familiar. I sling the door open without really meaning to and step into the alcove. Albert is about midway across the pub, limping, and the redheaded guy I saw at the video store—Dan, I think is his name—is pretty much holding him up. A ribbon of blood trails down Albert's arm all the way to his hand. His right eye is almost swollen shut and bruises have bloomed across his jawline.

"Who is it?" Matilda whispers beside me.

I turn to look at her. "It's Albert. I think he saved us."

I'm really hoping he saved us, anyway. The possibility that my attacker is still on the loose with a gun is too much to entertain.

"Oi," comes Albert's voice. He sounds annoyed, but his eyes are shining. "Told you to stay put till I came for you, didn't I?"

It takes everything I've got not to crush him in a hug right now, but he's clearly injured, and anyway that would be weird. "You did. Sorry. I heard your voice, and I…"

Dan supports him until he reaches the bathroom door. "Is everyone okay?" He gazes over my shoulder at the gaggle of people behind me.

I nod, stepping to the side so he can see. "We're fine. What about you? And what about—*him*?"

If Albert knows it was the same guy who attacked me on the heath, he isn't letting on. I don't think he saw him closely that night. But Dan the redhead, loitering against one of the wood panel walls in the bathroom alcove, *did* see him. The grim set to his mouth tells me he knows. He remembers.

It seems like a huge coincidence that the same guy who attacked me on the heath also attacked the pub while I was in it.

"We'll take care of it," Albert says, and Dan shoots him a wry look. Albert must sense it somehow, because he turns to him with a scowl. "Finish the job completely this time, eh? I'd prefer not to meet this particular one again."

This particular…what? Gangster? Murderer? How many of these guys does Albert run into on a daily basis?

The pub door opens again, and I jump—but it's only Isaac.

"No sense accusing anyone of anything," Dan mutters, crossing his arms as Isaac reaches the back of the pub and surveys us with a curious stare. "You know that wasn't our fault."

"Fair enough." Albert wipes at the stream of blood on his forearm, smearing it across his skin. "Just do it properly this time, lads."

They're talking about this like I talk about washing the dishes after dinner. Isaac is already checking his phone, and Dan is staring out into the pub, fuming about something—probably Albert's attitude. It might not be the best time to ask the question I'm about to ask, but I have to do it anyway.

"It was him," I say, looking at each guy in turn. "Wasn't it? Doesn't that seem like a really weird coincidence?"

Albert's eyes shift to Dan's. Isaac stares at his phone like I haven't spoken. To their credit, they don't pretend not to know what I'm talking about.

"I thought last night was a random attack," I say in a scratchy whisper. "Was it something else?"

I can feel the trickle of people behind me as one by one, or sometimes in pairs, the pubgoers evacuate the bathroom. Matilda pats their backs and reassures them that everything is okay, they can go home now. Many of them shoot grateful looks at Albert. Others keep their eyes on the floor, and I wonder if they'll try to forget this night ever happened, or if they'll immediately tell the first person they find. A few of them ask questions—"How did you know? Why haven't the police come?"—but Albert simply waves them off. They're too shell-shocked to persist.

"Seems too coincidental to be random," he says. "But they wouldn't seek you out unless they had a good reason."

Something about the way he says "they" makes me pause. "They who?"

"The Mortiferi," says Dan, pushing away from the wall. He steps toward me with his arms crossed. "If they're hunting you, they're probably trying to—"

He stops short, probably because my eyes are the size of baseballs and my jaw has dropped to the floor. "I'm sorry, what was that word you just said?"

"That's enough, Dan." Albert's voice is almost a growl.

I step forward. "You said 'Mortiferi.'"

He looks from me to Albert and then shakes his head. "Uh, it's nothing, really. Don't worry about it."

"You said they're hunting me," I go on. "Who's hunting me? Are the Mortiferi people? A gang of some kind?" I look to Albert for clarification, but he's still glaring at Dan. He shakes his head the tiniest bit and then turns back to me.

"Rosie, you've already met Isaac," he says, and Isaac gives me a sharp nod. He looks marginally less irritated about my existence, which seems like a step in the right direction. "But I don't believe you know the jokester of the group. This is Dan Mason." He grimaces at Dan, who's leaning against the wall again, looking sullen. "Sometimes he talks a lot."

Dan bobs his head at me. There's a scattering of freckles across his nose that darken as his cheeks flush with embarrassment, or maybe anger. "Lovely to meet you," he mumbles.

Albert puts a hand on my shoulder. "I'm going to take Rosie back to our place for a bit." He leads me toward the door, clapping each of his friends on the shoulder as we pass. "Cheers, guys."

"You owe me breakfast in the morning," Dan replies with a grin. I get the feeling it's hard to get on Dan's bad side, and even harder to stay there.

Isaac nods at Albert, but his lips press into a tight line when our eyes meet. I shift my gaze away from him and follow Albert out the door.

FIFTEEN

"**I** WANT ANSWERS," I SAY AS WE SCURRY ACROSS THE road to the heath. The wind cuts across the open space as if it's angry at us, and the smells of Blackheath cover us in a strange mixture of grass, daffodils, and cinnamon. "Specifically, I want answers about the word 'Mortiferi.'"

Albert is a little out of breath. "As soon as we're safe, you'll get them."

We jog about a minute to Talbot Place, a mere hint of a street with several large buildings that overlook the heath. The building we stop in front of is massive. The body of the structure is made of antique-looking bricks, the darker kind with mortar smeared here and there. The front door is black and guarded by a pair of white columns, Pantheon-style.

"Seriously? This is your house?" The disbelief in my voice borders on disdain.

He laughs and shakes his head. "Not the whole thing. It's divided into flats. We live in #2."

"Oh." I hadn't seen them in the darkness, but now I can tell there are other doors with columns on either side of this one. "For a second there, I thought you were disgustingly rich."

"That'd be nice, but no. Not even close. We all work to cover expenses. The flat is paid for, which helps." He shoves his hands in his pockets. "Things are tight, but we make it work."

Somehow, I hadn't considered that Albert might have a job. I guess I thought his parents supported him like mine support me. I wait tables at The Chicken Cottage on weekends, but not to pay the electricity bill. My paychecks go toward things like movies and clothes.

Now that I think about it, Albert hasn't mentioned his parents at all.

"Where do you work?" I ask.

"Isaac and I both work at the library. Casey works at a Topshop in the city. Dan does gardening on the weekends."

I bite back a grin. "You're a librarian?"

"Yeah," he says with a smirk. "A librarian who could throw you through a wall for not paying your late fees."

He presses his thumb to a small electronic pad where the keyhole should be. Something inside clicks loudly and he opens the door.

"Why do you..." I begin, gesturing at the thumbpad.

"We need a little extra security around here. Keys are too easily lost and copied."

Dark wooden floorboards creak beneath my feet as I follow Albert inside. He sets his wallet on a long, narrow cabinet, its green paint chipping at the edges. An iron chandelier dangles above our heads and casts a soft yellow glow over the entryway. Right in front of me is something I've always wanted in my own home one day—a spiral staircase with an iron railing and wooden steps. To the left of the stairs stands a white coat rack. A colorful mass of jackets and scarves hangs from it in a cheerful tangle.

Albert shuts the door and methodically locks a series of deadbolts.

"There," he says. "We're safe now. The thumbpad unlocks them all from the outside, but only for us."

I nod like this is all normal and fine. Like I haven't just been hunted down by a monster and taken inside the fortress of a time-manipulating, monster-fighting librarian.

"Right," he says, moving closer to me. "Tea?"

I nod again, afraid to use my voice. There's something weirdly intimate about being inside Albert's flat, as if seeing his home has finally convinced me he's a real person. That he's not some superhero who appears when there's trouble and then vanishes when his work is done. He has a home, and he drinks tea, and right now he's probably relieved to be alive.

He pushes a door next to the staircase and holds it open while I walk through. The scarred wooden floor continues into the living room, where a worn Oriental rug lies surrounded by two lumpy sofas and a sagging armchair. A large square coffee table covered in books and newspapers sits in the middle, and the whole room is dimly lit by two brass lamps perched on a couple of scratched-up side tables.

Albert leads me to one of the sofas and offers me a soft red blanket, which I drape around my shoulders as I sit down. It smells like nutmeg and soap. I tuck my legs underneath me and lean on the arm of the sofa, which creaks in response.

He gestures to his blood-streaked shirt. "I'll just go get cleaned up and put on the kettle. You okay for the moment?"

I force a smile. "Fine. Not bleeding, unlike some people."

"Par for the course," he says. His eyes fall to my throat.

"What?"

He nods at my neck. "You do that a lot, I've noticed."

I'm fiddling with the gold rings on my necklace, but I didn't realize it until he pointed it out. I can't believe I still haven't taken it off. What is wrong with me? "Oh. Yeah, it's just a stupid habit. The necklace was a gift from…a friend."

He watches me for a moment. "So, how bad is it?"

What? How could he possibly know about Stephen? I haven't mentioned him, I'm sure of it. And unless he somehow heard about my breakup from Paul…but when would they have crossed paths?

I clasp my hands in my lap and clear my throat. "Well, it's—I mean, it's not that bad, really. Not anymore. How did you—I mean, did someone tell you—"

He tilts his head. "I'm not sure what you're talking about, but I meant my face. How bad is my face?"

Well, that's mortifying.

Albert touches a couple fingers to his puffy eye. "This feels fairly impressive. Is it as huge as I think it is?"

I'm nearly overcome with the urge to throw myself out the window, but it's only a few feet to the ground, so it wouldn't have the desired effect of putting me out of my misery. Of course he was talking about his face. I'm an idiot.

"Well…" I look from his swollen eye to the welts on his jaw to the gash on his arm. "You look awful, actually. On a scale of one to ten, ten being the very worst you could ever look, this is probably a seven."

"Am I worse than Dan? Because that's something I just can't live with."

I smile, wondering if he cracked a joke because he knows I'm on the verge of tears.

"Make yourself comfortable," he says. "Like I said, I'm going to clean up a bit, and then I'll bring you tea. Maybe some biscuits, too, if you're lucky."

"They're called cookies," I murmur, nestling deeper into the cushions. Exhaustion is seeping through my bones and I'm not sure how long I can hold it off.

"Fine then," he says with a laugh. "Cookies. Although you know it isn't wise to argue with someone who's just offered you a sugary snack."

He disappears through the door to the foyer and jogs up the spiral staircase. His footsteps creak far above me; they sound too far away to be on the second floor, so his room must be on the third.

When he comes back to the living room—de-bloodied, wearing a long-sleeved crimson T-shirt and a different pair of fraying jeans—the difference in his appearance is so striking, it makes me sit up.

"Better?" he asks as he crosses to the other side of the room.

I run a hand through my hair. "Uh, yeah. Better."

Something flutters inside me as he smiles—a long-dormant ripple of warmth. I shake my head and squash it back down; whatever it is, it's a fluke. The weight of my necklace reminds me that my heart has been destroyed twice—shattered by Papa's death, and the pieces scattered into oblivion by Stephen's rejection. A breakup isn't the same kind of pain as losing my grandfather, but still, it hurts. I'm not ready to open up whatever's left of me to someone else just yet.

"Tea, then," Albert says. "Yeah?"

I smile. "Yeah. Thanks."

He pushes through a swinging door into a small yellow kitchen. I only catch a glimpse of the room before the door falls shut, but it looks cozy and clean, with a round wooden table and a large window overlooking the backyard.

A sharp pain begins in the base of my skull and works its way toward my forehead. I close my eyes and massage the back of my neck, wishing more than anything that I could crawl in bed and sleep for the next twenty hours. Mom is probably expecting me to call for a ride home any minute, but I can't leave now. Not when I'm finally going to get some answers.

I get out my phone and pull up Mom's number. My fictional date with James is about to run later than expected.

SIXTEEN

THE RUSTLE OF TURNING PAGES DRAGS ME OUT OF slumber and back to the real world, where I am curled up on Albert's couch beneath a plush red blanket.

My eyes fly open and I push myself to a sitting position. The pain in my head is still going strong, but that's not the worst of it. Memories of what happened in the pub explode in my mind all at once, like the finale of a fireworks show on the Fourth of July. I let out a small moan, closing my eyes to block the images. It doesn't work.

"Hi there," Albert says. His voice is doing that rumbly thing again. I swear I can feel vibrations in my bones when he speaks. "I was wondering how long you'd sleep."

I heave one eyelid open. He's sitting in the armchair across from me with an open book on his lap. Something looks different about him. Not his hair, not his clothes—

"You wear glasses?" I say.

"Only late at night, when my contacts get dry." He slips them off—simple black frames—and rubs at the lenses with the hem of his shirt. "Why? Do I look funny in them?"

"Late at night?" I echo. "Wait—what time is it?" Before he can answer, I grab my phone off the table. "Twelve-thirty? Holy crap! I bet my parents are freaking out right now!" I leap from the couch, but my ankles get twisted up in the blanket and I barely avoid tumbling into the coffee table.

"I don't think they are, actually," he says as I struggle to free my tangled feet. "Your mum texted ten minutes ago asking if you were still at the movie with James. I texted back 'yes' and she responded with a smiley face."

He was looking at my phone. That's kind of weird, but at the same time, he saved me from causing Mom and Dad any more grief.

I sink back into the couch. "Oh. Thanks."

"No problem." He seems relieved. I bet he expected me to be angry that he'd picked up my phone while I was sleeping. I still have a bunch of texts from Stephen—irrelevant things, like logistics for getting dinner before prom and whether or not we wanted to go to the afterparty. I hope he didn't see those. And I especially hope he didn't see the texts Stephen sent me the night I caught him with Rebecca in her bedroom. There are only two of them, and although the first is fairly repentant, the second simply says, "Maybe we should break up."

Amazing how it took us six more weeks to actually get there.

I run my bottom lip between my teeth. "James is part of my alibi for tonight, which I'm sure you've figured out. My grandmother's friend set me up with him. I think he's a jerk, but my family doesn't know that."

"You don't owe me an explanation," Albert says.

He's right, but somehow I want him to know anyway. "So nobody's freaking out about how late I am?"

He shakes his head.

145

"I still need to go home soon." Truth be told, I'd rather stay here. Albert's house might be drafty and filled with thrift-store furnishings, but it's cozy and it smells a little like coffee.

"I'll drive you," Albert says.

Is he kidding? He's got a bandage wrapped around his forearm and more bruises than I can count. "It's not that far. I can—"

"You're not walking home." His tone is final. The rebel in me rises up indignantly, and my body follows suit, lifting me to my feet and squaring my shoulders.

"Listen," I begin. "There's no reason for you to—"

He stands up and walks toward me, limping just a little on his right foot. "I can tell you're not the kind of person who likes to be ordered around, but the thing is, I'm absolutely not letting you walk home on your own. It doesn't matter how close your place is. You can fight me on anything else, but don't fight me about getting you home safely."

The irritation that had sprung up in my gut retreats like a wounded soldier. I cross my arms, trying to maintain my tough exterior. "Fine. But I don't believe for a second that you'll be able to drive with your arm like that, so why don't you let me do it?"

A slow grin crosses his lips. "It's a manual. Five-speed. Stick shift. Can you handle it?"

I once learned how to drive a stick shift. The car was a Volkswagen Rabbit with a diesel engine, and it belonged to a guy I dated briefly (without telling my parents) in ninth grade. He turned sixteen that spring and thought it'd be cool to be my driving tutor on our secret dates. I destroyed his clutch and he broke up with me shortly thereafter.

"I've driven one before," I say, but my voice is so empty of conviction that we both laugh. "Okay, no, I can't handle it. But can you really drive like this?" I wave my hand from his head to his feet. The puffiness around his eye has gone down a bit, so I suppose he'll be able to see, if nothing else. There's an icepack on the table next to his chair; I guess he was icing it while I slept. Beads of condensation drip off the plastic onto the wood.

Albert holds up a hand, palm-out, like he's being sworn into office. "I'm fine. It's not the first time I've been in a fight." The hand drifts to his face, where he runs a finger absentmindedly along the scar by his ear. How did he get it? He sees me eyeing it and gives me a knowing smile.

"It happened at a party a couple years ago. This wanker was snogging Casey in the kitchen, but when she wanted to stop, he wouldn't back off." He swallows, and it's like he's seeing the guy again, feeling that fury he must have felt watching his sister get harassed. "She hit him a couple times—she's good at that—but it wasn't enough. I told him to get away from her. He took a swing at me, missed, and decided it would be more effective to come at me with the scissors that were lying on the counter."

My jaw drops. "You got stabbed in the face with *scissors*?"

"He caught me off-guard." His fingers fall away from the scar. "I was trying to get Casey out of the kitchen and didn't see what he was doing until—well, you know."

"Until he stabbed you in the face with *scissors*," I say. "What happened then? Did you beat the crap out of him?"

"I, uh…" He clears his throat. "I handled the situation."

I feel one side of my mouth tug upward. "Which means?"

"Okay, yes, I 'beat the crap out of him.'" He echoes my words in a terrible impression of a Southern accent and then groans. "That was awful. Remind me never to do that again."

"Jolly good, right you are, mate," I say in an equally bad English accent.

We laugh, but fall silent quickly. Albert brought me here to tell me about the man—men?—hunting me, and the word "Mortiferi," yet we haven't discussed either. I hope he's not planning to put it off until another time, because I'm not leaving this house without answers.

"So," I say. "About tonight."

He inhales a long breath, all traces of humor erased from his expression. "The man who came in the pub was the same man who attacked you on the heath. But you already know that."

I nod.

"We thought we had him under control after the attack on the heath, but before we could dispose of him at our flat, several of his friends showed up. My mates and I can handle a lot, but this was over our heads. We had no choice but to release him and bar the door."

Wow. So Albert and his friends aren't as bulletproof as I thought.

I rub a hand over my arm; it's cold without my blanket, but I'm afraid that any extraneous movement could ruin this moment. I'm getting answers, and I'm not willing to risk losing them. "Who is he, though? Do you know?"

"He's part of a…gang, I guess you could say. A huge, very dangerous gang." Albert's eyes seem to darken as he speaks. "And if this one man is after you, I'd wager they're all after you. The Mortiferi."

Something curdles in my stomach. How did Papa know about them? And why would he say that word into my mind in his last few moments of life? I want to ask, but Papa's final warning echoes in my mind: *Protect our secret.* The secret must be his ability to speak into my mind. But am I supposed to protect it from everyone, or only from the Mortiferi? And perhaps more importantly, can I speak into minds now? Was that the talent he gave me?

I lock my eyes onto Albert's and try to direct a single thought at him.

Can you hear me?

He lifts his eyebrows and my heart rockets into my throat. But then he says, "Why are you staring at me like that?" and I look away with a sigh.

Maybe it just takes practice.

Pieces of the puzzle swim around in my mind—Papa, the Mortiferi, the attack on the heath, the attack on the pub. My thoughts are so jumbled; all I see are images of the would-be shooting combined with Papa's frantic expression as he died. There are so many questions I could ask, but the only one I manage to whisper is, "What do I have to do with all this?"

My question was directed internally, but Albert answers. "I'm not sure." His eyebrows pinch together. "There's a reason they're targeting you; we just have to figure it out."

Albert and his friends have saved my life twice now, and I barely know them. Isaac doesn't even like me. I don't understand why they're going to all this trouble, and the uncomfortable truth is, I don't know if I would do the same for someone else.

"Why are you doing this?" I ask. "Helping me, I mean. Why do you care?"

He shrugs. "It's what we do."

"But Isaac doesn't even seem to like me." For some reason, this really bothers me. I think it's because I didn't ask for any of this—feeling the Pull, getting attacked on the heath, finding myself in the middle of a mass killing. And I feel like Isaac silently accuses me of causing trouble every time he looks at me. Like I did all this on purpose.

Albert scuffs his bare foot on the floor. "It's not that he doesn't like you. He's just protective. Very few people know what we can do, and that's the way we prefer to keep it. Our methods are much more effective when nobody knows to expect us." He looks down. "He's convinced I told you too much."

I gape at him. "Is he worried I'll call the news or something? Because I'm pretty sure they wouldn't believe me."

"He's just being cautious, that's all. He'll come around."

"I hope so. He scares the bejeezus out of me."

"That's a very country thing to say for someone who hates country music," he says with a grin.

"Yeah, yeah. Sometimes the Nashville in me bubbles over a little."

The corners of his mouth twitch. "I should get you home, but first…" He crosses the room to the door that leads back to the entryway. "There's something I want you to see."

I follow him through the door to a small closet set behind the coat rack. It's tall, narrow, and painted the same color as the wall.

"I never would have seen it if you hadn't shown it to me," I say, waiting as he pushes his thumb against a pad above the doorknob. It's the same kind of thing I saw out front. These people are serious about avoiding keys.

"Yeah, that's kind of the point." The lock buzzes open and he twists the knob, looking at me over his shoulder with one arched eyebrow. "Behold, the closet of secret spy equipment."

White shelves fill the narrow space from top to bottom. Papers, flash drives, compact binoculars, and lots of other things I can't identify sit clustered on each shelf. A plastic tub full of cell phones has been pushed against the back wall. The whole space is packed with boxes of things labeled CODES and COMS and BADGES (that last one has "alphabetical order, please" scribbled beneath it). I have a feeling I could dig through here and find a fake nose, or maybe a pen that doubles as a poison dart gun.

"Well?" Albert says, and even though I'm not looking at him, I can hear the smile in his voice. "Are you intrigued?"

It takes me a moment to form words. "And where do you keep the wigs and fake mustaches?"

He laughs and picks up a square of white cardstock from the box labeled COMS. Rows of small black dots arch from the surface of the paper. "These are coms. Short for communicators. We stick one on our clothes. I prefer shirt collar, but Casey puts them on her bra strap—" he rolls his eyes "—and then we put another one just inside an ear. They're two-way, so it doesn't matter which one you put where. You can talk into and hear out of all of them."

I squint at the black dot, which is about the size of a pencil eraser. "Are they picking up our conversation right now?"

"No, no. You have to practically eat them before anything comes through." He places his lips against one of them. "Like this."

"So someone heard you say that?"

"Maybe. But I don't have a com in my ear right now, so if anybody says anything back, I won't know."

"And what's in here?" I point at the box labeled BADGES.

"Identification cards." He slides the box off the shelf and hands it to me. "Isaac isn't much fun at a party, but he makes a wicked fake ID. Though he is a bit of a prat about people putting them back in order."

I thumb through the pile of cards: British Museum staff, Harrod's salesman, HSBC employee—the fakes go on and on. Albert, Casey, Dan, and Isaac stare up at me from each one, their faces pinched into professional frowns.

"Why would you need all these?"

"In case we need to get into one of these places. We usually take a few with us if we know we're going to be in the area. When someone's just bombed a building and we've only got a few minutes to stop it from happening again, there's no time to ask for a visitor's pass."

My eyes grow wide. "Has that happened?"

He fishes through the stack of cards, pulling one out from the center. *Royal Observatory Staff* stretches across the top in red, with Albert's face underneath. He holds it up with a grim expression.

"Someone bombed the Observatory?"

"Yep. That was one of our biggest Pulls ever. Casey and I were in the park when it happened. Between the two of us, we managed to Pull back almost twenty minutes—adding more people to a Pull increases your time exponentially. It took us a while to find the bomber, but when we saw a man wearing a thick black coat in the middle of August, we figured he was the guy. Casey pointed him out to the security guards. They found explosives strapped to his chest."

My mouth goes dry. "How did you stop him from setting them off?"

"We almost didn't. One of the guards tackled him when he put his thumb on the button. Then another one knocked him out with a club. If either of them had waited half a second longer…"

I nod. "When did this happen?"

"About a year ago."

I stare at the ID card without seeing it, imagining the horror of what could have been. The people who would have been killed. The panic that would have spread through the city. And they stopped it, but no one would ever know, and they would never be thanked for saving all those lives. "I had no idea you were so proactive about all this."

"We try to be, although we don't do as good a job as some of the others. And we're still trying to perfect a Collective Pull."

"You mean, like you and Casey Pulling together?"

He nods. "There are seven Servatores in Paris who claim to have Pulled back three hours by working together." He returns the Observatory ID card to the stack and sets all of them back on their shelf. "But you know how Parisians are," he says with a shrug. "Always trying to convince you their croissant is bigger than yours."

I laugh, setting off another wave of pain and nausea. I press my fingers into my temples with a quick groan.

"Come on, let's get you home," Albert says. "Your fake movie should be getting out about now."

"No, hang on." I reach for a remote-type thing. "I'm not done snooping around."

"I'll let you snoop later." He guides me toward the front door. "If you stay out with James any longer, your parents might not let you see him again."

"And wouldn't that be tragic."

"It would be if it meant you couldn't come 'round anymore."

The fluke warmth starts to bubble in my chest again, but I extinguish it before it can turn into heat. "Take me home, Batman," I say.

SEVENTEEN

RAIN POUNDS THE WINDSHIELD OF ALBERT'S black Renault as he turns onto Camden Row. The wind flings water across the road in sheets—just a typical night in London, everyone doing their best not to get completely drenched after five minutes outside.

"Aren't you glad you chose to spend your summer in sunny Britain?" he says over the squeak of the windshield wipers.

I laugh, but his joke reminds me that he has no idea why I'm here. In all the confusion, he hasn't asked. "I would rather deal with rain any day than sweat in the Tennessee heat."

"Ah, it can't be that bad."

"It is," I say. "It's like walking into a sauna that's inside an oven. And the oven has caught fire."

He turns to me with a grin. "And you're saying that's not better than English weather?"

"I'd take drizzle over solar flares any day."

"*Solar flares,*" he repeats. "I had no idea you could get so dramatic about weather."

I give him a wry look. "Says the guy with an unnatural aversion to rain."

"Right," he says. The humor leaves his eyes, and the retort I expected doesn't come. What did I say? Did I misread some part of our banter?

"Don't forget to tell me where to stop," he says, drumming on the steering wheel.

"Here."

He stops the car outside Nana's house. I turn to him, planning to apologize for whatever I said to upset him, but he's staring at something over my shoulder.

"What?" My head jerks around to the window. Someone must be after me again—but no, the street is empty. I look at him. "What's wrong?"

"Nothing." He clears his throat and meets my eyes. "Just a bit tired, I guess."

A beat of silence passes between us. I know he's not just tired, and I'm pretty sure he knows I'm on to him, but I don't want to push the issue too far. That look on his face, though—he knows this house.

"You've been here before?" The words tumble from my mouth before I can stop them.

His eyes are guarded. "Why would you think that?"

"Because you're staring at my grandparents' house like it's a poisonous snake. What's going on?"

"Nothing," he says, but I don't buy it.

"Is something wrong with the house?" I ask. "Should I not go inside?"

He shakes his head, looking almost hurt at my question. "If the house was dangerous, I would tell you."

"Then why are you looking at it like that?"

He starts to speak again, but the words die on his lips as something else through my window catches his attention. Paul is leaning against the doorframe, clutching it to keep his balance. He grins at me and gives us an erratic wave.

I close my eyes. Surely this isn't happening. "He's been drinking again."

"Is that your brother?" Albert asks.

"Yes. Hang on a sec." I roll down the window just enough to shout through the crack. "Go back inside, Paul. I'll be right there."

"Hey, Ro-sie," he calls, drawing out the "o" in my name. "Where have you—oh." He shuffles through the rain to the car and peers through the opening at the top of the window. Water drips from his nose down the inside of the glass, and I lean away from him. "Is this the famous James? Did y'all have another—" he winks "—super-hot date?"

"Go back inside," I say. "You're getting soaked."

"It *is* James. Wow, you were right. He's a hottie."

"Paul!" I unbuckle my seatbelt and throw the car door open. It hits him and almost knocks him to the ground. Guilt assaults the anger that had monopolized me only a second ago. I should have been more careful.

"Ow, Rosie, that hurt!" He glares at me and rubs his hip.

"Well, you should have moved when I said to." I can't keep the venomous words from slithering out of my mouth. I get out of the car and push him back toward the house, fuming as the rain pounds down on both of us. I'm angry at Paul for acting like an idiot again, but I'm mostly angry at myself for being a jerk.

"Sorry," I call over my shoulder as the rain plasters my hair to my neck. "Let me just get him in the house. I'll be right back."

But Albert shakes his head, glancing at the clouds through his window. "No, just go inside. We'll talk later."

"What? No! I want to talk now!"

"Get out of the rain. We'll talk soon, I promise. Just go inside!" He rolls up the window and lets up on the brake so that the car rolls forward. He's waiting to make sure I get in the house before he leaves.

"There you go with the rain again," I say under my breath. I spin around and tug Paul to the door by his elbow. "Why did you have to do that?"

"Do what?" He stumbles into the entryway.

I shut the door behind us and lock the deadbolt with more force than necessary. "I was in the middle of something important. And you interrupted it. Again." He leans against the wall. "And I see you've also been getting into Nana's liquor cabinet."

"Shh! I think Mom's still awake in their bedroom. And for your information, I didn't steal Nana's liquor. I've been at a pub in Lewisham. It's called The Black Swan, and it's friggin' awesome."

I push my wet hair back from my face and stare at him. His forehead is streaked with dirt. "You need a shower, first of all. And secondly, how did you get out of the house? Mom and Dad said you weren't going anywhere unsupervised."

He shrugs with a sly smile. An image of his bedroom window comes to me—the tree outside it would make a perfect ladder.

"You snuck out?" I say, and his smile widens in confirmation. "Paul, come on, you can't do that! It's dangerous! And how did you even get beer? You're fifteen!"

"We're in Britain, Rosie." He's speaking slowly, like I'm a child. "There's not really a drinking age."

"Actually, it's eighteen." My voice is so sharp it could cut glass.

He gives me an exasperated look. "Sure, but nobody cares as long as you've got money."

"*I* care," I say. "I care about you, Paul, and I don't want you sneaking off to shady pubs with—who were you with, anyway?"

"No one." His gaze drops.

I take a deep breath, desperately hoping he won't say what I fear. "Were you with *them*?"

"If by 'them,' you mean Max and Luther, then yes." I open my mouth, but he keeps going before I can tell him off. "I know what you're going to say, but I don't care. I had a great time tonight."

I wrinkle my nose. "Your breath smells like a frat party."

He bursts out laughing and collapses against the wall, clutching his stomach.

"It's not funny. Do Mom and Dad know you snuck out?"

His face turns serious. "No, and you better not tell them. They got home a couple hours ago and went to bed. Luckily, I got home first, so they thought I'd been asleep the whole time. I'm sure they'll want to hear all about your second date with James in the morning."

I arrange my face into a neutral expression. "Mom and Dad told you I was with James?"

"Of course they did," he says with a smirk. "Because that's what you told them. But it's funny, because when you came home just now and I asked if the guy outside was James, you didn't answer me." He flings his hand in the direction of the street, and then lets it smack into the side of his leg. "So was it James? Or was it—" he lifts one eyebrow suggestively "—someone else?"

I cross my arms. "Why would that even occur to you?"

"Because Nana has been asking James's mom to text her pictures of James so she can show him off to all of us. And that guy?" He flicks his head toward the front door. "Wasn't him."

I rub my eyes. Boy, it'd be nice if I could find my way out of this conversation.

"So," he says. "Who was the guy in the car?"

"None of your business."

Mom and Dad's bedroom door opens slowly, and Mom peeks out. Her eyes droop with fatigue. How much time is she spending on this Traitor's Gate essay? Between that, Papa's funeral plans, and Paul's shenanigans, it's a wonder she's still walking.

"Hey, Rosie," she says with a tired smile. "Thought I heard you out here. Paul? What are you doing up?"

He flicks his head at me. "Just talking. I was getting a drink when she came in."

Oh, I bet he was. Out of the liquor cabinet.

"I'll leave you two alone, then," Mom says. "Just wanted to make sure everybody was okay. Did you have a good time, Rosie?"

She's looking at me with so much hope. "Yeah, it was great. James is awesome."

"Good." She glances back into the bedroom. "I'm going to hit the sack. Love you both."

"Love you too," I say, then shoot an expectant look at Paul. He gives Mom the "bro nod," a classic signal of camaraderie among high school guys who consider themselves too cool for handshakes. Mom rolls her eyes at him, but smiles before she closes the door.

As soon as we hear the bed creak beneath Mom's weight, Paul's eyes narrow like a cat about to pounce. "Has Dad met him? Because if he hasn't—"

"Yeah, I know. Trust me. I am very well acquainted with Dad's dating rules." Three years of nine o'clock curfews and weekly discussions about physical boundaries have pretty much worked their way into my body's cellular structure at this point.

He shifts his weight. "So you're going to introduce him to Dad?"

"No!" Oops—probably shouldn't have said that so quickly. "I mean, there's no reason to, because we're not dating. He's just a friend."

"A friend," he echoes witheringly. "Yeah. Mom and Dad aren't going to buy that."

"Which is why I'm not telling them."

He arches an eyebrow. "So I guess you don't want me to tell them, either."

"No, I don't." I let my chin drop to my chest. "Which means I won't be telling them about The Black Swan."

"Exactly." He rubs his hands together, then turns around and eases up the stairs. "Nice doing business with you."

I shoot a dark look at the back of his head. What a slimy little punk. I wish I could hate him properly, because that way, I wouldn't be so worried about him. "If you sneak out again, I'm telling Mom and Dad. I don't care if you tell them I lied about James. You have one more chance to stay away from Max and Luther before I do something drastic."

How many times have I made this threat? It sounds empty even to me, now.

"Oh, you will not." His voice is melodic with victory as he lugs himself up the rest of the stairs, gripping the banister like it's the only thing anchoring him to Earth. "Night, Rosie-posey."

After making myself a cup of Earl Grey in the kitchen, I curl up on the sofa in the front sitting room. Nana's house has two sitting rooms—one down the hall next to the kitchen that also houses the dining table, and this one on the front of the house. It's my favorite room, probably because of the book-clogged shelves that cover an entire wall. A large window stretches in front of me, showcasing a spectacular view of somebody else's back door.

Nana and Papa's ancient television sits in the corner, wedged between a stack of magazines and a wobbly side table. I pick up the remote, point it in the general direction of the TV, and let it fall to my side without pushing the power button. I could use a little quiet time right now.

There's a portrait of Papa and Nana on their wedding day that sits on the bottom shelf of the bookcase. My dad gets his wide smile from his father, that's for sure; if I could take away the dated clothes and hairstyles, this photo of Papa would look just like Dad. Nana is smiling too, with her head tilted slightly toward her new husband.

They look so happy and in love. Indestructible.

But now, they—as a couple—don't even exist. They've been reduced to part of a whole. And it feels like my family is headed the same way.

EIGHTEEN

THE MORNING OF PAPA'S FUNERAL DAWNS AS appropriately as possible—gray clouds that seem content to hover indefinitely over Blackheath and a fine drizzle mixed with fog.

The sanctuary of All Saints' Church is a rich blend of white columns and wooden pews, with thick red carpet running down the center aisle. The ceiling peaks far overhead—a stretch of open space with windows at the very top, which might allow for sunlight on another day, but today only provide a gloomy reminder of the mournful weather. At the front, next to the pulpit, is Papa's casket. It's white and smooth. Thick brass handles jut out from its sides, handles that six men will grip to lower my grandfather's body into a rectangular hole. The burial process suddenly seems barbaric. Who decided it was a good idea to lock someone's body inside a box and then heap dirt on top of it? What kind of final farewell is that?

I shift on the hard pew, smoothing my black dress over my legs—or rather, Mom's black dress that she let me borrow. I don't know why I didn't pack anything to wear to Papa's funeral. We knew this would happen sometime between now and August. It was silly to leave my black dress at home.

Silly, or maybe hopeful.

To my right, Dad sniffles, and a thousand hairline cracks race through the supporting walls of my heart. He's trying not to cry, probably because of all the times he's reprimanded me for sobbing over things I couldn't change. His voice rings through my head. Words I've heard so many times I've lost count. *Crying doesn't help anything, Rosemary.* I'm never Rosie or Rosebud in those moments, just Rosemary. Formal and distant.

I let my eyes drift over to him. His face is worn and pale. If he feels me looking, he doesn't show it; his gaze is fixed on the front of the sanctuary.

The crowd files in reverently, but somehow, they still manage to be loud—rustling skirts, clicking heels, murmured condolences. There are more people here than I expected. I know Papa was loved in the community, but the church is nearly at full capacity. I lean forward just enough to peek down our row; is everyone else falling apart like Dad?

Mom is staring straight ahead, too, with her hair extra moussed and her lipstick extra drab. Her eyes are dry, but she's clutching tissues in her hand like she's afraid they might fly away. Nana's next to her, breathing in uneven spurts. Her eyes are glassy and her hands seem like they're working independently from the rest of her body, clenching one second, wiping themselves along her skirt the next. She keeps opening her mouth a little as if she's going to say something, but she never does. And then there's Paul, slouching at the end of the row in his wrinkled black pants and a jacket nobody realized was navy until twenty minutes ago. The last time I saw him in a suit was our cousin Amy's wedding, when he was six and holding a pillow with a fake ring tied to its middle.

A hush goes over the crowd, and I swallow a sudden rush of panic. This is really happening. Papa's funeral is right in front of me. Surrounding me.

My talent is yours, dear girl. Take it and conquer.

But I don't know how to speak into minds like he did. What am I supposed to conquer? The Mortiferi? I hardly know what they are, much less how to conquer them.

And whatever you do, always protect our secret.

Oh, Papa. It seems you had a lot of secrets.

I close my eyes as all the familiar questions blaze across my brain. I can't handle them now. Today is for mourning. The Mortiferi—whatever they are—will have to wait.

Music pipes through the organ, a collection of swollen notes that fills the sanctuary. Nana must have chosen the hymn for this moment. It was Papa's favorite, a tune he used to whistle while he shaved in the mornings. Hot tears gather in my still-closed eyes as I remember the shrillness of his whistle, the rush of water in the pipes as he rinsed his razor. The words run through my head in time with the organ's melody.

For the beauty of the Earth, for the beauty of the skies
For the love which from our birth, over and around us lies
Lord of all, to Thee we raise
This our hymn of grateful praise

When I open my eyes—still brimming with unshed tears—the organ is silent, and in place of the rich music is a vacuum of soundlessness that makes me squirm. I hate the spaces between moments, those few seconds when one thing is over but the next has yet to begin. So as the priest begins his slow migration up to the pulpit, I turn my head just enough to scan the crowd.

He's here. Albert. Sitting in the back with Dan, Isaac, and his sister Casey. It's odd to remember the first time I saw all of them at the video store. They seemed so carefree and comfortable. Now, they're stiff and grim, with shadowed eyes and somber frowns.

What in the world are they doing at my grandfather's funeral?

"Dearly beloved," the priest begins, but I barely hear him because my eyes have locked on Albert's sorrowful face, and the shock of seeing it—seeing *him*—has sent my heart on a full-throttle escape mission.

"We are gathered here today to celebrate the life of Edward Clayton," the priest goes on.

My heart pounds on the wall of my chest and then crawls up my throat until I feel like I might suffocate. I look back to the pulpit and wrap my fingers so tightly around my necklace that the rings leave dents in my flesh.

"Many of us knew him as a friend." The priest gestures at the crowd in general. "Others loved him as family." He nods towards us and Dad looks at the floor. "But some of you never knew him personally; you only knew *of* him, and that is what brought you here today."

What does he mean, people knew *of* him?

Nobody else in the sanctuary seems confused. Everyone is watching the priest as if he hasn't said anything odd. A few people are smiling and one man nods enthusiastically.

Why would people know *of* Papa without actually knowing him? And why would that bring them to his funeral?

I look over my shoulder at Albert. He's watching me.

"Turn around," Dad whispers harshly.

I obey.

CHARLTON CEMETERY LIES TO THE NORTHEAST OF All Saints' Church. It is packed with rows of headstones and lined with pathways—a horrible alternate version of the heath. Until today, Charlton Cemetery was just a cemetery. Now it's Papa's new home. The low rows of granite markers remind me of tiny sentries standing guard over their wards, and it's as if I can hear them whispering to me along the breeze: *You're not meant to be here. This is no place for the living.*

But I *am* here. And so is Papa, being lifted out of the hearse in his white box by a group of men I've never seen before. I still don't know what the priest meant by people knowing *of* Papa. I tried to ask Dad, but he didn't respond.

The burial passes in much the same way the service did—so slowly I fear it will never end, and then over in a breath, too suddenly for me to realize what's happening. Papa's already being lowered into his grave, and I feel like we just got here, like I only just shuffled my way to the front of this green tent and stood by Nana while her hands shook. Dad's still snuffling loudly on my other side—has he stopped crying at all since the funeral began?—and even though I can't see Mom, I sense what she's doing. She's crying quietly into a tissue, unwilling to let her emotions truly show. It's the same thing she did when Carter had his accident and my little brother's world began to unravel. She sniffled, wiped away a couple of tears, and told us to watch TV while she made spaghetti and garlic bread.

I cast a sideways glance in her direction. She's nodding sadly at the well-wishers and blotting her tears with the crumbling tissue, carefully avoiding eye contact with everyone.

She won't say anything about the funeral when we get home. I guarantee it.

Papa's coffin hits the bottom of the grave with a soft *thunk*, and Nana tosses a handful of dirt on top of it. The priest mutters some empty stock prayer, and then I hear soft footsteps trailing across the spongy grass as people begin to leave. It's over for them. They'll go back to their jobs and complete families and normal lives, and we'll do—what?

The same thing, I suppose, except it won't really be over for us.

I lost track of Paul somewhere between the car and the cemetery, but I see him now. He's standing at the side of the group, about two yards away from everyone, glancing at the grave and then down at his shoes. He does this kind of thing—the shifty-eyed, I-don't-know-where-to-look thing—when he's feeling lost. I want to reach out to him. But when his eyes meet mine, he turns away, and I don't have the energy to persist. So I let him go. Not for good, just…for now.

The handful of dirt from Nana's palm sits on top of Papa's casket like a bizarre little hat. Bits of earth tumble down the glossy surface and into the cavernous hole. I should be crying, but my eyes are stubbornly dry. I can't look at his grave anymore. It's worse than being sad, this feeling. It's an emptiness that sucks all my emotions dry. I turn to the side, trying to look like I'm not desperate to get away from this place—and that's when I see him again.

I knew Albert must have come to the burial, but I haven't seen him since the service. Now, though, he seems impossible to miss. He towers over everyone around him, black hair blown unruly by a sudden gust of wind. He's staring into Papa's grave.

I turn to Dad, focusing on the collar of his jacket instead of his eyes. It takes more than one nudge for him to notice I'm trying to get his attention.

"I'm ready to go," I say when he turns to me.

He nods. "Take Paul home with you." His voice is so frail. "I think we'll be a while yet."

Mom gives me an empty smile from Dad's other side. Nana keeps looking at Papa's grave; I don't think she even heard me. Tears roll down her face unchecked. It feels wrong, this blankness inside of me. Instead of closure, I feel like all my emotions have been erased.

Paul is loitering under an elm tree in the corner of the graveyard near the exit. He looks up when I start to move, and I hold up my index finger, telling him to wait a minute. He scowls. If anyone's more desperate than me for all this to be over, it's Paul. But there's one more thing I want to do before I leave.

I have to talk to Albert.

He's unflinching as I approach, a statue of a man in a black suit. But when I say, "It looks like we have more to talk about," he cracks a sad smile.

"You knew Edward," he says quietly, nodding toward the grave. "You're his family, I assume, since you're staying at his house. He was your grandfather?"

"Yes. And you knew him too, since you're here," I say. "And since you recognized his house when you dropped me off."

He chews briefly on his bottom lip. Then he looks around the cemetery as if he's afraid of being overheard. "I know this is a bit much to ask, but can you get away today?"

"Probably not," I say. "I need to be with my family."

I look back toward Papa's grave. A few stragglers still stand in and around the tent, but most have left for cars or taxis or the Charlton train station. One man with white hair looks over his shoulder at me and then turns away, ambling toward the gate. I bet he was one of Papa's friends. Maybe a member of one of the committees Papa loved so much. I wish I could say hello, learn his name, maybe chat about his memories of my grandfather. But the man is walking quickly now with his head down. He doesn't want to talk.

"Come to my flat tomorrow, if you can," Albert says. "We'll be able to talk uninterrupted." His shoulders are tense and his eyes shift from one section of the graveyard to another, lightning quick.

"What are you looking for?" I whisper.

His eyes cut to me—sea green against a canvas of ivory skin. "I'm looking for them."

Them.

"The Mortiferi," I breathe.

His nod is almost imperceptible. "It may not be safe for us to talk in the open anymore. I don't know how much they know about me, or you. There are too many unanswered questions. But my flat is safe—you remember that, I'm sure."

"Of course." I cross my arms, suddenly cold. "I'll try to get away tomorrow. When should I come?"

Paul's voice, ragged, carries over to me from the elm tree by the gate. "Rosie, are you coming?"

I turn around. "One more minute, okay?" Then, without waiting for an answer, I look back at Albert. His thick eyebrows are furrowed as he scans the cemetery.

"I work in the morning," he says. "Come after lunch, if you can manage it. If not, I'll find you another time."

"All right." I edge toward Paul. The cemetery is starting to suffocate me, even though we're outside in the open air. "Until tomorrow, then."

"Until tomorrow," he replies in a quiet voice. Then he turns toward Papa's grave, and I turn toward my brother, who carries an eerie reflection of death in his eyes.

It's like I can almost see the life leaving him just like I watched it leave my grandfather.

NINETEEN

ALBERT'S BEDROOM HARDLY QUALIFIES AS MORE THAN a closet. There's a single bed pushed into one corner with a rumpled quilt strewn over its lower half. The pillow has fallen to the floor, landing perilously close to a half-full glass of water. The opposite corner houses a brown leather armchair, its surface raw and worn. If I look closely, I can almost see the imprint of Albert's body; he sits with his back pressed into one of the arms, probably so he can look out the foggy window. The glass needs a good cleaning, but thanks to the room's third-floor location, it provides a stunning view of the heath in spite of the smudges.

Albert and his sister share the top floor of the house. Her room is across the hall from his, and although I haven't really seen it, I did catch a glimpse of bright orange walls as we passed her door. Dan and Isaac share the second floor, which is laid out identically to this one.

Albert moves to the low nightstand that separates the desk from the bed. He switches on a brass lamp, bathing everything in a soft yellow glow.

"Thanks for coming over," he says, gesturing to the leather chair. "I know it must have been hard to leave your family, with the funeral yesterday and all."

I smile as I move across the room. "It wasn't that hard, actually. Mom and Nana have gone into full-blown organizing mode. You've never seen so many extra-large plastic bins in your life. And the label situation is completely out of control." I shake my head, settling into the chair while Albert perches on the edge of the bed.

He smiles too, but it's not enough to chase the sadness from his eyes. "What about your father and brother?"

I guess he's not going to let me leave them out, regardless of how much I'd like to. Dad's robotic movements and half-aware responses are enough to send me over the edge, but combine them with Paul's self-imposed solitary confinement in his bedroom upstairs (what is he *doing* in there?) and it's too much for me to think about, let alone discuss.

My eyes travel along a crack in the blue wall to the metal desk, which is covered in scratches and dents. Papers and pens lie scattered across its surface, while other random things—paper clips, receipts, loose change—have been thrown into a large glass jar that sits on the corner. To the right of the desk is a tiny closet with the door halfway open. Some of Albert's clothes are hung up properly, but most of them are clumped together on the floor.

"They're surviving," I say.

"I'm so sorry, Rosie." His voice sounds hollow. "How did he...how did it end? I mean, if you want to talk about it. We don't have to talk about it." His expression is strained, like he's fighting the same level of emotion I am—except, unlike me, he's winning. His face is a carefully arranged mask of control, but I see the tangle of disbelief and despair behind his eyes.

"He had cancer," I begin, and Albert nods like he knows this. And I guess he does know, thanks to whatever connection he had with Papa. "But he ended up having a heart attack. And right before it happened, he—"

Suddenly, I don't know how much to say. The truth is that Papa spoke to my mind, that he mentally said the word "Mortiferi" and told me, without actually speaking, that he was passing "the talent" to me.

I glance at Albert.

He stands up and saunters to the window, leaning against it with his arms crossed. "Something strange happened, didn't it?"

I lick my lips. "Yes."

"What?" His voice is a croak—the only hint of turbulence beneath his composed exterior.

There's really no way to say this without sounding crazy, but I have the weirdest feeling he already knows what I'm going to tell him. "He talked to me, only he didn't use his voice. It was like I heard it…in here." I tap my temple. "He said something about passing his talent to me. And then he said—or thought—the word 'Mortiferi.'"

Albert's expression is glazed, as if he's thinking about something so hard that he's forgotten where he is. Then he takes a deep breath and lets it out slowly. "Rosie, your grandfather had a secret."

I slide to the edge of the chair. "Tell me."

He sticks the tips of his fingers into his pockets and then rakes them through his hair. Worst-case scenarios race through my head—Papa led a secret life as a mobster, or Albert is the product of some alternate family Papa had. What if Albert and I are related? What would that make us—third cousins? Or would this be one of those "once removed" situations I've never quite understood?

"Edward Clayton was one of the most active Servatores of our time," he says with carefully measured words. "He's averted more disasters than Casey, Dan, Isaac, and me put together."

A strange sloping sensation makes me grip the arms of the chair.

Papa? A Servator?

"He's saved dozens of lives, usually without anyone knowing what had happened," he goes on. "Your grandfather was a Servator legend."

He's got to be kidding. "I've known Papa all my life. If he could manipulate time, I would have known about it."

Albert looks at me closely. "Would you?"

The word "yes" is on the tip of my tongue, ready to break loose. But...would I have known?

We come to London for eight weeks a year. That's it. I haven't really grown up around Nana and Papa. In fact, when you get right down to it, their presence in my life was never consistent. Sure, we've spent a lot of time talking, but keeping a big secret from us would have been pretty easy for Papa to do.

And, come to think of it...I remember something about Papa saving someone's life. Dad mentioned it, maybe four or five years ago, but I can't recall any of the details.

"Wouldn't people have made a big deal about all the lives he saved?" I say. "My grandmother? My dad? I remember something about Papa rescuing a person from some kind of accident, but that's it. Wouldn't they have talked about the other saves?"

"Not if they didn't know. He made the news more than any of us, though—locally, anyway."

"He made the news?" So that's what the priest meant. Some of the attendees only knew *of* Edward Clayton because they'd read about him in the news.

I throw my hands out to my sides. "How could people not know you're saving all these lives?"

"Think about it. We rewind time. We make situations play out differently. Nobody knows what would have happened if we hadn't intervened." He bites his bottom lip, then mumbles, "Except you, of course."

I stare at the floor while my brain spins into overdrive. Papa was a strong man, sure, but he was hardly the superhero Albert's making him out to be. I can't reconcile this mega-Servator legend with the cardigan-wearing grandfather I knew.

"Tell me how you knew him," I say.

Albert sits on the bed with a loud creak. Thanks to the room's tiny dimensions, he's unnervingly close to me, even from my station in the leather chair.

"I met him when I was thirteen," he says.

His voice is so soft that it nearly blends with the chatter of the rain against the windows. I hadn't noticed until now that it had started back up again.

"He came to speak to our school about courage. How to be a hero even when you're afraid. Even though only a few of his saves were public knowledge, it was enough to earn him a nickname. People called him the Blackheath Savior."

"The Blackheath Savior," I echo. The name feels good in my mouth. I could say it a hundred times and still find it impressive.

He nods. "While he was speaking in our auditorium, a girl had a seizure. She fell out of her chair and started convulsing so violently that she cracked her skull on the floor."

He looks down at his hands, which are clasped between his knees. He's running a thumb over his palm. Rough callouses spread from the base of his thumbs to the edge of his hands. He didn't get those from shelving books, that's for sure.

"She stopped breathing at one point, and everyone panicked. I looked at the stage and there was Edward, standing there with his eyes closed. He held his hands out in front of him and then everything started spinning. I felt like I was getting sucked into a black hole. There was a bright flash of light, and then we were all sitting calmly in the auditorium, just as we had been a few minutes before. The girl was in her seat again, listening to Edward speak." He straightens up, making the mattress complain. "Any guesses as to what happened next?"

Oh, I have a guess. I can see it playing out in my head because I've seen how Albert operates. "He stopped her seizure from getting out of control."

"Yep. He came down into the crowd, pretending to choose volunteers to reenact one of his saves, but in reality he was just placing himself near her. He caught her when she fell out of her chair, and they were able to keep her from hurting herself until the convulsions passed."

"And you and Casey were the only ones who felt the Pull." I imagine younger versions of Albert and his sister sitting together in an airy auditorium, feeling something inexplicable. Something that would change their lives forever.

"We were losing our minds," he replies with a laugh. "I asked the bloke next to me if he felt it, and he looked at me like I was insane. I remembered the way Edward closed his eyes, and the way he held his hands out, right before everything rewound. Casey didn't want to ask him about it. She was afraid I was wrong, that he'd think we were crazy. But I had to know. I approached him after the assembly. He listened as I told him what I'd felt, and then he gave me his card. Told me to phone him if I wanted answers."

"Did you call that night?"

He shakes his head. "For weeks, I swung from one side to the other, hurrying to the old payphone down the street but then never actually phoning him. I must have chucked his card in the bin and fished it back out a dozen times. Eventually, though, I went through with it."

I fold my legs into the chair and rest my elbows on my knees. "Is that when he told you about the Pull?"

"He told me a little on the phone, yeah. Enough to convince me he knew what I'd felt, and that it was something real." Albert mimics my position on the bed and leans toward me. For two people who aren't even sitting on the same piece of furniture, we are oddly near each other. "So many strange pieces of my life clicked into place during those few weeks."

"Like what?"

"Casey and I both knew we could Pull. We'd done it before accidentally. It requires a huge amount of focus, but sometimes, that focus takes the form of panic." He fiddles with the edge of the quilt—a patchwork type thing, the kind Nana used to make before the arthritis in her knuckles put a stop to it. "We didn't have a name for what we'd done, and Casey didn't like to discuss it. Talking to your grandfather was like the sun coming out after years of rain."

"Why did he never say anything about this?" I didn't mean to let the hurt creep into my voice, but there it is. "It seems weird that he never told us."

Albert gives me an understanding smile. "Didn't want people thinking he was a lunatic. That's why we all stay a bit underground. It's hard to save lives when you're trapped in a mental institution."

"Right," I say. "So he kept up with you all these years?"

"Yeah. We lived in the dorms at school—this bloody pretentious place with gates and gargoyles." He rolls his eyes. "But he visited all the time. He practically became a father to us."

I wait a beat before asking my next question. "Where's your real father, Albert?"

His eyes shift to the floor. "He's away."

"And your mother?"

He starts to answer, but an eruption of thuds and a panicked shout—"Al, get down here, quick!"—from the ground floor sends both of us rocketing toward the door.

"What is it?" I yell.

Albert's eyes are lit with alarm. He flies out to the landing and grips the banister, leaning over the staircase. "I don't know. Hang on."

He's halfway down the first flight of stairs and I'm hot on his trail. We can't see anything, but the grunts of the struggle have grown louder. Glass breaks somewhere below, and I flash back to the pub, to cowering inside the men's bathroom as Albert defended my life.

I won't cower this time.

A wiry, dark-haired woman with a vicious face is trying to force her way into the house. Dan has his whole body pressed against the inside of the door. He's holding a broken beer bottle in one hand. Every time the woman sticks her arm through the gap in the door, Dan jabs it with the broken bottle, causing the woman to howl in rage and jerk her arm back out. She's like a zombie, only faster and more aggressive than the lumbering creatures I've seen on TV. There's a lump of horror in my throat that I can't swallow. When Dan sees Albert, the panic in his expression recedes a fraction.

"Not the biggest of problems," Dan says with a grunt. "Just a Bestia. Still, she's got a bone to pick over something. Help?"

"Go back upstairs," Albert calls to me over his shoulder. He throws himself against the door and the woman growls in protest. "Get in my room and lock the door."

Even though he can't see me, I shake my head. There's no way I'm sitting on the sidelines again.

TWENTY

THE WOMAN IS SCRAWNY, WITH DIRTY, GRAYING SKIN and wild eyes. She's not in her right mind; the evidence lies in every miscalculated grab of her hands, every rage-filled shriek that follows Dan's repeated bottle-jabs.

"Ran out for the mail and this lovely bird tried to follow me back in," Dan says to Albert, his face strained with effort. "Couldn't close the door fast enough."

"Don't worry about it; let's just get her out of here." Albert throws his weight against the door. His hands turn white at the edges from the pressure. Even with Dan doing the same thing next to him, the gap in the door keeps getting wider.

"Bit strong for a Bestia," Albert remarks pointedly.

"Look at her!" Dan cries, adjusting his footing. "What else could she be? Certainly not a Magus, is she? Does she look capable of enchanting anyone?"

Suddenly the woman's entire rain-streaked head thrusts, snarling, through the gap in the door. Dan's shoes squeak as he scrambles for traction, but he can't find it—the gap in the door is a few inches wider now. Even though Dan recovers quickly and throws himself against the door, the woman thrusts one bony arm into the house and rakes her claw-like fingernails across Albert's neck.

"Isaac!" Albert shouts. "Get in here!"

"He and Casey went out, mate," Dan says. "It's just you and me."

Except that it isn't.

I leap off the stairs and wedge myself between them. If another body against the door is what they need, there's no reason I can't be that body. But, as expected, Albert turns to me with fire in his eyes.

"Rosie! What do you think you're doing?"

"Helping," I grunt. Man, this *Bestia* is strong. "What does it look like?"

Albert shakes his head. "I don't want you down here—"

His words cut off as a hand clamps down on the woman's face from outside the house, pulling her away from the door. It slams shut with the sudden loss of pressure, but Albert flings it back open so hard it bounces off the wall. He and Dan leap onto the front stoop. Isaac, who must have come home just in time to see what was happening, has the woman in a headlock.

"To the cellar," Albert says. "Take the outside stairs, though. I don't want her in the house."

Isaac nods.

"What's in the cellar?" I ask.

Albert watches Isaac drag the Bestia halfway down the front stairs. "A disposal system."

The words give me a sick feeling. "What kind of disposal system?"

Isaac lets out a sudden howl as the woman's ragged fingernails rake across his forearm. He loses his grip and she tries to escape, but Albert darts through the door and catches her arm. She wails, wraps her free arm around Isaac's neck, and all three of them tumble down to the sidewalk. Dan leaps down the stairs after them, trying to help wrestle the Bestia back toward the house, but she slips out of the fray and darts across the street to the heath. Albert, Isaac, and Dan sprint after her.

I hover in the doorway as the fight migrates onto the heath. The rain has lightened, but the ground is still a wet mess. Dirty water sprays around the group as their feet scramble to gain traction in the mud. Albert jumps on the woman's back and punches her in the ribs, in the face, wherever he can reach. The woman swings her arms uselessly as Albert tightens an elbow around her neck. But then she throws Albert to the ground. He hits hard, flat on his back, and his face crumples in pain.

"Oi," calls a raven-haired girl running up the steps to the house. It's Casey, Albert's twin. "You must be Rosie." Her eyes—that same sea-green as her brother's—shift from me to the violent scene on the heath. "Since the three of them are occupied, you and I will stay in here. It's good to have one Servator whose hands are free, just in case."

She slams the door and her fingers fly down the line of deadbolts. Her movements remind me of a lioness—careful, calculated, and fluid as water. She's thin, but not skinny. The lean muscles in her arms twitch with every twist of a lock.

"Don't worry," she says, mistaking my open mouth for a sign of confusion. "They can get in if they need to. Those three, I mean. We don't use keys, we use—"

"Your thumbs," I finish. "I saw."

"Yes, that's right." She smiles, and it's a wide, welcoming kind of thing that sets me so at ease, I nearly forget the fight outside. "Let's go up to Al's room. We'll have a good view from up there, and I'll know if I need to Pull."

We jog up to the third floor and into Albert's bedroom, where Casey locks us in. There is only one deadbolt this time—a detail I failed to notice before.

"Now," she says, moving to the window Albert leaned against only moments ago. "Let's see what's what."

"Aren't you worried about them?" I gaze over her shoulder to the heath. We're just in time to see Albert land a vicious punch to the woman's ribs. The force of the blow makes me wince. I know how he fights—I've seen it firsthand. But the power he delivers in a single jab takes me by surprise every time.

"Not terribly." She waves a hand at the fight. "It's three against one, and she looks like a Bestia. I'll fight if they need me, of course, but like I said, it's useful to have one Servator not tied up in the skirmish."

"Albert used that word, too," I say. "'Bestia.' What does it mean?"

"It means 'beast,' of course." She smiles and offers me her hand. "I'm Casey. Don't think we've met properly." Her voice goes quiet. "So sorry about Edward. We attended his funeral—but you know that, I suppose. Al said he spoke to you at the burial."

I nod, noticing the redness in her eyes and the worry that lurks just behind her confident demeanor. She's acting like she's not upset, but I see it in the slump of her shoulders and the false smile she keeps giving me. It's the same smile Nana wore when we first arrived. The one that didn't reach her eyes.

"Thank you," I say, and I want to talk more about Papa, but a cry of pain from the heath jerks my attention back to the fight. "Are you sure they're going to be okay? That woman is a monster."

The Bestia has jumped onto Isaac's back, and for one horrifying second it seems like she's getting the upper hand. Then Isaac flips her over his shoulder and lands a kick to her stomach. A few people have gathered around the edge of the heath, and several are on their phones, probably calling the police about the three guys who appear to be attacking an innocent woman. A couple of men run out to help her, but as soon as they get near the fray, Albert shoves them back.

"The Mortiferi are all monsters," Casey says. "They're used to it."

So Casey thinks I know what the Mortiferi are.

"That woman out there," I say. "What is she, exactly? Is a Bestia the same as Mortiferi?"

Her gaze turns piercing. "You don't know what the Mortiferi are?"

"Albert told me they were a gang, but somehow that feels like an incomplete definition."

"A gang," she says with a sigh. "I love my brother, but honestly. A *gang?*"

"I need to know," I say, punctuating every word with as much insistence as I can.

"Well," she says. "I'll tell you what Albert didn't. But I've got to warn you, it's not pretty."

"I'm fine," I say, squaring my shoulders. "I can handle it." This may or may not be true, but either way, I can't take one more minute of suspense.

Casey gives me an appraising look. "Okay then. A Mortifer—that's the singular form, you know—is a person whose soul has been darkened by sorcery."

My eyebrows arch. "Sorcery? Come on."

She shrugs. "It is what it is, mate. Believe it or not."

It's true that I've seen some crazy stuff lately, but this seems too far over the top. If Casey's telling the truth, then the man who attacked me on the heath and then came into the pub was filled with black magic. So is the Bestia woman who just tried to break in.

"Sorcery," I say again, letting the word soak in my mind. Is it possible that black magic exists? That people could be infected by it like a disease?

I'm having a hard time telling reality from fantasy these days.

A gunshot echoes from the direction of the heath. We both jump. Casey flies to the window, black hair billowing behind her like a cape. Her jaw goes slack and she exhales in a rush.

"What?" I shout. I want to look out the window, but I'm frozen in place, unable to do anything but watch her reaction.

She spins around. "I don't know. I… Stay here for a minute, okay?"

I force myself to the window. Albert, Dan, and Isaac are stumbling toward the house, their faces stricken with panic. A man with white hair is running in the opposite direction, toward the church, and it looks like he's got something in his hand—it must be a gun. Even though the man's hair suggests he's old, the powerful way he runs proves otherwise. Something about him seems familiar, though I don't know why; I'm sure I don't know him.

Only the Bestia stays behind. She lies in a mud puddle, fingers of crimson leaking into the murky water beneath her.

Clutching the banister, I fumble down the steps and reach the ground floor just as the guys burst into the house. All three of them are cut and bruised. Albert presses one hand to a gash on the bridge of his nose while twisting the deadbolts into place with the other.

"What happened?" Casey demands.

"Al knocked her out, exactly as he should've," Isaac replies, examining the deep scratches on his forearm. He licks his lips. "Then this white-haired bloke came out of nowhere and shot her."

Silence.

"Dead?" Casey asks.

Dan nods, a sharp movement. "For sure."

More silence. The anger on their faces doesn't make sense.

"The woman who tried to break in and attack all of us—she's dead?" I ask, just to make sure I understand the situation.

They nod.

"It's worse now than if she were still alive," Casey says, but whatever explanation she might have given dies as her brother's threatening gaze lands on her.

"What's worse?" I say.

More silence.

I shift my weight and cross my arms. "No one's going to tell me?"

Albert's gaze flickers to mine. "The woman out there—the Bestia—she knew your name, Rosie. She said it while we were moving the fight onto the heath. They're hunting you and I'm sure it has something to do with your grandfather. If they realize you're aware of them, they'll track you even more viciously. They might—"

"Wait for me under a willow tree in the middle of a storm?" I say flatly. "Or maybe even follow me to a pub and try to gun me down?"

He presses his lips together. Isaac gives me a steely gaze as blood drips freely from his forearm to his fingertips. Casey's mouth keeps opening and closing, like she's trying to say something that will ease the tension but she can't figure out which words to use. Dan's gaze is locked on Casey, and for once, his eyes carry no hint of amusement.

Finally, Casey says, "They're hunting you? Rosie, you didn't tell me that. If I knew they'd marked you specifically, I never would have told you anything."

Albert rounds on her. "You told her? What did you say?"

"She told me what you wouldn't," I say, pinning him with my eyes. "She told me what they really are."

Albert looks at me. The muscles in his jaw tighten. "Is that all she told you?" His gaze flickers to Casey, who gives him a shaky nod.

"Yes," I say. "But there's more, I know there is. And if you won't tell me, then I'll just find out another way." I peer through the peephole in the door. "Is it safe to go home?"

Albert shakes his head. "You can't walk alone. I'll drive—"

"No, you won't." My vision has practically gone red. "You think you get to decide all these things for me. What I'm allowed to know, where I'm allowed to be while you fight, how I'm allowed to get home. I'm involved in this, whether you like it or not, and it's time for you to start treating me as one of you."

On some level, I feel the foolishness of what I'm doing, but that awareness is no match for my rage. I wrench open the door and fly down the steps, racing as fast as my legs will carry me all the way to Nana's blue door. Maybe Albert's trying to protect me, but I'm in too deep for that. There's a connection here, some common thread running from Papa, to Albert and his friends, to me, and then to the Mortiferi.

Albert's voice echoes in my head. *She knew your name, Rosie. They're hunting you.*

Terror shoots through my gut, but I shove it back down. I don't care if information makes me vulnerable. I can't live in ignorance just for the sake of personal safety when so much else seems to be at stake.

I'm going to find out just how deep this rabbit hole goes.

TWENTY-ONE

AFTER LUNCH THE NEXT DAY, I BEGIN OPERATION Figure-It-Out-Myself.

The Internet might be useless when it comes to information on Servatores and Mortiferi, but that doesn't mean information about them doesn't exist. If the Servatores really are centuries old, there must be a record of them somewhere. And if there are records, they would probably date from well before the time of technology, which means they would be written on actual paper. So instead of spending my day experimenting with different search term combinations, I'm using something most people have forgotten all about—the library. There's a small one in Blackheath, but it's so tiny, I doubt it has a large archive collection.

My best bet is Greenwich.

North Greenwich Library sits near the Naval College, facing the Thames. It looms three stories tall, and its walls are gray stone with white trim and rugged wooden doors. A hint of mold edges the window frames, and the metal bike rack out front is rusted and bent. To the left of the building sits a red telephone booth, the kind that is somehow quintessentially British, yet never actually used for making calls. A group of French schoolchildren are currently seeing how many of them can fit inside.

I push through the front doors into a cool lobby with white marble floors. Straight ahead is the main room, with carved wooden archways separating fiction from nonfiction. To my right is a long glass countertop with a massive clock hanging on the wall behind it. Two men, grim-faced and gray-haired, sort through a stack of thick reference books behind the counter. They spare me a glance when I pass, but don't offer any help.

That's fine with me; I'd rather not be noticed.

I amble toward the center of the lobby, where a metal stand shows a map of the building. I'm on the main floor with fiction and nonfiction books. On the floor above me are the children and teen sections, and above that, reference. That's the most likely place for what I need, but there's a small note at the bottom of the map. I bend to read it.

Special Collections located in basement.
Hours M-F, 8:00—4:00.

"Aha," I mutter. "Jackpot."

The old men behind the glass counter frown at me.

With an apologetic wave, I move to the staircase on my left and try to keep calm as I hurry down it. Whatever the Mortiferi are, and whatever my grandfather had to do with them, I don't need Albert to spoon-feed me information whenever and however he feels like it.

At the bottom of the stairs, I reach a rusted metal door with a keypad set into the wall next to it. Even though I have a feeling it won't work, I grab the handle and give it a tug. Locked.

"Huh," I say, stepping back to examine the keypad. There's an intercom below it. I press a small white button and wait.

A low, uninterested voice comes over the speaker. "Yes?"

"Uh, hi. I'm here to..." Uh-oh. I didn't expect to have to explain myself so quickly. "I'm here to do some research."

Something clicks softly above me. It's a white security camera in the corner above the door.

"Bet you are," says the voice, which carries an oddly familiar tone. "Hang on."

The intercom clicks off and I wait, arms crossed, without knowing who or what I'm waiting for. After about a minute, the door swings open and—

"Isaac?" I feel my nose scrunch up. "I thought you worked at the Blackheath Library."

He regards me with a tired expression. "Nope."

Long pause.

"Great," I say. "Well, I..."

One of his eyebrows twitches. The rest of his face remains stoically uninterested.

"You know why I'm here," I whisper, leaning close to him. "Will you help me?"

His stare makes me feel like I'm covered in ice. I'm sure he'll refuse me after I ran out on Albert last night, but then he backs into the hallway behind the door and gives me the tiniest flick of his head. Assuming he means for me to follow him, I dart through the door and stretch my strides to match his.

This section of the building looks more like a medieval dungeon than a library, with low wooden rafters and cool stone walls. The floor is hardwood, scarred by decades of dropped books, pointy heels, and—knowing the English—the occasional fumbled cup of tea. Although given how fragile most of the things in this collection probably are, tea may not be allowed down here at all.

At the end of the hallway lies another set of doors. They're metal, with small windows set into their centers. Instead of a keypad, Isaac holds his ID card up to a scanner, which beeps and releases a mechanism inside the doors. He pushes one of them open and holds it for me as I walk through.

"The special collections room," he whispers.

The space is vast and cluttered, with wide-planked floors and walls made of the same stone as the hallway. Since we're underground, the walls are uninterrupted by windows—something that would probably bother me if I wasn't so distracted by the dozens of aisles filled with file cabinets, plastic-wrapped volumes, and what look like treasure chests. The air carries the tangy scent of old paper and ink. I close my eyes and I can almost feel the secrets swirling around me. Long, wooden tables extend down the center of the room, with three chairs on each side and green glass lamps in their centers.

"Where should I start?" I wave at the vast expanse of materials on each aisle. "I don't really know what I'm looking for."

"Start wherever you like. Just make sure your hands are clean, and be careful when you turn the pages." He gives me the closest thing to a smile I've ever seen from him. Then he turns around and heads for a desk at the back of the room.

"Wait a second! Aren't you going to help me—you know? Find what I need?"

He looks over his shoulder. "I let you in. That's all I'm willing to do."

I plop down at one of the tables. I suppose I can't expect him to be loyal to me over Albert, but I was hoping he'd steer me in the right direction.

"Isaac," I say, and he turns around again. "Let's keep this between us, okay?"

His gaze shifts to something over my shoulder. "Might be a bit difficult to do that, mate."

I swivel around. Albert is standing behind me, expressionless. He's wearing a black T-shirt and uncharacteristically nice jeans. A nametag on the pocket of his shirt reads *ALBERT S*. It's the gold-colored plastic kind that pins on, the same kind I have to wear during shifts at The Chicken Cottage. For a brief moment I picture Albert working at my restaurant, his arms laden with trays of deep-fried wings and thighs, offering more sweet tea to greasy-lipped customers. My mind rejects the image instantly.

"You both work here?" I say to Isaac. "Why didn't you tell me?"

Isaac shrugs. "You didn't ask." He turns his back to us and saunters to the desk.

I face Albert with narrowed eyes. He gives me a wry look. "I told you I worked at the library," he says.

"I assumed you meant the one in Blackheath." I hold my hands up. "Trust me, I didn't come here looking for you. Why this one, anyway? There must be two or three libraries closer to your house."

"I have my reasons."

"Hmm." I lift my chin. "Well, I have some research to do. My primary sources—" I give him a significant look "—aren't much help, so I'm taking matters into my own hands."

He frowns as I stand up. "You don't take no for an answer, do you?"

I let out an indignant laugh. "Did you expect me to just give up? How could I be involved in all this without knowing every possible detail? You say it's dangerous for me to know about the Mortiferi—"

He winces and looks around. "Not so loud."

"—yet you've admitted they're hunting me. My grandfather died saying their name in my mind. If you won't tell me anything else, then yeah, I'll figure it out on my own."

He stares at me for a long moment. Maybe he's going to throw me out.

I wait.

He chews his bottom lip.

Finally he says, "Come with me," and walks toward the back of the room. There's no door over here, so I'm pretty sure he's not throwing me out. Which means he's… helping me?

Oh, please let that be it.

Even though I sort of like the idea of digging through all these fragile documents without Albert's help, things will be much easier with his guidance. A thrill shoots through my veins as I follow him past the tables, through a maze of file cabinets and locked boxes and cluttered shelves, to the last aisle in the back of the room.

The light barely reaches back here, and the air seems even mustier than when I first came in. At the end of the aisle, behind a large black file cabinet labeled *Geological Sample Reports, 1954-1958*, is an ancient-looking wooden door with an iron lock and handle. The wood is a little warped and splintered; how old is this thing? A thumbpad sits just above the lock—same as the one at Albert's flat. He shoves the file cabinet to the side. It moves reluctantly, rolling on squeaky wheels.

"Keep close," he whispers, pressing his thumb to the pad. "It's dark in places and you can lose your footing." A mechanism in the door whirs in response to Albert's thumbprint and he pushes against the iron handle until the door creaks open.

"This door looks a hundred years old," I whisper. "How did the library wire it for thumbprint entry?"

"The library didn't." He turns to me with a grin. "Casey did."

"Casey?"

"She did the flat, as well. Anything electronic that seems rather amiss, she's probably responsible for. This library has always been owned by a Servator. That way, we can do whatever we want."

"But there are only a few Servatores in London. Who's the owner?"

He smiles sadly. "Until a couple years ago, it was this bloke named Ben Burgess. He was killed in the process of rescuing a young girl from her would-be kidnapper. The girl got away, but the kidnapper, it turned out, had a knife."

"Oh, man. I'm glad she was safe, but that's awful about Ben."

He nods his agreement. "Ben's will left the library to me; we were quite good mates, he and I, and all Servatores have a will. So until further notice—or until I kick the bucket—I'm the owner."

"What?" I laugh. "You own this entire library? Doesn't that take up a lot of your time?"

"Not really. The library is fully staffed, and I'm an excellent delegator. Plus, a busy staff doesn't have much time to ask questions or notice strange doors behind file cabinets." He gestures toward the space on the other side of the door. It's so dark, I can't see what we're about to walk into. "Go ahead. I'll close up behind us."

His position in the doorway forces me to pass close to him—close enough to smell the scent of rain he always seems to carry. My fingers leap for my necklace, and I rub my thumb over the gold rings as Albert shuts the door behind us.

"Is this the part where you kill me?" I whisper.

His laugh seems to fill the tight space. "Something tells me you'd tear my arm off if I so much as touched you right now, so I guess the killing will have to wait until you don't see it coming. Watch your step, and try not to panic."

I hear him crouch down, then stand back up. A light clicks on; he must keep a flashlight in here. As the beam travels from his shoes to the other side of the space, I can see we're standing at the top of a twisted stone staircase. The light barely reaches the first few steps before the rest are lost in darkness.

"I thought we were already in the basement," I mutter.

He moves past me to the top of the stairs. "Things aren't always what they seem. Be careful—these medieval staircases aren't exactly proportional."

I balk. "It's not really medieval, is it?"

"Eleventh century. The library was built on the site of an old prison. These stairs led down to the torture chambers."

"No way," I say as we ease down the first few steps. The stone wall is surprisingly cold beneath my fingers. "Torture chambers?"

"Don't worry; we use it for much nobler purposes now." He pauses and looks over his shoulder. Even in the dim light, his gaze is sharp and clear. "Last chance to back out, Rosie Clayton. Once you see what I'm about to show you, there's no going back."

"Nothing will stop me at this point."

He regards me for a moment. "Fair enough. Down to the torture chambers we go."

There's no rail to hold—just the stone walls that curve down around us like a granite cocoon. The air grows damper with every step and I force my breathing to stay even as the space constricts. Albert's flashlight bounces in his hand, sending the beam from one side of the staircase to the other, and I try to ignore the stains and cracks it reveals. How many people were dragged down these stairs toward a fate worse than death? How many screams ricocheted off these stones? How many of these stains are blood?

"Hey," Albert says, stopping. "Are you all right?"

I press a hand to my stomach. Now that I hear how strained my breathing has become, I understand his concern. "I'm okay. Just imagining things."

He's a couple of steps below me, which puts our faces at the same height. "Imagining what?" His voice is little more than a whisper, but it echoes around me as if he had shouted.

"People," I manage, waving around the staircase. "Here."

The flashlight hangs from his hand, its beam casting a white circle around our feet. For a moment, the only sound is my labored breathing and the pounding of my heart in my ears.

Then he says, "Right," and wraps his hand around mine.

All the air in my lungs seems to evaporate.

I jerk my hand back and stumble against the stairs, catching myself just before I start to tumble down however many are left.

"What are you doing?" I shout.

He throws a hand into the air. "Trying to comfort you!"

I stare at him.

He glares back.

"Oh," I say.

His expression is as closed off as a high-security lockdown gate. "Obviously, that was not a good decision."

"No, it was—it was fine." I clear my throat. "You just surprised me, that's all."

"Well, don't worry." He holds his hands up in surrender. The flashlight beam dances across my eyes. "I won't do it again. Come on, we're almost there."

He starts down the stairs again, but this time, he doesn't take them quite so slowly. When he's not burdened by a first-timer like me, he probably flies down this staircase. I hurry to keep up with the bouncing beam of his flashlight. Just when I'm about to shout at him to slow down, we hit flat ground.

"Another door?" I squint at the wooden entryway blocking our path. It looks identical to the one we first came through at the top of the stairs.

"Yep. We're almost there, I promise."

He presses his thumb to another electronic pad. We step through the door into a dark, musty corridor. I throw an elbow over my nose.

"Are we in a sewer?" I say, my voice muffled against my arm. It doesn't smell as awful as a sewer, but there's definitely a large amount of mold down here.

"No. We're in a thousand-year-old Servator tunnel." He swings the flashlight left to right, revealing a dirty floor punctuated by small, round drip marks.

"What do you mean, a Servator tunnel?" I pull my arm away from my face. If I'm going to be brave, I'd better be brave all around—even when gross smells are involved. "You say that like it's a thing."

He walks through the door, looking over his shoulder to make sure I'm following. Our footsteps echo softly against the walls, which I think are made of the same stone as the staircase.

"It *is* a thing. London hasn't always had trains, you know. Centuries ago, if Servatores needed to move quickly from one spot to another, tunnels like these were their best option." He pauses. "Of course, they've also been used for other things."

"Like what?"

"Hiding people, mostly."

My toe catches on an uneven stone and I steady myself on the wall. It's slimy and cold, and I have to stop myself from making a disgusted noise. "What people?"

"Most recently, the Jews." His voice is reverent.

I run a finger along the walls; they don't seem quite so disgusting anymore. "This was an escape route from the Nazis?"

I barely see the silhouette of his head as he nods. "One of them, yeah. The Servatores during World War II tried to stop Hitler by Pulling, but they weren't strong enough. They did manage to save some lives, though. And they smuggled everyone they could through these tunnels and into the countryside, where they hid them in the woods."

"Amazing," I murmur.

"Yes, quite." His tone has become formal, like he's leading an official guided tour. "The great majority of them were killed for what they did. The Mortiferi were recruiting heavily then, and given the imbalance between the two sides at that time, I think the Servatores must have known they wouldn't survive. But they fought anyway." His voice goes a little thick. "They didn't back down."

He stops in front of an ancient-looking iron gate. I stay a few steps behind.

"I'm sorry," he says quietly, glancing at me over his shoulder. "About the hand thing."

I shake my head. "It's fine. I shouldn't have yelled at you. It was an overreaction." The memory of that fire from his touch sears through my mind. I rub my arms, trying to get a grip on myself. It wasn't the first time he's ever touched me. But this time, without the element of an imminent threat, it seemed more…personal.

"I didn't realize you would *actually* try to tear my arm off," he mumbles, looking back to the gate. "That was supposed to be a joke."

"Sorry. It won't happen again. As long as you don't touch me, of course."

"Right," he says, tapping on the keyhole.

There is a *drip drip drip* of water coming from somewhere to my left. How far does this tunnel go? It definitely turns here, but we're not going to follow it anymore, apparently.

Still pointing to the keyhole on the gate, Albert says, "This one isn't quite as high-tech as the others. It's original to the tunnel."

"This gate is a thousand years old?" I step forward and run a finger along one of the iron bars. "You can't be serious."

"I am. We've repaired it now and again, of course, and replaced small parts of it, but the overall structure is original. You can almost feel the history coming off it in waves."

He reaches into his shirt and pulls out a thin red cord with a black iron key on the end, about three inches long, with jagged teeth and a few smudges of rust. He shoves the key into the lock with a metallic *screech*. The gate swings into the room behind it, and a new wave of apprehension mixed with excitement works its way through my body.

Albert goes in first. "Well," he says quietly, "here it is. London Servator headquarters."

TWENTY-TWO

MY VISION FILLS WITH BLUE WHEN WE WALK THROUGH the gate.

Nothing in the cavern is actually blue. It's just a result of the glowing screens and incandescent lanterns reflecting off the cave walls. The space reaches at least fifty feet overhead, but the distance from where I'm standing to the opposite wall is only half that. It's sort of like being inside a giant stone egg. The whole thing would have a claustrophobia-inducing effect if the ceiling wasn't so far up, but as it is, there's plenty of breathing room.

"Servator headquarters?" I say, giving Albert the side-eye. "Or Batcave?"

He lets out a small laugh. "Trust me, we've made our fair share of Batman references since we put this place together. But our reality is less impressive than Bruce Wayne's, I'm afraid. We've managed to tap into some of the CCTV cameras around London, which you can see here—" he gestures at the row of rectangular screens mounted on one of the walls "—and we use them to coordinate with other Servatores on patrol. I've been down here most of the day, communicating with Dan as he traveled the city."

I blink at the screens. It's hard to reconcile goofy, lanky Dan with someone who roams London and communicates with headquarters. It all seems so official. "Did he Pull today? I don't remember feeling any vortexes in my gut."

"He only Pulled once, and you have to be really close to the person who's Pulling to be able to feel it."

"Ah. So why did he do it? What happened?"

A wrinkle appears between his eyebrows. "A girl's boyfriend got a bit aggressive with her in an alley and then started to hit her when she refused his advances."

My stomach clenches. "That's horrible."

"We're not sure if he actually killed her or just knocked her out," he says grimly, "but either way, Dan came to her rescue. He even managed to bring a constable with him."

"So now she's safe."

He nods and looks around at the screens on the wall. "This is what we do. And now you know where we do it."

I take a few steps into the space. "Is anyone else here?"

"Not right now. We take shifts at headquarters. Isaac and Casey have afternoon duty."

"This all seems..." I frown. "More organized than I expected. And given the spy closet in your house, I had pretty high standards."

"We have to be organized," he says, trailing me to the center of the room. "It's the only way to fight the chaos."

He meets my eyes, and in the dim light I can see there's more to those words than just their surface meaning.

"And by chaos, you mean Mortiferi," I say in a low voice.

"Yes, exactly." He flicks his head toward the opposite side of the room. "Are you ready for some profound unpleasantries?"

I step closer to him. "Let's go."

He leads me to what looks like a bank vault. The door is sleek metal, with a large combination lock on the outside. Albert spins it right, left, right, and then the door unlocks and we're in.

I suck in a breath. "Holy. Freaking. Mother."

The room behind the bank vault door is the size of a typical high school classroom. The floor is white tile, and the walls and ceiling are made of metal. Running all the way from the left to the right are metal shelves, arranged into rows, with books and video cameras and file cabinets stacked on top of them. Some of the file cabinets have large white labels I can read from here.

Founders—64 A.D. Rome Consortio.

London Consortio.

Trahos, Centuries 1-2

Even though I don't understand a lot of the words I see, there's a deep sense of history here, a profound air of magic that sends the hair on my arms springing to life.

Albert gives me a knowing smile. "Everything you hoped for and more?"

I steady myself on the cool doorframe. "What is all this?"

"Records," he says. "Everything about our origins, our struggles, and our triumphs. Notes about each save, with names, if we can get them. Profiles of known or suspected Mortiferi. Patterns identified within their specific groups."

He looks at me, and I force my mouth to close. "From how far back?"

"All the way back. Second century."

"Second *century*?"

He nods.

I stare.

"Look," he says, moving to the left side of the room. "This is a record of the very first Servatores."

He opens the file cabinet labeled *Founders—64 A.D. Rome Consortio* and carefully lifts out a large square object wrapped in leather. He carries it to the end of the aisle and pushes a button, which sends a thin metal rectangle, roughly the size of the changing table in The Chicken Cottage bathroom, jutting out from the side of the bookshelves. On the metal table is a plastic bag with latex gloves inside.

"Document table," he explains, putting on the gloves. "They stay inside the shelves when they're not in use. Keeps them from getting dirty."

"Right," I say as he places the square object on the table and unfolds the leather.

Inside is a very old book with a crumbling exterior and pages that crinkle like autumn leaves. He slides a finger gently under the first one, turning it with a slow, deliberate motion.

"Now," he says, and I feel like I should hold my breath. "Come look."

I pad over to him and stand at his elbow. The first letter on the page is an elaborate drawing with painstaking detail and colors that used to be bright. It's so elaborate, in fact, that I can't even tell what letter it's supposed to be. An S, maybe? Or an R? And the rest of the text is so cramped and so—well, so *Latin*—that I don't have a chance of deciphering it.

"What does it say?" I whisper.

Albert leans closer to the page. "Been a while since I've looked at it. Let's see. 'Formed this fourteenth day of September, the brotherhood of the Servatores, now bound with common blood, vows to seek justice for the atrocities committed by Imperator Nero Claudius Caesar Augustus Germanicus—'"

"Nero?" I echo. "These men formed an alliance against Nero?"

Albert nods. "It was just a couple of months after the Fire of Rome, which Nero was suspected of starting. He was crazy and brutal to his own people—you know all this, I'm sure."

"Of course. But I've never heard of a brotherhood standing up to him."

I don't know much about Nero aside from the usual stuff—that he was awful and had syphilis and basically killed everyone in his path. If anyone confronted him, I can't imagine they would have survived very long.

"'Standing up' is a generous term," Albert says. "It was much more subtle than that, more underground. Similar to how we operate now. The fire was the last straw, and these men—the original Servatores—had been honing their powers for years as Nero grew more and more dangerous."

"What kind of powers did they have?"

He turns the page to an illustration of four men with long, ornate robes. "They were royal magicians, so anything from transfiguring one item into another to making small items disappear."

"But those weren't real tricks," I say, letting cynicism seep into my voice.

Albert lifts one eyebrow at me.

"No," I say, narrowing my eyes. "They were real?"

"Sure. Real magicians with real powers, some of which we Servatores retain to this day."

"Like communicating telepathically?" I say.

He smiles. "Spot on."

"Can you do it?" I step closer to him without really meaning to. "Can you speak into my mind?"

"Not at will," he says. "It's not like Pulling, which I can do fairly easily. To speak into someone's mind requires a great sense of urgency for us. More than just regular panic."

Papa certainly seemed distressed when he spoke thoughts to me in the hospital.

"So these magicians," I prompt.

He nods. "Eventually, they figured out a way to use their powers to fight Nero. He'd do something horrible, and they'd Pull, but they had a different word for it. *Traho.*"

"Traho," I echo.

"It's a Latin term they adopted for reversing small sections of time so you can stop something bad from happening, but there are all kinds of slang terms for it, depending on where you live." He shrugs. "We just call it Pulling."

Albert carefully turns a few more pages. I'm sure the text is fascinating, but the cramped words are hard on my eyes, and I look back to the shelves.

"Is all of this information about Servatores?" I ask.

Albert grins without letting his eyes leave the book. "If that were true, you'd probably punch me."

"You're really getting a handle on my personality."

"Give me a minute to put this away," he says, nodding at the book, "and we'll go to the deepest, darkest corner of the records room."

He wraps the book back up and stows it carefully inside the filing cabinet. Then he tugs off the gloves and seals them in the plastic bag, which zips back inside the shelf along with the document table.

The room is so still, yet so full of *presence*. I get the feeling I could spend hours in here by myself and never feel alone. Do these books actually contain magic? Remnants of the powers wielded by the early Servatores?

At this point, it seems anything is possible.

"It's back here," he says, gesturing to the far corner of the room. His steps slow as we walk. "None of us like to go back here, so I'm not sure what state we'll find it in. Hopefully, whoever went through it last left it tidy."

He leads me to the end of the last aisle, and when we reach it, I feel a shift in the air—a heaviness that settles on my shoulders and sinks into my chest, making me feel like I can't breathe quite as well as I should.

Albert is watching me. "You feel it?" "Yeah," I wheeze.

"There are things in this room," he says, "that we can only guess at. These books carry something with them, and every time we touch them, it's like they leak into us. I don't know." He rubs a hand over his face. "It sounds crazy, but I swear it's true."

"Let's not stay here too long, then," I say.

"Right. That's a good plan. So, this lovely corner of the room is where we keep information about the Mortiferi." He waves at the shelves, which seem less organized and dustier than the others. "We don't put much effort into maintaining it because, quite frankly, there isn't much new information to keep track of. We know who they are, and we know what they do."

He digs around on the bottom shelf. The weight on my chest has begun to feel like claws digging into my flesh. I'm not sure how much longer I can be here.

"Almost got it," he says, shifting what looks like a shoebox, then shoving an olive-green expanding file to the side. "Here we are."

When he stands up, I almost laugh at the book in his hand. It's a gray leather Bible with red embossed letters on the front cover.

"You know, they have the Bible online," I say flatly.

"Sure, but this is an official London Servator one." His eyebrows jump. "Much more exciting."

"Of course."

He flips the tissue-thin pages with considerably more speed than he used with the Roman book. "What I want to show you comes from the book of Numbers."

"I don't do math."

He tips his head back with a loud laugh. "Blimey, you know exactly how to bring down the house, don't you?"

"Sorry. This place has me on edge."

His fingers stop, go back a page, and run down the text. "Here we are. Numbers chapter thirteen, verses thirty-one through thirty-three. The language is a bit antiquated, so bear with me. Ready?"

"Sure," I say, even though I have no idea what I'm supposed to be ready for.

"'But the men that went up with him said, We be not able to go up against the people; for they are stronger than we. And they brought up an evil report of the land which they had searched unto the children of Israel, saying, The land, through which we have gone to search it, is a land that eateth up the inhabitants thereof; and all the people that we saw in it are men of a great stature. And there we saw the giants, the sons of Anak, which come of the giants: and we were in our own sight as grasshoppers, and so we were in their sight.'"

He looks up, and I meet his gaze.

He thumbs all the way back to Genesis, stopping at chapter six. "'And it came to pass, when men began to multiply on the face of the land, and daughters were born unto them, that the sons of God saw the daughters of men that they were fair; and they took them wives of all which they chose.'"

"Sons of God?"

Despite his attempts to act casual, Albert's eyes are alight with intrigue. "Angels. But because they're taking human wives, they have to be fallen angels. Also known as demons, though pop culture has more or less erased the connection between the two."

He adjusts his grip on the Bible and clears his throat. "'There were giants in the earth in those days; and also after that, when the sons of God came in unto the daughters of men, and they bear children to them, the same became mighty men which were of old, men of renown.'" He closes the Bible. "This is the King James translation, but there are other translations that give these giants a name—Nephilim."

"Nephilim," I say. "I've never heard the word before. So a Nephilim—"

"Naphil," Albert corrects. "Nephilim is plural."

"So a Naphil was the child of a demon father and a human mother?"

"Lovely thought, isn't it?" He shoves the Bible back on the shelf. "The Nephilim started out simply as a race of giants. You've heard of Goliath, I assume."

"As in, David and Goliath? Sure." I remember Sunday school lessons based on that story. Flannel boards with cutouts of little David and monstrous Goliath, and the slingshot David used to bring Goliath down.

"Yes, that's the one," Albert says. "Nine feet tall, extra fingers and toes, all that jazz. He was a Naphil. So were most of the Philistines, which were Goliath's people. Somewhere along the line, the Nephilim became murderous, conscienceless monsters. Most horrible things that happened, a Naphil was behind it. No rhyme, no reason. Just senseless destruction." He pauses. "Exactly the kind of thing you'd expect from someone with demonic blood in their family."

"But that blood must have thinned," I say. "Surely the families would contain more and more humans, and eventually, the Nephilim would die out. Right?"

"Their bodies became more normally sized because of human genetics," he says. "But unfortunately, their penchant for evil didn't dilute. The wickedness in their hearts—it wasn't a physical thing. It couldn't be tamed by any natural process. So now that you know all this, and given what you know about Nero, would you like to propose a theory as to what, exactly, Nero was?"

My eyes widen. "A Naphil descendant."

"Correct you are. And he began the Naphil practice of kidnapping hopeless people, giving them a sense of belonging within his inner circle, infecting their souls with sorcery, and then using them for his own despicable purposes. These soul-darkened people were called Mortiferi, and once they were in, they could never get out."

I tap my lips with my index finger. "Then Nero set fire to Rome, and the Servatores were born. But all they could do was try to reverse time and undo whatever he'd done. They couldn't stop the Nephilim or the Mortiferi completely."

"Right," Albert says. His smile is remorseful. "History would look quite different if they'd been able to do that. But they fought for peace, and they saved as many lives as they could, even though they knew the Nephilim were too powerful to defeat completely. Although…" He grips the back of his neck.

"Although?"

"Some of the Servatores were captured. Tortured for information. That's why the Nephilim, and now the Mortiferi, are aware of the Pull. They can't feel it, but they know how it works, and if they see one of us nearby, they assume we've sabotaged them."

"So these people fought evil, even though they knew they'd never defeat it altogether," I say quietly.

Talk about selfless. Talk about *brave*.

"If I can be a fraction as devoted to the cause as they were—" Albert swallows, then looks away. "Let's just say I never feel like I've done enough."

The emotions on his face are rawer than I've ever seen them. He lives every day of his life knowing it could be his last, and even then, he wishes he could do more. I've never felt quite so lazy as I do right now.

Papa was trying to tell me about all this. He must have planned to reveal his secret—at least, to me—before he died. But then he ran out of time, and all he could do was speak inside my head.

"This is why I was slow to tell you," Albert says. "They like to remain anonymous. Anyone who knows the details of how they operate is at great risk. Your grandfather was one of the only Servatores they feared, and now that he's gone…"

"They're becoming more active," I finish, and he nods. "But why are they targeting me? Is it just because I'm related to Papa?"

"I don't know. I thought about it, but if that were the case, it seems they would target your whole family."

"Right." I meet his eyes, bolstered by the courage I see there. "You'll tell me everything from now on?"

"Everything."

I give him a piercing look.

"I swear it," he says.

"I'm going to hold you to it." I pull out my phone and look at the time. "I better get home. Plus, whatever is in this room?" I cough and steady myself on the shelf next to me. "I think it's about to choke me."

He gives me a wry look. "Can I drive you home this time, or are you going to shout at me again?"

I press my lips together. If only the Pull could be used to take back stupid, reckless words. "About all those idiotic things I said to you—"

"Life's too short to judge people by their lowest moments," he says. "You were angry. If you can forgive me for keeping too many secrets, I can forgive you for running out of my flat with an armed stranger on the loose."

I pause. "You followed me, didn't you?"

His expression turns sheepish.

"Albert!"

He flings a hand in the air. "The man had a gun, Rosie. You really think I'm going to watch you walk out my front door without making sure you don't get bloody *shot*?"

We stare at each other.

"Of course not," I say quietly, because he wouldn't. He would rescue me even if I didn't deserve it.

He huffs in a way that is both maddening and weirdly endearing. "So," he says, gesturing at himself. "Forgiven?"

"Forgiven. And me?"

His eyes are locked on mine. It feels like he is looking past my flesh into my soul. Finally, in a low, rumbling voice that works its way deep into my bones, he says, "Forgiven. Always."

TWENTY-THREE

THE HOUSE IS EMPTY WHEN I GET HOME. THERE MIGHT not be sorcery in here, but the grief that settled within these walls on Papa's death day has taken up permanent residence with my family. It wraps its tendrils around my shoulders the moment I walk through the door, and as I creep down the hallway and into the kitchen, I swear I feel it trace a line of fear down my spine.

There's fresh coffee in the French press but no sign of anyone to drink it. I look around—for what or who, I don't know, it's not like drinking coffee is illegal—and then grab a mug from the cabinet.

Through the window in the back door, I can see the outline of Nana's gray head as she sits in her favorite wrought-iron patio chair. She's got her back to the house and a glass of red wine on the table next to her. The last thing I want to do right now is talk to her about Papa, and maybe that makes me a bad person—or maybe it just makes me human. Either way, I'd much rather curl up on the sofa in the sitting room and drink my coffee in silence, staring at the wall and processing everything I learned at the library.

But I can't. I won't.

There's no way I can ignore my own grandmother, regardless of how tired my brain is from the Mortiferi tutorial in the Batcave or how many reruns of *Big Brother* are probably airing on Channel 5 right now.

So I turn toward the door, take a sip of my coffee (black, because I just don't have the motivation to search for milk in the fridge), and brace myself for a mostly one-sided conversation.

One day, maybe things will feel normal again.

The kitchen door squeaks when I open it, but Nana doesn't turn around, so I walk to the chair next to her and drop into it. The hand that isn't occupied with the mug fiddles with my necklace, tapping the rings together so that they clink softly.

"It feels stupid to ask how you are," I say.

There's a rustle of movement as she turns to me. Redness tinges her swollen eyes, and she holds a bunch of tissues so crumpled they've practically disintegrated.

"I'm sad. But that's to be expected, isn't it?" She dabs at her eyes with the tissues and then reaches for the glass of wine on the table between us. "You know, I always tried to convince your father to move back here," she says, lifting the glass to her mouth.

She takes a long sip, oblivious to the way my mind is spinning. Nana tried to get Dad to relocate the family? Why did I never hear about this? London would've been a cool place to grow up.

"He wouldn't hear of it, though," she goes on, puckering her lips a little against the wine's bite. "Philip was smitten with Nashville the moment he set foot on Vanderbilt's campus as an exchange student. Smitten with your mother, too," she adds with a tearful smile. "There was no moving back for him after that."

I nod, but I have no idea what to say. Dad has told me the story of how he and Mom met probably a million times, but I've never heard the part about Nana asking him to move back home.

"I'm proud of him for going to America and getting a good job," Nana says. "Proud of the beautiful family he's raised. But selfishly, I think about how much Edward and I missed."

"I wouldn't have minded moving here." I kick off my flip-flops and wiggle my toes in the grass. "I like this city."

A long pause stretches between us.

Then Nana says, "I'm sorry you didn't have more time with him," and without even looking at her I know there are tears spilling down her cheeks. "It wasn't your father's fault," she blubbers, "but all these years I've blamed him for staying in America. Blamed him for choosing to live where he was happiest." She rubs the tissue over her eyes, smearing wetness across her skin. "I never should have indulged those feelings. But I missed you so much when you weren't here. We both did."

I reach for her hand as hot tears collect in my eyes. She latches onto my fingers and grips them so tightly it hurts. All she ever wanted was for her family to be whole.

Which is exactly what I've wanted ever since we started losing Paul.

"I love you, Nana," is all I can say. I feel strangely like I'm meeting my grandmother for the very first time. It's like she's been a cardboard cutout all these years—just a cheerful old woman who bakes cookies and chats about neighborhood gossip. Yet here she is, clinging to my fingers and sobbing into what used to be a tissue.

She clutches my hand even tighter and says, in a shaky voice, "I love you too, my Rosie. So much."

We sit like that for a long time, watching fat bumblebees drift from one rose to another. When I was in elementary school, I learned that bumblebees are a miracle of nature because, according to the laws of physics, they shouldn't be able to fly. Yet every summer, we see them doing the impossible like it's no big deal.

I'm pretty sure the miracle-bee theory has been disproved, but I like the idea because it reminds me of Albert. He does the impossible every day. Manipulates the laws of time to save others. Servatores throughout history have treated the Pull as a part of their everyday lives. Wake up, eat breakfast, take a shower, fight evil. Go to bed and start over the next morning.

"I want to ask you something," I say to Nana, and she looks at me. "I have a vague memory of my dad saying that Papa once saved somebody's life, but the details are fuzzy. Can you remind me what happened?"

I swallow, hoping she won't notice how nervous I am. It's not that I don't believe what Albert told me about Papa—I do. But I somehow need to hear it from someone else, and even though Nana supposedly doesn't know about Papa's secret life, she must have noticed something strange.

"Of course." Her voice is lighter than I've heard in days. "It was uncanny how often Edward managed to be in the right place at the right time."

A shiver ripples up my spine. "So it happened more than once?"

"Oh, yes. He became something of a local celebrity, you know."

I stare at my toes, where the orange polish I applied last week has begun to chip away. "No, I didn't know."

We sit for a moment, listening to the birds flutter through the hawthorn trees. I probably look calm on the outside, but my mind is spinning like crazy, still trying to reconcile the grandfather I thought I knew with this other version of Papa—the one who manipulated time to save others and acted as a father to Albert Shaw. Did he see Albert as a younger version of himself? Did Albert fill the void my dad left behind when he moved to Nashville? I knew Papa, but the Blackheath Savior is a stranger to me.

Fresh tears prick my eyes and I turn my face up to the sky, blinking them back.

"Nana," I say after a moment, "do you feel like telling any of Papa's stories? You don't have to, but I—"

"Oh, my dear, yes! In fact, I'd love to show you the clippings we saved. Just a second."

She darts into the house and then reappears on the patio before I can get too lost in my head. She's got a large book covered in faded blue canvas tucked under her arm, and when she sits down with it, her fingers trace the gold filigree along the edges. It's an instinctive movement, like she's done it so often she doesn't even think about it anymore. Some of the filigree has worn off where she's touched it.

"I must admit, I look at this quite often." Her weathered hands lift the cover and a musty scent escapes the pages. "Although I haven't opened it since he left us."

"Nana," I say, "it's okay if you don't want to—"

"Here's the first story that printed." She adjusts her glasses and peers at the paper with laser-like focus. I guess she's pretty eager for a distraction. "'Local Man Saves Woman from Falling Scaffolding.' Oh my, this was a good story."

She shifts the scrapbook on her lap to give me a better view. There's Papa, decades younger, giving a satisfied smile. An inset picture shows a young woman being examined by a medic. I squint to read the caption beneath the photo. *Eileen Jones of Lewisham was pulled clear of a piece of falling scaffolding by Edward Clayton of Blackheath.*

"Amazing," I murmur. "You must have been so proud."

Nana gives me a soft smile. "There's no 'have been' about it, my dear. I *am* so proud, and will be until the day I die." She clears her throat. "Tell me, dear Rosie. Do you know how I met your grandfather?"

"No," I say after a moment. Which is weird, because Nana and Papa have always talked about their dating days, going down to the pub and holding hands by the river. But I don't think I've ever heard about the day they met.

"This incident with Eileen Jones on the scaffolding wasn't the first time he saved someone," Nana says. "In fact, I'm the first person Edward Clayton ever saved."

My eyebrows shoot upward like they're launching into orbit. "Are you serious?"

"I am," she replies. "Would you like to hear the story?"

I blink at her. "Uh, yeah. I would." I can't believe I've never heard about this.

Nana adjusts her position on the chair, grimaces through another sip of wine, and says, "It happened when I was twelve. My best friend Abigail and I were walking along the Thames. Abigail's mother had popped into a shop for some bread, and we were supposed to be waiting just outside the door. Abigail was very disobedient, but I always went along with whatever she did because I admired her so much. So we were playing next to the Thames when Abigail got the bright idea to walk the rail like a tightrope."

"Uh-oh," I mutter.

"Exactly. When I saw how brave she looked up there, balancing with her arms out to either side, I had to try it for myself. I made it about five steps before I slipped."

"And?"

"At the exact moment my feet left the rail, I felt these hands clamp down on my arm. At first I thought it was Abigail, but then I was heaved back over the rail as if I weighed no more than a doll. I didn't open my eyes until I felt solid ground beneath my back. When I finally looked, your grandfather was staring down at me with the kindest smile I'd ever seen. In that moment I knew I'd never forget his face." She takes a deep breath. "It still turns my stomach when I remember how it felt to slip off that rail."

I rub at the goose bumps on my arms. If Papa saved her, she must have died the first time, or at least been seriously injured.

"Did it make the news?" I ask, peering at the scrapbook. Seems like she would have shown me the article if she had it.

"I didn't report it. Neither did Abigail. We were too afraid we'd get in trouble for not staying put outside that shop."

Nana clucks her tongue as if scolding her past self for her reckless behavior. "As soon as I stopped shaking, we ran back to the sidewalk where we should have been all along. Abigail's mother came out about five minutes later, never knowing what we'd been up to. I'm not sure if Abigail ever told her."

"And what about Papa?" I ask. "Did he just walk away after that?"

"Well, yes. He made sure I was none the worse for wear, and he left. Imagine my surprise when I passed him in the hallway at school the next day." She laughs, her face alive with the memory. "Even though he was two years older than me, we became fast friends. It was inevitable, really, that we'd fall in love. When someone saves your life, you feel a bit of a connection to them, you know?"

I nod, wondering if it always happens that way—if the first person a Servator saves holds a special place in their heart. What about Albert? Does he share an unbreakable connection with his first save?

The next page in the scrapbook holds another photo of Papa, a few years older than the last one. *Blackheath Man Prevents Armed Robbery*, the title proclaims. I skim the first paragraph; Papa had alerted police to a suspicious man who, a couple minutes later, pulled a knife on a convenience store clerk. Because the two policemen were already watching him, they were able to subdue him almost immediately.

"The right place at the right time," I mumble, shaking my head.

"Mm-hmm," Nana agrees.

The next page holds a story of Papa evacuating a café that later exploded due to a gas leak. Apparently some people accused him of setting that one up, although no one could prove it. In the next story, Papa must have been in his late fifties and had prevented a toddler from falling in front of a train at the London Bridge tube station.

"I wasn't even born when all this happened." I thumb through the rest of the book. "Why didn't anyone tell me?"

Nana shrugs. "I suppose we referenced it here and there, but you must not have realized what we were talking about. By the time you were old enough to understand, it was all fairly old news."

"What about this?" I ask, pointing at the last story in the scrapbook.

"Ah yes," Nana says. "He never quite got over this one—in fact, you heard him going on about it in the hospital, just before he passed. I wasn't going to save the article when it first ran, but he asked me to, so here it is."

The hair on my arms stands up as I read the headline. *Boy Killed by Bus on Greenwich High Road.*

A photo of the boy's weeping parents dominates the page. The father's arms are wrapped tightly around his wife's shoulders, both of their faces twisted with grief.

Gareth and Emily Long mourn the loss of their son Kieran, the caption proclaims.

According to the article, twelve-year-old Kieran Long darted in front of a bus trying to catch up to his friends after school. Although Papa was there to yank him back, his hand slipped on the boy's arm, and he couldn't grab him again fast enough.

At the very end, there's a quote from Kieran's father: *"Of all the times the Blackheath Savior has rescued people, he couldn't rescue my boy."*

Maybe this is why Papa never told any of us. He couldn't bear for us to know that he'd failed.

"The father, Gareth—his part of the story only gets worse, I'm afraid," Nana says. "He fell into excessive drinking after Kieran's death, and even though his wife threatened to leave him, he couldn't stop. The drinking led to financial trouble, which led to gambling, which eventually bankrupted them."

"So what happened then? Did his wife walk out?"

Nana hesitates. "In a manner of speaking."

I look at her for a moment, hoping my suspicion is wrong. "She died?"

"Yes."

"Of natural causes?"

We stare at each other. Then Nana gives me a one-sided shrug. "If taking an entire bottle of sleeping pills could be considered natural, then yes."

A lump forms in my throat. I look at the picture again. Gareth's face angles down toward his wife. His arm curves around her shoulders like he's trying to shield her from their cruel new reality. It's obvious, even from this one snapshot, how much he loved her.

Nana leans close to me. "Don't tell your dad about this next part," she whispers, and my stomach clenches at the dark tone in her voice. "A few days after Emily's funeral, Gareth showed up at the house looking for your grandfather. He was drunk out of his mind and Edward shouldn't have agreed to talk to him, but he did. For half an hour, they stood in the street while Gareth accused Edward of letting his son die on purpose. Said he had single-handedly ruined his life. His shouts were so loud that the neighbors called the police."

"So he was arrested?"

"Yes, but not before threatening to kill your grandfather."

My jaw drops. Someone threatened to kill Papa? Papa, in his tweed vests and his driver's caps, with his bright smile and cheery *hello* for everyone he passed? The idea is preposterous.

"He swore he'd take revenge when Edward least expected it. That he wouldn't rest until his son and wife were avenged. Nothing ever happened, though, and now that Edward is gone—" Her voice breaks.

"When did this happen? I don't see a date."

"About five years ago." Her voice has reduced almost to a whisper, even though we're alone. "Edward never told your dad about this, which is why you never knew. He didn't want your parents to worry."

"Aren't you concerned that Gareth is still out there somewhere?"

"No, no." She waves a dismissive hand at me. "They locked him up soon after the night he showed up here."

"In prison?"

"Mental institution."

"Oh."

I feel slightly better, but it's still creepy knowing there's some guy out there with a vendetta against Papa, even if he is locked up.

"I can't believe this," I say. "Papa saving so many people, this man coming after him… I wish I'd known more about it." I pause. "I wish I'd known *him* more."

Nana nods. "I know, my dear. I know."

Something in the margin of the article catches my eye. Someone's written two words next to the last paragraph, but the tiny, cramped text is almost impossible to read. "What does this say? Opus something?"

She leans over the scrapbook to peer at the words. "It's in Edward's handwriting. *Opus postremum.* Wasn't there the last time I flipped through these articles, I don't think." She sits back, staring at the tiny note. "What could it be?"

I shake my head. "No idea."

But knowing Papa, I bet it's important.

TWENTY-FOUR

My family is downstairs, including Paul. He's sulking in a corner of the couch, glaring at the TV like it's a teacher who's just given him detention. *Britain's Dance-Off Champion* is on. A girl in ripped jeans and a tank top is doing ballet while the judges beam at her. Paul looks like he wants to set her hair on fire.

"I'm going to bed," I announce.

Dad tosses the remote on the coffee table, where it lands with a clatter. "Don't blame you. Think I'm heading to bed myself."

He gives me a hug—more abrupt than usual, but at least he's somewhat participating in conversations again—and then heads for the stairs. I kiss Mom and Nana before touching Paul's shoulder. He squirms beneath my hand.

"Hey," I say. "We haven't really talked today. How was SPARK?"

He blinks and sighs loudly. "Fine."

Everything about his body language screams that he doesn't want to talk to me. I don't know why he's even down here; maybe Mom threatened to take away his rap

T-shirts if he didn't spend some time with the family. His eyes are heavy with shadows.

"Are you sure?" I mess up his hair with a swish of my hand. "You look really tired. Have you been sleeping—"

"I said I'm fine, Rosie!" He jumps to his feet and shoves past me so hard I stumble into the sofa.

Mom's jaw drops. "Paul Clayton!"

Nana watches my little brother with arched eyebrows. I open my mouth to shout at him, but he's already out of the room and clomping up the stairs.

"Wait for it," I say to Mom and Nana.

Slam.

"Sorry. I guess I pushed him too far." I give them a half-hearted wave and head for the stairs.

Paul and I aren't on the best of terms right now, but it still hurts that he can't realize we're all on the same team when it comes to grieving for Papa. He acts like he's so alone in all this—like he's the only one who's upset over what happened to Carter, the only one who loved Papa, the only one who feels overwhelmed and frazzled.

I still want to reach him. I still desperately want my brother back. But I'm feeling more defeated by the moment.

My bed creaks when I tumble into it and my eyes fall shut almost instantly, but my brain is whirring away like a helicopter preparing for takeoff. The things I saw in the Batcave flip through my mind like a bizarre slideshow— the blue lights that first struck me when we entered the crypt, Albert's smile as he showed me around, the screens on the wall, the records room with the pressure that bore down on my chest.

Sleeping tonight without some kind of sedative is about as likely as sprouting wings and flying back to Nashville.

As I'm considering the likelihood of coaxing my mom to part with one of her precious Ambien, there's a soft knock at my door. Paul pokes his head into the room. Something is different about his face—there's an alarm lurking in his eyes that has replaced the sulkiness I saw downstairs.

"Hey, buddy, what's up?" I haven't called him "buddy" in years. That nickname died when he entered puberty and no longer thought I was cool. I guess I'm using it now because I want him to feel safe with me, like he used to.

He loiters in the doorway like maybe he wishes he hadn't done this, but it's too late now. I leap out of bed, pull him into the room, and shut the door.

"Sit," I say, and he perches on the edge of the bed, rubbing his hands along the tops of his thighs as if he's trying to get warm.

"Well?" I ask. I don't want to jinx this by speaking too much or too soon, but someone has to say something.

He opens his mouth, then closes it and licks his lips. "Max and Luther," he says in a voice that's just above a whisper.

My heart rate speeds up. "What about them?"

He darts nervous glances between his moving hands and my bedroom door. Suddenly, he goes still and cocks his head, listening. I strain my ears but don't hear anything out of the ordinary, just the murmur of the TV downstairs and water in the pipes as someone flushes a toilet.

Clasping my hands in front of me, I pin him with what I hope is a firm, yet kind, stare. "Paul, what is it?"

But he's shaking his head. He's about to bail.

"Nothing, forget it." He rockets halfway toward the door like I've scalded him. He's fast, but I've always been faster.

"Nuh-uh," I say, blocking the exit. The time for walking on eggshells has passed now that he's attempted an escape. "Tell me about Max and Luther."

He runs a hand over his head and shifts his weight from one foot to the other. "It's probably nothing. But..." His hands twist together and then dive for cover inside his pockets. "The other night, at the pub, they introduced me to some guys. Older guys, probably in their twenties. They asked me a lot of questions about myself."

"Like what?"

"Where I was from," he says to the floor. "Why I was in town. They asked about my family. And I told them—" he swallows "—I told them about Papa. And then they asked about you."

Every drop of blood in my veins freezes. "You mean, they asked if you had any siblings?"

"No." He licks his lips and blinks. "They asked about you by name."

My heart is screaming in terror.

"And then," he goes on, "Luther said something to Max—I couldn't hear exactly what, but I heard the last part, and it was something about 'when we become' something. And then Max hit him on the arm and looked at me like he was afraid I'd heard."

"When they become what?" I say. My voice has been reduced to a whisper.

He shakes his head. "M—something. More. When they become more?"

Mortiferi.

Could that have been what they said? Could Max and Luther have become Mortiferi in the past few days?

Snippets of conversation tear through my head, things I was told by Albert and Casey.

The Mortiferi are all monsters.

These soul-darkened people were called Mortiferi, and once they were in, they could never get out.

They like to remain anonymous.

I remember the way they looked at me when we met, the way their presence seemed to darken the whole house. And my brother has slowly been attaching himself to them, all in the name of belonging somewhere.

I try to keep my breathing slow and my expression calm, even though it's all I can do not to freak out and shake him by the collar for not telling me this earlier. "Paul, don't ask me how I know this, but you need to stay away from Max and Luther completely. I know I've said that a million times before, but it's different now."

A loaded pause stretches between us. Paul frowns. "Do you know what they were talking about?"

Thank God he's listening. If I weren't so desperate to tell him what I know, I'd probably collapse in relief. "I know it sounds nuts, but they're not—well, they're not regular people."

His brow crumples in the middle. "What do you mean, not regular?"

How can I explain what I know without sounding like I'm making stuff up? "You just have to trust me. I could be wrong, but I think I know what they are."

"*What* they are?"

His expression has closed off just a little. My hands are trembling. "They're not exactly…"

He stares at me.

"Normal," I finish lamely.

His eyes are blank. He's sorting and processing everything I've just said, weighing it on a scale that will determine whether or not it's crap.

Finally, he blinks. "Whatever happened to your mugging story?"

I freeze. "What?"

"First, you told me Max and Luther mugged a girl on the heath." His voice has an edge to it that wasn't there a minute ago. "Now they're just 'not normal'?"

This is exactly what I was afraid of—that he would stop listening when I couldn't give him straight answers. "First of all, I stand by the mugging story because it actually happened. Secondly, you're just going to have to trust me that Max, Luther, and anybody else they associate with are dangerous people. They're pure evil, Paul." I rub a hand across my face. "Like, not-entirely-human pure evil. Which I know sounds crazy, but if you keep hanging out with them, I'm afraid—"

"Not entirely human?" He scoffs. "So they're what. Aliens?"

"No, that's not—"

He holds up a hand. "Here we go again with the melodramatic lies. Okay, then. If Max and Luther aren't human, then your date with James took place at Cinderella's castle, and your friend Albert is actually a unicorn in disguise."

"You know what, Paul? You came to me for help. I'm trying to help you, and you're making fun of me. There's a lot I know that you don't."

"How?" he says.

I stop. "How what?"

"How do you supposedly know all this about Max and Luther?"

"Oh. Um…"

There's got to be a way to divulge my insider information without mentioning Albert or the Servatores. If I bring up the Batcave under the North Greenwich Library, I'm officially toast as far as my credibility is concerned—not to mention it might make things more dangerous for Paul if he knows about it.

"You need help," he says, standing up. The disgust has returned to his eyes, and my heart sinks. "I'm totally cool with the possibility that Max and Luther are on drugs, or that they're alcoholics. I mean, they're at SPARK, right? So obviously something is off."

"Paul—" I start, but he shakes his head at me.

"They're screwed up just like I am, and I know that, so telling me they're not perfect isn't going to scare me." He throws his hands out to his sides. "But really, dude. Not human? Do you even hear yourself?"

Words churn in my mind—*just listen, give me a chance to explain more*—but I can't make myself say them.

"Right," he says. "Maybe Mom and Dad can find a reform camp for compulsive liars, and then we can both spend all day playing name games and hating our lives."

He slips into the hallway and shuts the door behind him.

I drop onto the bed, rubbing my face with my hands. How is it possible that my relationship with Paul just got worse? I thought we'd already sunk as low as we could.

There's only one person who would know what to do with Paul's information, and I've got to get to him as soon as I can.

TWENTY-FIVE

'M PACING ON THE SIDEWALK IN FRONT OF ALBERT'S house at an absolutely ungodly hour. We are *not* good enough friends for me to be knocking on his door at the crack of dawn, but after what Paul told me last night, I couldn't wait. Mom thinks I'm getting coffee in the village, which is a stark contrast to my actual mission—stopping my brother from associating with soul-darkened monsters.

The door opens and Albert appears. He's wearing blue-and-white striped pajama pants but no shirt, and his hair sticks straight up on one side. Creases from his sheets line his skin.

"Oh," I say. I don't think I've ever seen him in anything but jeans and a T-shirt. Seeing him all rumpled makes me feel…

…something.

I clear my throat.

"It's six-fifteen," he says, squinting at me.

I force myself to look him in the eye, which is hard because this is beyond embarrassing. "I know. I'm sorry.

How did you know I was out here, anyway? I didn't ring the doorbell."

He points to the wooden arch over the door. There's a small black box attached to its top. "Camera. It's hooked up to a computer that alerts us if someone hangs around too long. I've been watching you skulk around my doorstep for the last five minutes."

Perfect. I'm sure I haven't looked like an idiot at all.

"Listen to this," I say, ignoring the yawn he doesn't bother to hide. "Paul came into my room last night and told me he heard Luther say a strange word that started with M. And apparently, a couple older guys asked about me by name. All this happened at a shady pub in Lewisham called The Black Swan. Ever heard of it?" I'm talking fast. Too fast.

His eyes narrow to green slits. "How much coffee have you had?"

"A lot. I didn't really sleep last night. So? The Black Swan?" I hear the shrill tone in my voice, but I'm powerless to stop it.

He holds the door open and steps aside to make room for me. "Yeah, it's a dodgy place, all right. Can I get a shower and some breakfast before we dive into this investigation?"

"Sure," I say, trying to sound patient. "There's something else, too."

He raises an eyebrow.

"I want to try to Pull." I haven't said it out loud until now, and as the words leave my mouth, something inside me flutters. It's like I've done something very, very right. Something I didn't know I needed to do until this moment.

"Ah." He looks down. "Well, the thing is—"

"I know," I say, deflating a little. "You already said I'm not one of you. But I can feel it, right? And so could you, before you learned to control it. And Papa told me he was passing his talent on to me. What else could he have been talking about? I mean, I guess he could have meant the telepathy thing, but I already tried that and it didn't—"

"Hang on, champ," he says, rubbing his eyes. "I was going to say, the thing is, you actually might be able to Pull because you can feel it and your grandfather could do it, and guess what? The ability to Pull can be passed down to a blood relative. Not always," he says as I bounce on the balls of my feet, "but sometimes. And I don't know specifically how it's done, except that it involves a great deal of magic and sometimes it doesn't work at all—"

"Okay!" I cry out. He winces. "So let's see if I can Pull, and then we'll figure out what to do about Paul and The Black Swan. Sound good?"

"I don't think there's any stopping you," he says, giving me the side-eye. "But I'm determined to shower first. Dan's put the kettle on for tea, although more caffeine might make you explode." He motions for me to enter the house. "Go on into the kitchen. I'll be back down in a bit."

I walk through the foyer to the living room and pass the sofa, where my red blanket lies folded across the arm. I push through to the kitchen. Dan is leaning against the counter with his long arms crossed tightly, glaring at a bright red coffee maker while it splutters black liquid into the carafe below.

"Heck yes," I say to the full pot on the counter.

Dan turns to me with a mock scowl. His red hair looks even wilder than Albert's, and his freckles stand out on his pale skin. "Look," he says with exaggerated pain, "if you're going to walk into my kitchen and throw filthy language around like that, I'm going to have to hurt you." His expression darkens. "Don't think I won't make you drink decaf."

"You wouldn't dare," I say. "No one's that heartless."

He grins. "Cups are in the cupboard by the sink and milk is in the fridge."

I retrieve two white mugs and set them on the counter. Dan fills each of them nearly to the top while I wait, tapping my fingers against the countertop. It's quiet again—too quiet. And just like always, I'm desperate to fill the silence.

"Albert said you were making tea," I announce.

He grimaces as he carries our cups to the kitchen table. "Not strong enough today, love. Want to sit?"

I grab the milk out of the fridge and follow him to the table, adding white to the black until my coffee turns a soft gold. The kitchen is so small I feel like we should be running into each other at every turn, but somehow, the space doesn't seem too cramped. The round white table fits nicely into a bay window that overlooks the backyard, and the appliances are minimal, which keeps the room uncluttered.

"I never got to thank you for what you did at the Hare & Billet," I say as I sit across from him.

He shakes his head and gazes into his steaming mug. His eyelashes are the same shade of orange as his hair, long and delicate, and the blue of his irises is just visible through them. "Don't worry about it. Just a typical night in London, isn't it?"

"Not for me. And not for anybody else except you four." I laugh. "How do you do it?"

He looks up. "How could we not?"

To me, there are a million ways they could *not*. They could pretend their ability didn't exist, for one. They could walk away and let whatever happens happen. Lord knows it would be easier if they just acted like everybody else, like they were as much victims of the universe as the next person.

But they don't.

"Not everyone finds it so easy to put themselves in danger for someone else," I say, tracing the rim of my mug with my finger.

"Yes," he replies. "But not everyone has the ability we have, either."

He takes a long sip of coffee, and I turn my gaze to the window. The kitchen is on the back of the house, so we have a view of the small, overgrown yard. There's nothing in it but a pile of firewood in the corner, next to a big tree stump with an axe leaning against it. I wonder which of them chops the firewood when it gets cold.

"Albert told me you're Edward Clayton's granddaughter," Dan says after a while. "He was a great Servator and a great man. I'm sorry I didn't speak to you at the service; Casey and I weren't able to attend the burial." He pauses for a moment, as if he's wrangling his emotions into submission. "Someone always has to be on patrol, no matter the circumstances."

"How did you meet him?" I ask. "My grandfather. You obviously knew him well."

"Through Al."

"And how did you meet Albert?"

He wrinkles his long nose with a smile. Everything about Dan is long, from his gangly limbs to his pointy chin. "It's a bit embarrassing."

"I won't laugh. I promise."

"Not embarrassing for me," he says with a grin. "Embarrassing for Al."

"Oh, now you *really* have to tell me." I prop my elbows on the table. "Go on. I'm ready."

He leans back in his chair and laces his fingers behind his head. "We were at a mutual friend's party a few years ago. This gorgeous girl had been snogging him all night, but then she left with somebody else. He was trying to Pull so he could get her back and take her home with him." He chuckles. "You know the slang meaning of 'pull,' I assume. We've joked since then about him being on the pull that night and trying to Pull just to pull a bird."

I flash back to that night in the Hare & Billet when Albert first told me about the Pull. *It has nothing to do with kissing*, he said to me when I brought up the term's colloquial meaning. It seemed funny then. But now, I can feel my face arranging itself in disgust. Using something as important as the Pull just to get a girl? That doesn't seem like the Albert I know. I try to picture it happening, but I can't.

"He was too drunk to make it work, of course, so all he managed to do was exhaust himself. But I could feel him *trying* to do it, and I recognized the position of his hands—palms up."

The memory of Albert under the table at the pub comes back to me. I remember his open hands, the way he closed his eyes and went very still—and then everything swirled into a vortex, and the people who had been dead weren't dead anymore.

"I'd been Pulling for years at that point, so I figured he was either a Servator or he was insane. Either way, he seemed like a fun bloke. I walked up to him and asked if time manipulation was something he attempted for every girl, or just for the incredibly fit ones."

His face lights up with laughter. I move my lips into a shape that hopefully resembles a smile, but my stomach has turned to molten lava and sunk all the way to my toes. I stare into my coffee.

"You okay?" he asks, watching me closely.

There's a noise at the door. I look up to find Albert standing there with damp hair, wearing his usual uniform of frayed jeans and a T-shirt. This time, the T-shirt is a dusty shade of blue, and I wonder if he bought twenty of the same shirt in twenty different colors. They certainly look identical, with the pocket on the left side and a tendency to cling across his chest.

The flutter comes back—a fizz of bubbles deep in my gut. I blink and shift my eyes back to my coffee, wiping at a rogue droplet with my thumb.

"All right, Rosie," Albert says with a smile. I look up and force myself to smile brightly. "Ready to be trained in the art of Pulling?"

"Of course." I stand up and squash the seed of disappointment planted by Dan's story. So Albert tried to use the Pull to get some action. I bet every Servator in the world has done that at one point or another.

"Aren't you going to eat something?" I say. My voice sounds too sharp, my words too quick. I lick my lips and take a deep breath; let's try that again, without the accusatory tone. "Surely you don't want to do this on an empty stomach. Unless a full stomach would be worse, with the whole turning-inside-out feeling."

He slathers a slice of white bread with Nutella. "The last time I Pulled hungry, I passed out and nearly fell off a bridge." He devours the whole thing in two enormous bites. "Right. Let's go upstairs."

TWENTY-SIX

"**S**O HOW IS THIS GOING TO WORK?" I SAY AS I SETTLE into the brown armchair in Albert's room. "Do I need someone to save? You're not going to have to hurt yourself or anything, are you?"

Albert crosses the room to the window, where a timid sliver of sunlight seems to be requesting permission for its existence. It stretches from his left temple down to the right side of his jaw as he leans against the window frame, and for a moment it looks like he has two faces, separated by a stripe of pale gold. But then a cloud shifts, and the two faces merge into one.

"Nah, don't worry," he says with a grin. "If somebody has to be hurt, I'll make Dan the guinea pig."

"Very funny." I tuck my knees into my chest. "Seriously, though. How do we do this?"

He moves to the bed and sits carefully on the edge of the mattress. We've sat like this before—me in the chair, him on the bed. But I have a feeling this conversation won't be anything like that one.

"Even if you have the ability to Pull," he says, "you won't be able to do it unless you're desperate to change something. Not at first, anyway. With more practice, you'll be able to do it whenever you want, but it will take a while."

"Okay." The half-gallon of coffee I've had is starting to burn a hole through my stomach. "So what do I do?"

"In a real-world situation, you'd check your watch right before you Pulled." He holds up his left wrist to show me the black watch wrapped around it. "Otherwise, after you've Pulled, you have no concept of how much time you've bought."

"And if I don't have a watch?"

"We'll need to fix that soon. In the meantime, we'll start with the fun bit."

He extends his hands, palms up. "Hold your hands like this, and focus on the exact moment you want to relive. Picture as many details as you can. If you do it right, your fingers will touch something that's not there." His mouth twists as he searches for the right words. "It'll feel like a handle, but you don't have to move your hands to grab it. You just use your mind. And once you've got your mental fingers wrapped around the handle, you Pull. Make sense?"

I mimic the position of his hands. "You just used the phrase 'mental fingers' in a sentence. Of course it doesn't make sense."

"I know, I know," he says. "It sounds ridiculous. Let's focus on finding your motivation." He looks around the room as if my motivation could be lurking in a corner or behind a book. "Something needs to happen that you want to change."

I give him a significant look. "Like another chance at getting in somebody's pants?"

He freezes and looks at me like I'm a cat about to take a swipe at him. When he speaks, his voice is low and even. "What are you talking about?"

"Dan told me how he met you," I say, feeling heat creep up my neck. "At that party, where some girl made out with you all night. He said he felt you trying to Pull so that you could leave with her."

"Oh." He cocks his head to the side. "What does that have to do with anything?"

"Nothing. I—just forget about it."

"Does that upset you?"

I look down. "I spent half the night going through my grandmother's scrapbook of the Blackheath Savior," I begin. "I'd started to think of the Pull as a gift. A way to make the world a better place. But now I'm afraid that you use it for your own purposes, too."

Albert's face hardens into an expressionless mask, and I squirm beneath his stare. Why did I say that to him? He's saved my life multiple times since I got into town, and now I'm suggesting that all he cares about is getting girls.

"I was a different person three years ago," he says.

Regret climbs up my throat and starts to choke me. "You don't have to—" I begin, but he holds up a hand. The words die in my mouth.

"My dad had just left Casey and me. He moved to New York. Said he needed a fresh start in a new city."

The disdain in his voice is almost a tangible object I could pick up and toss around.

"He's a barrister, and a really successful one, so he paid off this flat, paid our tuition through graduation, and told us to call our uncle in Worcester if we needed anything. It wasn't that big of a shock when he left—he worked all the time, so we were used to taking care of ourselves—but it still hurt, being abandoned like that."

I've wondered about his parents—why he and Casey live in this flat with two other guys, how they manage their expenses with nothing but part-time jobs. But I didn't expect that the answer involved abandonment, and I didn't expect to get the answer by making a fool of myself.

Were Dan and Isaac left by their families, too?

"My answer to that hurt was, quite simply, to have as much fun as possible." He runs a hand through his hair. "I went to parties almost every night. Drank anything I could get my hands on. Took drugs whenever I could find them. Hooked up with girls I cared nothing about."

I lick my lips; my mouth has gone unbelievably dry. "And now?"

"And now I'm clean. In every way." His eyes are locked on mine. "Sure, I've got regrets—loads of them. But I'm not that bloke at the party anymore. I haven't had a drink in two years. I haven't taken a hit of anything in two years." He swallows. "I haven't been with a girl in two years. In fact, I don't even pay attention to girls unless—"

I watch him closely. "Unless?"

His jaw clenches once, a flutter of muscle that ceases almost instantly. "Never mind. The important part is that your grandfather dragged me out of all that. He's the one who helped me sort out my life."

I'm dying to ask him where his mom was when all this happened, but judging from his reaction last time I asked about her, that's probably not a good idea.

"I'm sorry," I say. "I shouldn't have brought that up. It's none of my business."

He doesn't respond. His expression is carefully neutral, and it's all I can do not to beg him to say something.

Finally, he stands up. "Do you still want to try to Pull?"

"Yes." I get to my feet. Maybe if I can appear calm, I'll start to feel calm. "But I don't know what to use for motivation."

He crosses his arms. "Do you have something special I could destroy? It needs to be something you love, but not something you can't bear to lose. Once it's gone, it's gone; I won't use energy on a Pull to get it back for you. But you need to really feel the loss of it. You need to want it back."

My hand flinches toward my necklace. Albert catches the movement.

"You said a friend gave you that," he says, "the night I brought you to my flat for the first time. I asked you about it because you kept touching it."

I pinch the golden rings tightly. Part of me wants it to stay around my neck forever; the other part can't get rid of it fast enough. If the necklace is gone, it will feel like my relationship with Stephen is really over—for good. No going back. No second chances.

And I just don't know if I'm ready for that kind of finality.

"That's what I said." I clear my throat. "But I lied. It was a boyfriend."

He looks from the necklace to my eyes, and back again. "A current boyfriend?"

"No. We broke up." *We broke up.* It's the truth, and yet it's so laughably incomplete. Alternate phrases run through my mind, various ways of communicating the fullness of what happened.

He shattered my heart the day Papa died.

I found him betraying me with another girl in April.

The relationship we spent two years building fell to pieces the moment I left his sight.

"It's time I took it off," I blurt. And then—no, *no*. I can't be crying—not here, and not about this necklace. But the tears are coming hot and fast, and even though I manage to wipe them away before they fall, I can't hide them completely.

Albert watches me, stone-faced. "Sometimes," he says, "we need a little shove from the nest."

He reaches beneath my hair and feels for the clasp. His fingers trace warm paths over the back of my neck. I let my eyes fall shut. There's a small *click* as he unhooks the clasp, and I open my eyes to see it dangling in front of me. It looks so fragile in Albert's hands, like it's made of thread instead of metal.

"You're sure this is okay?" he asks.

I shrug. "Not really. But that's the right answer, isn't it?"

"It is," he says with a sad smile. I feel like he understands. It's in the way he looks at me with long gazes that drape around me like a cloak.

"All right then." He nods toward the door, pocketing my necklace. "Let's go downstairs."

We swirl down the staircase to the ground floor and I follow him into the living room, through the kitchen, and out a back door that leads to the overgrown yard. We walk until we reach a tree stump near the axe I saw earlier. Albert stretches my necklace out on the stump and picks up the axe, testing its weight in his hands. I can tell he knows how to handle it.

So that's where those callouses came from.

"Last chance to back out," he says with a half-smile. "Ready?"

"Well, mostly—"

WHACK!

In one swift motion, my necklace is halved. He swings the axe over his shoulder and brings it down again, right where the two rings link together. They fly apart and one piece of the necklace lands in the grass. He picks up part of the chain and tosses it into some scrubby bushes over the fence. Then he flings the remaining parts onto the roof.

And just like that, my last connection to Stephen is gone.

Every bit of breath in my lungs whooshes out. I stare at the spot where my necklace lay only a few seconds ago.

"So?" he says. "How do you feel?"

I stare at him with my mouth open. "I don't know."

"Think about it. Wait until you have an answer, and then tell me."

My neck feels strangely naked without the necklace, and my chest has constricted a little. "I feel kind of freaked out," I say.

He leans the axe against the stump, keeping his eyes on the blade. "Do you want it back?"

"Yeah." I frown. "But not as much as I thought I would."

I've dreaded taking off that stupid necklace, thinking it would bring me to my knees with grief—but it hasn't.

Albert gives me an approving nod. "Well, let's give it a go. Close your eyes."

I close them. He shuffles through the grass toward me. A breeze whispers through the yard, lifting a few strands of hair across my mouth.

"Think about the moment you want to go back to. Pick something recent, like when I laid your necklace on the stump."

I picture the scene.

"Focus on it with everything you've got. Hold your hands out, palms up."

I'm concentrating so hard that sweat is beginning to bead on my forehead, and I'm really starting to regret my breakfast of coffee with a side of coffee.

"Reach for that moment with your mind. Want it like you've never wanted anything else in the whole world." He's standing very close to me now. So close I can feel his breath on my forehead. "Picture as many details as you can. The way the necklace lay on the stump. My voice when I asked if you were ready."

I think about the necklace, but then my mind drifts to the moment he picked up the axe. The tension in his muscles as he balanced it in his grip. The way his eyes crinkled at the corners when he said *Last chance to back out*. The satisfaction on his face as he watched it fly to pieces.

I open my eyes. His face is inches away from mine.

"Did you feel the mental handle?" he asks.

"No." I swallow, letting my hands fall to my sides. "I don't think I want the necklace badly enough."

He watches me for a moment. Then he says, "We'll try again later. Once you know what you really want."

I meet his gaze. "What do you mean, what I really—"

"Until then," he goes on quickly, "now that you're privy to all our secret Servator information, I have an adventure for you. That is, if you're available tonight?"

I squeeze my eyes shut, pretending to think really hard about my schedule. "My parents and Nana are busy going through Papa's things, and my brother is being a grade-A jerk, so I'll probably watch some TV by myself and go to bed at nine. I'm swamped."

"Right," he says with a smile. "I'm going on patrol downtown tonight. Do you want to come with me?"

"I don't know. What do you do on patrol?"

His smile widens. "Only one way to find out."

TWENTY-SEVEN

A<small>T SEVEN O'CLOCK, I LEAVE NANA'S HOUSE TO MEET</small> Albert. He's waiting for me just a couple houses down the street. His eyes are focused on the ground; he hasn't seen me yet. I wonder how long he's been pacing up and down that bit of sidewalk, and whether his hands have had a single moment of freedom from his pockets.

"Yo," I say when I'm near enough to be heard.

He looks up, eyebrows arched.

Yo. Did I just say that? Did I actually just walk up to Albert Shaw and greet him with a cheery *yo*?

"Sorry," I say as my cheeks burn. "Apparently I was a nineties rapper in another life. Won't happen again."

This coaxes his lips into a smile. "You seem a bit nervous."

"Hmm." I nod slowly, as if considering a piece of particularly insightful information. "Perhaps. So, where are we off to tonight?"

He grins. "A counter question—how did you escape the house?"

My stomach tightens with guilt; how many lies have I told my parents since we arrived? They'd think I was crazy if I told them the truth, though. I'm just trying to keep them from losing whatever remains of their sanity, which means it's totally justified.

Right?

"James and I are seeing *Les Mis* on the West End," I say, giving my hair an exaggerated flip. "We're high-society like that."

"Obviously."

He's still smiling, and I'm glad he can't see how much the lying bothers me. No matter what I say to try to justify it or how tightly I try to pull the wool over my own eyes, I know what I'm doing is wrong. I just can't face revealing the truth yet. Not about Albert, not about Papa, and certainly not about the whole talent-transfer thing. Mostly because I don't fully understand any of it, which means I can't effectively explain it.

"Hey," I say as Blackheath station comes into view. "Did you know my grandmother was the first person Papa ever saved?"

Albert nods. "Edward told me the story several years ago."

"Who was the first person you saved?"

The silence that follows is so long that I wonder if I asked the question out loud, or if maybe I only thought it.

"Nobody I knew," he finally says. "Some bloke who fell off a ladder while painting the outside of his house."

We enter the deserted Blackheath station and dig our Oyster cards out of our pockets, tapping them on the circular readers and slipping through the partitions. After taking the train to Charing Cross and picking up another one to London Bridge, we end up on a busy sidewalk downtown while Albert coms his sister. He keeps his back to the street so that no one will notice him talking into his shirt collar. His face is mostly shadows in the dusky light, green eyes glinting whenever the setting sun catches them.

Albert finishes his conversation and turns to me. "Good news. Casey's covering my patrol so that you and I can relax."

I like Casey, but she doesn't seem like the type to just randomly offer her brother a night off. "Really? Why?"

"You've had a rough go of it, haven't you?" he says quietly, leaning in so that no one will overhear. "And to be honest, so have I. Might be nice to have a bit of a rest."

Our eyes meet, and I see the gift he is trying to give me—an evening in central London, just the two of us. No grieving family. No messed-up brother. He's trying to give me *fun.*

This night was never about going on patrol.

"Casey's a bit of a loose cannon, but she can handle anything that crosses her path," he says.

I guess he thinks I'm not responding because I doubt his sister, when really, it's not that at all.

"Sometimes I wonder if she's tougher than I am, you know? But if she has an emergency, I've still got this." He pulls his ear down, showing me the tiny black com stuck near his ear canal. If Casey needs something, all she has to do is call, and Albert, Dan, and Isaac will come running. "So no worries, yeah?"

I clear my throat. "Yeah. That's great."

"Stay close to me," Albert says, turning toward the street. "Mortiferi or not, London isn't the safest city in the world."

I ease toward him until our elbows brush. "I'll try not to slip away."

No matter how many times I come to London, I'm always amazed at its constant motion. Men and women in business suits rush along crowded sidewalks. Herds of pre-teens migrate from one clothing boutique to the next. Cars, buses, and taxis race around corners and through roundabouts on their way to a million different destinations. The Thames surges through the middle of it all, rising and falling twenty-three feet each day—a fact I learned from Papa years ago.

Albert and I walk up Borough High Street at a quick pace. I cast sideways glances at him as we dodge loud tourists and irritated locals; something about the way he moves is distinctly South Londoner. It's a definite swagger, but not a strut. He exudes confidence, but not arrogance.

He slows down as we reach London Bridge, and I match his pace. "You know," I say, "I always thought London Bridge should be fancier."

"It's funny—the original was sold to an American," he says. "I believe it's located in Arizona now. Londoners joke that the man who bought it actually meant to buy Tower Bridge."

He nods toward the elaborate structure a little farther down the river, glowing with colorful lights. It looks like a postcard, all lit up like that, and I have the weirdest feeling of being on a stage with a painted set. Like I could knock the towers over with a bump of my elbow and they'd fold, nothing but cardboard.

"I'd pick Tower Bridge over London Bridge, given the choice," I say. "Any structure that gets its own song should look the part, don't you think?"

This earns me a laugh. "It's not exactly a cheerful song, though, is it? 'London Bridge Is Falling Down?' Do you know where that song came from?" He smirks in a way that makes me think I probably don't want to know, but of course I can't resist.

"Go on," I say with mock irritation. "I know you're dying to tell me, Mr. Librarian."

His voice instantly transforms into the same professorial tone I heard in the Batcave. "There are lots of theories, of course, but I believe it's about the Vikings pulling the bridge down during their attack in 1014."

"Wow, that's kind of morbid." I imagine the bridge tumbling into the river under a hail of flaming arrows while metal-clad Vikings cheer on the destruction—all while "London Bridge" plays merrily in the background. I can't imagine how such a lighthearted melody was born out of such horror.

"Ever thought about 'Ring Around the Rosy?'" Albert says, pulling me out of my weird London Bridge daydream. "That one's about Bubonic Plague. 'Ashes, ashes, we all fall down.' As in, fall down *dead.*"

"Charming," I say with a scowl. "I'm so glad we teach that song to children."

We reach the end of the bridge and continue on Borough High Street. We're silent as we walk, and when the Tower of London appears on our right like something out of a medieval fairy tale, Albert says, "Awfully pretty to be the site of so many nightmares, eh?"

"Yeah. It always makes me feel a little ill." I pull out my phone and check the time. "Whoa! How is it already 8:30?"

"Well," Albert says, "when I met you on Camden Row, it was already early evening. It was a ten-minute walk to the train station, and the better part of an hour and a half to get from Blackheath to this point, so when you add it all up—"

"You get a punch in the gut," I finish, lunging at him with my fist. He stops me, even though he's nearly incapacitated with laughter, and manages to get both my wrists in a death grip before I can come at him again.

"You think you're so hilarious," I say, failing to keep a smile from my face.

"That's where you're wrong. I *know* I'm hilarious."

I roll my eyes, still grinning. "Are you done?"

"Yeah, yeah." He lets go of my wrists and hooks my hand on the crook of his elbow.

"You're escorting me now?" I ask, nodding at our hand-elbow arrangement. The callouses on his hand scrape over my skin, and I picture him swinging that axe in his backyard as he sliced Stephen's necklace into smithereens. Give him a plaid shirt and a beard, and he could pass for a lumberjack. A lumberjack with a South London flair, of course.

He shrugs in response to my question. "Dangerous city, remember?"

"Of course," I say. "But it seems considerably less dangerous when you're with a time-manipulating bodyguard."

"Does that make you Whitney Houston, then?" He gives me the side-eye. "Is this the part where we sing 'I Will Always Love You?'"

My jaw drops. "You've seen *The Bodyguard*? I didn't think anyone under thirty knew it existed!"

"Casey's got a thing for older films, and her obsession with Kevin Costner is legendary," he says with a laugh. "I'm pretty sure he couldn't Pull in *The Bodyguard*, though, so we'll take a rain check on the musical number. It just wouldn't fit our situation."

I sigh dramatically. "Too bad. I've always wanted to do that song as a duet."

"Next time," he says in a wistful tone. He pats my arm and gives me a one-sided grin.

There's a smile spreading across my face—I can feel it. And it's absolutely massive, and I can't make it stop, and the worst part is I think I know why it's there. Oh, sweet mercy. What am I going to do now? How am I supposed to function with all these *feelings* going on?

His eyes narrow. "Why are you smiling like that?"

I snort out a laugh. "I—nothing. It's nothing."

"I don't buy it, but I will say your poor lying skills are fairly endearing. Are you really not going to tell me what that enormous smile is all about?"

He's got to stop asking questions. I'm not prepared to answer them just yet, and if he keeps pushing me, I might blurt out something really embarrassing.

"Look," I say, letting my arm fall away from his. "I'm just a little punchy from this week, that's all. I'm sorry."

He stares at me.

"Seriously. There's nothing else to it."

"Hmmph," he says, but I hook my hand on his elbow again, which seems to pacify him. This time, I manage to hold it together—except for the smile. That, I can't shake. No one, not even Stephen, ever made me smile this idiotically.

My necklace has been gone for a few hours, but I just now feel free.

We continue walking toward Tower Bridge in silence. The breeze flutters my hair over my shoulders as I gaze out at the river, which twinkles and whispers under the city lights. When I turn back to Albert, I notice he's scanning the crowd with a sharp focus. His posture is rigid.

"I'm no expert on relaxing," I say, "but you don't seem terribly calm right now."

His eyes slide from the river to my face. "Sorry. It can be a bit hard to switch it off sometimes. Do you like pizza?"

It takes me a second to follow his subject change. "What? Oh, yes. Of course."

"Great. Let's grab a bite, yeah? I'm a bit peckish."

He guides me down a small access road that runs several feet below street level. There's a restaurant called Strada at the end of the road—a small Italian place with a few metal tables on the sidewalk. The smell of dough and tomato sauce drifts past my nose and my stomach clenches with hunger.

"It's nothing fancy," Albert says, opening the door. "But the *pizetta pollo* will blow you away. And yes, you have permission to make fun of the way I just butchered that pronunciation."

I laugh. "I would have butchered it worse. And for the record, 'not fancy' is my favorite kind of food."

"Mine too. How about we get takeaway and eat it on the bridge?"

"That sounds amazing." I nod at one of the outdoor tables. "You mind if I sit out here and text my mom while you order? Here." I fish a ten-pound note out of my pocket.

He waves the money away. "I might let you pay next time."

Next time?

Hmm. So he expects there to be a next time.

As Albert disappears into the restaurant, I pull my phone out and sit in one of the cold metal chairs.

It's just now intermission, I type to Mom. *Okay if I'm home late? James wants to go out for coffee afterwards.*

Ugh. More lying. But what am I supposed to say? *I'm with a guy who can rewind time and we're on a secret outing-type thing. Might be home a bit late. XOXO, Rosie.*

Yeah. Lying is the better option. Doesn't make it any easier to stomach, though. When my phone buzzes, it almost startles me out of my seat.

Fine. Glad you're having fun.

I grimace and shove the phone in my pocket.

"Okay," Albert says, coming out of the restaurant. He's got a pizza box in one hand and two cans of Coke pinned between his arm and his ribs. "Ready to go?"

"Wow, that was the fastest service *ever*."

He shrugs. "When you save the owner's life, you get to jump the line. And you get free food." He nods at the pizza. "So now you definitely don't owe me any money."

He saved the owner's life. Of course. "Man, I'm impressed! You've got connections everywhere."

"Yeah," he says with an exaggerated sigh. "It's a burden, being as cool as I am. I try to bear it gracefully."

"I was going to offer to carry something, but after that line, you're on your own."

He laughs. "Fair enough."

We walk back up to the road that leads to Tower Bridge. I run my hand along the blue rail, not really thinking about anything in particular, just enjoying the breeze and the chatter of everyone around us.

"Everything okay?" Albert asks as we reach the bridge.

I look at him. "Yeah. I'm good."

"What are you thinking about?"

"Nothing," I say. "I should be thinking about my grandfather, or the Mortiferi, or my brother, but I'm not." I smile. "It's nice."

Albert adjusts his grip on the pizza box as we approach the first tower. "Good. You deserve a break."

We follow the sidewalk to a circular lookout point lit by a single streetlamp. Albert leads me to the edge of it so we can overlook the Thames. He sets the pizza box on the stone ledge and hands me a can of Coke, its surface already dripping with condensation.

"Actually," I say, "there is one thing bothering me."

"Oh? What's that?"

"The whole James thing. I hate lying to my parents, you know? Especially right now. It feels icky."

He stares at me with a funny look on his face.

"What?" I say.

He turns back to the river and pops the top of his drink. It hisses and he brings it up to his mouth to catch the overflowing fizz. He swallows, wipes his lips, and says, "Rosie, you're not the only one who's been holding back around here."

I pick up a slice of hot pizza and blow on it, trying to act casual. "Oh?"

"Remember earlier, when you asked me about the first person I ever saved, and I said it was the guy on the ladder?"

"Yeah."

"Well, it was, but..." He hesitates with a piece of pizza halfway to his mouth. "Your question reminded me of the first person I *should* have saved."

"And who was that?" Again, the look on his face tells me I probably don't want to know—but this time, there's no hint of playfulness.

"My mother. She died when I was six." He takes a huge bite of pizza, as if he's trying to distract himself from what he's just admitted.

My heart sinks. I pop my Coke open and take a long, slow sip. For the first time maybe ever, I don't have the urge to fill the silence.

Then he speaks again.

"Casey and I were absolute terrors during the summer, running amok with nothing to do but cause trouble, so Mum had taken us to Greenwich Observatory as a diversion. A huge mass of black clouds appeared as we were leaving. Mum thought we could make it home before the storm hit, but the moment we set foot on the heath, the lightning started." His eyes slide out of focus, as if the memory is replaying itself right in front of him.

"A bolt of lightning struck my mother as we ran across the open space. She died instantly."

I stare at the water. So that's why he never mentioned her.

"Casey and I had no idea what to do. We just stood in the rain and screamed. But then something strange happened. I was so distraught that I began to subconsciously *will* her alive. My hands came out in front of me as if acting of their own accord, and I knew what I had to do. I'd never done it before. I'd never even heard of it. But that afternoon, I Pulled for the first time. And then we were running across the heath again, and I was trying to shout over the sound of the storm that we had to change course, that we had to take cover somewhere, but neither of them could hear me. I tugged on my mum's dress and tried to point her toward the trees, but she was afraid of standing too close to them in the rain." He lets out a bitter laugh. "She thought they would attract lightning."

"And so it all played out again," I finish. "You saw your mother die twice."

He nods, his lips tight. "I tried to Pull again the second time, but it wouldn't work. It was like I wasn't strong enough. Pulling takes a huge amount of energy, and doing it twice in a row is impossible."

"And Casey couldn't do it yet?"

"No. She didn't Pull until she was ten, when one of her friends choked on a grape in the school dining hall. Dan and Isaac were ten when they first Pulled, as well. I think that must be a pretty typical age for a Servator to discover their ability."

"How did you manage to do it at six?"

I'm trying to imagine a first-grader rewinding time, even by accident, and it's impossible to visualize. He must have looked so small on the heath, crouched over his dead mother, hands out in front of him. I wonder if anyone saw him. I wonder how badly it hurt when he realized he'd managed to reverse the scene but couldn't stop it from happening all over again.

He shrugs. "I don't know. I didn't try it again for years after that. In fact, I convinced myself I'd imagined the Pull. That it was something my mind had constructed as a result of my panic."

"And the guy on the ladder was your second Pull?"

"Yep. It was almost exactly one year before Edward spoke at our school and I began to learn who I truly was."

A group of skateboarders with glow-in-the-dark boards whiz past us, whooping and hollering, and the mood is broken.

"Let's talk about something else," Albert says, taking an enormous bite of pizza.

"Okay. Like what?"

"You choose."

I think for a minute before it comes to me. "Have you ever heard the phrase *opus postremum*?"

He stops chewing and looks at me, one corner of the pizza crust poking out between his lips. "Hunngh?"

"Yesterday, when Nana was showing me all the news stories about Papa saving people, we found it in one of the margins. She said it was Papa's handwriting."

He swallows the pizza quickly. "What story was it written on?"

"The one about a young boy, Kieran Long. Papa tried to save him, but the boy died. I couldn't find anything about that phrase online other than its Latin translation, 'final work.' Why would he write that on one of his articles?"

Albert squints at the water like the answer is written there, drifting along in the current. "I have no idea." He pauses and tilts his head. "Surely he didn't believe…"

"Believe what?" My heart is racing. It feels like this is important—some clue about my grandfather's true identity, and maybe a glimpse into his death.

Albert's expression is almost remorseful. "The *opus postremum* is the idea that after a Servator dies, their spirit hangs around to make one last save. A spectacular one, something they wouldn't have been able to do when they were alive. Then they depart for the afterlife."

"So you think he was investigating it or something?"

He shoves the rest of the pizza in his mouth and wipes his hand on his jeans. "I don't know," he says, his tone full of doubt. "Nobody gives the idea any credit because there's no evidence to prove the theory. It's an urban legend at best, one of those hypothetical 'if the *opus postremum* was real, what kind of save would you want to make?' kind of things. I highly doubt he believed it was true. Maybe he was just wishing."

"Oh." Disappointment sits in my stomach like a brick. For a moment, I'd believed there was a chance Papa might still be here. But he's gone. I watched him die and I went to his funeral. Papa is in the ground beneath a granite headstone. He can't do anything for us, or for anyone else.

"So this is what you do in your spare time?" I say, eager to lighten the conversation. "Hang out with girls on bridges?"

He grins. "What, my life isn't as glamorous as you were hoping?"

"I wasn't hoping for glamour. I just thought I might see you save someone's life again. Maybe mine. You know, something boring like that."

"Even when I'm officially on patrol," he says with a shrug, "it's usually uneventful. The whole thing is a game of odds. If we happen to be nearby when someone's in danger, or if someone at headquarters alerts us to a problem and we get there quickly enough, then we can change the event. But otherwise, there's nothing to be done. And given that there are only four of us in the city now that Edward is gone…"

"The odds are stacked against you," I finish.

"Definitely. But full moons have a way of producing more action, so the others may have a more eventful night."

I glance up at the perfect sphere of a moon, which casts a silver glow over the city. "Oh, right. Werewolves and all that."

"Yes, exactly. They'll be out any minute."

Lights dance along the river's surface, glittering in the waves of its tide. Every cell of my body is tuned into Albert—the sound of his breathing, the smell of his shampoo, the warmth of his arm against mine. I turn to him, and he cuts his eyes to me.

"Why do I have a feeling I know what you're going to ask?" he murmurs.

"Because you're psychic, obviously." I wince. "Sorry. Pretend I didn't make a joke just then."

He turns toward me fully and I mirror him so that we stand face to face.

"I'm guessing you're wondering why I let my sister take over for me tonight. Why I suggested we get dinner. And why I keep insisting you stay close to me."

I raise an eyebrow. "Wow. You're good."

"I can give you some space, if you want."

"No," I say, reaching for his hand.

He stiffens at first, but then laces his fingers through mine. He smiles at me—full of fire, a deep, radiating heat that melts my bones and makes my stomach all fizzy.

"Rosie?" he says, and my heart speeds up until I'm scared it might give out. "I know we haven't known each other long, but I want you to know—"

Rowdy voices pierce the air and we turn toward the source of the noise. It's coming from the docks below the bridge. There's a patio area with a fountain of a dolphin tossing a girl into the air. And on that patio are three guys, all of whom I recognize.

"You've got to be kidding me," I fume.

Albert follows my gaze. "Isn't that your brother?"

TWENTY-EIGHT

PAUL STAGGERS AROUND THE FOUNTAIN WITH HIS HAND on his stomach, laughing. He's been drinking again—I recognize all the symptoms, even from here, because I've seen him like this far too often. I bet he's been at that Black Swan place again, even after my warnings to stay away from Max and Luther.

"So these are the prats he's hanging out with?" Albert asks, eyeing the trio below us. Max and Luther are with my brother, naturally. Just the sight of them sends a ripple of disgust down my spine.

"Yep. There they are, in all their glory." I scowl at the patio, where Max is lighting up a cigarette. He offers it to Paul, who accepts it and takes a long, slow drag.

"He doesn't even smoke," I whimper. "At least, I thought he didn't."

There was a small crowd on the patio, but the three teens in dark clothing must be giving off a bad vibe, because everyone heads back up the street to the bridge. They're all alone down there now, just three guys and an aura of trouble.

"Hold on." Albert squints at Max and Luther. "They look familiar."

I thought he knew exactly who they were, so I'm a little surprised to be explaining their identities. "Oh. Yeah. You beat them up on the heath after they mugged that girl. That was the first time we ever talked."

The first time I ever saw his pale green eyes. The first time I watched him willingly put himself in danger for someone else. The first time I learned things are truly not always what they seem.

"Ah," he says. "Yes, I remember. So why is your brother hanging around with them?"

"He thinks they're cool," I say in a weary voice. "I told him what I saw, but he thought I was making it all up. He's really sensitive about being told what to do." I kick at the wall in front of me. "He's so freaking stubborn."

Albert lets out a long breath. "Stubborn, or desperate?"

"Both." My stomach sinks a little. It's much easier to be angry with Paul than to empathize with him.

An elderly man and woman straggle in from the other side of the docks, but as soon as they see the three drunk guys, they hurry past with their heads down. The old man throws a glare over his shoulder and mutters something in Luther's direction.

Whatever he said, Luther didn't like it. He looks at Max and then nods toward the old man's back. Max grins. Paul misses the exchange because he's staring into the fountain.

"Albert?" I say. My voice carries a warning tone.

"I know," he mutters. "I'm watching."

Luther darts toward the couple while Max watches with a smirk. Luther grabs the old man's arm and pulls him back toward the fountain, making him stumble. His wife screams and reaches out for him, her fingers grasping nothing but air.

"Oh, no," I breathe. "No, no, no."

When they reach the fountain, Luther pulls a knife and holds it to the man's ribs. Max gets in his face. The old woman falls into hysterics, sobbing and reaching for her husband.

"Come on!" I shout, taking off toward the road. But Albert grabs my arm and pulls me back.

"Not yet," he says. "Hold on."

Hold on? What in the world does he want me to hold on for? A small crowd begins to gather around us as people notice the scene. Someone needs to *do something*.

"What is wrong with you?" I jerk my elbow out of his grasp. "We have to help them!"

He leans close to me. "Wait," he says. "Can't you trust me after all we've been through? After all you've seen?"

I blink, letting my eyes fall away from his face. "Of course. But—"

"Then wait." His voice is rough. "Let me do this the right way. If I Pull at the wrong time, I won't have the strength for a do-over. It's wise to wait until we know what happens for sure."

I turn back to the scene below. Logically, I know Albert knows what he's doing. This is the kind of thing he deals with multiple times a week. But my body is raging with the impulse to *do something now*, and I don't know how much longer I can hold myself in check.

"What's going on down there?" a woman to my left cries out. "Somebody call the police!"

Even though the action centers around Max, Luther, and the old man, my eyes drift toward my brother. He hovers at the perimeter of the patio, hands traveling from his back pockets to his hips, uncertainty radiating from his entire body. Then he crosses his arms and glances up at the bridge. Does he see me? His stare is so empty.

A jagged scream pierces the air. Luther's knife has found its way into the old man's ribs.

He sinks to the ground, blood sprouting across his shirt, eyes blank with shock. His wife falls to her knobby knees and crawls about two feet before collapsing on the ground. People fly into an uproar around us; shouts fill the air and fingers zoom over cell phones. A couple of men start running in the direction of the fight. Luther looks over his shoulder and scowls at the crowd. He slides his knife out of the old man's ribcage and takes off with Max, who grabs Paul's arm and drags him along.

"Albert!" I scream. Whatever he was waiting for, whatever cue he needed to spring into action, this has to be enough.

"I know," he says, checking his watch. "It's time."

He draws in a deep breath, holds his hands in front of him, palms up, and closes his eyes. His fingers never move, but I can tell when he starts to Pull because of the suctioning in my gut. The vortex strengthens, just as it did on the heath and just as it did in the pub. It feels like my body is going to rip itself to shreds, and right when I think I can't handle the pressure anymore—

A blinding flash of light.

We're standing on the lookout point, holding hands. The patio is empty; Paul and his friends haven't arrived yet. But the panic I felt only moments ago—or moments in the future, I guess—hasn't changed at all. I don't know how any of the Servatores think clearly in these situations, knowing what's coming and what they have to do. I think I'd crack. The only thing keeping me from crumbling right now is the guy next to me, standing rigid with determination and blowing a soft stream of air through his lips.

I turn to him. "How much time do we have until they stab him?"

"About four minutes. Stay up here, okay?" He drops my fingers. "I'm going down to the dock."

"No way. He's my brother. I don't sit on the sidelines anymore, remember?"

He opens his mouth to argue, then closes it and pulls his lips into a tight line. "Fine. But if I tell you to run, you run. Got it?"

"No problem," I lie.

We sprint back past the crowd of onlookers and hang a right down the small access road that leads to the docks. Strada, the pizza place we ordered from earlier, sits on our left. Only a few minutes ago we were walking along the bridge, and I wasn't thinking about anything. I was just enjoying the evening. Enjoying Albert.

And now the night is tainted with blood.

"How are we going to stop them?" I ask, panting.

Albert's breathing is much steadier than mine. "I'm going to intercept the old couple before they get to the fountain, but I'll have to cross the patio to do it. Hopefully I won't run into your brother and his friends. The Mortiferi know who I am. If they see me, they'll recognize me."

Just before we emerge into the open, I hear the laughter—deep, loud, full of malice. My stomach plummets all the way to my feet.

They're already here.

Albert skids to a stop and swears under his breath, then tugs me into a small parking lot to our left. We squat between a van and a convertible. "I thought we had more time before they showed up," he says, and grits his teeth with a growl of frustration. "I didn't Pull back far enough."

"It's okay." I nod, willing myself to believe the words I'm about to say. "We can still do this. You've dealt with worse before, right? At least these guys don't have guns."

"Not that we know of," he mutters.

We press ourselves against the van's cool metal and peek around the front bumper. Max and Luther are only a few yards away, and suddenly I notice something about them that makes my breathing stutter.

There's a faint orange glow in their pupils. If it wasn't so dark, I probably wouldn't be able to see it. But it's there—just like the orange glow I saw in my attacker's eyes on the heath.

"Their eyes," I croak.

Albert follows my gaze. "They're Mortiferi. Recently changed, from the looks of it. When black magic enters a soul, it leaves a burn trail on the inside of the person's body. You can only see it in the dark."

"A burn trail?" I never thought of sorcery as a tangible thing, an object that could physically manifest on someone's flesh. The idea makes me clutch my knees to my chest.

"I can't take them on my own," he says, and lifts the collar of his T-shirt to his mouth. "Hey lads, you there?"

I lean in to hear Dan's voice in the com. "Yeah, mate. You all right?"

"I'm going to need some help, soon as you can get here. Just below Tower Bridge, by that dolphin fountain you're always making fun of."

"What's up?"

Albert licks his lips. "Trying to keep two Mortiferi from murdering an old man, and I've got to get Rosie's brother away from them. We think they're trying to recruit him."

"Right. I'll head that way, but it's gonna take me a few minutes. I'm just leaving Canary Wharf."

"Where's Isaac? Is he closer?"

Isaac answers, his voice deep and serious. "I'm near Hyde Park."

Then Casey: "And I'm in Stratford. We'll get there as soon as we can, but Dan's your best bet."

Anxiety crosses Albert's face. "All right. Hurry, Dan."

"On it, mate."

He drops his collar and shifts his weight, steadying himself on the van behind us. "You said Paul met them at his reform camp?"

"Yeah. SPARK."

He nods. "That's the kind of place the Mortiferi go to recruit. Reform camps, AA meetings, psychiatric wards... anywhere there's a good chance they'll find broken people."

I squeeze my eyes shut and try to keep my mind from flying in a million panicked directions. "Are you saying they want to turn Paul into one of them?"

"I'd bet a lot of money on it. The Mortiferi prey on insecure, troubled people because they're so eager to belong somewhere. SPARK means your brother probably fits that description."

"We've got to get him away from them."

"I will, but I can't take on two Mortiferi by myself. These two aren't Bestia; they're Fortes."

"Fortes?" A nugget of knowledge from my show choir days tickles the back of my mind. "Does that mean 'strong?'"

"Yes. Fortes are new converts. They're incredibly angry and dangerous, but smart enough to act normal. On the other hand, Bestia are nearing the end of their existences as Mortiferi; they no longer have control over themselves, and they're fairly easy to subdue."

I think back to the Bestia that tried to break into Albert's house. It took Albert, Dan, and Isaac to bring her down. What do these guys consider hard to subdue?

I raise my hand like I'm in a classroom. "I could help you fight them."

He considers me for a moment. "Fair enough. If an opportunity presents itself, take it. But Rosie, I'm serious about this—they will kill you without hesitation. So let me and the others handle the majority of the offense work, yeah?"

"Okay, but why can't we take them on our own? You beat them up by yourself on the heath."

"They weren't Mortiferi then. If they had been, I'd have seen it in their eyes—and there's no way I would have fought them alone."

I squint at Max and Luther, who are chucking rocks into the Thames. "You really think they were changed that recently?"

"Things would have turned out much differently if they'd been Mortiferi that night."

We peer around the bumper again. Paul looks pale, but maybe it's just the streetlamps. Max and Luther seem different than I remember, and not just because their eyes carry that soft orange glow. They're bigger. Their faces are more angular, and their mouths droop at the corners.

I shiver. "Is my brother…"

He squints at Paul, who's the farthest away. "Still human, as far as I can tell."

Max starts shouting curse words at the Tower Bridge crowd and Luther doubles over in laughter. Paul observes the scene with a blank stare. Everything is about to go seriously downhill and it's up to us to stop it.

"If I'd known what Max and Luther really were, Paul wouldn't be in this mess right now," I say. "I would have locked him in the house and guarded all the exits if I had to. But he wouldn't listen to me, and I gave up."

Albert looks at me. "It's not your fault."

But it is.

"The old couple should get here any minute now," he says.

They arrive almost instantly, as if Albert had somehow summoned them. The old man shoots a disapproving look at Luther and says something to him, something I still can't understand, but I have a better view of the rage on Luther's face this time.

Albert takes a deep breath. "Here we go." He stands without making a sound. "Stay here for the moment, okay? It's possible we can avoid a fight altogether. Not likely, but possible. And Rosie?"

I give him a questioning look.

"Don't forget to run if things get bad," he says.

And then he walks away.

TWENTY-NINE

THE MOONLIGHT SHINES ON ALBERT'S BLACK HAIR AS he moves closer to the fountain. I'm cold in his absence and I rub my arms. I have no idea what his plan is, but I have a bad feeling it could go spectacularly wrong. And if it does…then what?

"Good evening," he says to the elderly couple, keeping his face turned away from Max and Luther. "I'm afraid the docks are being closed off for the night. Repairs on the fountain." He waves in the direction of the fountain, which is, in fact, spitting erratically from one of its spigots. "Would you mind moving onto the street?"

The old man is still glowering at Max, Luther, and Paul. His wife tugs on his sleeve until he turns around.

A few yards farther down the dock, Max grabs Luther's elbow and points at Albert.

"Crap," I mutter. Even though he's doing his best to hide his face, they recognize him. Paul, oblivious to the brewing trouble, kicks a rock and stares out at the river.

"So sorry for the inconvenience," Albert continues, stepping closer to the baffled couple. "Do you mind?" He gestures toward the road, a hint of desperation in his voice.

"Who are you?" says the woman, eyeing Albert's ratty jeans and T-shirt. "You don't look like a policeman."

Max and Luther watch the exchange from beneath furrowed brows. When I first met them, they seemed like a couple of punks with hooded eyes who liked to sneer at everyone. But now, there's something more sinister in their expressions. Something feral and deadly.

"I'm not a policeman," Albert says to the old man, "but I work for the city."

Well, I suppose that's true, in a way.

They give him dubious frowns. I can almost see Albert's mind whirling as he searches for a way out of this.

"Oi!" Max shouts. "Shaw!"

The old couple seems to sense that something is off. The woman clutches her husband's arm as they hobble to the road and out of sight. If nothing else, the old man is safe. Now we just have to get my brother away from these guys before they try to turn him into one of them.

This is about to be a full-on confrontation, and there's no sign of Dan, which means Albert needs help.

I take a step closer to the patio. Albert seems to move in slow motion as he turns toward the fountain to face the two Fortes. Paul, finally tuning into the trouble brewing around him, looks from Albert, to Max, to Luther. His cloudy-eyed expression confirms that he's either too drunk or too stoned to fully process what's going on. I've seen him under the influence plenty of times, but I've never seen him quite so out of it before.

"What did you see, Servator?" Luther demands.

I'm confused by his question at first, but soon realize what he means. Albert is interfering with their troublemaking, so they know he must have rewound something. They just don't know what.

"Don't worry about it," Albert says. He steps back, in the direction of my hiding place. "Not a big deal."

"You Pulled," Max says. "You wouldn't be down here otherwise." The *s* whistles through a gap in his upper teeth. He takes two steps toward Albert and Luther does the same.

Paul continues to stare at the scene from the other side of the fountain, mouth hanging slightly open. If I could just get to him without being seen...

Albert places one hand on his lower back with the palm facing me. His fingers flicker toward the street. *Run,* he's telling me. *Go. Now.*

I don't move.

When Luther pulls the switchblade out of his pocket and flicks it open, something twists in my chest. They might not have guns, but a knife in the hands of a psycho with a damaged soul is plenty dangerous.

"Easy, mate," Albert says, backing away from them. "It's not worth it, okay? Just let it go."

But they come faster, faces contorted with anger. I look around for a weapon—a stick, a rock, anything—but come up empty. Dan is nowhere in sight; what if he can't get here for some reason? What about Paul? He's ambling around the fountain with a vacant expression. What's wrong with him?

I have to do something.

Anything.

My feet move one, two, three steps into the soft light of the streetlamps. I don't say anything, but it doesn't matter. Their eyes are drawn to me like a magnet.

From the other side of the patio, Paul tilts his head and squints at me in an unfocused sort of way. "Rosie?"

THIRTY

Albert shakes his head when he sees me. His eyes are sharp. *You promised*, they say to me. *You promised you'd run.*

I never had any intention of leaving him here—not after the heath, and certainly not after the pub.

"Paul," I say in a shaky voice. "Come here."

Luther looks from my brother to me. His upper lip curls upward just enough to seem canine, like he's a wolf preparing to attack. "He's not going anywhere."

I clench my fists at my sides. My temper is dangerously close to boiling over, but there's just enough terror mixed with it to keep everything subdued—on the outside, at least. Inside, I am a monster about to unleash a whirlwind of fury on this would-be killer.

But my brother speaks, and the rage slips from my mind at the sound of his voice, far away and lost.

"Why can't I go?" he slurs. "Maybe I want to talk to my sister. She's nice. Isn't she?" He sways on the spot and steadies himself on the railing by the river, closing his eyes.

His body is here, but where is my brother?

"Paul is going home with Albert," I say, forcing the words over the lump in my throat. "You can have me instead."

"What?" The question explodes from Albert's mouth. Redness floods his neck and face and he's staring at me like I've just transformed into a dinosaur.

"It's me you want anyway," I go on, my eyes locked on Luther's. "I'm the one who can Pull. My brother can't do anything."

Ah, lying. Even now, I can't get away from it. I'd like to Pull, and I'm trying to learn how to Pull, but can I actually do it? Nope. Here's hoping they don't realize that.

Max narrows his beady eyes. "What do you mean, you can Pull?"

They're listening. It's more than I hoped for, and now that my plan seems to be working, I don't really know what to do. To be honest, I hadn't counted on getting this far. I figured someone would have thrown a punch or attacked with a switchblade by now.

"I mean exactly what I said. I'm Edward Clayton's granddaughter. But you already knew that, didn't you? The night you came to my grandparents' house, you knew who we were. My brother told you." I pause, hoping I'm right. "Then you saw the picture of Edward in the sitting room, and you knew it was true."

Luther's eyes flicker to Paul's face.

"So," I say, keeping my expression as hard as possible. "You've been hunting us because we're related to Edward Clayton, and you're worried we inherited his ability to Pull. Right? You thought since he was dying, there was a chance he'd pass his ability on to us, and then you'd have two more Servatores on your hands."

He glares at me. At any second, he could decide I'm not worth talking to—and not worth keeping alive.

"Here's the thing," I go on. "I'm the one who's a threat to you. He's not." I flick my head in Paul's direction. "So make the trade, me for him."

Max and Luther exchange a look. "How about this?" Max says. "We'll take both of you."

What if Paul and I both get kidnapped by the Mortiferi tonight? Mom and Dad would never know where we went. Or, even worse, what if they found us—but we'd been damaged by black magic?

"Not a chance." Albert grabs my elbow and pulls me behind him. "You're not leaving here with either of them."

Luther grimaces. "Sure we are. Because you're not leaving here alive."

"Wouldn't bet on that," calls a familiar voice from the access road. Dan strides across the patio, his red hair standing up in windblown curves.

"Dan Mason," Max says with a sour face. "This ain't your fight."

Wow. Albert wasn't kidding when he said the Mortiferi know exactly who the Servatores are.

"It is now," Dan shoots back. He looks at Albert. "All right, Al?"

"Yeah." Albert pulls his collar up to his mouth. "Casey, Isaac, we're gonna need a ride out of here. St. Katharine Docks."

Paul is staring into the sky with his arms at his sides. I wonder if he even hears us talking.

My eyes jump to Albert; every inch of his body radiates raw power. His fists clench and the corners of his mouth pull down. They're about to fight, and now that Dan's here, I can focus on rescuing my brother.

"Last chance," Albert says, his voice dangerously low. "Either you walk away, or we eliminate you."

"You have no idea what you're dealing with," Max says.

Albert narrows his eyes. "I know exactly what you are."

Luther lunges for Albert, face twisted with fury, the blade he holds glinting silver in the moonlight. I dive toward the side of the patio. If they need me, I'll help. Otherwise, I'm going for Paul.

I crouch next to the tree and look up just in time to see Luther taking a wild swipe at Albert's ribs with the knife. Albert jumps to the side. The blade misses by an inch.

Paul has moved to the opposite side of the patio, closer to the water. He sinks to the ground and stares at the river with his arms propped on his knees. If I skirt the edge of the patio, I can stay in the shadows and nobody will see me.

A loud grunt snaps my attention back to the fight. Max lowers his head and dives into Dan, wrapping his arms around his waist. The two of them stumble in my direction before Dan regains his footing and pushes back.

Luther is a few yards away from me, knife slicing through the air. He brushes his oily black hair out of his face and jumps toward Albert, who sidesteps the attack. Luther lets out a primal growl and runs full speed toward Albert. The tip of the knife is aimed directly at Albert's stomach. He leaps out of the way, but not quite fast enough. The blade catches his side.

Dan looks up just in time to see Albert get cut. He throws Max to the ground so that he hits the pavement flat on his back and curls up, breathless. Dan leaves him there and runs toward Albert, launching himself into Luther a fraction of a second before his blade takes another swing at Albert's stomach. The two of them tumble across the concrete, Dan keeping a frantic hold on Luther's knife hand. Albert dives toward Max and tackles him as soon as he gets to his knees. They crash to the pavement in a tangle of limbs.

Max is lying face-first on the concrete. Albert has one hand on Max's head and is digging a knee into his lower back. With his free arm, he grabs Max's wrist and wrenches it so that the Mortifer screams in agony.

I ease into a crouching position and creep around the edge of the patio, closer to Paul.

"Dan!" Albert yells as his face strains with effort. Sweat slips down his face and drips from his chin.

Dan and Luther are fighting on Paul's side of the patio. They dance around each other, Dan continually leaping out of the way of Luther's blade and looking for a chance to attack.

"Can't help ya, mate," Dan shouts back as Luther's blade swings twice. "Got my hands full!"

My brother is lying on his back under a tree, staring at the branches above him. I'm only about fifty feet away from him now.

Albert throws a look in Dan's direction. Then he lands a full-throttled punch into the back of Max's skull. His face smacks the pavement and a river of blood spills from his nose. His eyes roll back in his head as he falls unconscious.

Albert straightens his back, keeping his knee pressed into Max's spine. From the pocket of his jeans, he produces a bundle of zip ties and holds one in his teeth while pulling Max's wrists together behind his back. He binds them once and then uses another zip tie to bind them again.

With one Mortifer down, Albert leaps to his feet and hurries to the other side of the patio. Dan's back is pressed against the railing. He leans backward over the water, clutching Luther's forearm in his hands and struggling against it to keep the knife away.

Albert jumps onto Luther's back and brings his elbow down onto the base of his neck. Luther lets out a sharp cry of pain. The knife falls from his fingers and his head swivels as he tries to pry Albert from his back. Dan snatches the switchblade from the ground and turns it on Luther.

"Urrgggh."

My attention snaps back to Max, lying on his face in front of me. His head lifts a degree and he spits blood onto the pavement. A tooth falls out of his mouth.

I look away, suppressing a gag.

Max wriggles his shoulders, confused as to why he can't move. When he figures out that his wrists are tied, he starts trying to roll onto his side. At first I don't know what he's doing, but when I see him pulling his hands underneath his butt, I get it. He's trying to move his hands in front of him.

"No way," I shout, but he's already got his legs halfway through his arms.

I rush toward him, but he's too fast—his hands are in front of him now. He gets to a sitting position and has just enough time to give me a triumphant smirk before I drive my knee into the underside of his jaw.

He doesn't even make a sound. His eyes roll back in his head—again—and his body goes limp. Briefly, I wonder if I've killed him, but then Luther tumbles across my path. He rolls onto his side, clutching his arm against his stomach. Albert and Dan appear on either side of him. Dan looks at Albert, who nods.

As soon as Dan's foot connects with the side of Luther's head, I know it's over. Luther slumps to the ground without so much as a twitch. His body is contorted at an unnatural angle, the whites of his eyes gleaming through half-open eyelids.

Dan pulls zip ties out of his pocket and bends over Luther, securing his wrists in the same way Albert secured

Max's. "Think we can get them home before the cops come?"

Albert rubs his shoulder with a grimace. "Dunno. Sure hope Casey's close."

They both look at me. I'm standing next to Max, who is neither in the same place nor the same position as Albert left him.

"What the— Rosie?" Albert calls in a panicked voice. He runs a few steps in my direction and then slows as he reaches me. "What happened? What did you do?"

"What needed doing," I say.

"Right," he says, examining Max's unconscious form. "Good work, Clayton. Dan can tend to him. Let's go get your brother."

We hurry to the other side of the patio and I fall to my knees when we reach him. His breathing comes in shallow gasps and his eyes stare into the sky, glazed over. He's worse than I thought.

"We've got to get him to a hospital," Albert says. "I only hope it's something that can be treated."

"What do you mean?"

"Just that they may have given him something… unnatural. But we won't know until we have him looked at."

My stomach twists. "Unnatural, or supernatural?"

"I don't want to waste time speculating. Let's just get him up."

Something clicks behind us.

"Or not," says a deep, ragged voice.

My eyes meet Albert's, and his expression reflects the dread I feel in the pit of my stomach.

"Turn around," the voice says.

In slow motion, I look over my shoulder. A man with white hair stands behind us, his face hard with cold rage. One glimpse and I'm positive he's the man who shot the

Bestia outside Albert's flat. The fingers of his right hand are woven into Dan's hair, pulling his head down at an angle. His other hand presses a gun to Dan's temple.

The man is familiar—and not just from the shooting on the heath. When he shot my attacker, I'd been all the way up in Casey's room, too far away to see his face. I know him from somewhere else, too.

"Back away from the boy," he says, his eyes darting between Albert and me.

I throw a desperate look at Albert. He replies with a tight nod and holds his hands up, then takes a few steps back.

I hesitate too long. The man cracks his gun across Dan's face, and Dan cries out as his nose splits open. "I said *move*," the man growls.

Swallowing a sob, I force my feet to move away from my brother. It feels like ripping off one of my legs.

Dan's bloodied face is pinched with panic. His freckles stand out even more now that his cheeks have drained of color, and he shakes under the white-haired man's grasp.

"That's good," the man says as Albert and I back away from Paul. "Good. Keep moving. Now, hands on your head and face the street."

We turn toward the access road and stare into the darkness—and that's when we see the police cars barreling down the street, sirens wailing and lights flashing. They screech to a stop and officers spill onto the patio.

Who called the cops? Wait a minute—there was a crowd on the bridge before Albert Pulled. I look up, and sure enough, there they are. In all the chaos, I hadn't even noticed them.

There's a splintering sound behind us, followed by a howl that makes my blood run cold. Albert and I spin around to see Dan jerking free from the white-haired man, who is doubled over. The gun drops onto the cement with a clatter. The man cradles his arm, which hangs loose like it has been pulled out of its socket, and screams.

Dan ducks toward Albert and me as the police swarm the injured man. I take off in the direction of my brother.

"Paul!" I shout as I reach him. "Talk to me!"

His head jerks from one side to the other as he gasps for air. "Help!" I scream in the direction of the policemen. "My brother needs help!"

Two policemen jog toward us, one of them speaking into a walkie-talkie. They kneel beside Paul and shine their flashlights in his eyes.

"We got one that looks like he's on something," the one with the walkie-talkie says to someone on the other end. He turns to me. "What did he take?"

My throat tightens. "I don't know."

It seems to take a decade for the ambulances to arrive, but once they do, everything moves faster. Paramedics appear next to my brother. They lay him on a stretcher and one of them checks his vitals while the other secures the straps. I stand at a distance with my hand over my mouth, choking on panic.

"He'll be okay," Albert says, appearing next to me.

A hand squeezes my elbow and I look up. Dan stands next to us, his face already covered in purple welts. He opens his mouth to say something, and then closes it, looking weak.

"All right, load him up," one of the paramedics says.

I rush toward them. "Can I come with him?"

"No room," one of the men replies as they carry Paul toward the nearest ambulance. "Meet us at the hospital."

"Which one?"

"St. Thomas. The police can bring you."

I close my eyes and remind myself to breathe. If Paul doesn't make it through this night, I'll never forgive myself for failing to lock him up in Nana's house when I had the chance. I should have been more assertive with him. I should have forced him to listen to me, or at least told Mom and Dad what he was up to, even if it meant temporarily sacrificing his trust.

"Anything from Casey?" I say to Albert, more to distract myself than anything else.

"Not yet, but I'll check in with her. She must be close." He gives me a long look. "It's not your fault, you know."

I feel my mouth open, but I'm too off-guard to reply. He saw what I was feeling, and he said exactly what I needed someone to say—

"I can't let you go," says a voice behind me.

I spin around to face a police officer in his late twenties. The droop to his mouth suggests he'd rather be anywhere but here.

"Roberts," Albert says with a huff. He gestures toward Paul's ambulance as it pulls onto the road. "Surely you're not going to question us now, when her brother's just been taken to the hospital."

I look at Albert, then at Dan, for clarification as to who this guy is. Neither of them seems surprised to see him, and Albert obviously knows him fairly well. But neither of them returns my stare.

"You can see," Albert goes on, waving a hand at the scene around us, "that this is not exactly the best time for a trip down to your office. We can answer your questions tomorrow, once Rosie's made sure her brother is okay."

Roberts puts his hands on his hips and sighs. "Unfortunately, I'm not just going to question you. I'm going to arrest you."

THIRTY-ONE

"**A**RREST US?" ALBERT SHOUTS, JUST AS DAN SAYS, "What for?"

Roberts holds up his hands. "We got a lot of conflicting calls about a fight by Tower Bridge. About half the witnesses said they'd seen a man matching your description"—he nods at Albert—"antagonizing two other men. There was an argument, and then a fourth man with red hair appeared and initiated a fight."

"We didn't antagonize them!" Dan cries out, his face flushed. "They were—" He stops and gives Albert a look of barely controlled frustration. There's nothing else he can say without sounding like a lunatic.

"Roberts," Albert says. "Please. You have to understand. We were acting out of self-defense."

It's close to the truth.

Roberts seems to be considering something. He steps closer to us and we lean in automatically. "They said you two didn't stop when the other blokes were down. That you knocked them out cold and tied them up. This much, at least, is true." He nods behind us, where Luther and Max are being inspected by several paramedics. "And some of them said"—he shifts his attention to me with a raised eyebrow—"that a girl kicked one of them in the head when he tried to get up."

We turn to the crowd of onlookers above us. Tower Bridge is packed with witnesses, and roughly half of them think we're the bad guys.

"I kneed him, actually," I mutter.

Roberts's lips pull into a tight line as we turn back to him. "I've worked loads of cases involving you lot," he says, nodding at Albert and Dan. "And it always seems like you're defending someone else, even when things turn violent." He lowers his voice even more. "But because of how many people say that you were the instigators of all this, and because it's already quite late, my chief inspector has ordered me to hold you overnight. You'll be questioned in the morning and hopefully released."

A bubble of panic rises in my throat and explodes from my mouth in a single word. "*Hopefully?*"

His expression hardens. "Yes. That's the best I can do; I can't go against my chief's orders. If your friends had taken my previous advice to heart and left the crime fighting to the police, you might not be in this situation."

"No!" I shriek. "You can't do this! My brother— I have to go to the hospital! What if he's not okay? What if he—" I can't bring myself to finish the question.

"I'm sorry," Roberts says again, and even though I believe him, it doesn't make this any better.

Dan glances toward the other officers, who are watching the medics load Max and Luther into a second ambulance. The white-haired man is still on the ground and I wonder if they will take him to the hospital, too, or if they'll just pop his shoulder back in and arrest him on the spot.

I'm hoping for the second option.

Dan takes a subtle step closer to Roberts. "What if we run?" he whispers. His eyes dart toward the rest of the policemen. "Could you stall them?"

Roberts shakes his head. "You'd only be making things worse for yourselves. Let's get this over with." He nods at an officer behind him, who approaches with three sets of handcuffs. He hands one of them to Roberts.

"Cuffs?" Albert says with a scowl. "Really?"

"It's protocol. The sooner you get in the back of the car, the sooner I can start working on getting you released."

"Where are Casey and Isaac?" I whisper at Albert while Roberts handcuffs him.

He shakes his head. "They must've gotten held up."

The other officer moves behind me and pulls my hands together. I close my eyes as the cold metal clamps around my wrists.

THE HOLDING CELLS ARE COLD, WITH BRIGHT BLUE GATES that click loudly when Roberts locks us in. A narrow bed with grimy linens sits wedged into a corner of each cell; I wonder when the sheets were last changed and how often they're washed. Judging by the brown stains, not often. My toilet provides zero privacy. A couple of flies buzz above the water, fighting. Or mating. Either way, I have to cover my nose and mouth to keep from gagging at the smell.

"This is cozy," Dan says from the cell he and Albert share next to mine. He runs his fingers over the split on his nose and perches on the edge of the bed. "Never been in this station before. What were you doing on this side of town, anyway, Roberts?"

"I was actually trying to track down the man with the white hair," he says, hooking his keys onto his belt. "We never found him after he shot that woman in Blackheath, but this evening we got a tip that he was hanging around Tower Bridge."

"Who is he?" I ask.

Roberts shrugs. "He didn't have any identification on him, but he'll be fingerprinted at the hospital." He looks at me through the bars. "I know you're worried about your brother. I'm going to get you out of here as soon as I can."

Albert slams his hand against the bars. "You don't understand what kind of danger her brother is in! Those two guys—they're not just a couple of thugs, and the man with the white hair is working with them somehow; I'm sure of it!"

"You know who they are?" Roberts says, tilting his head. "Tell me."

Albert's jaw works. "Just let us out. We have to get to the hospital."

"Why?" Roberts moves closer to the cell. "What is it you think you can do that the doctors can't? How are you always in the right place at the right time?"

Silence.

Roberts looks at Albert for a moment, frustration lining his face. "Fine," he says. "Have it your way." He pulls a walkie-talkie out of his back pocket and clicks it on. "Mark?"

A voice comes through from the other side, edged with static. "Sir?"

"Need you to watch some hooligans for me tonight. Can Alistair cover for you out back?"

There's a pause. "Yes sir, coming over right away."

He strides to the door and puts a hand on the knob. "Mark is a new guard and doesn't quite know the ropes yet," he says with his back to us. "He lacks confidence.

Common problem in society, of course, but most unfortunate for a guard."

He leaves without looking at us.

I rest my forehead on the metal bars and close my eyes, taking deep breaths. Roberts is trying to help us get out. He's not making it easy, but he's trying.

Albert pulls his shirt collar up to his mouth. "Case. Where are you?"

He chews his lip while she responds.

"Is Isaac still with you? Okay, stop swearing and listen. We *were* at the docks, but then a load of crap went down and now we're in jail. Rosie's brother got in with a couple of Mortiferi, and we think they've drugged him. They're all at St. Thomas—of *course* we knocked them out, stop interrupting—we have to get to the hospital to make sure they don't get to him again. It'll take all of us to bring them down, if it comes to that." He pauses as footsteps come down the hall. "Borough High Street, Casey," he says quickly. "Bring Isaac. You've got to get us out of here!" He drops his collar and leans against the wall with his hands in his pockets.

I barely notice when the door opens. My thoughts are stuck on one thing Albert said that I hadn't even considered yet—what if another Mortifer comes for Paul before I get to him? What if they drag him off somewhere and turn him into one of them?

What if it's not drugs in his system, but the beginning of his transformation into a Mortifer?

A large guy with sweat stains in every crease of his tan uniform enters the room, huffing as though the walk from his previous post nearly did him in.

"Right," he says, trying to sound authoritative. It comes out too forced to be convincing. "I'm supervising you three tonight. Don't do anything you'll regret, yeah?" His fingers fumble over the baton on his belt.

He moves toward a desk in the center of the room and then drags the chair back with a screech. Someone left a newspaper—*The Sun*—which he opens with a rustle. It hides his face completely, and the three of us start shooting visual messages at each other.

I spread my hands out to my sides and give Albert a *What do we do now?* look through the bars that separate our cells. He stares at me, and I can tell he's trying to come up with something, but finally he shakes his head. He's got nothing.

Dan shrugs and mouths *Casey*. We just have to wait on Casey and Isaac to get here. But what are they going to do? How could they possibly get us out?

Something else needs to happen.

I turn toward the guard, still invisible behind the sports section. "So, your name is Mark?"

He peeks over the top of his paper. "Yeah."

"I'm Rosie." I smile. Please, oh please let me come off as charming and not suspicious. I need him to think I'm cute and innocent.

He gives me a shifty look and then raises the newspaper again.

"What are you doing?" Albert whispers. I ignore him.

"I have a question, Mark," I say. "It's, um…kind of embarrassing."

He folds the paper and lays it on the desk with an expression that is one part irritation, two parts anxiety. I'm making him nervous just by talking.

"Where am I supposed to use the bathroom?" I ask.

He looks past me into the cell, where the fly-infested toilet sits in the corner.

I follow his gaze and laugh. "Yeah, I don't really want to contract any diseases while I'm here. And I'm pretty sure making me use the bathroom in front of three men is illegal, especially since I'm only seventeen. Isn't there somewhere else I could go?"

"No," he says with false firmness. "Either use the toilet or hold it." Insecurity haunts his eyes. Mark is not used to being in charge of anyone, especially a girl.

"It's not really a matter of holding anything," I say with a small laugh. "I, um…need to take care of something. A feminine issue. So unless you want to watch me do that…"

A shadow of horror flits across his face. I'd find it funny if I weren't so desperate for him to heave himself out of that chair and open my cell door.

"Right," he says. "Just, ah, let me…" He glances around the otherwise empty room as if looking for someone to help him, then picks up his walkie-talkie. It looks like a child's toy clenched in his thick fingers. "Are there any available guards who can help me with a small situation?"

"I'm covering for you out here, mate," comes another male voice across the walkie-talkie. Probably Alistair, the other guard. "What's going on?"

"Are there any female guards here tonight?"

Pause.

"Seriously, Mark, you know it's just me and you. What's going on? Need me to switch posts with you? It'd be okay, you know, since it's your first week and all—"

"No, no," Mark says quickly. He glances at me as his face flushes red. "I can handle it. Never mind. All's well."

He clips the walkie-talkie back on his belt and stands up, fingering the key ring that hangs from his belt loop. "I'll take you to the toilet down the hall," he says to me. "Under one condition."

"That I don't try to escape?" I give him a wry look. "Unless there's some kind of trap door in the bathroom, I think you're safe."

"There's no trap door," he says firmly.

I widen my eyes. Hopefully, my fake worry will pass as genuine; I'm so close to success. "Can we go now? This is about to be an emergency."

Mark lets out a resigned sigh. Then he unlocks my gate and I slip through. I can feel Albert's eyes on me, but I don't dare glance in his direction. Just because Mark is new on the job doesn't mean he's stupid. I do my best to look docile, yet desperate for a toilet.

"Right," Mark says to Albert and Dan. "Don't try anything. We'll be back in five minutes."

Dan rolls his eyes. "What do you think we're going to do? Bite the bars in half?"

Mark's lips press together. "Just five minutes. Stay where you are." He grabs my arm and tugs a pair of handcuffs off his belt.

"What?" I protest. "How am I supposed to—you know—if I'm handcuffed?"

"Just till we get to the loo." He pins my wrists together behind my back and clicks the handcuffs into place. "Let's go."

He gives me a little push so that I walk in front of him. We exit the main holding area and turn left down a hallway. Our footsteps echo along the cement block walls, which are painted a depressing shade of taupe. One of the fluorescent lights above us flickers and dies, throwing a section of the floor into shadow. At the end of the hallway, looking out onto Borough High Street, is a glass door with iron bars on the outside.

And on the other side of that door is a beautiful black-haired girl with panicked eyes.

Mark lurches in surprise behind me. "Whoa! What—"

Casey beats on the door and twists her head around frantically. "Help me!" she shrieks. "Let me in! I'm being chased! Help! HELP!"

Mark stops in his tracks. I spin to face him. "Aren't you going to let her in?"

He's sweating again. "Uh…"

"She's in trouble!" I shout.

He wavers for another moment, but then Casey flings herself onto the door and claws at it while throwing a blood-curdling scream through the glass.

"Don't move!" Mark says to me. He hurries to the security desk and pushes a button underneath it. The door buzzes and Casey wrenches it open, her face flushed. She scrambles through the metal detector, which offers a feeble *beep* of protest. Then she hurls herself into Mark's arms. He catches her, his hands fumbling over her back, and falls into the wall behind him.

She lifts her face from Mark's shoulder, panic replaced with satisfaction. "Thanks, mate."

Two things happen simultaneously—Casey's right hand brushes along Mark's hip and slips the baton out of its holster. Her left hand dips into the waistband of her jeans, underneath her shirt, and pulls out a gun. She aims both weapons at Mark's head and takes several steps back.

My plan was to try to use my phone—which Roberts conveniently forgot to confiscate—in the bathroom. Casey's plan was to storm the place with a gun. I will never be on her level.

Mark's mouth opens in silent shock and his breathing turns to gasps. "Wh…what…?"

"Casey!" I shout. My body is buzzing with adrenaline.

"Don't you dare," she says through her teeth as Mark's fingers drift toward the walkie-talkie. He closes his mouth and holds up his hands.

Casey stands perfectly still. Her hair twists in wild tangles around her shoulders. "Give me your keys. Put them on the floor and kick them over to me."

He hesitates for a second, then slowly unhooks the key ring from his belt and drops it on the floor.

"Kick," she commands.

He kicks—a stuttered motion that paints a clear picture of his unfortunate gym-class days. The keys skid across the linoleum and stop in front of Casey's leopard-print flats.

"And the walkie-talkie."

Sweat cascades down his face. "Please don't shoot me."

"I will if you don't do what I say." She cocks the gun, sending an ominous *click* echoing around the space. "The walkie-talkie."

He drops it with a loud clatter and kicks it over. Casey squats on the floor and places the baton beside her, keeping the gun pointed at Mark. She hooks the key ring on her thumb and clips the walkie-talkie onto her belt loop. Then she picks up the baton and steps sideways, in my direction.

"Do. Not. Move."

Mark nods shakily, staring at the floor.

Casey keeps the gun on him until she reaches me. Shoving the baton into her waistband, she separates the keys with her free hand. Her grip falters and the keys fall to the floor, their metallic clinking magnified by the concrete wall. Mark eyes her as she bends to pick them up.

When he thinks she's not looking, he takes a tiny step toward her.

"WHAT DID I SAY?" she screams, swinging the gun toward him.

He freezes, swallows several times, and sinks to the floor. "I won't do it again."

"That's right. You won't."

Casey's eyes are bright with adrenaline as she stuffs the gun into her waistband and chooses a key from the ring's endless options. Her breathing accelerates as she moves behind me, trying key after key on my handcuffs, none of them working. I stare at the ceiling, waiting to feel the lock release.

Something moves in my peripheral vision.

Mark lunges toward the security desk and grabs the phone. A *click* sounds above our heads, followed by his flustered voice over the intercom.

"Help on main floor! Alistair! There's a woman with a—"

Casey pulls the gun out of her jeans and fires.

THIRTY-TWO

MARK GRABS HIS THIGH AS THE BULLET LODGES JUST above his kneecap. Screaming, he falls to the floor and writhes in agony.

"What did you do?" I shout. My voice sounds like it's coming through a thick layer of cotton.

"Albert said to break you out of here. So that's what I'm doing." She stows the gun in her waistband again and pushes on my shoulders until my knees bend. "Get on the floor and pull your legs through your arms."

I can't focus on what she's saying through Mark's screeching and the ringing of my ears. "What?"

"Get. On. The. Floor."

I lower myself to the floor and she rolls me onto my side. "Now. Put the handcuffs underneath your bum and pull your legs through. Quick."

This is the same move Max tried when he was on the ground by the fountain. Casey helps me shove my legs through the loop of my arms until my feet scrape over my hands. I push up from the floor, still trapped in the handcuffs but much more mobile with them in front of me.

A crazy thought occurs to me.

I'm pretty sure shooting a guard isn't going to turn out well for Casey, and maybe—just maybe—I can erase what she's done and get us to this same point some other way. I have to want it, though. Really want it.

Closing my eyes, I muster my desire to change what happened.

Reach for the mental handle, I think.

I hold my hands out in front of me.

"What are you doing?" Casey cries.

Search for it. Curl your fingers around it.

I close my eyes and try to block out Mark's moans of pain, but my fingers find nothing.

Focus on the exact moment you want to return to.

The moment Casey appeared at the door. I picture it in explicit detail.

There's still nothing…

…no, wait. There's *something*. I'm touching something!

"Get up," Casey hisses. "Now. Hurry!"

The mental handle. I feel it!

"Wait," I say, because I'm pretty sure I could get a grip on that handle if I just had a few more seconds—

But Casey's hand is wrapped around my wrist and she's tugging me to my feet. Whatever I felt, it's gone now, and my heart is heavy with frustration and disappointment. That might have been the moment I Pulled for the first time.

"If you Pull, I'll just have to do all of it again," she snaps.

Anger bubbles up inside me. "Not necessarily," I say as she examines the lock on my handcuffs. "There might be another way—"

"There might be, but we need to save our energy for a Pull that really matters. Not one that might make things more convenient." With a nervous glance at Mark's whimpering form, she drops my cuffed wrists and grabs my elbow. "No time to unlock them here. We gotta get the boys. Show me where they are."

I'm about to argue with her again, but then Mark groans loudly and I remember the other guard is probably on his way down here. Casey follows me as I run down the hall to the holding room, where Albert and Dan are standing with their faces pressed between the bars. They let out a string of swear words as we burst into the room, and I can't blame them. They just heard a gunshot and Casey looks like a lioness running down her prey, tousled hair flying around her shoulders and eyes sharp with focus. I don't know how I look, but if it's anything like I feel, then I'm pale as a ghost and rigid with fear.

"Who fired a gun?" Albert demands, his face tense.

"Me," Casey says as she shuffles through Mark's keys. "I've just screwed us all by shooting that guard in the leg, but he didn't give me a choice. The good news is that I got his baton, too."

"You did *what*?" Albert shouts.

She pushes her hair away from her face. "I'm sorry! He tried to stop us!"

Albert and Dan both gape at her.

"Casey," Dan says slowly, "surely there was another way—"

"There wasn't," she shouts, and he holds his hands up in surrender.

Mark's walkie-talkie, which is hanging from Casey's belt loop, clicks on. "Mark, you there? Where on the main floor are you?" It's Alistair, the guard who took over Mark's outdoor patrol.

We all freeze.

"Hurry, Case," Dan mutters.

"I'm hurrying, I'm hurrying."

She flips through a few more keys before finding one that looks a little larger than the others. We hold our breath as she shoves it into the lock. It doesn't turn.

"Pick another one," Dan says, shooting worried glances toward the door.

"Shut *up*, Dan, I'm going as fast as I can."

The walkie-talkie clicks on again. "Mark. Come back, mate. You all right? Was that a gunshot?"

"Somebody has to respond," I say. I unhook the walkie-talkie from Casey's belt loop and hold it—with both hands, since I'm still handcuffed—through the bars. Albert takes it from me and clicks the button on the side.

"Yeah, mate," he says in a terrible impression of Mark's wobbly voice. "I'm here. Gunshot, did you say?"

There's a long pause. Then Alistair's voice again. "Who is this?"

Albert grimaces and throws the walkie-talkie on the ground. It clatters across the floor and bumps into Dan's feet. "He knows something's up. Casey?"

She thrusts another key into the lock. It doesn't fit. "Working on it, working on it."

An exclamation sounds in the hallway. Alistair must have come to investigate and found Mark bleeding on the floor.

We all stare at Casey, who's flying through keys at the speed of light.

"Why aren't you trying them all?" Dan snaps at her.

"Because they're too small, the key has to be something like"—she holds one up, longer and thicker than most of the others—"this."

Footsteps pound toward the door as she sticks the key in the lock. It slides in with a jagged clicking sound. She turns it to the left.

The lock opens.

Dan and Albert burst from the cell. We all run toward a door at the back of the room, opposite from the footsteps coming down the hallway. Alistair erupts into the room just as we're leaving. His baton is drawn and he looks ready to use it.

"Hey!" he shouts, but we're already through the door and sprinting down another taupe hallway.

I push myself to run as fast as the others, but the handcuffs are making it almost impossible to build up any speed. Casey and Dan are way ahead of us. Albert's holding back because of me. My heart screams and my lungs burn for air; my legs threaten to give out. The hallway turns right and we skid around the corner. The echo of Alistair's pounding feet trails us. It doesn't sound like he's getting any closer, but we're not losing him, either.

An alarm wails above our heads. Red lights flash on the walls.

Please let us find a door. Please please please.

"HERE!" Casey screams as we run past a narrow alcove. I only catch a glimpse of her as we speed by, but I think she's standing next to an exterior door.

We almost fall over each other trying to change directions. Albert grabs my arm as we stumble after her through the door and into the parking lot. We tear past a row of police cars to the parking lot gate, duck under the automated barrier, and race to the sidewalk on Borough High Street. A black Fiat slows next to us and Casey wrenches the passenger door open. "Get in!"

Albert shoves me into the car and then tumbles in behind me. His shoulder rams my hip as we crawl over the center console into the backseat. Dan climbs in behind us and Casey leaps into the passenger seat, grabbing onto the headrest as Isaac slams his foot down on the gas. The air fills with the smell of burnt rubber as we peel away from the curb.

Isaac swerves into traffic. He shifts gears and presses the pedal to the floor. We roar around cars, buses, and black cabs before turning onto a main road and matching our speed to everybody else's.

"So," Isaac says drily. His dark eyes find mine in the rearview mirror. "How'd it go?"

"Casey shot a guard," Dan says.

Isaac lets out a low grunt. "That complicates things."

"Look," Casey says. "There wasn't another option, okay? He was calling for help! If I hadn't shot him in the leg, we wouldn't have had time to get out of here, and then Rosie's brother would be d—"

She cuts her sentence short and I realize she's staring at Albert. His expression is clearly telling her to shut up.

"Can I have those keys, Casey?" he says pointedly. "Rosie might like to have the use of her arms back at some point."

She tosses him the keys and he pulls my hands into the space between us. The fourth key he tries pops the lock open and I throw the handcuffs to the floor. "Thanks."

"No problem."

"How much farther to the hospital?" I ask, rubbing the raw spots on my wrists.

"Couple of minutes," Isaac says. "I'll stop the car near the entrance. Since you four have a price on your head, I'll go inside and find your brother. If there's any trouble, I'll com you." He looks at me in the mirror again. "No use showing your faces unless we've got Mortiferi to fight."

I nod and start biting my nails, a habit I thought I kicked last year. Casey transfers the gun and baton from her waistband to the glove box, and then turns on the radio.

"To see if they report us," she explains as Isaac frowns at her.

She turns the volume up, but I can't hear what they're saying. I can't hear anything. I know Isaac is right, I shouldn't go in the hospital unless Paul is in serious danger, but I'm not sure I can resist the temptation.

"Hey," Albert says in my ear.

I look at him.

"It's going to be okay. Isaac is going to walk into that hospital and find your brother. If he needs protection, we'll back him up. There's a good chance we'll all be arrested again before the night's over, but Paul will be okay." He tries to give me a smile, but ends up wincing. "Ouch," he says, reaching for his eye.

Without thinking, I touch the deep purple bruise that has bloomed at the outside corner of his eye. The skin is swollen and he flinches a little as my thumb skims over it.

"Sorry," I say absently.

He shrugs. "I'm used to getting beaten up."

"No, I mean I'm sorry for everything." My hand drops to his cheek. I brush over it with my fingers and then drag them over his scar before letting them fall away.

He closes his eyes for a moment. "You have nothing to be sorry for."

"I'm not sure about that. My presence here seems to have caused extra work for you."

"Servatores have been fighting the Mortiferi since ancient times." He manages a small grin. "It's not like you started it."

I nod, wanting to feel better, but the knot of guilt in my stomach doesn't ease. Albert must see it in my eyes, because he slips his hand over mine.

"We're almost there," Casey says, turning the radio down. "Everybody ready?"

"Yes," I say. The hospital appears through the windshield, and immediately I know something's wrong.

Police cars swarm the parking lot, their lights flashing so brightly I have to squint. Half a dozen officers mill around on the sidewalk, talking to distraught nurses and scribbling things on notepads. Dread reaches into every part of my body; something very bad has happened.

We pull into a bus stop lane in front of the hospital. Isaac puts the car in park and unbuckles his seatbelt. "I'll find out what's going on."

"I'll come with you," Dan says, and we all look at him. "Oh. Right. Price on my head. Never mind, I'll stay here."

Isaac opens the door. "Don't go anywhere unless you absolutely have to. I'll be back as soon as I can." He slides out of the car. Casey climbs over the gearshift to the driver's seat.

"Something happened to Paul," I say, watching Isaac walk up to a policeman. "What if they've gotten him out somehow and changed him?" My voice breaks on the words.

Casey looks at me over her shoulder. "Then we'll find him."

"We don't know that Paul had anything to do with this," Dan says. "It might be a coincidence."

I nod, but I'm not even close to convinced.

Isaac's dreadlocks swing across his shoulders as he talks to the cop. The policeman's expression is grim, and he's shrugging a lot. I can't see Isaac's face because his back is to us, but the tense set of his shoulders sets my nerves on edge.

Finally, Isaac turns around and strides back to the car. Casey cranks the engine and reaches across to open his door.

"He's gone," Isaac says breathlessly as he lands in the passenger seat.

The car explodes with questions, and I blink a dozen times, trying to clear the fuzziness from my vision. His words hang in the air like a fog.

"I'll tell you more once we're moving," he says. "Drive, Casey."

She pulls out of the bus lane and filters into traffic. "Okay. What's going on?"

Isaac turns around to face me. "The white-haired man came in at the same time as your brother. On the way to the hospital, a paramedic put his shoulder back in its socket, and that was the only injury he had. When they parked, the white-haired man forced his way out of his ambulance and ran over to Paul's. Then he pulled a knife out of his boot and stabbed one of your brother's paramedics. The other medic almost subdued him, but he didn't move fast enough. The white-haired man got into the driver's seat and drove away with your brother still in the back."

Dan is shaking his head. "That's ridiculous. He did all that with a knife? No way. It's impossible."

Albert looks at him. "Not necessarily. Not if he's desperate for something."

"Desperate for what?" Casey says.

"No idea, but I think we'd better find out."

I brace myself on the seat in front of me. I don't really care how my brother was taken hostage; I just care about finding him.

"Where did they go?" I say, my voice gritty.

Isaac shakes his head. "Nobody knows. The ambulance was found a few miles away, parked on the side of a highway. There's no trace of the man or your brother."

For a moment, the only sound in the car is the soft hum of its tires on the road. I stare out the window, my eyes burning with tears. They spill over and drip silently down my cheeks.

"This isn't over, Rosie." Albert puts his hand under my chin and pulls it around so that I'm facing him. "It's not over, not by half. Okay? We don't know for sure what they're planning to do with him, and we're going to find him. Right now."

"How?" I say. "We don't know where he is. We don't even know who the white-haired man is. Does he look familiar to you?"

"From the heath, you mean?"

"No. From…somewhere else."

Albert shakes his head. "I have no idea who he is or what he wants with us. But we're going to figure all this out. We'll find Paul. I promise."

"You can't promise me that. You have no idea—"

"Rosie, you need to calm down." His voice is low and even.

"Don't tell me to calm down. My brother is supposed to be in the hospital, but he's not." I reconsider. "Actually, he shouldn't be there because I should have taken better care of him. I should have worked harder to get him to stop hanging out with Max and Luther. I should have realized that SPARK wasn't what it seemed. I should have told Mom and Dad about him going to that stupid pub. I should have—"

I stop short. I can't believe how obvious this is.

"I know where he is," I say. "He's at the pub."

Albert frowns. "Which pub?"

"The Black Swan! Remember when I told you what Paul said about it? How he heard the word 'Mortiferi' there? Maybe he—*they*—went back. I know he's been there with Max and Luther before, and if they've been turned into Mortiferi, maybe that means something."

Isaac and Albert exchange a look in the mirror.

"So that's where we're going, then?" Isaac asks. "The Black Swan?"

Albert nods. Casey pulls a U-turn and presses the pedal to the floor.

THIRTY-THREE

THE BLACK SWAN SITS IN A GLOOMY CORNER OF Lewisham, surrounded by elm trees and nearly lost in darkness. The only light comes from one streetlamp on the corner, but it's too far away to illuminate much of the building. Most people probably don't even know it's there. It's the kind of place mothers tell their children to avoid if they happen to realize it exists. No respectable man would find himself ordering a pint at this bar.

Of course the Mortiferi use it as a gathering place. It oozes with secrets and shadows.

We drive past it first to get a good look at the outside. The wood is rotten in several places, and the red door, which might have been charming once upon a time, is covered in dents and stains. I'm afraid to speculate on what those stains might be.

The door is closed and the windows are dark. We drift farther down the street until Casey finds a place to turn around. I check my phone. It's after one in the morning.

And I have fifteen missed calls.

"Crap!" I clap a hand to my forehead. "I left it on silent!"

Albert looks at the phone over my shoulder. "Your parents?"

"Yes! They probably think I'm dead!"

"You should call them before we go in," he says, and I don't like the note of finality in his voice because I know what it means—depending how things go, this could be my last conversation with them.

"What am I going to tell them?" My heart feels like it's slowly being pinched in two. I try to take a deep breath, but my lungs won't expand all the way.

Albert's eyes droop with sympathy. "That's up to you."

I nod, trying to keep my hands from shaking. Mom seems like the safest option right now, so I call her cell, holding my breath.

But it's Dad that picks up after half a ring.

"Rosie!" he shouts in a voice that's half-anger, half-relief. "Where have you been? We've rung you a million times!"

"I know. I'm so sorry." My voice strains against the sudden tightness in my throat. "I put my phone on silent and forgot."

"You forgot. Of course you did." He huffs. "Well, I hope you're close to home, at least. Are you okay?" There's a rustling noise, followed by my mom's voice in the background. "Yes, yes, it's her!" Dad says in a muffled voice.

"I am close to home," I tell him as we approach the pub again.

"And you're okay?"

I hesitate.

"Rosie, tell me what's going on. Where are you? Are you still with James? And have you heard from your brother? He's missing. Must have snuck out of his bedroom window. He's not answering his phone."

I close my eyes and grip the back of my neck. "I've... sort of heard from him, yes."

"What does that mean? Do you know where he is? Is he okay? Why aren't either of you home yet?"

I take a couple deep breaths. "Dad, something happened tonight. Paul's in trouble."

There's a pause. "Trouble," Dad growls.

"I can't tell you the details, but I'm going to take care of it. I'll be home soon." I close my eyes tight, hoping I'm telling the truth. "I gotta go, Dad. I love you."

"Rosemary—"

I hang up and press the power button until my phone cuts off.

"Keep it on you," Albert says, his face grim. "We might need it."

I nod and slip the phone into my pocket. Casey gives me a sympathetic look from the driver's seat.

Albert snakes an arm around my shoulders and leans close to my ear. "I can't promise everything will be okay," he says. "But I can promise I'll do everything I can to get you and your brother home safely tonight."

I meet his eyes, and he gives me a sad smile.

"Thank you," I whisper. "I hope you're right." I look from him to Casey, then to Dan, and finally up to Isaac. "You guys—" I begin.

"We know," Isaac says, a smile transforming his face. It's the first time he's shown any kind of positive emotion toward me, and I'm caught off guard by the comfort it brings.

"We do?" Dan asks.

Casey widens her eyes at Dan. "You don't have to say it, Rosie. We're in this together."

"But you don't even know my brother!"

"We risk our lives for strangers all the time," Dan points out.

"Sure," I say, "but do you walk into places that might be swarming with Mortiferi all the time?"

There's a beat of silence.

"Nah, we tend to avoid those," Dan says lightly. "Although, now that you mention it, this *is* more efficient than trying to take them out one by one."

Casey pulls into a gravel driveway and we crunch our way to a grassy unloading area behind the pub. A black van is parked there, but the front seats are empty. Casey steers us past the van and parks behind a couple of rusted blue garbage bins.

"We don't know that anyone is here," Albert reminds me. "We might go in and find an empty building."

"Yes," I say, "but then what?"

"We keep looking. We're with you, Rosie, whether you like it or not. Oh—we better take the guns."

Stretching over the center console, he opens the glove box and pulls out the gun Casey used, then another one. The first, he keeps; the second, he offers to Isaac.

"I don't get one?" Casey says in a scandalized tone. "Do I need to remind you who broke you out of prison tonight?"

Albert gives her a wide-eyed stare. "Do I need to remind *you* that you SHOT A BLOODY POLICE OFFICER?"

Her gaze falters, but she says nothing.

Everyone unbuckles their seatbelts and climbs out of the Fiat. I follow them slowly, guilt and apprehension tangling in the pit of my stomach.

The beam from Albert's flashlight dances over the back of the pub and then focuses on the crooked wooden back door. While the front door is a worn shade of red, this one looks like it used to be painted green, but the color has faded and peeled down to the bare wood in most spots. When Dan pulls it open, the hinges squeal in protest and one of the lower corners drags in the dirt, creating a fan shape in the scrubby grass.

We stare into the dark pub. The space stretches in front of us like a black hole, empty and silent.

I let out a breath. He's not here.

Albert shifts next to me. "We should go in anyway. Maybe we'll see something that will lead us to Paul."

"Are you sure we have to go in the back way?" Casey asks, eyeing the thick cobwebs that hang from the doorframe.

"Unless you'd like to get arrested for breaking and entering," Dan replies. "Seems you'd be a bit more inclined to lie low, after what just—"

"I know what I did," Casey snaps. "No need to keep bringing it up. If we're going in, then let's go."

We stand outside the open back door and stare into the inky interior, none of us eager to be the first one inside. Albert shines his flashlight into the pub, illuminating mismatched wooden tables and chairs, a bar with several stools clustered around it, and a dartboard in the far corner. The whole wall behind the bar is covered with shelves of liquor bottles.

The light travels up, revealing a low ceiling with exposed wooden beams; then down to the wide-plank floor. The walls are paneled with wood that, at some point in the distant past, was painted a deep shade of maroon. Just like the back door, a lot of the color is chipped and faded.

The flashlight continues its slow trek around the room. A cockroach scurries away from the circle of light and vanishes behind the bar.

"Charming little place, isn't it?" Casey mutters behind me.

Isaac grunts.

"All right, chaps, we don't have all day." Albert holds the flashlight high and looks back at the rest of us. "I'll go first. Nobody wanders off on their own."

"Don't have to tell me twice," Dan says.

The scuffing of our shoes along the wooden floor echoes loudly in the empty pub. Albert swings the light left to right. Something chatters to our left and we all jump. Albert aims the flashlight into the corner just in time to see a mouse's tail vanish into a small hole in the baseboard.

"Bloody hell," Isaac says in a low voice. He turns to me, and in the dim light, all I can see is the outline of his features. "Are you sure this is where your brother has been coming?"

"That's what he told me," I say with a shrug.

Nobody speaks for a few moments.

"Empty," Albert finally says. He looks at me. "Totally empty."

My chest feels like it's caving in.

"What now?" Casey asks.

"Let's think of another possibility," Albert says. "Could he be somewhere else? At SPARK?"

I shrug. I feel so helpless. "I guess that's the next best option."

Albert moves toward the back door and holds it open while Casey, Dan, and Isaac slip outside. I stop as I pass him, leaning close so that the others won't hear me.

"I don't want to risk everybody's lives," I whisper, locking my eyes onto his. "I'm desperate to save Paul, and I'd gladly sacrifice myself. But you? Casey, Dan, and Isaac? What if we save Paul, but lose one of you?" I shake my head. "I need you guys, but I'm terrified someone's not going to get out of this alive."

He leans close to me. "No one's forcing us to do this. We could bail at any moment."

"But you won't."

"That's our choice, not yours."

Just as I'm opening my mouth to reply, I hear a strange sound coming from the outside of the building. I frown at Albert and he does the same at me. Slowly, we move into the night and Albert lets the door fall shut. It's almost more of a feeling than a sound—a distant pulse in the ground beneath our feet.

Following my train of thought, Albert points down with a questioning look on his face. I nod.

Dan calls from the direction of the garbage bins, where the car is parked. "Al! Rosie! What are you doing?"

The three of them are watching us with confused expressions. Isaac already has the driver's door open. We wave them over.

"Listen," I say as they reach us. "Do you hear something?"

They stand still, concentrating, until Casey speaks up. "Is it a sort of drumming?"

"Yes!" I whisper.

"Yeah," Dan says. "I feel it more than I hear it."

Albert nods. "It's coming from below us."

"Could there be a staircase inside that we didn't see?" Dan asks, rubbing his chin.

I eye the black van. "It's not coming from the van, is it?"

Dan hurries over to it and listens. He turns around, shaking his head.

"What's that thing over there?" Casey points past all of us into the darkness.

On the ground, leaning against the building, is a square shape. As we approach it with the flashlight, details come into view: two metal doors with rusty handles hinged onto a stone foundation.

"Looks like a storm shelter or something," I say when we reach it. The drumming is stronger over here, although it's still just slightly more than a vibration in the ground.

"Or a bomb shelter." Albert curls his fingers around one of the handles. "Want to check it out?"

No one replies. Finally, I grab the other handle. "Let's do it."

Albert gives me a stiff nod. "On three. Ready? One… two…three!"

We yank on the handles, but they only rattle against each other.

"Locked," Albert says.

"Hope the kit's still in your car, mate," Dan says to Isaac.

Isaac nods. "It is."

"I'll get it," Albert says.

"What kit?" I whisper, but he's already jogging through the darkness in the direction of the Fiat, carrying the flashlight with him. We wait in almost complete darkness while the beam dances around the car's interior. He returns about a minute later with a silver briefcase in his hand.

"Hope I put the key back in after last time," he says, opening the case. He hands the flashlight to me, and I crouch next to him as he removes things from the case and places them on the grass. There's a square piece of cardstock covered in coms, two small sets of binoculars like the ones I saw in the closet at his house, several switchblades, a couple of sleek black cigarette lighters, bandages, antiseptic cream, a roll of gauze, and another flashlight. When he reaches the bottom, he says, "Aha. There it is."

He picks up a black velvet bag and loosens the drawstring around it. When he holds it upside-down over his palm, a long, narrow piece of metal falls out.

"What is it?" I ask.

He holds it up for me to see. "Skeleton key."

I lean closer. It's silver, with a Victorian-style loop design at one end and a single metal tooth at the other. The middle part is smooth, made to slide easily into almost any lock. "It looks ancient."

"That's because it is. But so is this lock." He creeps toward the metal doors and motions for me to hold the light over his shoulder. "The great thing about London is—" he lines the key up with the mouth of the lock "—everything tends to be really old—" he wiggles it in until the lock swallows it almost up to his fingers "—which means this skeleton key can get us access to almost anywhere, as long as the locks haven't been modernized." He twists the key and the lock groans open.

"Okay then," he says, tugging the key until it pops back out. "Let's take some of this stuff with us and see what we can find."

He hands a switchblade to each of us. Dan grabs the extra flashlight and turns it on.

I put a switchblade in my pocket and sidle up to Isaac, trying to keep my voice steady. "Am I supposed to kill them?"

"You can if you need to," he says, "but the blades are mostly to distract them. Don't kill unless it's unavoidable."

"Why not?"

"Gotta burn them alive," he says. "It's the only way. Kill the body without fire, and the remains of the sorcery inside will escape and possibly infect someone else. That's why the white-haired man shot that Bestia on the heath before we could get to her. He knew we'd erase the black magic inside her, and he wanted it to find a new home inside an innocent person."

I stare at him with my mouth open, stomach churning.

"Burning them is a bit disturbing the first few times you do it," he says, looking a little sheepish. "Sorry. Shouldn't have said it so bluntly."

"No, no, it's fine. I'm—fine." My mouth tastes like bile. "Fire. Got it."

I watch Albert drop the skeleton key into his pocket, along with a switchblade and a lighter. He picks up the square covered in tiny black coms and walks over to me.

"If you get separated from me—which I won't let happen, but just in case it does—you need to wear a couple of these."

He peels off one of the black dots and eyes my neckline for a minute. "I hate to say it, but I think Casey might have the right idea for you girls." He slides the collar of my shirt to the side and sticks the com to my bra strap. "Your shirt will help keep the com in place, but you'll be able to reach it quickly if you need to."

I nod, but his eyes don't meet mine. "And this one," he says, sticking a second com into my ear. His face hovers close to mine, and his fingers graze my jaw as he pulls his hand away.

"You have your knife, yeah?" he says.

"Yes."

He hesitates a moment, then shoves a lighter in my hand. "Here. Take this."

I roll it from side to side in my palm. I can't imagine setting another human being on fire. I won't let myself think about Paul. What if they've already—no. Not going to think about it.

"Are you sure about this?" I ask.

"It's just in case you need it. Don't worry. I have one too."

"But how do I—you know—terminate them?" I shift my weight and try to control my wavering voice. "Do I just light their clothes on fire?"

"You can. They'll probably put it out before it kills them, but it will definitely slow them down." He fiddles with the binoculars, unfolding them, re-folding them, putting them in his pocket.

I place a hand on his arm. "Albert."

He looks at me, his expression tight.

"I'm going to be fine."

He shakes his head. "I'd feel a lot better about this if you would just drive the car to your grandmother's house and lock yourself in your bedroom."

I heave an exaggerated sigh. "Too bad I can't drive a stick."

One corner of his mouth twitches in a smile. "I knew you'd say something like that."

"Pardon me," Dan says loudly. "There are Mortiferi to be flambéed. Shall we?"

"All right." Albert lets out a long breath. "Everybody do your best to stay out of sight, and if you need to run, then run."

THIRTY-FOUR

AN HEAVES ONE OF THE METAL DOORS OPEN WHILE Isaac tugs on the other one. The pounding grows clearer and we all shoot grim looks at each other. Albert and Dan aim their flashlights into the dark, cramped space. There are few things that terrify me more than dark, cramped spaces—especially one that potentially contains a horde of angry, soul-blackened non-human beings. I'm almost tempted to take Albert up on his offer of locking myself in Nana's house until this is over, but my brother's life is at stake. Not to mention the Servatores who are putting themselves in danger to save him.

A flight of stone steps, surrounded by walls of packed earth, descends deep into the ground. Cracks run through some of the stairs, and in some spots, large chunks have crumbled off. Albert moves closer and points the light straight down. The hole goes too deep to see where it ends.

"Okay," Casey says. "It's now or never, lads."

"I'll go first." Dan steps up beside her.

Casey nods at him. "I'll be right behind you."

He offers his hand to her. She takes it, and they move toward the mouth of the staircase. Dan gets in first, pointing his light ahead of them.

"Nothing to worry about," he says, although the words carry a hint of unease. "It's the Stairway to Hell. You know, that *other* Zeppelin song. Not quite as popular, but—"

"Would you please get a move-on?" Casey pushes on his shoulders and he stumbles down a few steps. "Sorry," she says to me. "Nervous joker."

I smile. "Believe me, I get it."

Only the top of Dan's head sticks up above ground level, his hair even brighter than usual in the light from Albert's flashlight. It disappears as Casey follows him down.

"You two go next," Isaac says. "I'll be last."

"Right," Albert says to me. "Let's go."

I don't fully appreciate how small the entrance to the staircase is until Albert's bulky frame fills it.

"Bit tight, isn't it?" he says, almost lying on his back to get down the first few stairs.

"Yeah," I reply, stepping in after him. "And look at this. The ceiling is wood." Right above the stairs are several thick wooden beams, holding the earth in place.

The thought of being buried alive creeps into my mind, and I shudder. That would definitely be the very worst way to die, yet here I am lowering myself into a pseudo-grave. I follow Albert down the stairs. A few pebbles dislodge behind me as Isaac brings up the rear. He doesn't say much, but his presence has a way of comforting me.

Something inside my chest constricts a little more with each step. The walls are too close, the ceiling too low. My breathing speeds up in the stagnant air; I want to turn around. There's no way to see what we're walking into. I struggle to keep my balance on the narrow steps and try to convince myself to hold it together.

"Okay, it's opening up," Albert finally says in a loud whisper.

A few steps later, I'm able to stand upright. Albert still has to duck his head a little, but at least he's not hunched over like a caveman anymore.

"Blimey, it reeks down here," comes Isaac's voice from behind us.

I agree, but I'm afraid that if I try to speak, I'll betray the terror that's climbing slowly up my throat.

We march deeper in silence. The air grows stale and leaves a bitter taste in my mouth every time I inhale. My hands collect a layer of grime from where I keep my balance on the earthen walls. The pounding sounds louder, but still far away.

"How far down do you think we are?" I ask, wiping sweat from my forehead. My voice is a shaky whisper, and anyone who can hear me knows I'm freaking out.

The back of Albert's neck shines with moisture in the dim light. "No idea."

"Too far," Isaac adds, and although his voice is just as deep as ever, it carries a hint of apprehension that sparks a fresh round of fear in my gut.

Dan and Casey are moving faster than the rest of us. They have disappeared into the darkness below. Beads of sweat have gathered on my upper lip; it's been getting progressively hotter as we descend.

"They're at the bottom," Albert says, his breathing labored.

I peer over his shoulder. Casey and Dan are standing on flat ground with their backs to us. I can barely see them in the beam of Albert's flashlight; Dan has switched his off.

"What is it?" I ask as we reach them.

"Turn off your torch," Dan says. "We'll be able to see it better."

Albert clicks it off, throwing us into nothingness.

Isaac stops a couple of stairs above me. "What in the world?"

We're standing at the mouth of a tunnel. There's a faint green glow pulsing along with the beat of the noise. Everyone's faces look sickly in the strange light.

Casey whispers, "Should we turn the lights back on?"

"I don't think so," Albert replies. "I think we need to keep a low profile from here on out." He tucks the flashlight into the waistband of his jeans, next to the gun. "I'll take the lead this time."

The tunnel smells like mildew and sour milk. I cup my hand over my nose and mouth as we walk, hoping I won't throw up from the stench. The pounding grows louder as we move farther into the tunnel. It vibrates through the wooden beams above our heads and tickles the bottoms of our feet through the ground. The green glow brightens with every step, projecting waves of light onto the dirt walls.

After a few minutes of walking in a straight line, the tunnel begins to curve and the pounding changes. It's not just a drumming noise that I feel in my feet; it's a heavy bass rhythm that charges through my toes, up my legs, and into my heart. The closer we get to the source, the more I feel it in every cell of my body. And there's another component, too—a sort of electrical whining layered on top of the bass line.

"It's like the club from hell," Dan says.

I nod, even though he's not looking at me.

We keep walking.

The tunnel curves back the other way, but we don't get far before Albert comes to a screeching halt and backtracks until he almost runs into me. I put a hand on his back to stop him.

"What is it?" I say.

He shakes his head. "I don't know." Isaac appears on my left and Albert looks at him, then back at me. "We're going to go scope everything out. Stay put."

I lean against the dirt wall but push away quickly; the bass that thumps through it makes my teeth hurt. Isaac and Albert move ahead and crouch on the ground next to the tunnel wall. The green glow is much stronger around the curve.

Albert and Isaac mutter to each other, but the noise of the club makes it impossible to hear what they're saying. I turn around to talk to Casey and Dan—but look away immediately. I only saw them for a second—her tear-streaked face lying on his shoulder, his lips pressed to her hair.

We could die down here.

"Hey," Albert says.

He's coming back. Isaac lingers ahead of us, hovering on the perimeter of whatever lies around the bend. He takes a few steps forward, in the direction of the noise and the green glow.

I shoot Albert a panicked look. "What's he doing?" I can barely hear my own words over the electric music.

He leans down to my ear. "We think they're all on some kind of drug. Nobody noticed us when we were up there." He nods toward the place he and Isaac crouched. "Isaac is experimenting to see if anybody recognizes him."

"And what if they do?"

"If they hurt him, one of us will Pull and we'll try something else."

I nod in the direction Isaac walked. "What's in there?"

Albert's lips press into a tight line. "It's not for the faint of heart."

"I'm not faint of heart."

"All right, then," he says. "Go look."

I take a few steps forward, fingers tracing along the wall as I round the curve. Then I come to the end of the tunnel, and...

Whoa.

It really *is* the club from hell.

The room must be the size of a football field, maybe bigger. Wooden beams crisscross the domed ceiling, some providing structural support, others providing a place to hang the cages.

It takes a moment for me to register what I've just seen.

Cages.

Revulsion surges through my body as I stare at the swinging metal crates containing teenage boys and girls. At least a dozen of them dangle from the beams, each holding a single prisoner. All the captives lie on the bottom of their cages, motionless. And below each one is a large bowl, dug into the ground, filled with some sort of green burning liquid. Even though the flames spiral into the air, the cages are free of scorch marks.

Hundreds of Mortiferi fill the arena. They dance to the bass line of their electronic music, laughing in high-pitched shrieks at nothing in particular. Some cluster around the bowls of fiery liquid. Every few seconds, they dip a hand into the liquid and slurp it from their palms.

Albert touches my shoulder. "I think there's a strong possibility your brother is here," he says.

I nod, unsure whether that's a good or bad thing.

He points to our left. "Look. Isaac has made it halfway around the room without anyone noticing."

"What does that mean?" I ask. "Do you think they can't see us or something?"

"I think they can see us," he says, speaking right into my ear so I can hear him. His breath tickles my skin.

"But whatever drug they're on is keeping them from recognizing us. Or keeping them from caring, maybe."

We watch the Mortiferi for a moment. They drink ecstatically, lapping the green liquid from their hands and closing their eyes in delight.

"So what do we do?" I ask.

He surveys the floor for another minute. When the Mortiferi aren't drinking, they dance to the beat of the horrible music, waving their arms and throwing their heads back.

"There's only one way to blend in," he says after a moment. "Dance."

I raise my eyebrows. "What do you mean, blend in? I thought they wouldn't notice us."

"They won't." His eyes flicker upward. "But he might."

The white-haired man sits on a pedestal on the far side of the room, his eyes sharp and discerning. Whatever drug the others have taken, he most certainly hasn't.

And unlike the others, his eyes aren't glowing.

"His eyes," I say. "They're normal."

Albert arches his eyebrows. "He must still be human."

"Human? But he looks like he's in charge."

"Yeah, he does. Not sure what's going on." He holds out his hand. "May I have this really awkward and terrifying dance?"

"If you're trying to lighten the mood, it's not working."

"Then why are you smiling?"

"Just trying to act the part." I take his hand and pull him toward the bizarre dance floor. He says something over his shoulder to Dan, who nods and leads Casey in the opposite direction. They keep to the perimeter but mimic the motions of the people in the center of the arena, draping their arms around each other and letting their bodies move to the bass line. After a moment they drift into the crowd and I lose them.

We venture slowly into the horde of Mortiferi. The mass swallows us, pushing us along in its current as we try to copy their movements. At first, my body won't cooperate. I'm trying too hard. I'm too worried about the others.

But after a couple minutes, it gets easier. We glide deeper into the mob, and I start to relax. It doesn't make sense; I shouldn't feel so comfortable. I fight the sensation for a minute or so, but eventually I can't remember why I'm supposed to be worried.

How could anyone be upset in such a wonderful place?

Albert gives me a lazy smile as his hands wind around my waist. My fingers drift up his arms, lingering on the swell of his biceps before tracing along his shoulders and coming to rest around his neck. The heavy air clings to us like water.

"It's beautiful," I say to Albert, looking around at the green flames climbing up from the bowls in the ground.

He grins, and I watch the reflection of the flames in his eyes. "Not as beautiful as you."

His lips barely curve upward as he drops his forehead against mine. I close my eyes and drink in the feeling of his chest as my fingers explore it. We move like one person, swaying to the pounding beat, bathed in flickering green light. My hand travels into his hair, and I kiss his ear, then his neck. Why have we never done this before? God, it feels good. He plants his lips on my shoulder, up my neck, along my jaw, and onto my cheek. I close my eyes, and I can feel his lips coming closer to mine—but then he pulls away with a glazed-over smile.

"Let's get a drink," he says, which is weird because I was just thinking the same thing.

We move toward one of the bowls and stand over it for a moment, admiring the way the liquid swirls and bubbles. Steam rises from the surface, but it's cool, and I breathe in the flowery scent with a sigh.

I cannot live without it.

Albert and I lean over the edge of the bowl at the same time and reach for the lovely green liquid. Because Albert's arms are longer than mine, his fingers break the surface before I can reach it—

And the moment he touches the green liquid, he roars in pain.

THIRTY-FIVE

HIS SCREAM SLAMS ME BACK INTO THE REAL WORLD. I blink furiously and cup my hand over my nose. There might be drugs in the green liquid, but there's also something in the air, sedating my brain so that I forget what's happening. Focusing is like trying to stay awake after taking a sleeping pill.

The chaos around us camouflages Albert's yowls of pain, but the white-haired man could notice us any second. I grab Albert's wrist and pull him toward the side of the club behind a cluster of Mortiferi who are passing around some kind of pipe. The smoke drifts past my nose, and I make the mistake of taking a deep breath; the smell is so delicious it nearly drives Albert from my mind. I could join in on the dancing and take a drink from the green liquid, just for a moment; what harm would that do?

But Albert makes a grunting sound through his teeth, and I shake my head roughly to clear it. I pinch my nose shut until we're clear of the smoke.

Once we reach the wall and we're as far as we can get from the crowd, I examine his hand. It's red and blistered, as if he stuck it into a fire. His forearm tenses beneath my fingers.

"I'm sorry," is all I can say. "I'm so sorry, Albert. I don't know how to make it stop hurting."

"It's not as bad as it was at first," he says, but his expression is twisting in pain. "I'm just glad you didn't touch it."

"Why does it burn you, but not them?"

"Because it's full of dark magic." He stands up straighter and gazes across the arena. "Let's focus on finding your brother. Do you see him in any of these cages?"

My eyes float up to the dome above us. I can see six cages from here and at least six more hang farther away. The two closest ones are girls; the other four are guys. None of them are Paul.

"No," I say. "But I can't see into those." I nod toward the other side of the massive room, where more cages dangle over green flames. Paul could be only a few yards away. My heart races as I search for his floppy brown hair, his angular shoulders—but the view just isn't good enough from here.

"Right. Let's move in that direction." Albert nods toward the far side of the arena. "Try to keep your head down."

A group of Mortiferi jostles us as they pass on our left, flowing in the same direction we're trying to go. Albert pulls us into the current and we keep our eyes on the floor. I'm trying to focus on finding Paul, but the club is starting to hypnotize me again. The thumping of the bass line, the hum of the electric music, the crazed dancing, the swirling green light…

Wake up, Rosie. I pinch my arm hard and squeeze my eyes shut a couple times. *Wake up and find your brother.*

We pass a cage I haven't looked into yet. I wait until the white-haired man looks the other way. Then I crane my neck to see into it.

"Girl," I say into Albert's ear.

He nods.

The tide of Mortiferi curls around another bowl of burning liquid, and I glance into the cage above it. A boy, but not the one we're looking for.

I put both my hands on Albert's back and walk on my toes so that I can talk into his ear. "All these people in the cages. They're missing, just like Paul. Are we going to leave them here?"

"We'll do our best to save all of them," he says, "but let's find your brother first."

The white-haired man surveys the crowd, mouth twitching with a satisfied smirk. Once again I'm struck by the familiarity of his features.

Who is he? Think, Rosie.

But it won't come to me. I tear my eyes away from him in frustration.

We skirt around another bowl of flaming liquid. Dan and Casey are several yards away, working their way around the room. I want to wave at them, but I'm scared it will attract too much attention. Instead, I stare at Casey, willing her to feel my gaze. She looks up.

"What's wrong?" I mouth as she and Dan head our way.

She points behind her to the side of the arena Albert and I are trying to get to. I follow her finger to a cage that's so far out it almost bumps the wall. A boy is draped across the bottom of the metal crate, his bony hands sticking through the bars. Other than that, I can only see a mop of brown hair and one eyebrow.

But it's enough. I know my brother when I see him.

"Yes!" I shout, tugging on Albert's arm. "That's him!"

He follows my gaze. "I'll com Isaac."

"Don't worry about it," Casey says as they reach us. Their eyes are slightly unfocused, but her voice sounds clear. "We already did. He's coming this way. Al, what happened to your hand?"

He flexes his fingers experimentally. "The green stuff burns like hell. Don't go near it. I'm okay, though," he says before anyone can ask how bad the pain is. "Paul. We're focusing on Paul. My hand can wait."

"How do we get to him?" I try to keep the hysteria out of my voice. It doesn't work.

Albert's face tenses as he looks at Dan and Casey. "No idea."

We migrate across the floor until we're below Paul's cage. My little brother is hanging from the ceiling like a caged animal, drugged into delirium.

I lean against the wall, trembling. The others gather around me, looking just as sickened as I feel. A glance at the white-haired man confirms that he still hasn't noticed us. I don't want to think about what will happen if he does.

"Right," Albert says. "Let's think of a way to—"

He stops short when a deafening clang of metal on metal resounds through the room. We clap our hands over our ears and bend low to the ground as the cages begin to lower toward the bowls of fiery liquid. The Mortiferi shriek with delight at the descending humans. I grimace against the noise and squint at the dirt floor.

Albert's voice breaks through the chaos. "Get up, Rosie!"

A strong hand grips my arm and jerks me to my feet. I stumble because I'm trying to run faster than my feet can move. The Mortiferi are moving toward the cages, pressing in on us, blocking our way. It takes me a second to realize they haven't noticed us at all—it's the prisoners they want.

Albert pushes them aside to create an escape path for us. They fall over and get right back up, never seeing him. He pulls me along behind him, but there are too many bodies in our way; even with as many he shoves to the side, we can't get anywhere.

A scream of rage slices through the air. It's so loud it carries over the music, the shouting, the deranged laughter.

I glance over my shoulder to confirm what I already know has happened. We've been spotted.

Albert drops a collection of swear words and throws more dazed Mortiferi out of our path with one hand. He keeps the other hand around my arm. Dan and Casey are a few feet away, making even less progress than we are. I can't see Isaac anymore.

I hear the white-haired man shouting, but I can't understand him. The Mortiferi respond, though, and within seconds, every pair of eyes in the room is trained on me.

Me.

The cages reach the bowls of fire and dangle a few inches above the surface. When the metallic cranking stops, I realize none of the Mortiferi are talking. Everything is quiet. Even the thumping bass and electronic music have stopped.

The silence is worse than the shrieking.

A wall of Mortiferi encircles us. Albert tries to push one of the women to the side, but instead of falling over like before, she shoves him hard and he staggers into a Mortiferi man. Their eyes are far more focused than they were a minute ago. They're not attacking; they're just standing there, blocking our way. There are no gaps between them, and the new aggression on their faces stops Albert from pushing any more of them around.

I search the arena for the white-haired man, but I can't find him. Dan and Casey are behind us, and Isaac is to our left.

We've been herded together like cows going to slaughter.

Albert's hand snakes behind his back, into the waistband of his jeans. He looks at Isaac, who seems to understand. He nods and reaches into his own waistband.

I'd forgotten Albert and Isaac have guns.

"Rosie," Albert says out the side of his mouth. "Listen to me very carefully."

I step closer.

"Isaac and I are about to start shooting. The Mortiferi will attack us and forget about you, at least for a moment. I want you, Casey, and Dan to run back up that tunnel and get as far away from the pub as you can."

"Are you insane? Why can't you just Pull?"

"I will if I need to," he says. "But now's not the time."

"Al," Dan pipes up from behind me. "I'm not leaving you two here on your own." He pulls out a switchblade and flicks it open. His face looks like it's carved out of stone.

Suddenly, the mob of Mortiferi parts down the middle. The white-haired man appears, his lips curling up at the corners in a way that makes me shudder.

"Well, well," the man says, and my veins fill with ice at the sound of his voice. "This is quite unexpected."

He surveys the ring of Mortiferi and then says something to them in a harsh, guttural language. They take a collective step back.

"Rosemary, isn't it?" he says to me. He looks at Paul, still lying on the floor of his cage, the whites of his eyes peeking through his eyelids. "And Paul. Rosemary and Paul Clayton, grandchildren of the great Edward

Clayton." His tone drips with disgust as he says Papa's name.

My eyes travel down to his hand. It hangs by his side just like it normally would, except for one thing. It's clutching a gun.

The gun that killed my attacker on the heath before she could be properly terminated.

The gun that almost killed Dan.

He tilts his head down and to the side, and suddenly his face clicks with an image in my brain. Two images, actually. I inhale sharply.

"I know who you are," I say.

He scowls. "No one knows who I am, girl."

"No, I recognize you. You're Gareth Long."

His expression freezes.

"Aren't you?" I say, trying to keep my voice steady while fear bubbles in my stomach. "You were at my grandfather's burial. You looked at me but left before I could talk to you."

He stays perfectly still, but anxiety ripples behind his eyes. I remember how he watched me at the cemetery, how he turned away when he realized I'd noticed him.

"Your son Kieran was killed in Greenwich a few years ago, hit by a bus on the High Road. I saw a photo—"

"DON'T TALK ABOUT MY SON!"

He strides toward me and shouts another command to the Mortiferi. A huge man nearby steps up behind Albert and twists both his arms behind his back. I hear grunts of pain and look around to see that the same thing has happened to Isaac, Dan, and Casey.

Gareth Long reaches me quickly and presses the cold barrel of the gun to my head. My body goes numb with terror; sweat gathers under my arms and on my upper lip, and suddenly I'm thinking about my dad, my mom, Nana, Paul. Stephen smiles at me from countless memories, and

Albert's green eyes crinkle at the corners. Gareth's face is purple; he will pull the trigger any second now and I will be dead, gone forever, just like Papa.

"You're stupid if you think I would actually shoot you," Gareth hisses into my ear.

I can't respond.

"What kind of revenge would that be?" he goes on. The gun digs harder into my skull. "Teenagers die every day. I would know, after all." He laughs, and it's a horrible grating sound that makes me squeeze my eyes shut. "I want Edward Clayton to pay for what he did to my son. I want him to hurt like I hurt."

"That's all this is?" I say. "Revenge?"

A slow smile spreads across his face. His teeth are brown at the roots. "I watched them lower your grandfather's godforsaken body into the ground, and it was one of the greatest moments of my life—until now."

Spit froths at the corners of his mouth.

"He'll know the exact moment when his grandchildren become one of us," Gareth says, "and it will kill him all over again. You're just like him, I bet. Doing good when it's convenient. Saving lives if it's not too much trouble."

"He did everything he could for your son," I say. "What happened wasn't his fault."

A beat of silence hangs between us. Gareth's face is twisted with grief and anger. In spite of what's happening, I almost feel sorry for him. Losing his son destroyed him. Destroyed his whole life.

"Don't do this," I say. "These people—these *monsters*—they'll turn on you as soon as you change us. I don't know how you're still human, but they won't let you stay that way. They'll either kill you or they'll make you one of them."

His expression falters.

"You could get us out of here," I say. "You could escape with us, and we would help you. Listen to me, Gareth." His eyes flicker to mine. "You don't have to do this."

There is a pause that seems to last a year.

Then the pressure of the gun leaves my head and relief floods my body. I look up. He's staring at me.

"Come on," I whisper. "Let's escape. All of us, together."

The corners of his mouth tremble. There is so much longing in his eyes. He blinks like he's trying to clear his vision, and for one glorious moment, I think I've convinced him.

But then his face turns hateful again, and he aims the gun at my head. There's a scuffle behind me, and Albert cries out.

Gareth says, "Hold him tighter! Don't let him get away from you!" Then, to me: "Maybe I *will* kill you after all. Your brother would be enough for us."

"NO!" I scream.

"No," he echoes thoughtfully. "You're right."

And then he fires a bullet into Albert's chest.

THIRTY-SIX

I CAN'T MAKE SENSE OF WHAT I'M SEEING. IT'S WRONG, so terribly wrong that it can't be real. Albert cannot be crumpling to the ground while the Mortifer who was holding him backs away. Albert's hands—one of them still blistered from the green liquid—claw at his chest. Those hands are supposed to be saving lives. They're supposed to guide me safely through the crowded streets of London and leaf through ancient books in the Batcave. But now there are crimson splotches on his T-shirt that rush together until they've conquered all the white fabric in their path, and his hands are turning red, and I don't understand why.

His eyes dim as he stares into the middle space between us.

Casey's scream makes me breathe again, and understanding crashes down on me.

Albert is dying.

I start to shake.

Albert is dying.

No.

Isaac, Casey, and Dan thrash against the Mortiferi that hold them back, but they can't break free. Their anguished shouts fill the air. I can't believe all it takes to keep them from Pulling is to restrain their hands. A memory surfaces of standing in Albert's bedroom while he told me how to Pull, and when I close my eyes, I can almost hear his voice again.

Hold your hands with your palms facing up and focus on the exact moment you want to return to, he told me. *If you do it right, your fingers will touch something that's not there.*

I know what he's talking about. I felt it in the police station, right before Casey jerked me to my feet and the worst night of my life became hell.

They can't Pull because they can't get their hands free. It's that simple.

I close my eyes. I reach for the mental handle—

Focus. Focus on the moment you want to reach.

The tunnel? The empty pub? Dancing with Albert?

I picture Albert's face as we danced, the way he told me I was beautiful. I reach for it with all my might—

"Rosie," Albert croaks, and my concentration shatters.

He opens his mouth, but I don't know if he's trying to speak or breathe. Either way, he fails. The life goes out of his eyes. I can't feel anything. The scene has gone two-dimensional and I must be dreaming. I'll wake up soon and everything will be fine.

Casey screams again, but this time it's the word "No" ripping from her throat. The sound stops suddenly when Gareth turns around and shoots her. The man who was restraining her drops her to the ground. She barely twitches before going still.

I see Isaac and Dan shouting at the top of their lungs, but I can't hear them. My breaths come too fast and too hard. Black dots explode in front of my eyes. I sag against the Mortifer behind me and he jerks me up by my arms, sending a sharp pain through my shoulders that radiates up my neck.

Gareth has his gun aimed at Dan. He's going to kill him, and then Isaac, and then Paul and I will be changed into Mortiferi. Paul hasn't moved since we found him. He might be dead, too.

Gareth's face appears in front of mine. His eyes are bloodshot and shifty, and whatever pity I felt for him before is long gone. This man is a deranged killer, a psychopath with no respect for life. I cannot feel sorry for him, no matter what he's lost.

"It's time," he says to the Mortifer holding me. "Put her in the cage with her brother. We'll do them together. Let me just finish these two."

Rough hands push me forward and I fall to my knees, only to be yanked onto my feet again. My shoulders pop and pain sears the length of my arms. A woman sneers at me as she opens Paul's cage. I try to dig my feet into the ground as the Mortifer pushes me toward the bowl of fire, but two gunshots behind me confirm that there's no longer any hope of escape. They're dead. All of them.

But I can still find a way out of this. And maybe I can Pull.

My heartbeat is strangely steady as I stand before the door to Paul's cage. As the Mortifer pushes me inside, I kneel next to my brother. He doesn't react to my presence. I should feel his neck for a pulse, but I can't bring myself to find out if he's alive or not.

I lie down and close my eyes.

Maybe it won't hurt.

Gareth is saying something to the Mortiferi in that guttural language. They're cheering, laughing, chanting. The cage lurches; they're going to lower us into the bowl of green liquid. Gareth shouts another string of incomprehensible words and the Mortiferi roar in excitement. Then he turns toward the room and holds his arms out as if embracing the twelve cages and their victims.

Since the alternative is to give him the satisfaction of watching me panic, I let my mind go blank. I block out the voices. The insides of my eyelids glow with the room's soft green light. I will stay calm throughout this process. I will not beg for my soul.

He would like it too much.

A sound like wind whispers across my mind. It isn't outside my head because there's no way I could have heard it over all the noise. Words take shape in my consciousness; I don't hear them, don't see them, but somehow I understand them anyway.

I am here.

Chills sweep over my arms. I know that voice. I've heard it—*felt* it—like this before. First in the chaotic hospital room, and again when I was attacked on the heath.

"Papa?" I whisper.

Yes.

I sit up quickly, ignoring the stabbing pain where the Mortifer wrenched my shoulders. Gareth gives me a sharp look. My excitement must show because he strides over to our cage, his expression full of wicked delight.

"He's here, isn't he? Edward Clayton, the Blackheath Savior, is here for his *opus postremum*."

Tell him you don't know what he's talking about.

"I don't know what you're talking about."

"Yes, I'm sure. Well, it doesn't matter. You'll be one of us in a second, and there's nothing the ghost of your grandfather can do about that. Tell me," he says in a smug tone, "is he going to save you? Is he going to break you out of this cage with his spirit strength?"

I give him an even stare.

"The *opus postremum* isn't real," he goes on. "These people—" he gestures to the Mortiferi "—have thoroughly educated me on your precious Servatores. They know everything about your grandfather and these friends you brought along. And guess what they told me the Servatores *can't* do?"

I glare at him.

"Change things after they've died. Interfere with the natural course of events. Oh, they might drift around for a while before they depart, but they're completely useless as spirits." His mouth turns up in a horrifying smile. "But Edward can watch what happens to you. And I hope he does. I want him to witness every moment of your grand transformation."

Hold your hands out, Rosie, Papa says inside my head. *Palms up.*

I try to move my arms, but my shoulders hurt too much. *I don't think I can.*

Something like an electrical current shoots from my core, through my elbows, all the way to my fingertips. I let out a little yelp as my hands come out of their own accord.

A trace of doubt crosses Gareth's eyes. "What are you doing?"

Now: Pull.

The Mortiferi frown at me, confused.

I don't think I can, Papa.

"LOWER THE CAGES!" Gareth shouts, staring at me with wide eyes. He stumbles backward toward his pedestal, the gun dropping from his fingers. "LOWER THEM NOW!"

I close my eyes. Although the scene around me has turned more chaotic than ever—the Mortiferi screaming, cages lurching slowly toward the green liquid—my mind has created its own bubble of peacefulness. At first I think

I'm in shock, that my brain is trying to shut out the horror of what's happening, but then I realize that's not it at all.

Papa is doing something inside of me.

Images flip through my mind like a photo album. Snapshots from the past few hours appear in a flash and are replaced almost immediately. We're in the Fiat. Isaac is talking to the cops at the hospital. I'm on the phone with my dad. We're parked behind the pub. The black van is already there. We're inside The Black Swan. Albert is searching through the kit. We're going down the staircase with our flashlights.

Then the images stop.

You weren't there at the right time, Papa says. *I can guide you, but you have to Pull. I am not strong enough to do both.*

My mind spirals out of control. *I have to Pull?*

Yes. I have managed to slow things down around you, but I don't know how long I can do it. You have to Pull quickly. I will put you where you need to be.

The Mortiferi are moving as if they are underwater, their expressions taking too long to change, their strides drawn out in slow motion. Even Gareth Long's frantic gestures seem sluggish.

My eyes drift over the arena to my executed friends. Casey's black hair fans around her head like a dark halo; Dan's laughing face is pale and drawn; Isaac's wise eyes stare without seeing.

And Albert.

Unless I can pull this off, I'll never see his smile again, never feel the softness of his shirt against my cheek, never hear him laugh at his own lame jokes.

My hands are still in position. I close my eyes and search the corners of my mind, looking for the handle. At first, just like in the police station, there is nothing.

Then: *something.*

This, Papa says. An image of the back of The Black Swan, barely visible through the darkness, projects itself onto my mind. *Focus on it.*

I focus.

I haven't seen this scene in real life, I'm sure of that. There's no Fiat parked behind the garbage bins. No black van. No Albert, Casey, Isaac, or Dan. No me.

I adjust my mental fingers on the handle that's not quite there.

I love you to the end of the universe, my sweet Rosemary, Papa says. *Now—Pull.*

I take a deep breath, and I draw the handle toward my body.

Swirling colors. Imploding stomach. Pressure on my limbs from conflicting directions. A liquid feeling in my bones. And the *whooshing* sound that threatens to shatter my skull. A vortex opens up inside my chest and I'm sucked into it, turned inside out, and spat out the other side. Pain stabs through my head and my body crumbles into a million pieces. It's worse than the feeling of being next to Albert when he Pulls—so much worse.

The last thing I hear is the sound of my own deafening scream.

THIRTY-SEVEN

LIGHT. FAINT, BUT IT'S THERE. SOMEONE IS TALKING. A girl. She sounds familiar, but I can't place her voice.

"Is she okay? What happened?"

"I don't know. I don't know how we got here." A guy, breathless with worry. His voice catches on the next words. "Why isn't she waking up?"

Pressure under my jaw, followed by another male voice, this one deep and full of command. "She has a pulse."

"Unngh."

"There! Did you hear that?"

My mind perks up. Did I make that moaning sound?

"Unnnnngh."

Yes! That's me!

"What in the bloody hell happened? Why are we out here again?" Another guy.

My eyelids crack open. Light green eyes stare down at me, sparkling in the beam of a flashlight.

A name comes to me. "Albert?"

He falls back and rubs a hand over his face. "Oh, sweet holy mother."

And then I remember *everything*.

"Albert!" I shout, pushing myself upright. "You're—How did—"

I gasp between the sobs that choke me. My vision floods with tears and I can't support myself anymore, so I sink to the ground. A strong pair of arms wraps around me and squeezes. My face is squashed against a solid chest and I cry into it, breathing in Albert's unmistakable scent, clenching the back of his T-shirt in my fists.

"It's okay," he says to me. "We're okay."

I look at him. "Do you remember?"

"Yeah," he says slowly. "I remember going down those stairs and ending up in a huge room. I remember the Mortiferi. And I remember—" He pauses. "I remember dying."

He looks at me, and then at the others. Casey's eyes are unfocused. Dan massages his forehead. Both of them lean against the Fiat, which is parked behind the garbage bins, right where we left it. I'm sure it's not supposed to be here yet. But I guess if Papa can get us somewhere we haven't been, he could get the Fiat there just as easily.

"What happened?" Albert says. He adjusts his position on the ground and curls an arm around my shoulders. My head rests on his chest.

"Papa," I say. "The *opus postremum* is real."

The three Servatores gape at me.

"Edward?" Albert whispers. "He Pulled one last time?"

"No," I say. "I did."

Silence.

"Tell us," Dan says, wonder laced through the words.

"Papa showed me what to focus on, and—I don't know. We're not supposed to be here yet, but he was able to give me this image to focus on, and then—"

Tires crunch on gravel somewhere to our left. Albert edges away from me and creeps toward the garbage bins. He peeks through the gap between them.

"Black van," he whispers. "Unmarked. Headlights off. Same one that was here when we pulled up earlier."

One of the van's doors opens and shuts, followed by another.

"Two men," Albert says. "Can't tell if they're Mortiferi, but I'd be willing to bet they are."

I prop my arms on his shoulders and look through the gap over his head. The two men yank the van's sliding door open. They wear black from head to toe, and even though it's too dark to see their features, one of them seems familiar. I squint at him, wishing he would turn around so I could get a good look at his face, but he's busy with something inside the van.

Finally a cloud moves and the moonlight filters through the trees. It hits his profile just as he turns to say something to the other man.

Recognition hits me hard. "James," I breathe.

"James?" Albert echoes in a whisper. "As in, *the* James?"

"Yeah."

He might have been an awful date, but there's no way having his soul darkened by sorcery is fair punishment for being a jerk. His eyes burn with an orange glow.

"Mortiferi," Albert whispers. "Fortes, at that. At least one, probably two."

One of them—the one who's not James—grabs something large from the backseat and places it carefully on the ground. It looks like an oversized black duffel bag.

James heaves another bag out of the van and lines it up next to the first one. The two Mortiferi treat the bags almost reverently as they move one after another onto the ground. James's hands falter over one and it tumbles onto the ground by his feet. The other man shoots him a look.

"What is that?"

The voice makes me jump.

"Sorry," Casey says from her post right above my head. "But what do you suppose is in those bags?"

"No idea," I say.

And then one of the bags moves. A sickening suspicion punches me in the gut. I count them quickly. Twelve. They're being unloaded near the metal doors that lead to the Mortiferi arena. When another one twitches, I know I'm right.

"People," I say, my voice a strained whisper. "My brother is in one of those bags."

My stomach turns as I imagine Paul, drugged and helpless, being shoved into a duffel bag and thrown into the back of a van. Albert moves away from me to join Isaac and Dan, who are crouched next to the Fiat. They talk in hushed tones.

Casey positions herself between the bins and peeks through the gap. "They're going to fight. You and I will stay here and provide backup. Try not to worry, yeah?" She looks over her shoulder at me. "It's three against two. I predict you'll have your brother back in fifteen minutes."

"Casey, you know it won't be that easy."

Her eyes flicker away from mine, then back. "Okay. So it might not be quite that simple. And there might be a hundred Mortiferi inside that pub. Who knows? We've never been here at this time before. Speaking of which, how far back did you Pull? Thirty minutes?"

"I don't know," I say. "Maybe Papa helped me go back farther than I would have otherwise."

"Maybe," she says, eyeing me. "If he didn't, though…"

She shrugs and leaves the sentence hanging.

Squatting at the edge of the left garbage bin, I press my hands against the grimy metal and peer around the side. The two Mortiferi work with their backs to us. Sweat shines along their arms as they transfer bags of people to the ground.

A figure moves in my peripheral vision and I jump, expecting another Mortifer, but it's Albert. His broad shoulders are tense with energy. He clenches his fists, then spreads his fingers wide. I can't see his face, but I know what it looks like. Tight, determined, ready.

The Mortiferi lay the last bag on the ground and gesture at the pub, arguing loudly. There aren't any windows on the back of the building, so there's no way to know if anyone's inside. It's too small to hold all the Mortiferi we saw underground, but that doesn't make me feel much better.

Dan appears behind Albert. It seems strange that Isaac isn't with them. When I turn around to look for him, he's on the ground next to the Fiat with a gun in his hand.

"Protecting you," he whispers in response to the question on my face.

"Don't they need you?" I ask.

"If they do, I'll leave you with the gun." He smirks. "You Yanks know how to use these things, right?"

"Us *Yanks*?" I cross my arms. "Say what you want about Americans, but not all of us are trigger-happy gun junkies. The last thing I want is to be responsible for a firearm."

A loud scuffling noise comes from the other side of the garbage bins, followed by several grunts. I whirl around to see what's happening.

Dan has knocked the unknown Mortifer to the ground. He straddles the man's back, twisting his arm behind him and pressing his face into the dirt. The Mortifer struggles and tries to get up, but Dan's fist slams into the back of his skull. The blow dazes him but doesn't knock him out. He flips Dan off his back and punches him square in the face. Dan howls as his nose erupts with blood. Cupping a hand over his face, he shakes his head quickly and then lands a hard kick to the man's jaw.

Albert and James are tangled up a few feet away. Every time Albert gets him in a headlock, James tosses him onto the scrubby grass. James gets in a few punches to the ribs before Albert knees him in the groin and he crumples to the ground.

"This might be easier than we thought," Casey says, grinning at me. She squints through the gap again. "See? Look."

She's right; Albert has wrestled James into an inescapable pretzel-type hold. Dan knocks the other Mortifer out and ties his wrists behind his back. The tension in my chest eases, and I glance behind us at Isaac. He's peering into the shadows to our right.

"See anything?" I ask in a low voice.

He shakes his head and tucks the gun into his waistband. "I'm going to help them load people back in the van."

He walks past the garbage bins, and I relax a little. Casey, who's balancing on her toes, sinks all the way to the ground and rolls onto her back. She covers her face and laughs.

"Wow, I really thought it would be worse than that," she says.

"I know. I can't believe—"

A chorus of enraged shrieks brings both of us to our feet. We dart out from behind the garbage bins and stop in our tracks.

At least twenty Mortiferi stumble out the back door of the pub, eyes on fire.

THIRTY-EIGHT

HALF OF THEM CLUTCH LIQUOR BOTTLES AT THEIR sides—but instead of whiskey or vodka, they're filled with that same glowing green liquid. Their fiery pupils burn in the night, and the sight of all those luminescent eyes makes me stumble back a few steps, reaching for something—anything—to protect me.

"Oh," Casey breathes. "We were wrong."

Albert looks up at the sudden crowd. His grip falters just enough for James to throw him off his back. Albert tries to tackle him again, but James swings an arm into his face—and then he catches sight of me. His mouth twists into a hungry leer, and it fills me with terror.

But surely he's not *all* gone. Maybe there is something left of the guy who bought me a Just Coke on our horrible date. He's a Forte, just like Max and Luther. He still has his mind. Maybe I can reason with him and convince him to let us go.

"James," I say. "It's me. Rosie. Remember?"

He hesitates.

"From the Hare & Billet. We went on a date." I laugh, hoping it will trigger something human inside of him. "Come on, you remember, don't you?"

He takes a few steps toward me. Recognition flickers in his eyes. "Of course I remember."

Well, thank God. "Listen, I need your help with something. You can help me out, right?" I give him the coyest smile I can muster.

His mouth curls into a grin, but it's too sharp, too angular. "That depends how much you're willing to pay. I had big plans that night, *Rosemary*." He says my name like a curse word, and I step backward like he's slapped me. "Big plans to take you behind that pub, all the way to the end of the alley, and get my money's worth out of that date. But then you left." His smile becomes a sneer. "And you made a fool of me in the process."

He rushes at me, pupils glowing, sick ecstasy written all over his face. He's not James anymore—not really. He's a shell of James, an empty container housing nothing but memories and rage.

"HELP!" I scream, but screaming is the wrong thing to do. It's like a siren song to the Mortiferi. They all move toward me at the same time, and I back up so quickly I almost fall over. They surround me in seconds, but James is the first one to hit me. His fist cracks across my cheek and stars explode in my vision.

The scream that tears from my lungs is so loud that it feels like my head is splitting in two. I catch a glimpse of Casey's frantic face; a couple of Mortiferi are trying to restrain her. Even though she thrashes against their grip, she can't get free. I don't see any of the boys, but I hear the bang of gunshots and the thud of bodies hitting the dirt. Hands grasp at my arms and legs. Fists crash into my head. I shut my eyes and wait to feel the suctioning in my stomach. Someone will Pull. Someone will get me out of this. I would do it, but there's no way I can get my hands out, and I doubt I'd have the strength to do it again so soon.

James hefts me onto his shoulder and I open my eyes. Albert is on top of the van, kicking at the Mortiferi as they try to follow him. He glances at his watch, then puts his hands out in front of him and closes his eyes. I almost die with relief.

But the suctioning in my gut never comes.

Albert looks confused. He shuts his eyes tighter and tries again.

It's not working.

Oh, sweet mercy.

It's. Not. Working.

How can the Pull fail to work now, of all times? Is it because Papa helped bring us here, to a place and time we hadn't physically been in before? It's the only explanation, and I have no clue how to fix it.

The Pull, apparently, isn't an option right now.

"NO!" I scream, but we're already going through the door. Men and women with glowing eyes surround us. James is saying something to me, but it's in that horrible demon language and I can't understand him.

Finally he drops me on the wooden floor and the breath rushes out of my lungs. I throw my hands out in front of me, trying desperately to focus on getting us out of here, but I can't concentrate on any specific time. I can't feel the mental handle. I gasp for air, calling for Papa in my head, but there's no answer.

Albert said the *opus postremum* was for a Servator to make one last save. Papa saved all of us by helping me Pull. He can't do anything more.

Mortiferi close in on me. Every time I try to stand, someone shoves me back down. I can't understand why they haven't killed me yet, but then I remember I'm supposed to become one of them. Me and the twelve people they kidnapped, including my little brother. The thought burns like venom in my blood, but it also gives me a strange kind of fearless power. I didn't fight being put in the cage because I thought it was too late. But now?

It's not too late anymore.

When Gareth's face appears in the crowd above me, I'm not shocked. I'm not even scared.

I'm furious.

"Rosemary Clayton," he says. "I never expected to catch you this easily."

I search his eyes for any hint that he knows we Pulled, but all I see is fresh malice. His eyes roam my features greedily. To him, this is the first time we've spoken. He doesn't remember anything about the arena. He doesn't remember that Papa's spirit showed up to guide me through my first Pull.

As a leering smile spreads across his face, something moves behind the crowd. The Mortiferi are so focused on me that they fail to notice Albert and Casey squeezing through the back door. Albert's eyes are cold and hard. He aims a gun at Gareth Long's head.

"Get away from her." He pulls the back door closed behind him. Every eye snaps to the two Servatores. Casey holds the other gun; her jaw is set and she looks like she's dying to squeeze the trigger.

Something crashes into the back of the building and the walls shudder. Car doors slam. A glance through the window shows me what's happened—Dan and Isaac have rammed the Fiat into the back door. The Mortiferi can't get out. A couple of them try the handle, but the door doesn't budge.

For about three seconds, everyone just looks at each other.

Then voices explode around the room, confused and angry. Gareth lunges toward me and I scurry backward, bumping into a thick pair of legs. Hands come down on me from every direction and grab my wrists, my ankles, my shoulders. Gareth wraps his arms around my waist and jerks me toward him, but whoever's got my right arm isn't letting go. A man covered in scars glares down at me, his upper lip curled over his teeth like a dog. Gareth shouts at him and the man shouts back; neither of them wants to give me up. The others decide they want a piece of me too, and suddenly I'm being pulled left to right, front to back. It's as if every Mortifer in the room has decided to collect a Rosie souvenir. Arm? Leg? Makes no difference, there'll be plenty of pieces to go around.

They seemed obedient down in the lair before I Pulled, but now, they're too greedy to heed instructions. I guess they haven't had enough of the green liquid yet. Later, when they're saturated with it and breathing it in the air, they'll be fully submissive to Gareth's commands.

I lash out, kicking and flailing with everything I've got. I catch someone's kneecap with my heel and hear a satisfying *crack* followed by a scream. My elbow connects with Gareth's eye and he goes down, losing his grip on me.

"Rosie!" Albert shouts from a few feet away. He punches a man in the mouth and ducks under a woman's arms.

"Shoot him!" I yell at Albert, pointing toward Gareth.

He nods and tries to get a clear shot at Gareth, but there are too many people in the way and bullets are precious. I'm surrounded by Mortiferi, and there's no way out.

I catch sight of Casey behind the bar. She's scooping liquor bottles into one arm while holding the gun in her other hand. A couple of women block her path as she runs to the front door, so she slams the barrel of her gun into both of their skulls and they fall to the ground. Then she ducks as someone hurls a barstool at her head.

"They're coming!" she shouts at me. Then she sidesteps a Mortifer who's standing in front of the door and slips out into the night.

"Who's coming?" I cry out just as Dan and Isaac burst through the front door. The look in their eyes is no less terrifying than the Mortiferi's orange glow, and for the next few seconds I stand still, watching them work. The way they move seems almost choreographed, like some kind of lethal ballet. Dan leaps over the bar and hurls himself onto a cluster of Mortiferi. Isaac, more cautious in his movements, chooses one Mortifer at a time, administering a series of blows with surgical precision.

Isaac is about to break a chair over someone's head when something stops him. He pauses mid-swing, listening intently. I recognize that look; someone's talking over the coms. I put a finger in my ear, but there's nothing there. Mine must have fallen out in the fight.

Isaac waves at me frantically. "Get over here! NOW!"

I dive toward him just as the window shatters and something lands in the crowd. A massive fireball erupts in the middle of the room. For a moment, I'm blinded by the burst of light. It fades to an orange-yellow as shrieks fill the air and flames lick the walls. A couple of beams catch fire, and smoke begins to crawl along the ceiling.

The Mortiferi are howling. Albert scoots along the perimeter of the room, coughing; thank God he wasn't hurt. He vaults behind the bar to join Dan. Isaac and I run to the front door as he shouts into the collar of his shirt.

"Don't throw another one! We're coming out!"

We stumble onto the sidewalk. The bottom of Casey's shirt is in tatters; strips of it lie on the concrete. She's got three full bottles of liquor in front of her and she's wedging a wad of fabric into one of them.

"The green liquid doesn't burn," I say, because that's what all the Mortiferi were drinking out of the liquor bottles when they came out of the pub.

"I know." She looks at me. "I found some real alcohol on the shelves, though. They gotta keep up appearances for the human customers."

Customers like Paul. I should have remembered how he came home from this place smelling like rum.

"We'll take the others to the hospital," Isaac shouts as Albert and Dan burst through the door after us.

Dan and Isaac head for the back of the pub, where my unconscious brother and eleven others wait in the van. Albert stays out front with Casey and me. He puts his hands on his knees and coughs, wiping ash out of his watering eyes.

Casey holds her lighter under the fabric wick of her liquor bottle bomb until it catches, then shouts, "Out of the way, loves!"

Albert and I scramble down the sidewalk and cover our heads. A few Mortiferi have followed us outside. Two of them sprint down the street to safety, but the rest remain trapped in the inferno, screaming as the fire spreads around them.

Casey hurls the bomb into the doorway. It shatters on the doorframe and ignites on impact. The Mortiferi who were caught trying to escape dive to the ground, their clothes blazing. The front entrance is engulfed in flames within a minute.

The black van roars down the gravel driveway and screeches as it turns onto the road. I catch a glimpse of Isaac in the driver's seat as they pass and a small weight lifts off my shoulders. Paul is going to the hospital. Please, God, let him be okay. I can't handle it if all of this comes to nothing. If we can't save him—if we can't get help in time—

Breathe. Don't lose it.

Another Mortifer is trying to climb out the left window. He's got one leg over the windowsill when he looks up to see Casey lighting a bottle of rum. His eyes go wide, and he scrambles back into the building just before the bomb sails over his head. This time, the flames go all the way to the ceiling, which catches fire almost instantly.

The flames from the door spread to the windowsills, but a few more Mortiferi try to crawl through them anyway. They scream as the fire licks their flesh. Then they fall to the ground and limp away. Seconds later, the entire window is consumed and part of the roof falls in. There can't be any survivors.

But then I see him.

Gareth Long appears in the window. He's burned and bloody, but he's alive. He tumbles headfirst over the windowsill and cries out when he hits the ground. He grabs his shoulder; it's the same one Dan pulled out of its socket at the docks. It hangs uselessly from his side.

Casey picks up the last bottle. She lights the fabric tucked into the opening.

"Wait!" I shout, hurrying over to her. "I want to do it!"

The rage that boils inside me overflows. I grab the bottle out of Casey's hand. The fabric has already caught; all I have to do is throw it.

I pull my arm back.

I just have to move my arm forward and let go.

Just *throw it.*

Gareth is writhing in pain on the sidewalk. His face is twisted into an agonized grimace and he clutches his arm to his torso.

He's a murderer, I remind myself.

But he's not a Mortifer. His soul is still intact.

I can't do it.

I throw the bottle onto the roof. It shatters and erupts into flames. Another section of the ceiling crashes down.

"WHAT?" Casey shrieks. Sweat plasters her black hair to her face and her eyes are wild. "You're going to let him *live*? He tried to kill your brother! He tried to kill all those other people! He *did* kill us! And you leave him alive?"

Gareth writhes on the ground. The air fills with his screams.

"He's not one of them," I say. "He's still human. Plus, he obviously can't hurt us right now."

Albert puts a hand on her arm. "We don't have to kill him, not like this. We'll knock him out and take him to Roberts—"

"No!" She shakes him off and glares at me. "I thought you were going to kill him! After what he did—I can't believe—"

She puts both hands on her head, blinking back tears. Then she wrenches her gun out of the waistband of her jeans.

"Casey," I say carefully. "What are you doing?"

She doesn't answer. She doesn't even look me in the eye. Gareth Long's screams jump an octave as she approaches him.

She stops a foot in front of him and kicks him hard in the stomach when he tries to get up. He doubles over and curls up on the sidewalk, covering his face with his good arm. She points the gun straight at his head.

"Casey, wait!" Albert says, reaching for her. "There's no reason to kill him now. We'll just turn him over to the police and let them deal with it."

For a second, she hesitates.

Then she pulls the trigger.

THIRTY-NINE

I HARDLY FEEL THE STING OF THE CONCRETE AGAINST my knees as I hit the sidewalk and vomit into the gutter. Albert is shouting something behind me and I know I should get up, but I can't. The only thing that keeps me anchored in sanity is knowing that my brother, along with the other people who were trapped inside bags, is on his way to the hospital with Dan and Isaac.

I have seen so many people get shot tonight, but seeing Casey shoot Gareth Long point-blank—

It was so fast.

His legs jerked so hard.

"Come on," Albert says as he lifts me off the ground. His voice is muffled and suddenly I notice the high-pitched ringing in my ears. I can't get my knees to support my weight. Albert laces an arm around my waist and starts walking me away from the burning pub. He keeps my back to Gareth, but it's too late. The image of his last moment is burned into my mind.

"Where's Casey?" My voice sounds like it's coming from outside my body.

"She threw the gun into the fire and ran. I don't know where she went." His face is streaked with soot, and his arm trembles as he tries to support me.

I take a deep, shuddering breath. "So what do we do now?"

"There's only one thing I can think of," he says. "We call Roberts."

"The policeman? Why? Shouldn't we just go to the hospital?"

He shakes his head. "Think about it. We're on camera breaking out of that holding cell. Casey shot a guard in the leg. Now we've burned down a pub, and while I'd like to say none of us left fingerprints on anything that didn't burn, I can't be sure."

"So we're in trouble, is what you're saying."

"Yes—especially Casey. Fortunately, though, she won't be accused of shooting Gareth Long."

I turn to him. "Why not?"

"I shoved his body through the window while you were throwing up," he says. "He'll just be one more charred corpse in the building. But for the other charges, we're going to need some help."

I press my lips together. "Roberts can't be our only option. He's the one who arrested us in the first place."

"Only because he had to," Albert points out. "And you heard what he said just before he left that room. He practically told us to break out. Do you think he would have said that if he didn't want to help us?"

"Good point. You think he can really get us off the hook for all this?"

Albert shrugs. "If I tell him the truth, I think he'll do everything he can. Roberts has known something was up with us for a while now. He's dying for an explanation. If I give him one, and if he understands that we saved twelve innocent lives tonight, I think he'll work a little police magic on our behalf."

"Okay," I say. "But how do we get in touch with him?"

He glances at my back pocket. "You've got your phone, right?"

"Yeah."

"Look up Chandler Roberts. I bet he's the only one in south London."

I turn my phone on and search for him with shaky fingers. I keep punching in the wrong letters because my hands won't cooperate, and my phone takes forever to pull anything up, but finally I find an entry in the white pages for a Chandler Roberts in Blackheath.

"Is this him?" I say, handing the phone to Albert.

He pushes the call button and puts the phone to his ear. "We'll find out in a minute."

Roberts finds us walking up Vicars Hill. He drives past us at first, probably because our heads are down and we're close to the trees. The sun has come up a little, but most of the street still lies cloaked in shadows, as if it's reluctant to give up the night.

He stops his blue Citroën while we catch up to him.

"So," he says, rolling down his window. "You break out of prison, shoot a guard, burn down a pub, and then you decide to call me for a lift?"

"Don't tell me that's the worst thing you've ever heard," Albert says.

Roberts snorts. "Get in the car."

We slide into the backseat and Roberts starts driving. "You said you needed to go to University Hospital?"

Albert nods. "Yeah."

"And you'll tell me everything on the way there? How you're always in the right place at the right time? Why you're able to save so many lives? What happened tonight at The Black Swan with that white-haired bloke?"

"That's what we agreed to, isn't it?" Albert says.

Roberts's eyes narrow at us in the rearview mirror. "Then start talking."

I stay quiet while Albert explains who he is and what he can do. Roberts remembers my grandfather from the news stories, so I contribute a little to that part of the conversation, but my nerves are strung too tightly for me to focus on anything but Paul. I stare out the window in a daze, thinking about how much I would appreciate the sunrise if I wasn't on my way to the hospital.

An extended pause in the conversation brings my attention back to the car. Roberts has gone pale. I guess Albert held up his part of the deal.

"Do you really expect me to believe you can rewind time?" Roberts says with a scowl.

Albert shrugs. "I don't really care if you believe it or not, mate. The bottom line is that everything we did tonight kept twelve people from having their souls permanently damaged. Or, if you choose not to believe that, it kept them from being recruited by terrorists. They're all at the hospital if you need proof."

The car falls silent. We slow down and Roberts puts on his blinker. When I look through Albert's window, I see a sign for University Hospital, Lewisham.

"Is this it? Are we here?" I'm unbuckling my seatbelt and I've got my fingers on the door handle.

"This is it." Roberts pulls into a parking space and turns the car off. "Go inside, Rosie. I'm going to keep Albert here for a few more minutes."

I look at Albert. "Will you come find me when you're done?"

"Of course."

"Please don't arrest him," I say to Roberts.

He gives me a hint of a smile. "I'll see what I can do."

Everything from the parking lot to Paul's room is a blur. It's an eerily similar feeling to walking up to Papa's room with my family; I'm seeing things, but not registering them. I know I talked to a receptionist downstairs—I must have, because I'm wearing a visitor badge—but I don't remember anything she said, except that Paul is in room 312. They don't assign rooms to dead people, do they? I'm practically running by the time I turn onto Paul's hallway.

The door to his room is slightly open, and I screech to a halt just outside it. Will he still be the same Paul? Did we get to him in time? What are the long-term effects of whatever filth they doped him with? Tears sting my eyes, but I take a deep breath and knock softly, then poke my head inside.

Isaac and Dan are sitting by the window. Their smiles tell me everything I need to know.

"He's okay?" I rasp.

Dan stands up. "He's sleeping right now, but he's doing pretty well."

Paul is hooked up to about a dozen machines, all of them pumping and dripping things into him. His face is a deathly shade of white, but the beeps of the heart monitor are rhythmic. I sit on the edge of the mattress and push his hair off his forehead. He groans and cracks an eye open.

"Hi," I whisper. "I didn't mean to wake you."

"It's okay." He licks his dry lips. "Rosie?"

"Yeah?"

"Thanks."

I shake my head. "You don't have to—"

"No, listen," he says. "I don't know what I did this time, but these guys told me you saved my life. And…"

I wrap my hand around his. "And?"

"Things are gonna be different now." He's mumbling, eyelids fluttering shut. "I promise."

He's asleep again in an instant, his breathing deep and even. I don't realize how hard I'm crying until Dan and Isaac start patting my back and telling me he's going to be okay. I lay my head on Isaac's shoulder. He stiffens at first, but then wraps an arm around me. Dan mumbles, "It's okay, Rosie, it's okay, everything is okay," as I cry.

There's a hurried knock on the door and a nurse bustles in. "Hello, everyone," she says quietly. Then she gives me a smile. "Are you family?"

I pull away from Isaac, wiping my nose. "Yeah. I'm his sister."

She picks up his chart. "His blood work is at the lab. We haven't been able to identify the drug in his system yet. Something obscure, maybe homemade." Her expression darkens. "Whatever it is, it's nasty. Good thing we got him when we did."

She gives Isaac a significant look, and he puts a hand on my back. "They told us we would have to leave the room once you got here. Don't want to overwhelm him with visitors."

"Oh!" I put a hand on my back pocket. "I need to call my parents!"

"You'll have to go down to the lobby," the nurse says. "No mobiles allowed in this unit."

The last thing I want to do is leave Paul alone.

"Take her downstairs," the nurse says to Isaac. "I'll stay here with him. Got to change out his fluids, anyway."

We go down the elevator to the main lobby. My parents probably gave up trying to call me hours ago. I'm sure they've gone to the police, reported me missing, and sent out a search party.

My chest nearly caves in with guilt.

Isaac plants himself on a black leather sofa while I make a beeline to the farthest corner of the lobby. I dial Nana's home number and squeeze my eyes shut when it connects.

Dad picks up after half a ring. "Hello?"

"Hey, Dad, it's Rosie."

A strangled cry comes back to me. I cringe. My dad can't even say my name before he starts sobbing into the phone.

"It's okay," I say, straining to talk over the lump in my throat. "I'm okay, Dad."

The glass doors slide open and Albert walks in. He hurries over, gathering me into his arms.

"Dad, listen to me," I say. "Are you there?"

"Yes, Rosie, I'm here."

"We're okay." I sag into Albert's chest as my own words register: *We're okay.* We survived. A couple hours ago, I didn't think it was possible. "Paul and I are fine. He's in the hospital, but—"

"He's in the *hospital?* Where? What hospital?"

"University Hospital in Lewisham. He's stable, and—"

"We're coming," he barks. "Just don't go anywhere, okay? Stay where you are. Promise me."

"I promise, Dad."

I hang up and pre-empt Albert's questions with one of my own. "What did Roberts say?"

"Well, there's a reason he didn't bring the police car."

"Cameras on the dash?"

"Yep."

I drum my fingers against my phone. "So he doesn't want anyone to know he picked us up. Which means he's going to help us?"

"He's going to do everything he can."

"That's…incredible."

"Yeah," he says, breaking into a smile. "If he's successful, he wants all of us to consider careers in law enforcement. Except Casey." He looks down. "He thinks she's a bit too rogue."

"Still no word from her?"

He shakes his head. "She might have gone home, for all I know."

"So what are we supposed to do?" I ask. "I mean, about what happened at the police station and everything."

Albert sighs and runs a hand through his hair. "Well, since there's so much video and eyewitness evidence that we broke out of jail, Roberts has got his work cut out for him as far as getting us off the hook. But the pub is a different story."

I raise my eyebrows. "Oh?"

"Yeah. We actually drove over there just now, he and I. The place was swarming with cops, so Roberts left me in the car while he asked about what they found. As it turns out, they haven't found anything. All the evidence burned up. The Black Swan is so isolated, stuck back in that corner of Lewisham. I mean, there are houses sort of nearby, but nobody realized what was happening until people started passing it on their way to work. By that time, the place was burned to the ground."

I lower my voice, paranoid someone will hear us and raise the alarm. "But what about the Fiat? Surely they can trace the plates?"

"I'm sure they could," he says, lifting his eyebrows. "If there were plates to trace."

"The Fiat burned up, too?"

"Everything burned up. There's still a bit of a Fiat skeleton left, but no plates. When all those liquor bottles started to break under the pressure, the fire must have spread like crazy. All the trees around the building are gone. And when Roberts asked about bodies, they said they'd found some, but there was no way to identify them."

"No fingerprints?" This is the part I've been mostly worried about—that we left some glaring piece of evidence that would lead straight to us. I know fire tends to consume pretty much everything, but the people on *CSI* are always finding fingerprints in the unlikeliest of places.

"Not yet," he says, and I close my eyes in relief. "I told Roberts that Gareth was one of the ones who died in the fire, and—just for curiosity's sake—he did a little background check for me."

"And?"

"His wife committed suicide after their son died." I nod; I already know this part. "He was arrested several times for public drunkenness. He went to rehab for alcoholism three different times, but never got clean. He was arrested for harassment and public intoxication, and eventually subjected to a mental evaluation, which he failed."

"It was Papa," I say. Albert frowns, confused. "Papa's the one he harassed while intoxicated."

"Really?" He considers this. "Yeah, I guess that's not too surprising. Edward mentioned Gareth every once in a while. He was tortured by his failure to save Kieran Long."

I rub a hand over my face. "So how did Gareth get involved with the Mortiferi?"

Albert shrugs. "All I can do is guess. Want to hear my theory?"

"Sure."

He looks around to make sure no one is listening to us. "Remember how I told you the Mortiferi prey on vulnerable people? Well, one of their favorite places to recruit is the mental hospital. It's full of people who've been crushed by life and feel like failures because they can't overcome their problems without help. I'm guessing a Mortifer checked himself in to scout out some new recruits, and Gareth seemed like the perfect option. Gareth probably told him all about his son and wife, and how he blamed Edward for all of it. When the Mortifer figured out how much Gareth hated Edward, they struck a deal."

We're whispering now, and our faces are centimeters apart. "And you think part of that deal was that Gareth would remain human?"

"Must have been." He pauses as a man and woman hurry into the hospital with urgent expressions. They stop at the reception desk, and once they begin talking with the receptionist, Albert turns back to me. "I'm guessing another part of the deal was that the Mortiferi broke him out of the mental hospital. Gareth Long was reported missing from South London Psychiatric Ward nearly two years ago."

"But how did he become a leader?"

"Probably because he was their key to bringing down one of the most active Servatores in history. When Edward died, the Mortiferi didn't have much of a reason to hold up their end of the deal. I bet that's part of the reason he came after you and Paul—to reaffirm his value to them."

"I can't believe what he turned into," I say. "I know he was technically human, but that guy was a monster. A killer."

Albert shoves his hands in his pockets with a grimace. "You're right about that. It's amazing how un-human some people can be."

My family almost doesn't see me when they walk into the lobby. Mom is the first one to do a double-take. "Rosie!"

I'm in her arms in a second. Dad and Nana crowd around me, crying, scolding, and asking questions all at once. Dad pulls me into a hug that nearly crushes my ribcage, and Nana kisses my cheeks over and over.

"It's such a long story," I say. "Paul got in some trouble tonight and I—*we*—had to save him."

They follow my eyes to Albert, Dan, and Isaac, who are watching us uncomfortably.

"Rosemary Eleanor Clayton," my dad says in a thick voice, "as soon as I see my son and verify that he is alive with my own two eyes, you are telling me every detail about what happened tonight. Do you understand?"

"Yes," I say. "Dad, I'm really sorry, I know—"

He holds up a hand and closes his eyes as if my apology hurts him. "Please don't. I'm completely furious with you and completely relieved that you're okay, and I'm not stable enough to have a conversation right now." He takes a deep breath. "Take me to Paul. We'll talk later."

"Okay." I shoot an uncertain look at the boys.

"We'll be here," Albert mouths to me, and I nod before getting in the elevator with my family.

FORTY

WAKE BEFORE SUNRISE THE NEXT MORNING, BUT I
can't go back to sleep. Pushing back the covers, I pick up
my phone and check the time. It's 5:17. *One new voicemail.*

"Hey," Albert's deep voice says on the message. A
fuzzy warmth blooms instantly somewhere deep inside
me. "I hope you're sleeping. Call me when you wake up. I
have some things to tell you."

I dial the number to his landline. He picks up on the
first ring.

"Rosie?"

I smile. "Hey. Come get me and let's take a walk."

The stairs are cold under my bare feet as I tiptoe
down them, careful to skip the ones that squeak. Both
Nana's and Dad's doors are still closed. Mom spent the
night with Paul in the hospital; the doctors still haven't
identified the drug in his system—not that they ever will.
If the Mortiferi gave him the fiery green liquid, I don't
need to see drug test results to know it's not your typical
opiate. But they want to keep running tests, and they want
to keep him under observation until he's fully recovered.

He won't be out for a while.

I reach the first floor and rub the goose bumps on my arms as I walk into the kitchen. I was planning to make some coffee before Albert got here, but Dad and Nana are already sitting at the kitchen table, each clutching a steaming mug. The scrapbook of Papa's news articles lies open between them.

"Hi." My voice seems obtrusive in the quiet of the morning. "I thought you two were still asleep."

Dad pushes a chair out with his foot. "Want to sit?"

"Actually, I'm going for a walk." I eye the French press on the table. "With some coffee."

Dad and Nana look alarmed.

"You're going out by yourself?" Dad says. "I don't think you should—"

"No!" I laugh. "No. With Albert. He's coming to get me."

Albert met my family briefly in the hospital, and although he sort of explained who he was and how he knew Edward, he left out a lot of details. They know he helped to save Paul's life, but other than that, I think they're still pretty confused.

"Are you going out in your pajamas?" Nana asks in a scandalized tone.

I grab a mug from the cabinet and head for the table. "Nobody else will be out, and Albert won't care."

Albert. Every time I say his name, that fuzzy warmth spreads a little further.

"Your mum texted me a few minutes ago," Dad says. "They're going to evaluate Paul at eight. She says he's looking better. More color in his cheeks."

"Good." I pour my coffee and stir in some milk and sugar. A soft knock sounds at the front door. "That's him," I say. "I won't be gone long."

Dad stops me before I leave the kitchen. "Rosie?"

I look back at him.

"When you get home," he says, "you'll explain everything. About the...what was it you called them at the hospital?"

"Servatores," I say. "And yes. I'll tell you everything." I look at Nana, whose eyes are filled with eagerness. "I'll tell both of you."

THE HEATH IS BEAUTIFUL ANY TIME OF DAY, BUT AT dawn it is spectacular.

Fog drifts across the ground and veils the church's steeple as the sun bursts over the skyline in pink and orange streaks. Albert's arm is curled around my shoulders, keeping me warm against the early-morning chill. Our shoes collect bits of wet grass and leave dark footprints in the dew. I breathe in the cool air and take a long sip of coffee, closing my eyes for a second as it warms its way into my stomach.

Unlike me, Albert changed into real clothes before going outside. He's wearing his tattered jeans—the same ones he's been wearing all week, which calls his laundry skills into serious question—and a gray Millwall Football Club T-shirt.

Millwall and Crystal Palace don't exactly like each other, but I haven't trash-talked him yet. I'm biding my time until next week's match, when I'll get to shock him with my detailed knowledge of the league.

As we near the center of the heath, Albert says, "Guess who came home around three o'clock this morning?"

"Casey?"

"Yep. Dan found her wandering around Hither Green Cemetery and brought her back. He's with her now."

It doesn't bode well for her emotional state if she was hanging out in a graveyard all night. "Is she okay?"

"Not really. I think she's second-guessing herself quite a bit."

I can't even begin to imagine how Casey is feeling right now. Even though I know she's killed Mortiferi before, it must be very different to kill someone whose soul is intact.

"I don't know if she regrets shooting Gareth or not," he says. "To be honest, I would've shot him in the pub if I could have. Or in the underground lair, or anywhere else. The only reason I didn't kill him there at the end was because he was injured, and I quite liked the idea of watching him rot in prison. Casey just wanted him finished at any cost. But now, I think she might feel guilty for shooting him when he was down." He stops walking and tugs a thin section of newspaper out of his pocket. "Have you seen this today?"

"No," I say, coming to a stop beside him. "You get a newspaper delivered to your house? That's so grown up."

He laughs. "Yes, I'm very mature. Have a look at the front page."

I set my coffee cup on the grass beside my feet and angle the paper toward the pale morning light. *Fire rages in Lewisham,* reads the headline. *Black Swan pub destroyed, dozens found dead inside.*

"Wow," I say. "You weren't kidding about *everything* burning up."

The photo of The Black Swan is unbelievable, like a poster for a disaster movie. The entire building has been reduced to a pile of black wood. There's no hint of the building's former shape, or the nasty paint on the door with the suspicious stains. All of it is gone—lost in an inferno caused by an angry Servator with Molotov cocktails.

"What about the underground lair?" I say. "Did they find it?"

"Yeah." He scans the article over my shoulder. "Just there, toward the end. 'The fire exposed a mysterious underground space that may have been an unlicensed club. Traces of an unidentified chemical were discovered in various locations within the space.'" He looks up at me. "The green stuff, I'm sure. Anyway, it goes on: 'Everything inside has been confiscated and destroyed, and its singular entry has been permanently sealed shut.'"

I look at Albert. "Do they really think it was just a club?"

"Well, that's what it looks like, you know? Unless you saw those blokes drinking the green stuff, you'd think it was just a rave or something."

"Right," I say. "Anything else about Max and Luther?"

I don't really care about Max and Luther, but I'd like to know where they are. They weren't fatally injured in the fight by the fountain. If they're still in the hospital, that's great—but I'll need to know where they go after that.

"We haven't checked with the hospital again," Albert replies. "After all that's happened, my guess is that they'll relocate to another part of the city. Or maybe a different city entirely. They're easily spooked, the Mortiferi. Don't like to feel threatened."

"You think they'll leave town because of what happened last night?" It's a nice thought, but it doesn't seem likely.

"Maybe," he says. "Whenever your grandfather eliminated a Mortifer, a lot of others would relocate for a while. So they'll probably go to Manchester or Birmingham. Find another group of Mortiferi to run around with for a few months. There are plenty more of them in London, though. Our problems don't go away just because Max and Luther leave." He rolls up the paper and stuffs it back into his pocket, squinting at me in the growing sunlight. "It's good to see your face again, Rosemary Clayton."

"We've only been apart for a few hours," I say, but I can't keep from smiling.

"I know." He squeezes my shoulders. "Are you saying that's acceptable?"

His tone is light, but I arch an eyebrow. "Is there something we should talk about?"

"Ah. Right." He rubs the back of his neck. "Yeah, there is, actually. I've been thinking, and…well…"

I give him a playful punch in the stomach. "Spit it out."

He grabs my hand and locks his eyes onto mine. A grin tugs at one corner of his mouth. "I'd like to get to know you better."

"Really." The warmth in my gut breaks free of whatever was left of its restraints. It unfurls into my chest, into my arms, and all the way down to my toes.

"Yep, really. In a dating sort of way."

I clear my throat and try to salvage whatever coolness I can. "So you're asking me out on a date?"

"I am." He smiles. "A second date. And hopefully one that doesn't end in liquor-fueled fire and emergency rooms."

I laugh, but my heart feels like it's slipping into my stomach. How could I have forgotten? How could I have thought this could ever possibly work?

"What's wrong?" His smile fades. "If you don't feel the same way, then—"

"No!" I cry out. "I mean—yes, I do. It's just…" I rub my eyes. "This trip to London is only for the summer. When August rolls around, we'll go back to Nashville. I'll start my senior year. I don't know when we'll be back. Nana is talking about moving in with us. Which would be great, but I don't know how often we'll be here if she's living with us in Tennessee." I look down. "Which means I don't know how often you and I will see each other."

The warmth begins to retreat, leaving a cold, dead feeling in my fingers.

His expression sags. "Oh."

We stand in silence. I stare at my shadow, stretched out beside me.

"Nashville," he says thoughtfully. "That's where Vanderbilt is, yeah?"

"Yeah." I shake my head with a laugh. "How do you know about Vanderbilt?"

"Well, you probably don't know this—between fighting for our lives and saving your brother, we somehow never talked about it—but I'm starting University this fall. I've been researching schools for the past year or so."

"Oh," I say, picturing Albert cavorting around pubs filled with beautiful college girls. "Where have you applied?"

"Several places. St. Andrews and King's College here. Michigan, NYU, and a few other schools in America. My dad may be a deadbeat as far as parenting is concerned, but he is loaded, and he's offered to pay my tuition for any school that accepts me. Casey, too. Assuming we're not in prison, of course."

"Of course." I toe a stray piece of earth, flinging it to the side with my shoe. "Where have you been accepted?"

"So far, Michigan, NYU, and the University of Chicago."

"Wow. Those are great schools." I sigh. "And they are all really far away from Nashville."

"Yeah, I know." A grin starts in the corner of his mouth. "But I hear Vanderbilt has extended their deadline for foreign applications."

I narrow my eyes at him. "You *hear*?"

"Yes," he says. "Google told me, just last night. It costs a little more to apply so late, but it can be done."

I shift my weight, hardly daring to believe that Albert Shaw could end up in Nashville. If he did—well, it would change everything. "Are you thinking about applying?"

He looks at the ground, then back up at me. "Filled out the application last night. Those other schools are in miserably cold places, and I'd like to get out of Britain for a while. Casey could come, too."

"But what about the legal issues? Breaking out of jail? Surely Roberts can't get you—*us*—totally off the hook."

"I know," he says, somewhat deflated. "But there is someone who can."

I give him a blank stare.

"Money talks," he says with a shrug.

It takes me another moment to grasp what he's getting at. "Your dad," I say quietly. "You told him?"

Albert nods at the ground. "Had quite a chat with dear old Dad this morning. I might have convinced him to pay off all the right people, as long as none of them suddenly develop a conscience."

I stare at him. "Oh."

"Yeah." He shoves his hands in his pockets. "I feel quite sleazy about the whole thing, to be honest with you. But if Roberts and my dad work together on this, there's a good chance everything will be dropped."

I feel sleazy about it, too, but there's another feeling bouncing around inside of me—*hope*. If Roberts can pull the right strings and Albert's dad can work enough financial magic to make all of this go away, then whatever's been building between Albert and me—it could actually happen. *We* could actually happen.

"Albert," I say slowly. "Vanderbilt is, like, three miles from my house."

His expression turns dark. "Ooh, three miles? Hmm. I'm not sure I can deal with that kind of distance."

I swat mercilessly at his arms and chest until his laughter turns to silent gasps. "Stop hitting me!" he says. "I'm taking you on a date, remember? If you'll quit beating me to a pulp, we might go somewhere fancier than Strada."

I stop. "Why would I want that?"

"You wouldn't." He wraps an arm around my waist. "And that's one reason I like you so much."

He pulls me in close and drops his forehead against mine. I'm pretty sure I could spend the rest of my life like this—enveloped in his arms, breathing his scent, watching the way his eyes smile even when his mouth doesn't.

I haven't reached for my necklace in days. The place it used to hang no longer feels so naked; in fact, those interlocking golden rings seem like a distant memory now. And Stephen...

"Your grandfather is so proud of you right now," Albert says quietly. "I know he is."

I squeeze my eyes shut as the memory of Papa's *opus postremum* comes back to me. I explained most of the details to Albert last night at the hospital—how Papa used his "last work" to save us. Paul woke up before I could tell him everything, though, so there are some key details he doesn't know yet.

"He told me he loved me," I say with a smile.

His eyes fill with wonder. "You've inherited something special from Edward, that's for sure. I wonder how he managed to speak directly into your mind while existing only in spirit form. I've never heard of such a thing. Maybe we can find something at the library—"

His words are cut short as I tilt my head back and pull his face down to mine for the kiss that's been a long time coming. He brings me a sense of comfort, of home. I don't know what this thing between us is, or if it will turn into anything at all. But I'm more than willing to explore the possibilities.

Too soon, he pulls away. "We're giving the neighbors quite a show. Come on—let's get you home before your family starts to worry."

He puts his arm around my shoulders and steers me back toward Nana's house. I bend down to hook the handle of my coffee cup on my fingers and then lace my arm around his waist as we walk across the heath.

"I'd like to meet your family," he says. "Properly, I mean. I didn't get a chance to say what I wanted to say at the hospital. And with things being the way they are—" he squeezes my shoulder "—I'd say it's high time they know exactly who their daughter's been cavorting with."

"You'll tell them everything?"

He plants a kiss on my head. "Everything. There's a lot I need to tell your Nana, especially. I want her to know how amazing her husband was, and what he did for Casey and me."

I smile, picturing Nana's face when she learns the secrets Papa kept for so long. I wonder if she ever suspected anything, or if she really believed Papa was just in the right place at the right time.

As I lean into Albert, I swear I feel Papa brush against my mind.

Well done, my sweet Rosemary. Well done.

ACKNOWLEDGMENTS

THE FIRST THING I SHOULD SAY IS THIS: THE MOMENT I tried to make a list of all the people who helped *Pull* become a real book, my head almost exploded.

So I stepped back, and I took a few days to consider this monumental task, and I ate a lot of fried chicken. Because if growing up in the South has taught me anything, it's that there is no better thinkin' food than fried chicken.

After the stepping back and the fried chicken and the thinkin', I decided to break down my acknowledgments into five categories:

1) People who read *Pull* when it was but a wee baby manuscript and helped me teach it some manners.

2) People who worked with *Pull* in its childhood and/or adolescence and helped me teach it to dress well, comb its hair, and smile properly.

3) People who supported me simply by existing.

4) Random things that kept my sanity from dissolving.

5) God (because if anyone should get their own category, it's Him).

So if you're still reading this (and if you are, bless you), let's get this party started.

CATEGORY #1: PEOPLE WHO READ *PULL* IN ITS INFANCY

I can already tell I'm going to forget someone.

Not because their critique didn't mean anything to me—ALL the critiques I get mean THE WORLD to me—but because I started writing this story in May 2011, and my memory is comparable to that of a goldfish (Oh look, a castle! Oh look, a castle! Oh look, a castle!).

So as much as I'd like to list ALL the people who read a very early version of the manuscript, I'm just not that confident in the remembering part of my brain. Instead, I'm going to say this:

To everyone who read my manuscript while you worked out, or while you rode the subway, or while your kids napped and you could have been doing a gazillion other things, or while your boss was looking the other way at work—

Because of your encouragement, this book is venturing out into the world like I always hoped it would.

Because of your willingness to sacrifice your valuable time, Rosie and Albert's story has become accessible to anyone in need of an escape.

Because of your support of me as an author and friend, I can continue to create stories and distribute them into the hands of the world.

Thank you, a million times. You deserve all the kittens in existence. Unless you're allergic to kittens, in which case you get a turtle. I'm pretty sure those are hypoallergenic.

CATEGORY #2: PEOPLE WHO READ *PULL* WHILE IT WAS GROWING UP

1. Agent Emma.

First up in this category has GOT to be my incomparable agent, Emma Patterson, with whom I have spent countless hours on the phone and over email, laughing and chatting and occasionally talking shop. She has a way of getting business done without making it feel like business. When an agent can make a six-month negotiation period with a publisher feel like the most exhilarating time of your life, you know you've struck gold. And when she brings you out of that six-month negotiation period with more publishing contract perks than you imagined possible, you know you've struck platinum.

Also: She makes a mean baked ziti.

So, Agent Emma, please accept this original haiku as a token of my undying love for you and my appreciation for everything you've done since we began working together:

You are best agent
I write you more books to sell
You have real* nice hair

(*Sometimes, grammar must suffer for the sake of art. I'm sure you understand.)

I look forward to many more years of manuscripts, scones, wine, face-to-face dinners, and fond memories of that one time you rejected my manuscript, but I didn't take no for an answer.

2. ALL The Editors.

BIG THANKS to each editor from Spencer Hill who worked on *Pull*: Anna Masrud, who gets extra sprinkles on her cupcake for being the first one who couldn't live without this story; Danielle Ellison, who refused to let me *tell* the story instead of *show* it; and Britta Gigliotti, who took the manuscript from great to amazing by pointing out all the small, yet very important, things the rest of us missed (OF COURSE THEY NEED WATCHES, HELLOOOO). Richard Storrs, thank you for your superb work as The Closer. Every "LOL" comment made me smile, and I'm so grateful for all the things you caught in the final round of edits. You are truly excellent at your job. DON'T EVER CHANGE, RICH.

3. Last But Not Least...

Jenny Zemanek, your design for this book's cover is the stuff of legends. There is not a single thing I would change about it. Thank you for giving me exactly what I wanted, even though I didn't know I wanted it.

CATEGORY #3: PEOPLE WHO SUPPORTED ME BY EXISTING

1. Rob Riley.

Obviously, my husband is the first one to be thanked here. Not only has he given me some adorable children, he's also given me the space, time, and energy to write books. He's indulged my creativity since the moment I began to write. He's never once told me it's not worth it, or that I'm wasting my (and his) time. In fact, whenever I have a breakdown about writing (LOL I know, authors have breakdowns every five minutes), we basically have this same conversation every time:

HIM: Why are you upset?

ME: BECAUSE WRITING IS HARD AND I'M NEVER GOING TO BE ABLE TO DO THIS

HIM: Well, do you want to do it?

ME: YES OMG

HIM: Okay. What do you need me to do so that you can be a writer?

ME: I DON'T KNOW JUST HELP ME NOT GO CRAZY

HIM: How about I do some laundry? And maybe cook dinner?

ME: OKAY

It isn't out of the ordinary for him to do those things (we are very much partners when it comes to our children and our household), but he has always made my writing feel important, even when I feared I was pouring myself into a pipe dream.

So thanks for that, Handsome Rob. I love you, even when you play your Irish music too loud. Thanks for forcing me out of bed every morning so that I'll actually do stuff and be a person.

2. Family People.

To my parents, Bruce and Barbara: Thanks for deciding you wanted another child. You guys made arguably the greatest contribution to this book because you gave birth to me. And you read that one ferret book I wrote when I was nine (remember how it was twenty chapters long and WAY more complicated than any nine-year-old's ferret story should have been?). I love you, and I am so glad you are my parents.

To my sister, Laura: I'm really excited we're friends now. Love you lots, Lars. (PS: I originally had the lyrics from a musical here, but I had to take them out because of copyright issues. I bet you can guess which lyrics they were, though…)

To my parents-in-law, Bellaire and Caron: If it weren't for y'all, I might not have survived this whole book thing. Thanks for Thursday afternoons, writing days in the summer, calling me just to see if I wanted a break, taking me shopping for "author outfits," and giving us all the date nights we could ask for. I love you guys.

To the rest of my family, I'm sorry I can't list you all by name. Just know you're awesome, and I love you, always.

3. Friends and Coworkers.

Magic City Literati: Y'all are my literary loves and I am so thankful for the friendships that have come out of our little group!

Sophie Hudson: Remember all those times you said, "Oh, I just don't have a book in me," and then TWO BOOKS LATER, you are officially an author? Hahaha. I treasure our lunches together and our many conversations about comfy pants from Old Navy.

David Balik: Remember that time I wrote you a letter that made you cry? I meant every word. Thanks for allowing my first book to be stocked in the school library. You rock.

Jon Carter: Your encouragement at the beginning of my writing adventure was a major part of all this. Thanks for being my English teacher back in the day, and for the camaraderie as we both pursued publication. You are a special kind of awesome.

Nicole Conrad: Remember the time I got my first agent and I danced around outside your classroom window? And all those times you read manuscripts for me and helped me make them better? Thanks for that. Also, thanks for your stories about spaghetti mishaps and tap-dancing shrimp. I'm going to use those in a book if it's the last thing I do.

Battle Group (hey Nicole, you're in this one, too!): Alisa Poole, Kristen Williams, Nicole Conrad, and Emily McNearney. Sweet mercy. What would I do without you? So many group therapy sessions in the basement (literally AND metaphorically). I love you girls to the moon and back. PS: DON'T LISTEN TO THE LIES. (I just feel like we should keep saying that randomly to each other.)

Lauren Beck: Thanks for reading this manuscript TWICE and helping me out with the Latin. I'm grateful for your friendship!

Chris Knowles and Ben Burgess: Thanks for letting me talk your ears off about an assortment of random things. Those moments were probably small to you, but they were huge to me.

Kendra Knowles and Cally Burgess: I LOVE YOU LADIES. Thanks for the texts, the coffee, the lunches, and the instantly deep conversations. I think we've only had five minutes of small talk since our friendships began, and that makes me so happy. Y'all are jewels of great price, and my life would be considerably emptier without you.

Robbie Hinton: Thank you for supporting me both as a teacher and as an author. You have embraced all facets of who I am, and I am proud to work for you.

Claire Stimson: Thank you for helping me with British-isms, and for that one Facebook chat. You know the one.

All My Students, Ever: Guys, there are over 1,000 of you, so I'm obviously not going to list you by name. Thank you for being excited with me about getting published, for reading my book and not realizing it was written by THAT Anne Riley, for reading my book while I was trying to teach you (those were always weird moments— how do you tell someone to stop reading YOUR book during YOUR class?), for asking me to sign stuff, and for indulging your inner book nerd with me.

Friends whose names I stole for random characters in this story: Thanks, and sorry. If you ever write a book, you can kill me off in it.

Everyone else who has read anything I ever wrote: THANK YOU from the bottom of my heart. You are amazing, and you enable me to do what I do.

CATEGORY #4: RANDOM THINGS THAT KEPT MY SANITY FROM DISSOLVING

Really, this section is just about *Gossip Girl*. I watched the whole series while editing *Pull*, and honestly, I think Blair and Serena kept me from going over the edge because I was too busy watching THEM go over the edge.

Thanks for that, Upper East Siders. XOXO.

CATEGORY #5: GOD

I'm a God-following person, and while I realize many of you might not be, I'd like to thank Him for the gift of creativity. I believe all art is sacred, and that includes the literary arts. Thank you, Jesus, for everything.

ABOUT THE AUTHOR

Anne Riley is an author of young adult fiction cleverly disguised as a high school Spanish teacher. She lives in Birmingham, Alabama, with her family. When she isn't teaching or writing, Anne enjoys playing with her kids and reading novels that become part of her soul. She's also really great at pretending to clean her house and putting off the laundry until it overtakes an entire room. Anne is not good at sports, despite having played volleyball for four years of her life, but she is a very talented coffee-maker. You can connect with her online at annerileybooks.com.

CPSI/
at ww
Printe
LVOV
477

20453